Some Other Tyme

STEFAN JAKUBOWSKI

Published in 2021
by
Zygmunt Stanley

ISBN 978-0-9574625-2-6

©2021 Stefan Jakubowski

Cover illustration by andrey_l/stockadobe.com
Cover and pages designed and typeset by Zygmunt Stanley

Printed by Gomer Press, Wales

THE AUTHOR

Originally from Reading,
Stefan moved to Wales in the latter part of the last century.
(He wishes to point out, he is not as old as that makes him sound!)
(Nia, his wife, wishes to point out: 'Oh yes he is!)
He lives with Nia somewhere in Carmarthenshire.

This book is dedicated to the memory of

NEIL JAMES

Thanks mate

THE GIST OF IT!

This is where I tell you how it is with Tom Tyme so far.

Tom Tyme is sixty-five and a time traveller – it runs in the family. He is not happy about it.

He has a familiar – something like a witch has – who has the job of training him.

He and his familiar have the task of righting wrongs.

He has a daughter called Lucy and two grandchildren, Kate and Marc.

Tom also has a famous son-in-law.

He also has a cat.

He also has a shed. He likes his shed. Sorry, he loves his shed!

He has a portable loo in his garden. It can transport him to any toilet in the world. It is also a time machine. And no, it isn't bigger on the inside.

He is sometimes told lies by his familiar; for his own good.

He never tells lies. Yeah, right!

Tom's best friend is Smokowski, a mysterious shopkeeper.

Tom has a bit of a fear where grannies are concerned. But I'm sure he will get over it.

He can be an old fart at times. Make that most times.

He has a magical saver. It saves him. (At least it has so far).

Tom wears a cap, one of those that have flaps that can be worn up or down. It is silvery grey in colour. It is also a universal translator.

He wears a grey corduroy suit, but the jacket doesn't match the colour of the trousers.

He lives in an invisible time-bubble that protects him in the present, should the past be changed.

He likes the odd cuppa.

He likes biscuits.

He also likes the occasional pint

Tom doesn't like spending money.

He is about to embark on only his third adventure. (That we know of.)

There, that is about it so far. Of course, I haven't mentioned Excalibur, King Arthur, Catranna, or Rufus, or why Tom is slightly afeared by grannies. I don't want to spoil it for you when you read his first adventure: Once Upon A Tyme.

So, there you have it, the gist of it. So, onwards and upwards, I say. Let's go see what trouble the old fool gets into this time!

CHAPTER 1

'Aaargh!' yelled Tom.

'Yowee!' shouted Tom.

'Aaargh!' yelled Tom again.

'Nooo!' exclaimed Tom.

'Flipping 'eck,' said Tom.

Tom was having a rough time of it.

'To your left!' shouted Cat, as the sun god Ra – not the real one – slashed at Tom with his weapon of choice, a large metal beetle on a long wooden stick, a remarkably sharp-edged beetle, ornate in its design, a beautiful thing to look on, all golden and shiny. But Tom had not the time to admire what the false Ra held in his hands. He was more concerned with dodging its downward arc.

'Waaaa!' screamed Tom, as his body moved to the left, just avoiding the beetle with an inch to spare.

'The right!' yelled Cat, 'to the right!'

'Oooo!' cried Tom, as his body jerked violently to the right; twice.

'That's it,' encouraged Cat, 'you've got him!' Which, as statements go, was slightly wrong and indeed premature. Because at the precise moment Cat uttered the words, Tom's trousers decided to give up the ghost and drop round his ankles.

Tom's trousers had had enough. No more twisting. No more dodging. No more doing more than was reasonably expected from a pair of trousers worn by someone in their mid-sixties. It was wrong. It was tiring. It was darn right unseemly!

'Oh!' exclaimed Tom, suitably embarrassed by the event while trying to retrieve the situation by bending his knees so he could recover his dignity.

The rampaging corporate-sponsored Ra who aimed to exploit the world – as some corporate business entity from the future felt the real Ra should have done – roared as he saw Tom's predicament.

'There's no time for that!' yelled Cat, as Tom's window of opportunity passed by and the false Ra once more bore down on the hapless pensioner. 'Stand up!'

And Tom did. Cat, you see, had been waylaid by magical means, a trap set by the rampaging false Ra to stop her from stopping him. But thanks to a magical loophole in the trap's makeup, Cat had been able to slip a little magic through to Tom to aid him in his hour of need.

1

That is to say, Cat had taken control of Tom's body, which was a bit of a boon for Tom considering the task at hand, a pensioner going hand to hand with a God, even if that God was nothing more than a corporate stooge. A rather large and strong and fairly magical corporate stooge. A rather large and strong and fairly magical corporate stooge who had decided to use his rather large hands rather than magic to destroy Tom. Him being a frail old pensioner like.

As expected, Tom wasn't happy about it. The controlling of his body, that is. Being mangled by a stooge God wasn't that appealing either. But no one wants to be a puppet. Someone else's puppet. Especially with their trousers round their ankles.

Tom stood up just as the false Ra leaned forward to land a telling blow. There followed a sickening thud as the top of Tom's head collided with the false Ra's beak.

'Sorry,' said Cat, grimacing.

'Ow-ow-ow,' said Tom, reaching for the top of his head and feeling the lump that was swelling beneath his cap. 'Ow!'

'Does it hurt?'

'Yes,' said Tom, flinching as he touched it again. Typical, he thought, just as the bruise on his forehead had nearly healed.

'Stop touching it then,' said Cat. 'Now move it.' She had seen an advantage for them as false Ra reeled backwards from the blow. She concentrated as hard as she could. She had to; Tom was not the most flexible of puppets. 'Use it now!'

A staggering Tom reached into his jacket pocket and removed a small phial filled with a dark liquid. The false Ra needed sprinkling with it. It would win the day. Tom knew not what it would do or why. Cat hadn't said.

'Now!' Cat, seeing their window of opportunity closing as false Ra looked to be recovering from the blow, concentrated all the harder.

Tom managed to dither; he wasn't feeling well; he managed to dally, his old bones and other things were feeling the strain; he struggled with the phials cork stopper, his vision had become blurry; he felt he was almost there, but almost wasn't going to be good enough!

False Ra had recovered and was now seeking revenge for his bent beak. His beetle on a stick held high above his head was ready to do some damage. He was going in for the kill!

Oh, no! thought Cat, trying desperately to get the old ditherer moving. And then suddenly, full connection. Tom immediately jumped to the left as the razor-sharp beetle whizzed past him and into the floor.

'Ra-ra-ra-ra,' growled false Ra, which probably meant he was angry at missing the old geezer with his trousers round his ankles.

Tom then bunny hopped level with false Ra. Then cartwheeled around him – not easy to do with trousers round ankles.

Cat was hoping he still had hold of the phial.

Tom's next move saw him flip backwards and land inches from false Ra's back. Teeth chattering from his landing, eyes boggling like those on a child's birthday card, tummy rumbling as it struggled whether to get rid of the breakfast it held, Tom tried to get a grip. And then, against all odds, the battle was over.

Tom's tummy had had enough, and the porridge with maple syrup that he had had for breakfast suddenly erupted forth, landing on Ra's back. Cat had grimaced. Ra had roared as a hot stickiness trickled down his back. Tom had suddenly felt a lot better.

Ra, in his fury, had spun around with fire in his eyes. He had raised his stick again. He had slipped on said porridge and syrup. He had landed on the floor with a thump. He had lain on the floor with the wind taken out of his sails. Ra was helpless as Tom, at last, got the stopper out of the phial and poured the black liquid onto him. Ra had dissolved and was no more.

Tom then, when released as if by magic – which it was – from his invisible strings, collapsed in a heap. As his eyes rolled in his head and his tongue lolled from his mouth, he had only one thing on his mind. Relief? No. Triumph? No. Tom raised himself on one elbow and looked at Cat, who had just materialised by his side. He tried to speak.

'Tom?' said a concerned Cat. 'You okay?'

He struggled for words, but at last, he managed to utter what was on his mind. 'Cuppa?'

We must now travel back two weeks to Tom's kitchen.

CHAPTER 2

Tom's kitchen two weeks earlier.

'What have you got there?' asked Cat, intrigued by Toms screwed up expression – his thoughtful look – as he studied something he held between finger and thumb. She had just returned from the pyramid she called home. Tom looked almost studious. He was sat at his kitchen table, the light from his laptop playing playfully on the creases and lines of his face.

'It's a raisin,' said Tom.

'A raisin?' said Cat, wondering where this was heading.

'Yeah,' said Tom, not taking his eyes from the raisin. 'I read about it on the thingumabob.' He nodded at the laptop.

'Interesting,' said Cat, still none the wiser by Tom's sudden interest in dried fruit.

'Used the entranet.'

'Internet,' Cat corrected.

'That's what I said.'

Should I ask? thought Cat, might as well. She took a deep breath. 'That raisin in particular or all raisins?' she asked.

'Any raisin,' said Tom. 'Them on the entranet says it's an art.'

'Staring at raisins?' said Cat, eyebrows knitting. She knew she shouldn't have asked.

'It's called thoughtlessness,' said Tom, 'it's supposed to make your life better.'

'How?' said Cat. She sighed as she realised she had been well and truly sucked in.

'I-oh drat,' said Tom as the raisin decided it had had enough of being stared at and squirted from between finger and thumb. Tom quickly bent to catch it but forgot about the kitchen table.

'Ouch,' moaned Tom as his thoughtlessness look turned to one of pain – not much of a difference. 'I've banged me forehead.'

Cat winced. This thoughtlessness seemed somewhat dangerous.

Well, nothing much happening there. But at least we now know how the bruise on Tom's forehead had got there.

Back to the present.

4

CHAPTER 3

The present.

Tom sipped at his cuppa. The ointment he had liberally applied and rubbed on his bits and pieces was doing what it said on the label, soothing, healing, warming, and making Tom smell like an old boy covered in embrocation.

'Lucky I did what I did,' said Tom between sips. 'Perfect timing is what it was.'

'Yeah, perfect,' said Cat, rolling her watering eyes. The smell from Tom's fumes filling the kitchen wasn't pleasant and made her slightly green about the gills.

'Pyramid schemes, wasn't it?' said Tom, referring to the reason some corporation had used a Ra doppelganger in its attempt to change the past. He yawned. Fighting false Gods was tiring. He suspected fighting real ones might be worse.

'So it seems,' said Cat, joining Tom with a yawn of her own. Grief, she suddenly thought, what was she doing? That was a dog thing, yawning when its human did. She shivered. To her mind, there was nothing worse than a pandering lapdog, unless it was a Victorian one. Cat had a thing about the Victorians.

Tom yawned again, but this time Cat had her wits about her. The indignity of the thing.

Tom put his cup on the table and yawned yet again. Blimey, he thought, I'm plumb tuckered out, the jumping about and all. Tom's head slowly lowered. It then jerked upright again. But gravity and tiredness held sway, and Tom's bonce gently lowered until it rested on the table. A snore followed.

Cat looked up at the sudden noise. Ah, she thought, could do with a bit of shut-eye myself. She curled up on the kitchen rug. A few moments later, she was with Tom in the land of Nod.

CHAPTER 4

The little bell above Smokowski's shop door tinkled as the door opened.

Smokowski, who was trying to retrieve a can, contents unknown, from the top shelf, winced. He cursed Tom and his flipping "entranet". His back hurt. It ached. It twinged. All because of a flipping raisin.

He should have asked his assistant Darren – he of royal blood – to get the can down, but a stock take was scheduled for tomorrow, not next week, so better he did it. Darren could be a tad slow. But as Smokowski was busy, the job of serving the customer that had just come in would have to fall to Darren.

'Darren!' yelled Smokowski, who then nearly fell from the stepladder he was on as Darren replied from just behind him.

'Yes?' said Darren, always eager to please even if that wasn't always the result.

'Could you serve the customer, please?' asked Smokowski, gingerly stepping down from the stepladder.

Ah, thought a grateful Smokowski as he placed a foot back on terra firma with no more damage done. He turned the can in his hand to see what it contained, but before he had the chance to look, he felt a sharp tug on his grocer's coat. He turned his head to find Darren gripping his sleeve and looking as if he had seen a ghost.

'Darren?' said Smokowski, frowning with concern at his assistant. 'You okay?'

But Darren didn't answer; he just raised a hand and pointed at something behind Smokowski.

Smokowski's frown deepened; he knew Darren could be a little odd at times but something in the way he was staring alarmed him. He slowly turned to see what had caused the look in Darren's eyes. The grip he had on the can tightened. If a weapon was needed, it would have to do.

And then he saw what Darren saw. The can dropped from his grip and landed on the toe of his boot. He felt nothing – steel toecaps. But it was doubtful he would have felt anything, anyway. Mouth open. Face white. It was Smokowski's turn to look as if he had seen a ghost.

CHAPTER 5

'Marc!' called Lucy from the foot of the stairs for the umpteenth time. 'You up yet?' Silence. 'MARC!'

'But it's Saturday,' came a reluctant reply.

'You still have to get up,' said Lucy. She sighed; it was a hard life being a single parent. She then remembered she wasn't a single parent; she was married to Darren. Lucy sighed again. It was a hard life being married to someone like Darren. No, she thought, a bit harsh. She smiled. Nothing wrong with Darren; he was just a little odd now and again, but who wasn't? She loved her husband. The kids loved their dad. She smiled again and resumed her haranguing of Marc. 'Come on. I've got a surprise for you.'

'Heard that one before,' came the reply from above.

Lucy smiled again. The boy was telling the truth. 'Okay,' she said in a matter-of-fact voice, 'but don't say I didn't tell you.' Lucy heard a huff and then movement from Marc's room.

'It had better be good,' drifted from above. The sound of a drawer opening followed.

'And have a wash.'

'Oh, mum.'

Lucy grinned and wondered why boys were so averse to using soap and water? She left the bottom of the stairs and went to the kitchen where Kate was having breakfast.

'I hope he does wash,' said Kate as her mum entered, a spoon full of breakfast hovering in front of her mouth. She wrinkled her nose in mock disgust and put the cereal in her mouth.

'I'm sure he will,' said Lucy, not sounding overly confident. She took a bowl from a cupboard and placed it on the kitchen table, ready for Marc's appearance.

'So,' said Kate, when she finished her breakfast, 'what's the big surprise?'

'All will be revealed when your brother comes down,' said Lucy.

Lucy is Tom's daughter. Kate and Marc are his grandchildren. Marc is twelve years old but acting as if he were in his teens. Kate is fifteen and well into her teens; no need to act. Darren – he of Royal Blood – is Smokowski's shop assistant and married to Lucy. Lucy knows nothing of Darren's past; even the time they had spent apart is hazy. Cat had seen to that. Lucy only knows of Cat as that stray that sometimes visits Tom. Cat had also seen to that. Only Tom, Cat and Smokowski know about Darren's past, what happened during the hazy part, and who he really is. But that's another story. Kate and Marc are Darren's children. Lucy sometimes feels she is the only adult among all of them. Today, though, she is determined to forgive all their little foibles. Today she is determined to be happy and upbeat. Something special is going to happen. Something as rare as a blue moon. Today her mother is paying a visit.

It was past ten before Marc saw fit to show his face, which, together with ears and neck, had a shiny well-scrubbed look to them.

Lucy was impressed; perhaps the day would go better than she expected. But she would still keep a pair of fingers crossed to be on the safe side.

'Right,' said Lucy, 'now we are all here, I shall reveal my surprise.'

'At last,' sighed Kate, looking at her watch. 'I'm supposed to be meeting Becky at eleven at the Mall.'

'And who are you expecting to drop you off there?' asked Lucy, knowing full well who that might be; mum the taxi service, that's who.

Kate rolled her eyes. 'Okay,' she said, pouting. 'What's the big surprise?'

Lucy upturned a saucepan for the occasion and now performed a drum roll on it with a pair of chopsticks. She finished with a flourish and revealed her surprise. 'Mum's coming to visit!' she announced, 'how cool is that?'

To Lucy's disappointment, the room failed to erupt with excitement. Instead, there was silence as Marc and Kate exchanged puzzled looks. The looks now fell on Lucy. Marc was also confused. He had always thought the madwoman with the chopsticks was his mother. Did he have another sister?!

'Nanny Tyme?' ventured Kate.

'Yes,' said Lucy, wondering who else Kate would think she meant – Darren's parents were just shadows existing on the edge of reality and not spoken or thought about. Cat had also seen to that. She would reveal their existence and identity when she felt the time was right, which could be never – 'and she's arriving late this evening and staying until Monday.'

'Your mum?' said Marc, relief washing over him.

'Who else did you think I was talking about?' said Lucy, now looking a tad puzzled herself.

'Er-no one,' said Marc, blushing. But then a thought. 'I thought she was dead.'

Lucy was shocked. 'Why would you think that?'

'Grandad always says "rest her soul" when someone mentions her.'

Relief. 'Just his little joke,' said Lucy, making light of it but wishing Tom wouldn't keep saying it, especially in front of the kids. 'She lives in Crewe.'

'Oh,' said Marc. 'Have I seen her before?' But before Lucy could answer, Marc realised there was a more important question that needed asking. 'Where is she going to sleep?' A very important question, as he suspected it might be his room that Nanny Tyme was going to sleep in. If so, he would need time to hide things from prying eyes. Things adults shouldn't know he possessed; teddy for one. Too old for one, pah! He frowned and pouted at the idea.

Lucy mistook the frown and pout as trouble brewing regarding the sleeping arrangements, but she was ready for it and had already decided on them. 'Nanny Tyme will be sleeping in my room,' she said, nipping that problem in the bud, 'I'll be on the sofa.'

'Have we?' said Kate.

'Have we what?' said Lucy, distracted because Marc's expression hadn't changed. 'You okay, Marc?'

Marc snapped from his thoughts. 'Er-yeah. Just got to go tidy my room.' Better safe than sorry, he had decided, still thinking of Teddy, which happened to be the name he had given his teddy. There was also Flopsy, his gorilla. Better hide her too. Marc got up and, without another word, walked to the bottom of the stairs before heading up them at a great rate of knots.

'Did he just…'

'He did mum,' said Kate, as bewildered as her mum was. 'Perhaps he's coming down with something?'

'I had better check on him later,' said Lucy, not quite believing she had heard right. Marc, tidying his room. Kate might be right; he must be coming down with something.

'Mum?'

'Sorry, poppet, what is it you wanted to ask?'

'Have we seen nanny Tyme before?' Kate honestly couldn't recall if she had.

'Yes, but you were very young.' Lucy smiled. 'Never mind though, you'll see her today. Who knows, you might remember her when you do.

CHAPTER 6

The can rolled under the counter flap and came to a stop at the feet of the customer. But this was no ordinary customer.

It was picked up and offered back to Smokowski. He was slow to take it, his eyes wide, his jaw slack. The can back in his hands, he struggled to form the words he wanted to say. Instead, he mumbled something that sounded like Yo-Yo.

'Yes, it's me,' said the customer, a stout lady in her late sixties wearing a tweed suit. A pair of comfortable leather walking shoes on her feet. Her greying hair, tight in a bun on her head. The horned rim glasses she wore on the bridge of her nose appeared to intensify the stern eye aimed at Smokowski. Looking severe had just been reinvented.

The woman now turned to look at Darren. 'Is this him?' she said, studying Darren as he visibly shrank under her stare.

'Er-yes,' said Smokowski, finding his tongue now that he was no longer under her direct scrutiny.

'Does he speak?' she asked.

'Now and then,' said Smokowski, Adam's apple bobbing.

'Good,' she said. 'Now tell him to toddle off and that I shall see him later.'

Smokowski looked at Darren and nodded.

Darren didn't need nodding at twice. He removed his apron and made for the door.

'Wait,' said the lady, in a voice that would stop a bull elephant in its tracks.

Darren froze on the spot.

'An Indian takeaway at about six-thirty. I feel like a Vindaloo.' She hadn't even looked at a still frozen on-the-spot Darren. 'Go on then shoo,' she said without turning around.

The next sound heard was the bell above the door tinkling as Darren exited the building as if his life depended on it.

CHAPTER 7

Tom stirred, and raised his weary head. He yawned. Nature was calling. A cuppa too many, perhaps. A heavy eyelid lifted to expose the eye it covered. Tom blinked. He blinked again. He closed that eye and raised his other eyelid, and blinked that eye. Now he opened both his eyes and did a synchronised blink. Suddenly forgetting its weariness, his head jerked upright. Tom's eyes were now wide. Then wider still.

'Cat!' he yelled.

CHAPTER 8

Now recovered from his initial shock at seeing what he had just seen and having regained his composure, Smokowski straightened and faced the lady. Her name was Mary, and she was Tom's ex-wife. It had been a long, long time since he had seen her, and for her to show up like this, unannounced, something important must be afoot. But he had another question to ask before he delved into what that might be.

'So,' said Smokowski, 'does Tom know you're here?'

'Mind fog, you know that,' said Mary, referring to Tom's lack of memory regarding their marriage. 'Can't be too careful.'

'But you still sent cards.'

'You know about that?' Mary mused on the fact. 'But of course, you do,' she said. 'There are ways.'

'A dangerous thing to do,' said Smokowski.

'She's my daughter.' Her features softened.

'And Tom?' Smokowski knew it had had to be done; the job, the secrecy, but he hadn't liked or got over the way it was done. To end their marriage like that, their family; it was cold.

'He's history.'

Smokowski's mind raced. Tom? Was that why she was here? Something had happened to Tom. 'He's… History?'

'My history Smokowski, my history.'

'Oh, right,' said Smokowski, relieved to hear that. For a second there…

'He's still your best friend?'

'Yes,'

'He will need you; he's wanted.'

'Tom?' Smokowski's mind raced again. A worried look crossed his face. 'Why, what's he done?' He would have added "now" but thought better of it. He began to fear the worst, then realised he had already feared that a moment ago. He suddenly feared the slightly worst.

'Nothing,' said Mary, realising she should have used her words more carefully. 'I mean, he's needed. The Ladies Institute need him. The BIMBOs need him. I need him.'

Relief popped its head around the door, but Smokowski wasn't going to let it in just yet; worry hadn't finished its turn yet.

'Why?'

'I've been promoted,' said Mary. 'Or rather I'm retiring and then being promoted.'

Smokowski was confused. 'But you're the President of the Ladies Institute. I didn't think you could go any higher?'

It was the reason Mary had had to disappear into the night all that time ago. As the President, there could be no room for anything or anyone else when in such a position. The name of the President was a secret. No one could know who she was outside of the inner circles of the Institute and the BIMBOs. Smokowski was the exception. It was for safety's sake, the Institutes, Mary's and for everyone she knew.

'Nor did I,' Mary admitted.

Smokowski was having trouble getting his head around what Mary was telling him.

'Promoted to what?'

'The head of the BIMBOs.'

There was a gasp from Smokowski. He was flabbergasted. 'The BIMBOs President?' He hadn't in his wildest dreams heard of such a thing, a non-magical in charge of the BIMBOs. (BIMBO is an acronym for The Edge and Field Intelligence Division.) (Well, they are a secret organisation.) 'But how?'

'The powers that be, decided it was time for change, and a non-magical should take the reins for a while.'

'And that non-magical is you.' Smokowski shook his head. He couldn't believe it.

'It is,' said Mary, 'and I found it hard to believe myself when I was told.'

Amazing, thought Smokowski, still wondering at the idea. He then remembered Tom. 'But what has Tom got to do with all this? You said he was needed?'

'He is,' said Mary, looking stern. 'He and Cat.'

'Why?'

'The Jam has disappeared.'

CHAPTER 9

Darren was highborn. Darren was a warrior. But that had been in another time and place. In this place, in this time, he was a bit of a doofus. A lovable doofus but a doofus all the same. It wasn't his fault; it took time to adapt, and Darren hadn't mastered that as yet. Not for want of trying, you see Darren looked at the world he now lived in with constant awe. Small slabs of glass that spoke to you. Wagons that travelled without horses pulling them. Giant metal birds with undigested people in them. Tom and Smokowski had explained most things to him, and he was getting there, to grips with the new world he now existed within. He knew how to work the DVD player – he loved films. So some thought of him as a child learning, some an eccentric – Lucy and the kids to name three – but to most who didn't know him, he was a doofus. But beware, if needed, Darren could become that fearless warrior again if danger threatened. Tom thought of Darren as all three of the above.

He arrived home wild-eyed, sweaty and worried, at a little past half-past five. Sweaty because he had run all the way. Worried because he wondered if Smokowski would dock his wages for leaving early. Wild-eyed because of what he had seen.

The door to the lounge flew open, causing Lucy to almost jump out of her skin.

'Grief Darren, give a girl a heart attack, why don't you,' said Lucy, holding a hand to her chest.

As Darren couldn't see a girl, whilst wondering why Lucy should want such a thing done, he decided to ignore the request and pass on the news. 'She's here!' he exclaimed.

'Who is?'

'She. Her.'

Lucy saw that Darren was in a bit of a state. 'Slow down. Here sit on the sofa.' Darren sat on the sofa. 'Now,' said Lucy, 'who is?'

'Your mother.'

'What!' Panic rose in Lucy's breast as she looked at the door Darren had just burst through, half expecting to see her mum standing there in the doorway. 'Here?'

'No.'

'No?'

14

'No, not here, here,' said Darren, 'there, here.'

'What?' said Lucy, trying to make sense of Darren's rambling.

'At the shop.'

'At Smokowski's?'

'Yes.'

'What's she doing there?' said Lucy.

'Visiting Smokowski, I think.' said Darren.

'Did she talk to you?'

'Yes, she said she would be here at about six-thirty and could she have a Vindaloo.'

Lucy's eyes widened. 'A Vindaloo?'

'That's what she said. At about six-thirty.'

Lucy stared at Darren and then at the coffee table. On it was a menu from the local Indian takeaway. She had been wondering if her mum would like a curry.

CHAPTER 10

'Cat!' yelled Tom with some urgency. He was looking round in horror and with a bit of "what the heck has happened-ness" thrown in.

Cat shifted in her sleep. She was having a wonderful dream involving fried chicken and lots and lots of fresh cream. She was not about to wake up without a fight.

'Cat!'

Cat shifted some more and stirred from her slumber. This had better be good, she thought, grumbling to herself as the chicken and cream drifted from her thoughts. She yawned, half raised her head and flicked an eyelid open. She then did a quicker version of what Tom had done earlier. Cat leapt to her feet.

'I need the toilet,' wailed Tom.

What the heck, thought Cat, ignoring Tom's plight as she stared at her surroundings in utter disbelief.

'But it's not there anymore.' Tom finished.

CHAPTER 11

'Jam?' said a mystified Smokowski. 'I've plenty of jam here.'

'The Jam,' said Mary in a serious tone.

Smokowski's eyes suddenly widened to the size of eye sized saucers as he realised what Mary was telling him. 'The Jam! Good grief. How?'

It was a mystery, Mary explained, who then elaborated on the consequences of it missing. Without it, the appointment and ceremony of the passing of the Jam to the new President, Mary's successor, could not go ahead. Without that going ahead, Mary could not become the new head of the BIMBOs.

'It will turn into a logjam,' said Mary. 'Things could get messy.' Mary's demeanour was grim. 'It could leave us in a very sticky situation.' Mary frowned. 'Pardon my unintentional puns.'

Smokowski felt he understood the gravity of the situation, but just to be sure. 'You're saying you can't retire or be promoted and the incoming President can't be appointed without the ceremony?'

'Not quite,' said Mary. 'I will still retire; the wheels are in motion, which means in a few days, the Ladies Institute will be without a President. At least until the Jam is recovered.'

It was Smokowski's turn to look serious. 'Grief!'

'Yes, but not only that, as the wheels are already in motion, there will be no President of the BIMBOs either.'

'But surely something can be done,' said an alarmed Smokowski.

'Sadly, nothing can,' said Mary. 'The wheels are in motion and will grind on, regardless.'

Smokowski lowered his head and shook it. 'That's bad,' he said, wondering if even Tom and Cat could get them out of this pickle.

'Oh, but it's worse than bad,' said Mary.

Smokowski looked up sharply. Worse? he thought. 'How?'

'If any new President cannot take their place at the head of the BIMBOs in the allotted time, for me, that's in a few days; the BIMBOs will shut down.'

An aghast, Smokowski couldn't believe what he was hearing. 'Why?'

'Because a new President will have to be elected, which means nominations for office, voting, it will take ages.'

'But surely they have contingency plans to cover such an eventuality?'

'That is the contingency plan. It's written in stone, and I mean literally.'

'But surely something can be done?'

'If not,' said Mary, shaking her head, 'it will be a catastrophe.'

An understatement if ever he heard one, thought Smokowski. The Institute rudderless, and the BIMBOs shut down. 'But surely someone could step in. A caretaker, perhaps?'

'That's not how it works.'

'Can't you do something? You're still the President.'

'If I could, I wouldn't be here.' Mary sighed. 'The wheels you see. I'm only President in name now because the process has already started. I'm being wound down. This is my shore leave if you like before I change ships.' She smiled grimly. 'A chance to tie up any loose ends. See family. But yes, something needs doing, but not by me. I have to go through the motions; to do otherwise might raise eyebrows. So that is why I am here, visiting a friend. You are now one of only a chosen few who know of the dilemma we find ourselves in.'

Smokowski looked glum.

'But cheer up,' said Mary, 'there's always Tom and Cat.'

'Yes,' said Smokowski brightening a little, 'but what can they do?'

'Find the Jam, of course.'

'Of course,' said Smokowski, feeling a little silly at not having realised their part in this before now.

'The thing is, we believe someone has stolen the Jam. To what ends we don't know, but it could be a deliberate move to destabilise both the Institute and the BIMBOs at the same time.'

It hadn't crossed Smokowski's mind that the Jam might have been stolen. It just put everything in a more dangerous light.

'Who would do such a thing?' he muttered as much to himself as Mary. 'And why?'

'Small steps,' said Mary. 'First, we must try to find the Jam. If we find that in time, problem solved; we can sort out the who-done-its later.'

'But if Tom can't find the Jam?'

'As I said, small steps are needed, one at a time, but we have more pressing problems to deal with first.'

'Okay,' said Smokowski, pulling himself together. Mary needed his help to contact Tom, and he would play his part. 'I'll call Tom this minute, and we can get things moving.'

'Ah,' said Mary.

'Ah?' said Smokowski.

'I should have said earlier; I'm afraid Tom and Cat are one of those problems I mentioned.'

Smokowski looked mystified.

Mary continued. 'We don't know if it's something to with the Jam or something unconnected.'

'You've lost me,' said Smokowski.

'I'm sorry I'm not making myself clear, am I? I'm not here to ask you to contact them. I'm here to ask you to find them. Tom and Cat are also missing.'

CHAPTER 12

Tom was right. The toilet wasn't there anymore. Neither was the kitchen. Nor was the cottage come to that. The bottom line was, excluding himself and Cat, everything that had existed before Tom had gone to sleep was now no longer there.

'What's going on?' he wailed, staring at the boulder that stood where his kitchen table should have been. His chair had gone, in its place a smaller boulder. His bottom cheeks hurt. His elbows hurt. And he still wanted to go to the loo.

Ignoring Tom's wailing, Cat sniffed the air. It made her a little happier; at least they could breathe. That wasn't the real reason for her sniffing, though. She was trying to get a sense of their surroundings. The air smelled damp, she noted. She looked to her left. To her right. Up and down. There was no doubt about it; they were in a cave. The question was, how had they got there?

Tom wailed again. He was jigging and jogging on the spot. Cat closed her eyes. It was going to be one of those days, was it? 'Go behind the large rock over yonder,' she suggested.

'But it's dark,' groaned Tom, only just noticing he couldn't see anything past the dim shapes of the boulders.

'You got your Saver?'

'Think so.' Tom saw where Cat was going; it could be changed into a light source. Rummaging in his jacket pockets began. It was a good thing he had put it back on after seeing to his bumps and bruises. 'Aha!' he exclaimed as he pulled something from a pocket.

'Got it?' enquired Cat, crossing her claws. A grumpy Tom was bad enough, but one with a full bladder.

'Drat!' was the answer. 'It's just me torch.' He went to put it back.

Cat looked on in dismay. 'Does it work?'

'What work?' said Tom.

'The torch.'

'Torch?' It took a moment. 'Oh. Torch.' If looks could bleat.

'Try it.'

Tom found the ON switch and pressed it. 'Aargh!' he yelled as the torch sprang to life and blinded him.

'It works then.'

Tom didn't reply; he was much too busy trying to blink the numerous dots from his eyes.

Cat decided to leave him to it and explore their surroundings. See if she could find a clue to where they were and, perhaps, to how they had got there.

Cat could easily traverse the rocky terrain within the cave without too much trouble with her cat vision. She made for the highest point she could see; a large boulder. In the distance, she could hear Tom bemoaning his lot with the occasional groan as some part of his body found a hard object he hadn't seen. At the top of the boulder, Cat was rewarded with a glimpse of light. It was faint and a way off, but perhaps a way out.

'Cat!' yelled Tom as he stepped from the rocks and boulders he had disappeared behind. Where was she? 'Where are you?'

'Here!' shouted Cat. 'To your left. About thirty paces.'

Tom shone the torch.

'Your other left.'

The torch beam now swung in the other direction and lit up the base of the boulder Cat was standing on. 'Where?'

'Move the beam up. I'm on top of the boulder.'

The beam slowly rose until it reflected in Cat's eyes.

'Wah!' yelped Tom, dropping the torch.

'You okay?' asked Cat, seeing the torch beam suddenly drop, then illuminate parts of the cave floor as it rolled a few feet across it.

'Er-yeah,' said Tom, recovering from his scare. He went to retrieve the torch. 'Just tripped over a stone.' He wasn't going to admit to Cat that her eyes had just scared the living pyjama's out of him.

He frightened himself, thought a grinning Cat as she listened to the odd oath drifting up to her. Eventually, the beam started to rise again.

'Got it,' yelled Tom.

'Good,' said Cat as the beam headed her way. 'I think I've found a way out.'

'Did you say a way out?' said Tom, as he finally reached the bottom of the boulder Cat was standing on.

Cat watched as the beam slowly travelled up the boulder and then watched it travel much quicker down again after it had shone on her.

'That you Cat?' Tom asked, after a moment or two of silence.

'Yes,' said Cat, wondering who else Tom thought it might be.

'Just checking.'

Cat wondered about Tom sometimes. Most of the time. 'I can see a light in the distance,' she said.

'Light at the end of the tunnel, eh?' said Tom, who was not as cheerful as he was pretending to be.

'I'll climb down, and we can go investigate,' said Cat, ignoring Tom's silliness.

They set off, Tom keeping close tabs on Cat, the beam of the torch darting here and there, looking for things that weren't there, but might be.

'Any idea where we might be?' said Tom.

'I might,' said Cat, instantly regretting saying it. She quickly changed the subject before Tom could question her on it. 'Have you washed your hands?' Weak, but thankfully it worked.

'Yeah,' said an indignant Tom. 'I used a wet wipe and some of that gel stuff.' He looked at the hand that was torch free. 'Don't half sting if you got a cut you didn't know you had.'

'Suspect it would sting if you did know about it,' said Cat. Just how much stuff has he got in those pockets of his? she wondered. They appeared bottomless. She might well investigate when they are back home.

Tom frowned as he looked at his hand. 'Suppose.'

'Look,' said Cat. They were much closer to the light now. 'I think there's a gap in the wall.'

'Where?' said Tom.

'There. To your— Over there.' Cat pointed with her paw. 'The light's coming through it.'

'Where?'

'Turn the torch off.'

He didn't like the idea of that but did it anyway. 'Oh, yeah,' said Tom, who could see it now, now that the torch wasn't pointing at it. 'You think it might be a way out?'

'We can but hope,' said Cat, looking up at Tom. She frowned. His silver locks were gone. 'Where did you get your cap from?'

'It was in my pocket,' said Tom, pulling open a pocket for Cat to inspect. 'Found it when I was looking for the gel. Oh, and I found the Saver.'

That was it; she would most definitely be checking those pockets out. 'Good,' said Cat, 'it could come in handy.' She started for the gap. 'Wait here.'

Tom was not about to argue. No point in both of them getting into trouble; if trouble was waiting. No, someone should stay behind. Guard the rear. He watched Cat disappear into the darkness. The darkness. He had forgotten to turn the torch back on. He soon remedied that. The torch sprang to life, instantly creating dubious-looking shadows. He quickly turned the torch off again. Now he thought he could hear things. The torch sprang to life again. The shadows now twisted and squirmed amongst the rocks like living things as the beam played here and there. He turned it off again. Grief, he thought, I hope she isn't gone too long.

CHAPTER 13

'Missing?' said Smokowski, taken aback, 'but I only spoke to him on the phone yesterday. He had just come back from a mission.'

'His time-bubble stopped registering yesterday evening,' said Mary. Smokowski looked grim. 'And Cat?'

'We had a fellow familiar check for her Aura. They couldn't find it. We believe she is with Tom wherever that is.'

'Could they be on a secret mission?' said Smokowski, clutching at straws.

'We checked. No mission instructions were sent, secret or otherwise.'

Smokowski ran fingers through his hair. 'So, what do we do? They could be anywhere. With anyone.'

'We can't rule out foul play,' said Mary, watching Smokowski closely.

The colour of Smokowski's skin visibly paled. 'Foul play?' The thought was horrifying.

'Some people are also of the mind that the timing of the Jam going awry and their disappearance is more than a coincidence.'

'Preposterous.' Smokowski couldn't believe his ears. Not Tom and Cat. 'You can't possibly think they took the Jam?'

'I don't,' said Mary, 'but it will cause suspicion in some quarters.'

'But they wouldn't.'

'I know, but we need to find them as quickly as possible to quash those thoughts so they can find the Jam. And we need you to find them.'

Smokowski saw the sense in that, but what could he do? He wasn't a traveller. He had a Hitchhiker – a device that allowed the owner to travel on the residue of a time machine's wake – but using that could take ages. And it would be totally useless if Tom had not used his time machine to take him to wherever he was now.

'I would like to help,' said Smokowski, 'but what can I do? I'm not a traveller, and the Hitchhiker would be next to useless.'

Just then the shop doorbell tinkled.

Drat, thought Smokowski, he should have locked the shop door; not a good time to have a customer.

But it wasn't a customer.

'And that is why you need help.'

The not a customer, wearing probably the scruffiest jumper on the planet, arrived at the counter.

'This is Willy,' said Mary. 'He's a traveller, and he's here to help.'

CHAPTER 14

After what seemed like hours of waiting – in reality, it had been only a minute or so since Cat had entered the light – Tom's worries worsened.

What if something has happened to her? thought Tom. What if he was now on his own? Tom fretted. Further what-ifs followed. Until. What if? No, he decided, he didn't want to think about what-ifs anymore, he couldn't take it, the thoughts. He just couldn't take it. 'What if?' he wailed instead. Tom was getting just a tad carried away. 'What if?'

'What if what?' said a voice beside him.

Tom nearly did himself a mischief. With a look of terror on his face, he looked down to see Cat standing there.

'You okay?' said Cat, a little concerned by Toms theatrics.

'I-I,' was all Tom could say.

'You pretending to be a sailor again?' said Cat, remembering the last time he had done that; they were almost keelhauled by the British navy but saved by the privateer Francis Drake who had a soft spot for cats.

Tom's heart was still in his mouth, but he had recovered enough, now he realised it was Cat and not some cave-dwelling nasty who had crept up on him.

'You shouldn't creep up like that. You should have said something.'

'I called you from the gap, but you were too busy wailing "what ifs" to notice. So I had to come over to see what was going on.'

'Oh,' said Tom.

'I think it best if you follow me and see what's on the other side.'

They reached the gap, and Tom peered into the light.

'You will have to crawl the last few feet,' advised Cat.

Tom's felt his knees twinge at the thought, but if it meant getting out of the cave, they would have to lump it. He doubted they would complain too much though, if it were just a short distance.

They finally reached the outside of the cave, and Tom found he had been wrong. His knees were having a right old moan.

'Ooh me knees,' groaned Tom as he attempted to get upright.

'You okay?' asked Cat, as Tom staggered about as a flamingo might if its legs were back to front.

'Give me a minute,' said a wincing Tom, 'just me knees getting their own back on me.'

While Tom and his knees settled their differences, Cat looked out at the view that would greet Tom when he found the time to look. 'It's as I feared,' she said, forgetting to think the words.

Tom slowly turned to Cat, his complaining knees forgotten about for the moment. Feared? The word was bad enough, but Cat using it was ten on the "time to be worried" scale. 'Feared?' he said, the hairs standing up on the back of his neck. 'What do you mean it's what you feared?' He then noticed for the first time the view that had met Cat when she first left the cave.

From where they stood, the ground steadily sloped down to meet a world of wilderness. Wizened trees, parched earth, stubby grass and running down the middle of it and disappearing into the distance was a road made from yellow cobblestones. Beyond that was a hill with a flattish top to it, a plateau, surrounded by a great forest and on it stood a green structure that could only be described as a green box.

The last part described to Tom as his eyes weren't anywhere near as good as Cats was. He could see the yellow road and surrounding wilderness, though.

'Blimey,' said Tom, forgetting for the moment that he should be worried, 'Oz!' His voice full of awe.

'Oz?' said Cat.

'Yeah,' said Tom, 'you know, where things come back to you when you throw them. You know. What's it called? Ah, that's it, Australia.'

Cat was puzzled for a moment. She knew of Australia, but none of the information or pictures she had looked at described or looked much like the view in front of her. There was only one conclusion. 'No,' she said.

'Oh,' said Tom, his heart set on seeing a kangaroo.

'It's bleaker than that,' said Cat.

Tom didn't think Australia bleak at all; he had seen a documentary. 'So, where are we then?'

'Somewhere we shouldn't be.'

Tom felt he had already gathered that, but something in Cats tone brought her earlier words back to him.

'Is it somewhere to be feared?' he asked, moving closer to Cat whilst casting furtive glances at his surroundings.

'Perhaps,' said Cat.

Good grief, thought Tom, is she going to tell him where they are or not? 'So, where are we then?' he asked.

'Nod, Tom. We are in the land of Nod.'

And if Tom had had any clue about what Cat was saying, he would have been a very worried and afeared pensioner indeed.

CHAPTER 15

Willy was five feet, nothing tall. Wiry of build. His hair wild, brown of colour, encompassing a fine bald spot of medium size. His nickname was "the monk". He didn't know that as no one was brave enough to say it to his face. A Traveller on secondment to the Ladies Institute where he took on the duties of Mary's bodyguard and chauffeur; car and time.

'You may have heard of him,' said Mary.

'Not that I recall,' said Smokowski, giving the little chap the once over.

'No?' said Mary. 'Then let me introduce you.' She took a step back and waved her hand back and forth. 'Willy, meet Smokowski and, Smokowski, please meet, Willy Warmer.'

Willy held out a hand and, a wide-eyed Smokowski shook it.

'Not the Willy Warmer?'

'In the flesh, sir,' said Willy, bowing his head slightly. His hair made a grating sound as it brushed his jumper. Hairdressers – when Willy went to one – had to discard their scissors for wire cutters.

Smokowski was most impressed; Willy was almost a legend in his own lifetime to those in the know. Why, there was even a rumour that the LISPS (Ladies Institute Special Participatory Services) (their version of the SAS) had used his name as their password once. The Institute profusely denied it while hurriedly changing it. But the rumour was that the odd LISPS division still used it. When asked, a spokeswoman for the Institute said it was "poppycock". A further spokeswoman later denied that the word "poppycock" was also a password.

'So, is that your real surname?' asked Smokowski.

'No,' said Willy smiling, 'it's Vonka.'

'Why don't you use that?'

Willy shrugged. 'Because when I told someone my name, the person I was talking to would laugh and ask if I had any chocolate. No idea why; got on my nerves after a while, so stopped using it.'

'Understandable,' said Smokowski. 'So, why Willy Warmer?'

'This,' said Willy.

'Ah,' said Smokowski, 'your jumper.'

'Never go anywhere without it, you see. Warmest thing I've ever owned.'

'Well,' said Mary, affording herself a small smile. 'And now,' she said, looking at her watch, 'I must go.'

'So, what do I do?' said Smokowski, who had momentarily put the reason Mary was there to the back of his mind. 'Where do I start?'

'Willy will fill you in on the details when he gets back.'

Mary headed for the door, which Willy held open for her. 'Nice to have met you again, Smokowski,' she said. She then left the shop happy. Smokowski would do just fine.

CHAPTER 16

The slope from the cave proved to be as promised, a gentle one, a mere meander. Something Tom and his knees much appreciated. A perambulation he may well have enjoyed on another occasion, but here and now, with his mind clouded by what Cat told him, he couldn't.

Nod, the land of, Cat explained, was the place your mind went to when you were asleep. Other lands of Nod existed, which Cat didn't go into, but they weren't this one. Tom kept a blank expression on his face as she explained this. This Nod was made up of millions of other Nods. These were where humans and Magicals travelled to when they slept. This Nod, the one Tom and Cats were in, was not either of theirs.

Needless to say, during Cat's explanation, Tom's mind wandered, which is technically another land of Nod, which Cat, if she knew his mind was doing such a thing, would have told him. Thankfully Cat didn't, and so Tom still kept his sanity.

'So,' said Tom as he reached the bottom of the slope, 'we are in somebody else's sleep?'

'Yes and no,' said Cat. 'We are in someone's dream.'

'So, we're asleep?'

'No,' said Cat. 'Nor are we dreaming,' she said, anticipating Tom's next question.

'So, are we—' said Tom, stopping when he realised Cat answered the question he was about to ask. He decided on another one. 'So, we are actually here? In the flesh, like?'

'Yes.' Cat believed she and Tom had woken from their lands of Nod in someone else's land of Nod. And that person was having a dream. One they had slipped into. A dangerous thing to do.

A long time ago, when Wizards could shake a stick at anything they wanted to, the practice had been called "Nod Napping". Magicals used it to get rid of rivals or anyone else they wanted to see the back of in a neat, no-mess way. The victim would find themselves in a dream in someone else's land of Nod, and when the person whose Nod it was, woke up, the victim would be trapped inside and dissolve along with the dream. No one would be any the wiser as to the person's fate. Thankfully, there surfaced the occasional survivor, and the evil practice came to light. Henceforth the act was condemned as black magic and banned from use, and any person fool enough to attempt it faced the threat of banishment from reality. But sadly, there was always someone desperate enough to chance their reality.

'How?' asked Tom.

'Sheer bad luck,' said Cat. Or someone put them there on purpose, she thought. She kept that to herself, though. Tom had enough problems on his plate. His knees for one. So for the moment, the how or why could wait. The more important and pressing problem was getting out of the situation as fast as possible before whoever's dream it was, woke up. But how they did that, she didn't know. She would have to follow her senses; they had come to her rescue on more than one occasion.

They reached the cobbled pathway and stepped onto it. Tom gave it the once over.

'More gold than yellow,' Tom observed. 'You don't suppose it is, do you?' He wondered how many cobbles he could fit in his pockets.

'Yes,' said Cat, bringing a gleam to Tom's eyes.

'Way-hey,' said Tom, ready to fill those pockets.

'Fool's gold.'

'Eh, you sure?' said a disappointed Tom, eyes no longer gleaming.

'Certain,' said Cat.

'Oh,' said Tom, who then took an idle kick at one and instantly regretted it as boot juddered against stone. 'Ow,' he hollered, 'me knee.'

'As I said,' said Cat, smiling, 'fool's gold. Now come on, we need to get a move on.'

Tom, giving Cat his best "what do you mean by that" stare, rubbed at his knee. Cat meanwhile ignored him and headed along the road.

'Where are we going?' said Tom, now rubbing his other knee out of habit.

'To find a way out before we disappear.'

Disgruntled, but now following – he didn't want to disappear – Tom called after Cat. 'How do you know we're going the right way?'

'I don't,' said Cat.

'What do you mean you don't?'

'Just that,' said Cat. 'Now, come on. Times wasting.'

Stopping in his tracks, Tom let what Cat said sink in; she didn't know? And worse, she sounded worried when she'd said it. Grief, he thought, Cat worried? They really must be in trouble. He quickly shuffled after her.

CHAPTER 17

Willy dropped Mary outside Lucy's home and started back to the mini-mart and a waiting, wondering, Smokowski.

Mary knocked on the front door. There was a bell push, but one never knew if they were working. She finally heard footsteps approach the door from the inside. The door opened.

'Mum,' said Lucy, holding the door open, 'come in.'

'Thank you,' said Mary. She stepped in and into an immediate hug. Taken aback, not being used to such signs of affection, it took a moment for Mary to react. But gradually, her arms rose, and she hugged back. It was. It felt. Undeserved.

An excited and nervous Lucy led her mum into the kitchen, where three expectant faces looked up as one. She didn't need to introduce them, but she did. Kate stood and gave her nan a hug. Marc hesitated, unsure if he should do the same, decided it wasn't the manly thing to do, so sort of bowed and then offered his hand. The corners of Mary's mouth twitched into a slight smile as she shook it.

'And this is Darren,' said Lucy.

Mary's turn to hold out a hand. 'Nice to meet you again,' she said.

'You've already met?' said Lucy, surprised.

'At Smokowski's,' said Mary, now smiling fully.

'Oh-yes, silly me,' said Lucy, feeling a tad foolish. 'Would you like to sit down? We've ordered the curry. It should be here soon.'

'That would be lovely,' said Mary, her smile fading a little. She regretted what she was about to do, but it was an inevitable part of her life. She whispered something under her breath. The next instant, her daughter and grandchildren froze in time.

Her emotions held in check, Mary turned to face a mortified and mystified Darren just as the doorbell rang. It works then, she thought. 'Can you get that please?' said Mary. 'And then we shall talk.'

Darren, his mind a whirr of questions, rose from his chair and started for the door as asked; he felt compelled.

'I expect it's the curries,' said Mary, 'but if not, just get rid of them.'

Darren nodded. 'Good lad.'

CHAPTER 18

The distance from the cave to the forest had been deceptive. Much shorter than Cat had envisaged. Much shorter to Tom's relief.

The forest had also changed; it had shrunk in size and was now more like a large wood. The only things that had stayed the same as when they had first seen them were the wilderness on either side of the gold cobbled road and the road itself. But it was a dream they were in and, they could take nothing for granted; they would need to be on their guard if they wanted to get out of it in one piece.

'What now?' said Tom.

'We go in,' said Cat.

Tom just knew she would say that. 'But it's dark in there,' said Tom peering into the wood's shadowy depth.

'You've got a torch,' said Cat, not about to take any nonsense from Tom.

Tom gurned, his nose crinkling, eyebrows arching to a point on either side; he looked like a demented pink bat, the flying kind. She's always got an answer, he thought. Well, two can play at that game. 'Ladies first,' he said, politely offering her the way.

'Losers last,' said Cat as she moved forward.

"Ere,' said Tom, 'no such thing as losers, it's the taking part that counts.' Not what he had said about the horse he had backed in the Grand National. Grief, he thought, what am I going on about? But before he could decide, he walked into Cat, who had stopped at the wood's edge.

'Oops, sorry,' said Tom.

'Shush,' said Cat.

Tom shushed. He gave Cat a questioning look. Then he heard it, a rustling noise interspersed with a clip-clopping sound. It was coming from the woods.

Suddenly a shape emerged.

'Ye gads!' said Tom, unnerved by the sudden apparition. He took a step back. A knight in shining armour with a hobbyhorse between his legs and two coconut halves tied to each knee had clip-clopped from the woods.

'Who goes there?' said the knight, 'friend or foe?'

Silly question, thought Tom, you could say friend and be a lying foe. He played along, wasn't hard. 'Foe,' he said. Whoops. 'I meant friend,' he corrected quickly, taking a further couple of steps back. 'Sorry.'

The shining knight quickly took a defensive stance, his coconuts clopping as he did, and unsheathed a large, shiny, razor-sharp potato peeler. He raised it above his head. 'Which is it?' he demanded, looking as threatening as a person in shiny armour and wielding an oversized potato peeler could look.

Not wanting to be peeled, Cat took charge of the situation. 'Friend,' she said in a conciliatory tone. 'We both are.'

The potato peeler dropped a little, but it stayed threatening because of Toms little slip of the tongue.

'Who holds your allegiance, friend?' the knight asked Tom.

Tom didn't like being put on the spot, mainly because thinking on his feet could give him vertigo. So he said Reading FC. He knew not why.

'Reading if-see?' said the knight. The knight was giving Tom's answer some serious thought. He wasn't convinced that the old man in mismatched clothing or the short hairy one were friends, but as he had never heard of the allegiance the old man spoke of, he erred on the side of caution, for now. 'Who is this Reading if-see?' Best not to remove the head of someone you later find to be on the same side as yourself. Especially if that someone happens to be important.

A good question, thought Tom, who was not that much of a football fan. He didn't even own a football shirt or a telly remote with your favourite team on it. No, what had brought Reading FC to his attention was their nickname, the Biscuitmen. Tom was most definitely a biscuit man. Cakes were okay but harder to dunk.

But would the knight know what a football team was? he pondered, he went with no. Perhaps he could tell him they were Biscuitmen. But again, he decided he better go with no. The man, if there was a man there in the armour, could be a woman, might think they belonged to some weird bakery cult or were rivals to the gingerbread men. Then it came to him. Perhaps it was what he had meant all along. Reading had a second, more recent nickname; the royals. What knight didn't work for some Royal or other.

'The Royals,' said Tom, not a moment too soon. The knight had raised his potato peeler again and had taken an impatient step forward.

'The Royals?' growled the knight, moving his peeler in an arc.

It was Cat's turn to take a step back. She readied to defend herself.

Tom would have done the same if his legs hadn't turned to jelly. His knees hadn't yet decided what they would do. Instead, he gripped his Saver tight and started thinking of something useful if the need arose.

The shiny knight raised his potato peeler even higher.

Tom raised the arm holding the Saver to see to his horror it was now a rose, thorns and all. 'Ow,' he said, dropping it as it pricked a thumb.

Meanwhile, Cat had raised a paw, magic at the ready. She just hoped it would work here.

The potato peeler in the knight's hand suddenly swished through the air. It came to a rest level with his waist and pointing behind him at a path neither Tom nor Cat had noticed.

'Why did you not say you were allied to the Royals?' said the knight, lowering his potato peeler. 'Please pass with the blessing of Artorius, protector of this land and its people.' The shiny knight then clip-clopped to the side on his hobbyhorse to allow Tom and Cat to pass.

'Follow the path, and you shall seek what you find.' The shiny knight held his potato peeler to his chest and bent his head in deference.

With two eyes firmly fixed on the shiny knight, one of Tom's and one of Cats, the duo cautiously ventured past him and onto the path, both taking backward glances as they travelled further along it. Only when they were out of sight of the shiny knight did they relax, and their breathing return to normal.

'I thought he was going to peel us,' said Tom, sucking at his pricked thumb. He had carefully retrieved the Saver and put it back in his pocket. Thankfully, it had now returned to its original form; a pen.

'What was all that royal nonsense?' said Cat, not mentioning the thumb as she didn't need to know. Not in the detail Tom would use to relate the story, anyway. They didn't have the time for it. But she was thankful for his nonsense all the same. It appeared to have saved them from a fate worse than… She didn't know what.

'Long story,' said Tom.

And as they didn't have time for one, Cat left her questioning there.

They walked on.

'Cat?' said Tom.

'Yes?' said Cat.

'What do you think he meant when he said, "you will seek what you find", shouldn't it have been you will find what you seek?'

Cat had noticed but put it down to nothing more than nonsense. It being uttered by a knight in shining armour, riding a hobbyhorse, wielding a large potato peeler and making clip-clop noises with his knees.

'Nothing,' said Cat, 'just dream nonsense. I shouldn't worry about it.'

They walked on.

CHAPTER 19

Willy arrived back just as Smokowski was turning the open sign to closed. As usual, he had waited beyond the normal closing time in case that elusive last-minute shopper, with a list as long as their arm, should turn up. More so this day, not knowing when he would open again. He had already written a note for the door. There was always Darren, but would that be better, leaving him in charge? He was still in a quandary about it.

'You ready?' said Willy, as Smokowski held the door open for him.

'I thought you were meant to fill me in on details?' said Smokowski, locking the door.

'Okay,' said Willy, 'Tom and Cat have gone missing, and we need to find them.'

'But I already know that,' said Smokowski, frowning.

'Mary said you were sharp.'

Smokowski narrowed his eyes.

'But before we go, I need a few things. You still open?'

'I suppose, for you,' said Smokowski, sighing. Still, it was a sale. Perhaps something small, but it all counted. He then smiled to himself. He doubted a comb was on the list. 'Right Sir, what can I get for you?'

'Great,' said Willy, 'I have a list.' He took one from his pocket, and it unrolled the length of an arm. 'Right, you got any combs? Metal ones?' He sighed. 'Don't last long with my hair. Better have all you got.'

Gobsmacked but thrilled but not wanting to show it, Smokowski put on the best poker face he could muster and set about the first of a list full of purchases. But in his head, his excitement could not be contained. KERCHING-KERCHING-KERCHING!!! he thought, as he gleefully filled a bag with combs.

CHAPTER 20

Tom and Cat travelled for what seemed like miles, but as far as they felt they had walked, the distance from them to the edge of the wood where they had entered always stayed the same. Tom didn't like it.

'No,' agreed Cat. 'We appear to be going nowhere fast.' And at this rate they might not escape, she thought. She also wondered what was with all the knights? So far, they had been waylaid by the hobbyhorse knight, a monkey wearing plastic armour wielding a very sharp banana, and a ferret knight wrapped in silver foil who apologised for not having a weapon but knew it couldn't be far away. What next?

Suddenly the path got narrower, and now the further they stepped along it, the further the edge of the wood became more distant.

'I still don't like it,' said Tom, after noticing the change.

'Nor I,' said Cat, 'but at least we seem to be getting somewhere at last.'

'But where?' said Tom.

'Who goes there?' said a sudden voice from nowhere.

'Who said that?' said Tom, spinning on the spot to see who had. He couldn't see anyone. 'Cat?'

'Down there,' said Cat, who could see who had spoken.

Tom looked down at his feet. 'Down where?'

'Here,' repeated the voice.

Tom looked in the direction it had come. 'Ye gads,' he said, which was fast becoming his new go-to expression of surprise.

Standing only six inches tall was another knight. This new knight, a mouse, was kitted out in a silver-painted matchbox and a silver thimble for a helmet.

'Friend or foe?' demanded the mouse.

'Oh good grief,' muttered Tom, 'not again.' He thought of saying foe again, just to wind the mouse up. What could it do? But he knew Cat wouldn't be best pleased if he did, so… 'Friend,' he said. There then followed the same sequence that had happened with the other knights. Allegiance? Royals.

'Please pass with the blessings of Artorius.'

They walked on.

'How many are we going to meet?' said Tom, the novelty of the knights wearing thin.

'Who knows?' said Cat, 'but I have the feeling we are getting closer to our goal.'

'Ah!' blurted Tom. 'That's it.'

'What's it?' said Cat, wondering if the pressure was getting to Tom.

'Why they keep letting us past.'

'Pray tell?' said Cat, all ears but not expecting many, if any, words of wisdom from the mouth of Tom.

'Football,' said an animated Tom, almost dancing on the spot.

'Football?' said Cat. No words of wisdom yet.

'Yes,' said Tom, 'football,' he made a round shape in the air with his hand, 'and goal.' He then made a kicking motion followed by the raising of his arms in celebration. 'Football, goal,' he said.

'And?' said Cat, thinking Tom's joints would have to pay for his dramatics later.

Tom stopped walking. 'Don't you see the connection?' he said. 'I mention football to the knights, and every time I do, it brings us closer to our goal.'

No, thought Cat, nothing wise there, move along now. 'But you haven't mentioned football to them,' she said, pouring water on his parade. 'I have,' said Tom.

'When?'

'Reading FC,' said Tom.

Cat could almost hear the "na-na-ne-na-na" playing through Tom's mind.

'Did you mention they were a football team?'

Tom thought about this. 'Well, not exactly,' he admitted, 'but the FC is short for football club.'

'And you think they know that?' said Cat. 'The knight on the hobbyhorse? The monkey? The ferret? The thimble wearing mouse? Any of them?'

A shadow fell across Tom's face. Now he thought about it; he hadn't even mentioned Reading FC to the ferret and the mouse. He looked confused.

'It's the royals bit,' Cat explained.

'But Reading FC and the royals are the same,' said Tom, hanging on for as long as he could.

'They obviously think it means something else,' said Cat.

She's right, thought Tom, finally admitting it to himself. What was he thinking? Then he had it. Lack of a cuppa! And it must be breakfast time by now. No wonder. He was lacking in vittals. Woe was he!

'But cheer up,' said Cat, reacting to the glum look that had spread across Tom's face, 'we must be getting close to the hill and perhaps getting out of the dream.' She hoped.

Tom cheered a little. 'You think?' he said.

'Why else would the knights keep getting smaller? Or the path narrow? If we weren't close?' Why she had come to that conclusion, she didn't know. But if it got Tom out of the doldrums. Something Cat would not wish on anyone; a doldrum Tom.

There was some logic to that, thought Tom, brightening up further. Perhaps there would be a kettle, teabag and cup waiting for them when they got wherever it was they were going. And maybe, he thought, a choccy biscuit. Suddenly Tom was no longer in the doldrums. Now, if only his shoulders and leg didn't ache so much.

And then, as if by magic, they found themselves at the foot of the hill.

'Blimey,' said Tom.

'Ditto,' said Cat, swearing that it wasn't there a second ago.

'Where'd the trees go?' said Tom.

A good question, thought Cat, this is too easy. Her senses had told her to head for the hill. But instead of the expected pitfalls she might have suspected they may encounter, trapped in a dream that someone didn't want them to escape from, their journey so far had been uneventful. Smooth even. Surely they should be fighting their way out? There were the knights who challenged them on the path, but they had hardly been deterrents. Cat peered up at the top of the hill. If their way out, as her senses were telling her, was something to do with the green object above, then why hadn't there been any attempts to stop them? Unless the knights were delaying tactics. Or perhaps they were leading Tom and herself away from escape? Maybe there was a trap waiting for them at the top of the hill? But her senses had not let her down yet. But then again, this was a dream. Whoa, she thought, we've got to go back. We shouldn't have trusted the knights. The whole thing's a trap. They had to go back. The cave. They should never have left the cave.

'Tom,' she said, turning from the hill. 'We have to go back.' There was no answer. 'Tom?'

But Tom was no longer there.

CHAPTER 21

Somewhere behind closed doors.

'You go.'

'No, you go.'

'I said it first, you go.'

'No, you didn't.'

'Did.'

'Didn't.'

And so it would have gone on if the man, sitting behind the desk separating him from the argument, hadn't suddenly slammed his fist on that desk.

'It's decided,' said the man, 'you are both going.' The man was relatively new to his job, his predecessor leaving under a cloud like he had, so was determined to make his mark. And splitting the assignment would be easier.

'But that's not fair.'

'What he said.'

There, thought the man, an agreement, easy when you know how. The latest Chief Traveller stood up and wandered to the front of the desk where two empty chairs stood facing the front of it.

To the untrained eye, the chairs looked empty. To the trained eye, the chairs would still look empty. Even the Chief wondered if they were still there as he looked. But they were. Two of the BIMBOs best. He could hear one of them scratching.

'Right Bob, I want you to tag along with Smokowski. Keep an eye on him and Willy and report back any developments I should know about.'

'Is that left chair or right chair?'

'Right chair.'

'But he hates me,' said Bob, who is also known as Invisible Bob.

'Then I have a suggestion for you.'

'What?' said Bob.

'Don't pinch his chocolate peanuts.'

Bob snorted at the memory.

The Chief now turned to the other chair.

'And you Bob, ears and eyes open, you have the rest of the job. Okay?'

boB – explanation coming – nodded but had a question. 'Did you say "chocolate peanuts"?'

'I did,' said the Chief.

'Then perhaps I should go in Bobs place,' said boB.

'You have your missions.'

It was boB's turn to snort his displeasure.

'Right, off you both go then,' said the Chief, 'and remember, they are secret missions. You tell no one, not even your fellow BIMBOs.'

'We won't,' said Bob and boB as one.

'Good.' The Chief clapped his hands. 'Go.'

The two chairs were now empty. At least they appeared to be. The Chief wondered. So, whistling a nonchalant tune, he casually walked past the chairs, brushing his hands on the seats as he did. No, nothing there. They had left. Good, he thought. 'Now,' he said, 'where's that hand gel?'

But Bob and boB had not yet left the room.

'The cheeky so and so,' said boB.

'What you said,' said Bob. 'Does he think we don't wash or something?'

Bob and boB were invisible, you see. But to be invisible, one had to be, well, not wearing any clothes. Thus why the incident with the chocolate peanuts in the pick-and-mix was such a no-no.

Not only did they have invisibility in common, but they were also cousins, distant cousins. (Many times removed, in fact, but that was not always their fault, to be fair.) Invisibility ran in the family, missing a couple of generations now and then, but in this generation, it had two. Two that happened to join the BIMBOs at exactly the same time. It also just so happened that they were both called Bob.

Confusing? Not really. You see, Bob, of chocolate peanut fame, who was to track Smokowski and Willy, spells his name the more traditional way. Whereas the other one, who was less traditional, spells his name in reverse: boB. That way, everyone knows who is who. What could be simpler?

CHAPTER 22

'Tom!' yelled Cat, desperately turning this way and that. Where's the old duffer gone this time? She then caught a glimpse of him out of the corner of her eye. He was grinning like a certain cat from a certain county and standing in the green box in a smaller rectangular box. It was only then that Cat realised she was no longer at the foot of the hill but at the top.

Panic rose. She had to get him out of there. Cat raced across to the green box that suddenly began to change shape. It was taking on the form of a small castle. The box Tom was standing in, now the entrance.

As Cat approached the castle gate, Tom smiled and beckoned her forward. He was holding something. A jam jar. A full jam jar. How? Why?

'Come on, Cat,' said Tom, holding out a hand, 'it's a lift.'

Box, gate, lift; however you wanted to describe what Tom was standing in, it felt like a trap. Certain they had been led up the yellow cobbled path, Cat yelled at Tom to get out.

But Tom wasn't for moving. 'There's nothing to fear,' he said, the inane smile he had adopted growing wider, 'they're here to help.' And without further ado, the shiny knight, the monkey, the ferret and the thimble wearing mouse appeared from behind Tom. Hands, two furry, one hairy and one gauntleted, reached towards Cat.

Cat recoiled from the hands. 'No, Tom, it's a trap. We have to get out of here. Come with me,' she pleaded. 'It's not a lift.' She was sure of it. 'Please.'

But Tom just smiled at her. 'Which button?' he asked. He was so pleased Cat had joined them.

'Press up,' said the monkey.

'Good idea,' said Tom, who smiled his crazy smile at Cat. He pressed the button. The doors closed.

Cat watched them shut, but only when the lift moved, did she realise she was now looking at the doors, not from the outside, but the inside.

How had that happened? thought Cat. The panic she had felt earlier now doubled in intensity. She had to stop the lift. Press the down button. If she was quick, she might be able to press it before anyone could stop her. Cat leapt into action.

But she was out of luck. There was now only one button; the up button. She landed on the floor, disorientated and near to meltdown. She was sure there were more buttons when she had leapt. She glanced up at Tom. He was still smiling as if he held the secret to happiness.

Beside him, peering around him, the other four occupants of the lift were glaring at her. They tutted as one, and each waved a finger at her as if she had been a naughty girl.

Cat backed away. This was crazy. They needed to get away. And what does Tom do? He finds a box to stand in and waves and grins like a lunatic amongst a menagerie of weirdness. That's what Tom does.

Tom looks at her, but this time the smile has gone, replaced by a look of sadness. 'They want to come with us,' he explained.

Cat starred at him. Tom could be stupid, but this. Well, it takes the biscuit. With that, she suddenly laughs. But not the laugh you hear with the joy of finding something funny. No, this was the laugh of someone on the edge.

'They want to come with us?' said Cat. 'Well, why not. The more, the merrier, I say.' She now squeezed her body into a corner of the lift as tight as she could. 'But on our head be it.'

The smile had returned to Tom's lips. 'They've had enough,' said Tom. 'They're fed up of having to prance about like namby-pamby knights. Their words. They want to be free.' Tom smiled a dreamy smile as everyone behind him voiced their agreement.

I'm going mad, thought Cat. Or... Her next thought sent shivers through her. What if the dream had already ended? What if this was it for all eternity? Trapped in a lift with an inanely smiling Tom, a shiny knight, a monkey, a ferret and a mouse with a thimble on its head. Oh grief, she thought, this *is* it, isn't it? If Cat had possessed a thumb, she would have been sucking it by now.

Just then, the lift stopped with a judder and made a bing-bong noise. The bing-bong heralding an announcement.

'All ashore who's going ashore,' said the voice of a rather posh young lady. 'And have an absolutely spiffing day.'

The doors opened, the floor lifted at an angle to become a slope, and everyone fell forward and tumbled out.

CHAPTER 23

It was the delivery from the curry house. Darren paid, said thanks, returned to the kitchen and emptied the bags of food on the table.

Mary followed him in. 'Smells lovely,' she said. 'Now, take a seat in the lounge Darren, I want to talk to you.'

In the lounge, Mary took sat down opposite Darren.

'What's going on?' asked Darren, bewildered and worried.

'Hush,' said Mary, 'all is fine, just listen, and all will be revealed.'

A glum Darren hoped so.

'I want you to close your eyes and empty your mind.'

'Why?' said Darren, not sure what was being asked of him.

'Trust me, Darren.'

'Will it help Lucy and the kids?'

Mary smiled. 'Yes, most definitely,' she said.

'Okay.' Darren closed his eyes.

'Tight now.' said Mary.

Darren squeezed his eyes tight.

'Good,' said Mary. 'Is your mind empty?'

Darren thought so. 'Yes.'

'Completely?'

'Yes. Wait, no.'

'What do you see, Darren? This is very important.'

'Shapes.' Darren concentrated harder.

'What sort of shapes?'

'I can't tell. They're blurry.'

'Concentrate.'

'I am.'

'Harder.'

Darren did, and a shape became as clear as a bell. 'I see something.'

'What do you see, Darren?'

He told her what he saw.

Mary frowned. 'Really?'

'Yes,' said Darren, slightly embarrassed. 'But there's more.'

Mary noticed Darren's eyes widen under his closed lids.

'What do you see now, Darren?'

Darren told her.

Mary instantly clicked her fingers, sending Darren into a deep sleep. She waited for a second or two, then whispered something into his ear.

CHAPTER 24

Sadly, the list had only been as long as Willy's arm, which was shorter than Smokowski's, but it had been long enough to put Smokowski in a better frame of mind regarding the shop closing for who knows how long; he should have asked. But never mind, Willy's bill was enough to cover at least a week's income should it take that long.

Smokowski whistled as he finished cashing up. He then got his jacket from the storeroom and prepared to lock up the shop.

Meanwhile, Willy was putting his wares into the boot of his car. Boot closed, he walked to the driver's side, opened the door and got in. There he waited for Smokowski to join him.

After checking the lock three times and a fourth for luck, Smokowski set off to join Willy. Two steps later, he returned to the lock a fifth time. One couldn't be too careful. Finally satisfied, he walked to the waiting car.

It was a classic old Ford Cortina. Smokowski approved. He opened the passenger side door and got in. The inside smelled of pine, even though a lemon-shaped air freshener hung from the rear-view mirror.

'Got it cheap,' said Willy, noticing Smokowski looking at it. 'I bought a bunch of seconds.' Willy delved under his seat and pulled out another air freshener, this one in the shape of a pineapple. He passed it to Smokowski, who sniffed it then coughed.

'What scent is that?' spluttered Smokowski.

'I don't know,' said Willy, 'I was hoping you would know.'

'Well, it doesn't smell of pineapple. I can tell you that.' Smokowski handed the freshener back to Willy, who poked it back under his seat.

'Didn't think it did,' said Willy, wrinkling his nose.

His seatbelt fastened, Smokowski was ready. He wasn't sure how he felt about Willy, but it wasn't about making friends right now; it was about finding Tom and Cat. 'So,' he said, 'where's this time machine of yours?' He hoped it wasn't going to be a portable loo like Tom's.

'Didn't Mary tell you?'

'No,' said Smokowski, now fearing it was worse than a toilet.

Willy chuckled. 'You're in it.'

Smokowski's eyes widened. 'But… How?'

'You'll find out soon enough,' smiled Willy. 'Ready? Buckled up?'

Though he was sure that he was, Smokowski checked anyway. 'Yes.'

'Let's go then.' Willy turned the key, and the car came to life.

Feet pressed firmly against the floor and hands tightly gripping the sides of his seat, Smokowski readied himself. He was now firmly braced. He had also closed his eyes. He didn't know what to expect from Willy's time machine, something that zoomed, he suspected, but whatever he was surely going to hang on for dear life until they arrived at their destination. Wherever that might be? Something else he now realised he had forgotten to ask. Tom and Cat's last known whereabouts, he supposed. Too late now, though.

The car vibrated slightly as the engine noise grew louder. The car started to move. Gradually gather speed.

This is it, thought Smokowski, his knuckles white.

And then, suddenly, the noise lessened, the car slowed, it came to a stop. It was all over. It had taken all but a few seconds.

Relieved it hadn't been as bad as he had expected, nowhere near as bad, Smokowski released his grip and opened his eyes. He wondered where they were. He looked out of the window and was surprised to see his shop. They were not in quite the same place as before, a little further along, but the shop it was. He turned to Willy. Questions needed asking. He found Willy staring at him, a concerned look on his face.

'You okay?' asked Willy. 'Only you look sort of strained.'

Smokowski then realised, even though it had only taken a few seconds to jump in time, there had obviously been stresses on the body he hadn't expected. 'How far did we go back?' he asked.

'Back?' said Willy, looking confused.

'In time?' They couldn't have gone back far as the shop still looked the same as when they had left it. A sudden fear then took him. If a small jump back had this effect on him, what would a large one do to him? There must be something wrong with Willy's buffers.

'We haven't,' said Willy, concerned again, 'we've only gone a few yards along the road. Thought you looked a bit peaky, so I pulled over.'

'What?' said Smokowski. 'But I thought we were going back to Tom and Cat's last known whereabouts.'

'Nah,' said Willy, 'no idea where that is. It seems it's hidden from us.'
'How?'

'Who knows,' said Willy with a shrug. 'Mary thought it best to start at Tom's cottage and take it from there.' Willy gave Smokowski the once over again. 'So, just going to drive over there. You sure you're okay?'

'Oh,' said Smokowski. 'Yeah, fine. Drive over there.'

'Okay then,' said Willy, shaking his head. 'Let's pootle!'

An embarrassed Smokowski shrank back into his seat as the car pulled away from the kerb.

45

CHAPTER 25

Darren woke with a start. In the hall, the broom cupboard door flew open.

Tom, Cat, and the menagerie of the weird tumbled forward and landed in a heap on the hall carpet. There followed four loud pops and a ping. Now only Tom and Cat lay on the hall carpet.

That was interesting, thought Mary, who had seen the whole thing through the doorway that led from lounge to hall.

Tom, with a dreamy smile still on his lips, sat up. He turned and saw Mary looking at him. That's weird, was his last thought before slumping unconscious onto his back. He would be out for a little while, but that was to be expected; he had just survived somebody else's dream.

'Catranna?' said Mary, noticing Cat hadn't yet moved. 'You with us?'

The journey Cat and Tom had just taken, from dream to reality, was dramatic on the body and mind, whether human or magical. But Cat was usually pretty resilient when it came to the strange.

'Cat?' called Mary from the doorway.

At last, there was a slight movement. Cat's ears twitched. She stirred. She suddenly shot bolt upright and sprang on the mat, the front door one, and hissed and clawed at the surrounding air.

'Ah,' said Mary, suddenly understanding. Paranoia. She should have expected it, well documented as it was. But even if she had realised straight away, she wouldn't have expected it in Cat. Tom yes. Something needed to be done, especially if she wanted to save the doormat. Cat had turned her claws to it. 'Darren!'

Not sure what just happened to him and what was going on now, Darren struggled to his feet. 'Yes?'

'Could you warm some milk for me and put it in a saucer, please?'

A strange question, thought Darren, but as the day so far had been far from normal, he accepted it and shuffled into the kitchen to find the milk pan.

Half an hour later, all was back to normal. If you didn't include the still frozen Lucy, Kate, and Marc. Cat had had her soothing warm milk. Tom had finally consented to stop searching for the monkey and drink the sweet tea Darren had made for him. Mary was ready with explanations after taking Darren aside to tell him to be quiet about what had happened before Tom and Cat had arrived. Darren, who wasn't sure what exactly had happened before Tom and Cat had arrived, now sat in the kitchen staring at Lucy.

'You put us in the dream?' said Cat, hardly believing her ears.

'Yes,' said Mary, 'but it was necessary, Catranna. Let me explain.'

This had better be good, thought Cat, remembering the indignity she had felt when she found out who had destroyed the front doormat. But first things first. 'Please call me Cat.'

'Cat it is then.'

'So?' said Cat.

The story Mary was about to tell was a long one.

Only a few knew of the Jams disappearance and its consequences. The Chief Traveller – Tom's boss – a small number of BIMBOs, Willy, and only until recently, Smokowski. All trusted with one reservation; Willy.

Even though Willy had been with her for years as her bodyguard and driver, she had this nagging suspicion of doubt about him. That somehow, he was involved. She didn't know why, couldn't put her finger on it, woman's intuition perhaps. She hoped she was wrong.

Bearing this in mind, when Mary, the Chief Traveller and a trusted BIMBO got together to plan how to find and retrieve the Jam they concluded that it might be best if Willy was otherwise occupied and kept well out of the picture while it was still wet. This is where Tom and Cat came into it.

When the Jams theft was discovered, everyone in the know decided that Tom and Cat were the only ones capable of finding it. Problem was, no one knew who else could be trusted. So an elaborate plan was secretly put into action.

Tom and Cat would disappear. With them supposedly missing and off the grid, they felt whoever had taken the Jam would no longer have them down as someone to keep an eye on. To complete the ruse and keep Willy occupied, he would be given the task of finding them. And to authenticate the situation to those who might be watching, an unsuspecting Smokowski would be drafted in to work alongside Willy.

It had been Mary's idea to place Tom and Cat in a dream. It was dangerous, but the only way to make it appear they had indeed disappeared. There was the danger that suspicion might fall on Tom and Cat, but it was a chance they had to take. Story told, it was time to digest it.

'Head of the BIMBOs,' said Cat, shaking her head in wonder. 'Wow.'

'I know, I couldn't believe it myself,' said Mary.

'Congratulations.'

'Thank you.'

The indignity of the destroyed front door mat appeared to be justified, thought Cat, that cloud lifting from her, but there were still questions she wanted the answer to.

'So,' she said, 'whose dream were we in?'

'Darren's, not too bumpy in there for you, was it?'

'Darren's?' said a mortified Tom, thinking of the vast space within Darren's head. 'Wasn't that doubly dangerous?'

Mary smiled. 'It had to be someone, and there is a lot of room inside that head of his. A lot less cluttered with thoughts. Besides, he seems harmless.'

'You haven't known him long enough,' muttered Tom.

'I thought it was the finish of us,' said Cat, 'you know, at the end.'

'Sorry about that. I couldn't pull you out any quicker than I did. Your extraction had to be timed to the second.' Mary became serious. 'Out too soon, and part of you might have been left behind. Too late and, well, it would have been too late. You would have been trapped there.'

Tom shivered. The thought of being trapped in Darren's mind was not a nice one.

'And the side effects?' asked Cat, 'have they gone for good?'

'Yes,' said Mary, 'sorry about that. Goes with the territory, I'm afraid.'

Cat was glad to hear it. The paranoia she had felt was not an experience she would wish on anyone. Sadly, though, it meant that happy-clappy Tom had reverted to the moany-groany one. Still, she thought, he could be worse, he could be moany-clappy!

Yes, Tom?' said Mary, who had noticed Tom's face appeared to be showing signs of constipation. It was as if he was struggling to put a thought into words.

'It's his thinking face,' said Cat, confirming Mary's thoughts.

'You know when we fell out of the cupboard?' said Tom, also adding confirmation.

'Go on,' said Mary.

'Was there…'

'Yes,' said Mary. 'Strange that. If I'm right, it would appear some of Darren's subconscious had tried to come with you when you left the dream. They couldn't survive here obviously, but interesting all the same.'

'What about the jam?' said Cat, only now remembering Tom had had a jar of jam in his hands when they left the cupboard.

'What jam?' said Mary, sitting up.

'Tom had a jar in his hand when we fell out of the cupboard.'

'I'd forgotten about that,' said Tom, sipping at an empty cup. Drat, he thought. Then he remembered the knight had said something strange to him, "you shall seek what you find." He mentioned it to Mary.

'I've no idea what that could mean,' said Mary, frowning, 'but the jam part sounds as if part of my subconscious may have connected with Darren's. A subliminal message, perhaps?' Mary got to her feet. It was time to move. 'Right,' she said, 'no more time to waste.'

'Oh,' said Tom, surveying his empty cup. Another cuppa would have been welcome. And a biscuit.

No time for that,' said Mary, seeing Tom's look of longing at the cup in his hands.

'One more question before we do,' said Cat, who had been quietly mulling over something for a while now.

'Go on,' said Mary.

'You're not a Magical, so how did you do all you did?'

It was a question worthy of an honest answer, but Mary would not divulge her secrets just yet. It was a need-to-know situation. 'Let's just say a friend helped me out,' said Mary cryptically.

'Fair do's,' said Tom, eager to get on his way now another cuppa was not on offer. 'Home then.' Home where cuppas and choccy biscuits were in abundance.

'No home, Tom,' said Mary.

'Why?' said Tom, his world falling about his ears.

'Because I believe Smokowski and Willy might be there.'

'Why?' said Tom.

'Like true detectives. they will be trying to find clues to the crime and where best to start but your cottage. It's what I would do.'

'Crime?' said Tom, worried.

'Our kidnapping,' said Cat, nudging his memory.

'Oh yeah,' said Tom, now recalling he had been kidnapped, or hadn't, or had but hadn't. He furrowed his brow. His head hurt.

'What next then?' said Cat.

Mary lowered her voice to a whisper. 'I've left you instructions in Lucy's bathroom.' She narrowed her eyes. 'You never know who might be listening.'

Too late for that, thought Cat, but played along.

'Okey-dokey,' said Tom, who had just had an epiphany. It had been cuppa led. 'Surely we need to get home so we can use the Loo?'

Cat and Mary stared at him. 'You know, the time machine.'

'Oh!' said Mary and Cat as one.

'You have a Saver, I believe?' said Mary.

"'Ere,' said Tom, all defensive like, 'that's supposed to be a secret.'

'It is,' said Mary.

'I should think so,' said Tom. 'What?'

'It's connected to your time machine,' Mary explained. 'You can call it to you in an emergency.' Then as an afterthought. 'As long as you are in a toilet, that is.'

Tom looked puzzled.

Mary exchanged glances with Cat. 'You didn't know?' said Mary.

Cat would have to admit she had forgotten it could do that.

'Course I did,' said Tom.

Cat and Mary gave Tom an enquiring look.

Time to move, thought Tom, before they ask questions. 'You coming?' he said, stepping into the hall. He gripped the Saver. He hoped he could work out how the flipping thing did what Mary said it could do.

'Wait a minute,' said Mary, before Tom could escape to the safety of Lucy's bathroom.

Drat, thought Tom, expecting the worst.

'I want you to take Darren with you.'

'Darren?' said Cat.

'Darren?' said Tom, not sure whether to laugh or cry.

'You may need a bit of muscle.'

Cheek, thought Tom, flexing a bicep that immediately cramped. He grimaced but managed to stifle a groan.

'Suppose so,' said Cat, wondering what was wrong with Tom. He appeared to be thinking extra hard.

'I'll stay here with Lucy and the children,' said Mary.

That's a point, thought Tom, where were Lucy and the kids? 'Where are they?' said Tom, rubbing his arm, 'I'd like to have a word with Lucy.'

'She's out at the moment,' said Mary, not wanting to upset him with the truth.

'Out?' said Tom.

'Gone to the Indian takeaway,' said Mary. And before Tom could ask. 'She's taken Kate and Marc with her.'

'Oh,' said Tom. 'Well, tell them I dropped by.'

'I will,' said Mary, offering a reassuring smile. 'Now off you go. I'll send Darren along shortly.'

While they waited in the bathroom for Darren to join them, Cat had a question for Tom.

'You didn't know that about the Saver, did you?' she said.

'No,' admitted Tom.

'Thought so,' said Cat.

'Should you have told me about it?' said Tom.

'Yes,' admitted Cat.

'Thought so,' said Tom.

They spent the rest of the time waiting in silence.

Darren wasn't long, and Tom, through luck rather than judgement, was able to summon his time machine the first time he tried. It materialised around them.

'Right,' said Tom, 'let's make tracks.'

'Wait,' said Cat.

'Why?' said Tom.

'We need the instructions.'

Cat quickly explained to Darren that Mary had left them instructions somewhere in the bathroom.

A couple of minutes later, they were still without them.

'That's strange,' said Cat.

'Perhaps she forgot,' said Tom.

'Perhaps,' Cat agreed. 'We had better go and ask her.'

'Wait,' said Tom, as Cat went to leave.

'What?' said Cat.

'Something has been bugging me since we arrived at Lucy's, and I feel I should know.'

'Know what?'

'I'm almost sure we've met before,' said Tom, 'but for the life of me I can't remember where.'

'What are you going on about?' said Cat, fearing he was suffering from some delayed reaction to the dream.

Nope, thought Tom, can't remember, he would have to ask.

'It's just that I can't quite place her.'

'Who,' said Cat.

'That woman we were just talking to. Who is she?'

Cat and Darren exchanged glances. Drat, thought Cat, he would have to ask that now.

CHAPTER 26

Eager to forget the episode in the car, Smokowski quickly exited it and led the way through Tom's back gate and headed for the cottage's back door. Tom had given Smokowski an emergency key, but that was to the front door, and as they didn't want to draw any unwanted attention, it was an option they couldn't risk.

The back door was locked as expected, so Willy set about picking the lock. Smokowski wasn't happy about it and knew Tom wouldn't like it, but they had little choice. Tom still hadn't forgiven him for snaffling a biscuit without asking, and that was months ago. What would he be like if he found out he was now breaking into his cottage? Sure, it was covered under good intentions, but Tom still wouldn't like it.

'Ah-ha!' said Willy, as the lock clicked open. 'Shall we?'

Willy opened the door and went in. Smokowski followed him but took a moment to look at the scratches around the keyhole. Whoops, he thought, wondering if Tom would notice.

Maybe he would, but at that moment, it was Smokowski who wasn't noticing things; things going on behind him at the bottom of Tom's back gate. To be fair, it was doubtful he would have seen anything, anyway.

Unseen by anyone, mainly because he was invisible, Invisible Bob had crawled beneath the gate and had arrived just in time to see the back of Smokowski as he stepped into Tom's cottage.

Invisible Bob started to run. He had to get inside. He hurried along the path, past the Portable Loo, past the shed and as the door closed, flung himself at the gap. He arrived just in time. Just in time for it to shut in his face.

CHAPTER 27

'What!' exclaimed Tom. 'But she's in Crewe!' Crewe and other minor details were all Tom had been allowed to remember of his life with Mary.

'Calm down,' said Cat, fearing a blown gasket. 'Let me explain.'

'But why didn't I know it was her?' said Tom. 'Did she know who I am?' The third person in the Loo, who didn't want to get involved, went to take a step back but didn't get very far, restricted as he was in a portable loo. 'Why was she at Lucy's?'

Tom's face contorted this way and that as it struggled to decide which look, it should adopt; worry, incomprehension, puzzlement, or none of the above. Finally, it settled on none of the above and chose suspicion. Tom turned this face towards Darren.

'Did you know about this?' he said, narrowing his eyes.

Darren gulped. Truth be told, he wasn't sure. He had recognised Mary at the shop, but he must have seen a photo of her somewhere. Hadn't he? He knew Lucy was expecting her. Or had he? He hadn't known Tom and Cat were in his head. Or did he? 'No,' said Darren, plumping for the truth, or was it?

Tom's narrowed eyes turned into mere slits. What else hadn't he been told? He remembered what Mary had said about Lucy and the kids. And thinking about it, why hadn't Darren gone instead of Lucy? Surely alone time with her long-lost mother wouldn't be time she would want to waste. Come to think about it, he had smelt curry when Darren had brought him his cuppa. He had ignored it, thinking he was smelling things, after effects of the dream. Now, something smelled again, and this time it wasn't curry. 'Has Lucy and the kids really gone to get takeaway?'

Now, this was something Darren did know. He gulped again. 'She's curry,' he said, surprising everyone, including himself.

'Curry?' said Cat, appalled. 'What do you mean she's curry?'

'I mean frozen,' said Darren, though still not making any sense but getting to the point in his own good time. 'They're all frozen.'

'All the curries are frozen?' said Tom, getting a little lost.

'I think he means Lucy and the kids are frozen,' said Cat, breathing a little sigh of relief that they would not have to identify a Lucy curry.

'Frozen!' said a horrified Tom, imaging Lucy encased in a block of ice.

'I suspect it's for their own good,' said Cat, thinking she now knew what was going on.

'How's that good for them?' wailed Tom.

'Better than seeing us fall out of the broom cupboard,' said Cat. 'How would we have explained that?' (Lucy and the kids didn't know Tom was a time traveller, Cat was a magical, or Darren was King of the Brits; the legend, not the music awards.) 'No, it's better this way.'

'But frozen,' said Tom, 'couldn't there have been a better way?' He was imagining them thawing and lying shivering on the floor. 'What if they get frostbite?'

Frostbite? thought Cat. Then the penny dropped. The silly old duffer. 'Not frozen, frozen,' said Cat. 'Frozen in time.'

'Yes,' said Darren, remembering what Mary had said, 'what Cat said.'

Tom's face wasn't sure what to do next. It plumped for realization, then relief. 'Right,' said Tom, his fears melting away. His eyes then narrowed again. 'You could have told me,' he said to Darren.

'Mary said not to,' said Darren, looking decidedly uncomfortable. 'She said you will have gone through enough with the dream. She didn't want to worry you.'

Tom looked at Cat. 'Did you know?'

'No,' said Cat, 'all news to me but perhaps for the best.'

'What happens when they wake up?' said Tom. 'Won't they wonder where Darren is?'

'I suspect Mary's friend will fog them,' said Cat, trying to reassure.

'Fog them?' said Tom.

'It's the same as glamouring but not as strong,' said Cat. 'A glamour was used on you just before Mary left.'

'So, that is why I didn't know who she was?'

'Yeah,' said Cat.

'So, she's the President of the Ladies Institute now?'

'So it would seem,' said Cat, who already knew. She also knew that it was the reason Mary had to disappear in the night and why Tom was glamoured. Not many others did.

'Why didn't anyone tell me?' said Tom.

'There was no point,' said Cat, 'you wouldn't have been able to hold the information for long.'

'What information?' said Tom.

'About the real reason for Mary leaving.'

'Mary?' said Tom.

'Your ex-wife.'

'She's in Crewe.'

'Yes, she is,' said Cat.

CHAPTER 28

boB, not to be confused with Bob, had a job to do; report on the goings on that were going on and report those goings on that were going on, back to the Chief Traveller. He had been given a list. He was looking at it.

Item one on the list: Report on Mary.

Item two on the list: Report on Tom and Cat.

Item three on the list: Get doughnuts.

boB screwed his nose up. It wasn't fair. Bob only had to report on Smokowski and Willy. And where was he going to get doughnuts from? boB gave a humph and folded the list, placing it back in the only place available to him. And now he thought about it, where was he supposed to put them when he got them? He decided he didn't want to think about that.

So, trying very hard not to think how rough sugar might be, boB set about the task before him of getting into Lucy's house undetected.

CHAPTER 29

Back door safely shut behind him, Smokowski crossed the kitchen to where Willy was standing. 'What now?' he whispered.

'We look for clues,' Willy whispered back.

'What do they look like?' Smokowski had never been big on detective stories.

Willy shrugged. 'Not sure, but I bet we'll know them when we see them.'

Smokowski wasn't sure what that meant, but he looked, anyway. 'Here,' he said almost immediately. 'I think I've found something.'

Willy was sceptical but sidled over. 'Where?'

'Here,' said Smokowski, holding up a cup. 'It's a cup.'

Willy could see that. 'How is that a clue?'

'It's Tom's cup.'

'How do you know it's his cup?' said Willy, taking no chances.

'It's says Tom's cup on the side of it.' Smokowski manoeuvred the cup so Willy could see.

Willy read it. It would appear to be Toms, but how was it a clue? He asked.

'It's still got some tea in it,' said Smokowski, tipping it slightly so Willy could see.

'Looks like coffee to me,' said Willy. Whatever it was, it was cold. 'Not really a clue, though, is it?' he said.

'Ah,' said Smokowski, all detective-like. He felt he might be getting the hang of clue finding. 'But Tom always finishes his cuppa.'

'But it's cold.'

'It might not have been when he left it.'

'Good point,' said Willy, rubbing his chin thoughtfully. 'Then it could be a clue.'

A nodding Smokowski was feeling pleased with himself. It was perhaps a step closer to finding Tom and Cat.

'Can I see?' said Willy. Smokowski passed the cup to him. Willy studied the contents, sniffed at them and then gave them a swirl.

'Well?' said Smokowski. 'Is it a clue?'

'Could well be,' said Willy. He suddenly looked grave.

'What's wrong?' said Smokowski.

'I'm only guessing,' said Willy, looking Smokowski in the eye, 'but it could mean he was whisked away before he could finish it.'

Grief, thought Smokowski, whisked away before you could finish your cuppa, diabolical!

Willy put the cup down as something else caught his eye. 'What have we here?' he said.

'What where?' said Smokowski, craning his neck to see past Willy.

'A note,' said Willy, waving it at Smokowski.

'What does it say?' said Smokowski, a sudden fear gripping him. What if it's a ransom note?

'Haven't got a clue,' said Willy.

'Is it in code?' said Smokowski, now fearing the kidnappers might be spies.

'No,' said Willy, passing the note to Smokowski, 'that's what it says.'

What a strange thing to write on a note, thought Smokowski. 'Haven't got a clue,' he read aloud, 'could it be cryptic?'

'I don't know,' said Willy, 'but I think we should deem it a clue.' He took back the note and studied it. 'Is it Tom's writing?'

'No,' said Smokowski, who knew Tom's scrawl anywhere, 'it's too neat and tidy.'

'Cats?'

'I don't think she can write,' said Smokowski, 'her paws would be too small to hold a pen.'

'True,' said Willy, 'but she's a Magical.'

'True,' said Smokowski, 'but I've never seen her write anything.'

'Okay,' said Willy, 'we'll leave it at that. But it does mean we may have two clues already.'

'Perhaps we should broaden our search?'

'Good idea,' said Willy, casting a quick glance around Tom's kitchen. He couldn't see anything else that might give them a clue as to Tom and Cats whereabouts, so why not? 'Where should we go next?' He figured Smokowski should lead the way, as he knew the layout of Tom's cottage.

It was decided to go room to room, starting with the closest to the kitchen. Smokowski led the way.

'Keep an eye out for signs of a struggle,' said Willy, as Smokowski, taking a step into the hall, suddenly stopped.

'Wait,' said Smokowski, peering into the hall. The mention of a struggle had given him food for thought. 'What if they're still here, bound and gagged?'

'Then job done,' said Willy. 'We'll untie them and then get the heck out of Dodge.'

57

'What if their kidnappers are still here?' said Smokowski.

'I've got a rubber mallet in me boot,' said Willy.

Smokowski turned and stared at him.

'To defend ourselves with,' said Willy.

'No time,' said Smokowski, thinking it could be of the essence. 'Follow me.'

Together, always on the defensive, always ready to run, they slowly searched the cottage until there was only one room left; the attic.

'You stay here and keep watch,' said Smokowski as they reached the foot of the steps that led to the attic.

'You sure?' said Willy.

Smokowski was sure and for more than one reason. As each room proved to be empty of kidnap victims and clues, it dawned on him they would have to search the attic. He would finally see what Tom kept in it. It was the only room in the house that Tom wouldn't allow anyone, including his daughter, to enter. And now he would find out what Tom didn't want anyone else to see, and his entering the room was all legit.

He reached the attic door. Any fear he might have regarding kidnappers was nothing to the anticipation he was feeling at finding out the secret of the attic. He, of course, hoped Tom and Cat would be in there and he could rescue them, but. The attic. He would have rubbed his hands together with glee under any other circumstances, but that wouldn't be right at the moment; Tom and Cat.

He reached for the doorknob.

CHAPTER 30

With Tom forgetting that he had forgotten what he was supposed to forget, the topic in the toilet returned to Mary's lost message. Something Tom hadn't forgotten.

'So,' said Tom, 'what now?'

A hand shot up.

'Grief,' said Tom. 'Really? Now? You can't wait?'

'Sorry?' said Darren. Then he realised what Tom meant. 'Oh-no, I don't,' he uttered. 'No.' A little crimson about the cheeks, Darren explained the hand raising. 'I was just wondering if perhaps one of us might pop back and ask Mary where it is.'

'Mary?' said Tom.

'Good idea,' said Cat, ignoring Tom's question.

CHAPTER 31

That's odd, thought boB, where is everyone? The place was quiet. He heard no movement.

He had just arrived, as ordered, at Lucy's, to keep an eye on what Mary was doing. He didn't know why. He just followed orders. But he had been told where to find her and who should be with her.

Sniffing the air, boB thought he could smell curry. Perhaps a family meal was taking place? Could account for the lack of noise, but he thought he might still hear the odd chatter of voices and clink of cutlery. He followed his nose to the kitchen.

As he thanked the deity of open doors, he hated squeezing under them, boB entered through the open kitchen door and confirmed what he had suspected; the place appeared to be void of people.

The smell still lingering, boB headed for it via a chair leg. From there, he used the edge of the tablecloth to climb onto the table. On the table stood several containers. boB took a deep breath. 'Ah, saag aloo,' he said, as the smell of the spices tickled his nostrils. I wonder if I can get the lid off? he thought. Sadly, as much as he tried, the container lid would not shift. He gave up and was about to kick the container in frustration when something caught his attention, stopping him. He pricked his ears. Someone was trying to tiptoe along the hall and not succeeding.

Quick as a flash, boB was back on the floor again and seeking somewhere out of harm's way. He now held his breath as the footsteps grew closer.

CHAPTER 32

It was decided Darren would be the one to venture forth and talk to Mary, just in case Lucy and the kids were no longer frozen; fewer questions. Tom and Cat would wait, concealed from view, until his return.

Tom helped Darren out with a gentle push, and Darren, for reasons only known to himself, tiptoed down the hall. Needless to say, he wasn't very good at it and stopped doing it after his second trip.

At the end of the hall, Darren stopped and listened. All was quiet. He stepped into the lounge. Surely he would have heard voices by now? Unless Mary hadn't released Lucy and the kids yet. But why wouldn't she do that? He tried a tentative call.

'Mary?' he half-whispered. The other half sounded more like a strangled plea. Oops, he thought. He tried calling again but in a normal voice. There was no answer to this either, so he slowly entered the kitchen.

It was empty. Where were Lucy and the kids? An awful thought then struck him. What if… He faltered, fear rising. What if… He faltered again; fear getting higher. What if? He couldn't bear the thought. He bit his hand. What if Lucy had taken Mary and the kids to the cinema? He grabbed a chair to steady himself. There was a film that everyone wanted to see. It had monkeys in it. Woe was he. Could they have gone to see it? He gulped. Without him?

No, the curries were still there. Perhaps they were upstairs? He quickly searched the rest of the house, only stopping when he got back to the bathroom.

'Cinema?' said Tom, wondering what medication Darren wasn't taking.

'Gone?' said Cat, which was more to the point.

They left the bathroom and went to the kitchen.

'This is odd,' said Cat, who had jumped onto the table. She had made sure her feet were clean. 'The curries are unopened.' She touched one container with her paw. 'And still hot.'

'Perhaps they'll eat when they get back from the cinema,' Darren suggested. A cinema visit had become his default scenario.

'What do you think, Cat?' Tom asked, concerned but not too worried. The woman they had spoken to had seemed sensible enough.

'I don't know,' admitted Cat, doubting they would have gone to the cinema, not when Lucy hadn't seen her mother for so long. Not the best place for catching up on each other's news, she felt. But wherever they had gone, why hadn't they started on the curries? 'But I smell a rat.'

Under the table, an invisible Adam's apple bobbed up and down as an equally invisible throat gulped.

'Do you,' said Tom, his face a mask of disgust. He prodded a container. 'Which one?'

She tried to stop, but it had become a habit. Cat could no longer stop her eyes from rolling where Tom was concerned. 'I mean with the situation, not the curry,' she said, shaking her head.

'Ah,' said Tom.

'What now?' asked a glum Darren, thinking of monkeys.

'Perhaps we should have a curry?' Tom suggested.

'Perhaps,' said Cat, 'we should start looking for Mary, Lucy and the kids.'

'The Victorian,' Darren suddenly blurted.

Cat frowned; she wasn't keen on the Victorians, though she counted Queen Victoria, Vicky, as a friend.

'Which Victorian?' said Cat, wondering how a Victorian could be here in the here and now.

'It's the name of the cinema showing the monkeys,' said Darren. 'Perhaps we should start there.' He then wondered if they would be in time for the feature. 'I'll just go look up what time the film starts.'

''Ere, what's this?' said Tom, noticing something sticking out from under a container. He removed it.

'What is it?' said Cat.

'It's a piece of paper with Darren's name on it,' said Tom. 'Perhaps this is his curry?'

'Looks like a note,' said Cat, noticing the paper was folded in half. She called to Darren as he rummaged through a drawer.

'Can't find it,' said a dejected Darren as he joined them.

'Here,' said Tom, 'what does this say.'

'Darren,' he said, reading the front of the message.

'He means inside,' said Cat.

'Oh,' said Darren, spirits bucking up a little, 'perhaps I'm supposed to meet them somewhere?' He opened the note.

'Well?' said Tom.

'Your dinner is in the fridge X,' said Darren, reading the note's contents.

'X?' said Tom. 'Who's X?'

'It's a kiss,' said Cat, as Darren showed her the note.

'Oh yeah,' said Darren.

They all looked at the fridge.

'I wonder what it is?' wondered Darren.

I wonder why he's not having curry? thought Tom.

Grief, thought Cat, thinking they were getting nowhere fast in finding Mary and the instructions.

'Does Lucy often leave your dinner in the fridge?' asked Tom.

Then again, thought Cat, perhaps they are getting somewhere. She asked Darren if the writing on the note was Lucy's? She had a hunch.

'Who else's would it be?' said Darren. But on closer inspection, he realised the writing on the note might not be Lucy's. Similar, but different.

Then who wrote it?' said Tom.

Cat thought she had a good idea who that might be but kept quiet as she didn't want another Mary conversation with Tom. She suggested they open the fridge to see what was in there.

In the fridge, they found another note with Darren's name on it, taped to a plastic container. Darren took it out, placed it on the table next to the curries and removed the note. This one just had his name on it; no message.

'Open the container,' said Cat.

'Rather take the money,' said Tom, showing just how old he was.

The plastic container was opened.

'What's in it?' asked Tom, expecting to see a salad or something equally disgusting. What was that stuff Lucy had tried to feed him? Quinier? Quinoier? Ken-wah? Nope, he couldn't remember. Couldn't say it either, as he recalled. That's it; he suddenly recalled, birdseed! That's what it was. But he was to be disappointed, or not.

'It's an envelope,' said Darren, removing it. But this one didn't have Darren's name on it.

'Open it then,' said Tom.

'It's not for me,' said Darren.

'Who's it for then?' asked Cat.

'You. It says, Cat pee tee oh,' said Darren frowning.

'Must be code,' said Tom, reaching for the envelope. He sighed when he read it. 'It says PTO.'

'That's what I said,' said Darren.

'It means, please turn over,' Tom explained. To be fair to Darren, he had never come across the abbreviation before. To be fair, it was doubtful he knew what abbreviation meant. Not his fault. Tom turned the envelope over.

'What does it say?' said Cat.

'Open in the Loo and only in the Loo.'

'Time to go, I think,' said Cat.

'But what about Lucy and the kids?' said Tom.

'We don't know when the film starts,' said Darren.

'First things first,' said Cat, leaping from the table. 'We need to read that note.'

'Fair do,' said Tom, suspecting Cat knew what she was doing. He grabbed Darren by the sleeve.

'But—'

'Come on.'

Darren relented, and he and Tom reached the lounge before Cat.

'You coming?' said Cat, who had hung back.

Tom looked around and frowned. 'Who you talking to?'

'Our friend under the table,' said Cat.

Tom stooped as low as his knees would allow him. 'I don't see anyone,' he said.

'You wouldn't,' said Cat. 'Everyone to the Loo.' She glared at an empty space by one of the table legs. 'Now!' She growled.

They all went to the Loo. Someone, perhaps needing it more than others.

CHAPTER 33

The Chief Traveller looked at his watch. They should be here by now? Perhaps. Unless something had gone wrong. He looked at his watch again. The hands hadn't had time to move. Drat, he thought. Calm down, he thought. I wonder how the Bobs were getting on? he thought. He was doing a lot of thoughting.

The Chief Traveller stood up. He sat back down again. He drummed his fingers. He stopped as it hurt too much. He put the drumstick down. How had it got to this? he wondered. He looked at the empty cup on his desk. A moment ago, it had been full of coffee. He could do with another one. He looked at the intercom. Grief, he thought, I could end up a chain coffee drinker. His finger now hovered over the button on the intercom that connected him to his secretary. And where were the doughnuts? He then remembered he had put them at the bottom of boB's list. Why had he done that?

The index finger of the Chief Travellers right hand gently caressed the button on the intercom. Should he? It was no good; he needed another cup of coffee. He pressed it. A voice answered.

'Ah, yes,' said the Chief. He knew he shouldn't; it would be his fifth that morning. Unless… 'Could I possibly have a cup of tea, please?' There, he had been strong.

'Sorry, sir,' said the voice on the other end of the intercom, 'I didn't quite catch that. Did you say a cup of tea or coffee?'

Had he asked for tea? He had. Good Man. Shouldn't have too many coffees. Could make one whizzy. Did he feel whizzy? 'Coffee, please,' he said. Drat! he thought.

'Yes, sir.'

'Just a moment.'

'Yes, sir?'

'I don't suppose there are any doughnuts to be had?'

'No, sir. Sorry, sir.'

'Just coffee then, please.'

He started to drum his fingers again.

CHAPTER 34

Once they were back in the Loo, Tom opened the envelope.

'What does it say?' said Cat. She hadn't forgotten about the intruder in their midst. Questions would be asked, but for the moment there were more important matters at hand.

'Dear all,' read Tom, 'sorry about the sub-ter-fudge.' He slowed to a stop and looked at Cat. 'Fudge?' he said.

'Subterfuge,' said Cat, guessing that subterfuge was what Tom was trying to get his tongue around.

'Ah,' said Tom, 'oh yeah, sorry about that.' He continued with the message. 'Sorry about the subterfudge, but I'm a cautious old so-and-so. The house is shielded, but one can never be too careful; who knows who might be listening? Or watching? Or who you can trust?'

Who indeed, thought Cat, growling so low that only Magicals could hear it. She wondered how the little intruder had got into Lucy's with a shield in place? Then decided he must have been already inside waiting when Mary had activated it. She gave another little growl.

Cowering in the corner boB, guessing the growls were aimed at him, was thankful he had gone to the loo before he had left the Travellers headquarters.

Oblivious to the growls and handy toilet habits of boB, Tom read on. 'That said, once you have finished reading this, you must head for the Travellers Headquarters. The Chief will fill you in on what is to be done next. Please don't look for Lucy, the kids and I. We are all safe. Mary x.'

'Who's Mary X?' asked a disembodied voice from on low.

Darren and Tom nearly jumped out of their respective skins. Cat had mentioned something about a friend, but it had gone clean out of their minds as the note's contents were revealed.

'Flipping kippers!' exclaimed Tom, hand on chest. 'Who's that? Nearly had a flaming heart attack!' Truth be told, there was nothing untoward going on behind Tom's ribs. He just thought a little melodrama might cover his faux pas regarding a certain Mary X. Grief, he thought, I'm as dull as Darren.

'Sorry,' said Cat, 'I should have explained, it's our little friend from under the table.' She growled again. 'We have a BIMBO amongst us.'

'BIMBO?' said Darren.

'Yes,' said Cat, 'and if I'm not mistaken, it's that chocolate peanut pilferer Invisible Bob.'

'Actually, it's not,' said boB, 'I'm boB, his invisible distant cousin, completely removed.'

'Removed from what?' asked Darren.

'I don't know exactly,' said boB.

'So, you are, technically, Invisible Bob then,' said Tom.

After a quick think, boB could see the point Tom was making. 'I suppose so, but we are quite different. I'm taller for one, and I don't pinch chocolate-covered peanuts.' He gave Cat an invisible, reproachful look.

'Fair do,' said Tom, thinking Smokowski would be pleased to hear that.

Introductions of a sort now over, minds turned back to the note and what Mary had written. Cat still had questions to ask the invisible one, but that could wait; he wasn't going anywhere.

'So,' said Tom, pleased no one had noticed his mistake, 'onward to Travellers HQ then.'

'What about Lucy and the kids?' said Darren with renewed concern for his wife and children even though the note said they were safe.

'Yes,' said Tom, suddenly remembering, thanks to Darren, that he too was worried about them, 'what about Lucy and the kids?' He let go of the flusher and went to open the door.

'Wait,' said Cat, 'I'm sure they're safe. Mary said so in the note. I doubt she would lie to us.'

'If you're sure,' said Darren doubtfully.

'I suppose,' said Tom, wondering who this Mary woman was.

'I'm sure,' said Cat. 'Now, we should make tracks. Tom.'

'Okay,' said Tom, taking on the look of the constipated. He had decided to get on with things. The sooner done, the sooner done, he thought. Or something like that. He concentrated. He concentrated on where they had to go. He reached for the flusher and concentrated even harder. He would never hear the last of it if he missed the Travellers Headquarters of all places. His fingers tightened on the flusher.

'Wait!' exclaimed a voice from below suddenly.

Tom immediately lost his concentration. 'Drat,' he said as his forehead de-creased. 'What gives?' When he tried to open his eyes, one of them wouldn't respond. He had been concentrating that hard. He tried to open it using his fingers. 'Ouch.'

'I have things to do first,' said boB.

'Things?' said Cat.

'It's what I'm supposed to do. It's my job.'

'Your job?' said Cat, wondering what was about to be revealed.

'Yeah,' said boB, 'I'm supposed to report back to the Chief Traveller when I've finished, and I haven't even got any doughnuts yet.' boB wasn't making a lot of sense to those listening. But something boB had said had caught someone's attention.

'Doughnuts, you say,' said Tom, thinking how well a doughnut would go down right then. Especially with a cuppa to dunk it in.

'Finished what?' asked Cat, keeping her suspicious mind on the ball.

'After I'd finished reporting on everyone I need to,' said boB. His little invisible shoulders immediately sagged. Had he just told someone what he wasn't supposed to tell? He had. His little invisible shoulders had now sagged as low as they could sag. He had just let the cat out of the bag, and it didn't like what it saw. 'Oops,' he whispered.

The glowering boB was now receiving from Cat was withering. 'You were spying on us!' she growled.

'Not exactly spying,' said boB, trying to keep the hole he was digging for himself from getting too deep, 'more keeping an eye on.' Sweat had started to not appear on his brow.

'And the Chief told you to do it?'

'Not…' But boB checked his tongue. He was already in a hole up to his neck, and it was exactly what the Chief had told him to do. 'Yes.'

It was a good job for boB Cat was a cat and not a dragon. Otherwise, the steam coming from her nostrils might have been a lot hotter. 'Why?' she demanded.

Amazingly, boB's shoulders managed to sink a little lower. They were just below his armpits now. 'I don't know,' wailed boB, breaking under Cat's steam but now telling the truth. 'He didn't say. He just told us to do it.'

'Us?' The word hung above boB's head like a sword of ice. Cold, sharp and likely to cause some serious damage.

Oh no , thought boB, I've only gone and done it again! Now there were two bag-less cats running loose. Three, if you counted Cat. Only she wasn't running; she was starring daggers at him. Only the truth would do now if he didn't want the hole he occupied to be filled in. 'Invisible Bob and me.'

'Invisible Bob?' said Tom, who had been thinking about doughnuts, ring ones with icing on them; best for dunking. 'Where?' He gave the floor of the Loo a quick scan but saw nothing. Something he would have seen even if Invisible Bob was there.

'Yes,' said Cat, 'where?'

'At Tom's,' said boB, 'he's spy——,' he gulped, 'I mean, he's reporting on Smokowski and Willy.'

Cat's eyes could barely be seen through the slits she was looking through. Enough was enough, she thought, time to get to the bottom of this.

'Tom,' said Cat, not taking her eyes off the space boB occupied.

'Yeah?' said Tom.

'Next stop the Traveller HQ.'

'Oh,' said boB, who slumped to the floor before his shoulders could beat him to it.

'Oh,' said Tom, who had been hoping for a doughnut.

'Oh,' said Darren, not wanting to be left out.

Cat just sat, steely-eyed.

Tom once more took on the look of the constipated as he gripped the flusher.

The time machine came to life. It shook. It rattled. It rolled. It shimmied – the time machine wasn't all rock-and-roll. It then wondered what the dickory dock was going on. Nothing to do with Mary's note or the shenanigans that had followed the reading, but to what was going on in Tom's head. Most confusing it was. Most confusing to be sure, it thought, as it shook, rattled, rolled and subtly shimmied to its destination. Wherever that might be.

CHAPTER 35

The doorknob turned slowly in Smokowski's hand. The moment of truth was near, but it called for caution, should Tom and Cat be inside, together with their kidnappers.

Holding his breath without realising it, Smokowski gently pushed the door open. But barely an inch had the door moved when Willy's voice rose in an urgent whisper.

'Someone's here,' he said.

'What?' said Smokowski, hand reluctant to release the doorknob.

'Someone's here. I heard a door open.'

Darn, thought Smokowski, so close yet so far. For a moment, he toyed with the idea of taking a quick peek inside the attic. But good sense got the better of him. What if the kidnappers were inside? What if others had returned from whatever kidnappers did when they weren't kidnapping? He quickly descended the steps.

'Quick,' said Willy, 'out the back.' The sound of the door opening had been at the other end of the cottage.

Together, the two of them made haste for the back door.

'To the gate,' said Smokowski, planning to get as far away as possible.

'No,' said Willy, 'too much open ground. The shed.'

Smokowski swung the door open and flew out, Willy hot on his heels.

Invisible Bob, who had just got to the window in the back door so he could peep inside, failed to get a grip and hurtled across the garden.

'Did you hear that?' said Willy, 'sounded like a scream.'

Smokowski hadn't and was more concerned about the note they had found. He halted abruptly. 'The note.'

'Here,' said Willy, waving it before Smokowski's eyes.

'Good man,' said Smokowski.

They returned to the task at hand and, with speed belying their age, scooted to the shed. To their relief, it was unlocked. They quickly closed the door behind them.

They made their way through the gloomy inside without knocking into anything – luck more than skill – and ducked beneath a grimy window. They peeked outside to see if anyone had seen them.

Minutes passed, and no one had yet appeared at the back door. They relaxed a little. All they could do now was to watch and wait. Smokowski peeked. Willy studied the note they had found.

On the lawn, Invisible Bob opened his eyes and groaned.

CHAPTER 36

'Landed,' said a dazed Tom, the ride had not been a smooth one.

'You don't say,' said Cat, dodging the kneeling Darren.

'Thank goodness,' said Darren, wiping the odd bit of mysterious carrot from his chin. The toilet had been his close companion nearly from the off.

'All okay?' asked Cat, trying hard to ignore the smell coming from the toilet. 'Perhaps you should flush it.'

Darren reached out an arm and pulled the flusher.

'Bob?' said Cat, not so much concerned with his welfare as his presence.

'Here,' said boB, who was upside down and resting on his neck, 'but I think all the blood in my feet may have collected in my nose.' He felt it; it was huge.

'Or you banged it,' said Cat.

'Ah,' said boB.

All sort of fit and well, Cat turned her attention to Tom. 'Well?' she said.

'Yes, thanks,' said Tom, 'a little dizzy, but I'm sure it'll wear off.'

'Good to hear,' said Cat, 'but I meant, well, what happened?'

The journey from there to here had been a little traumatic. Cat had known nothing like it from the Loo, even with Rufus, Tom's great uncle. The Loo had rocked, rolled, jigged, jumped, jackknifed – not an easy thing to do when considering it was a portable toilet – and shimmied violently; the Loo lost its cool on its way from one destination to another. Cat had even thought she had heard it utter "phew" when it finally arrived.

'No idea,' said Tom, who wasn't fibbing, as he didn't know for sure, but he had an inkling what might have caused the Loo's erratic behaviour. He decided to keep it under his hat. Cap.

'Never been travel sick before,' said Darren, struggling to his feet just as the door to the Loo opened. 'Oh,' said Darren, turning green and getting back on his knees as a waft of bacon and egg scented air flowed in through the doorway.

'Tom?' said Cat, looking at Tom accusingly.

'Blimey,' said Tom with little conviction.

'We are in a café,' said Cat, 'but I suspect you knew that already, didn't you?'

'Doughnuts,' said Tom, thinking he had better fess up.

'Doughnuts?' said Cat.

'I couldn't stop thinking about them,' explained Tom. 'And then I was thinking about a cuppa at home and going to the HQ.' Tom sighed. 'Sorry.'

'So you should be,' said Cat. She didn't want to be hard on Tom, but. 'The Loo is a complicated and delicate piece of equipment.'

'AMEN TO THAT SISTER.'

'Sorry?' said Cat, looking around.

'For not thinking straight,' said Tom.

'I gathered that,' said Cat, 'but someone spoke.'

'That was me,' said Tom, frowning.

'Not you,' said Cat, 'someone else spoke. They said, "Amen to that sister".'

'I didn't hear anyone say that,' said Tom.

'Me neither,' said Darren, feeling well enough to talk.

'Or me,' said boB, who was still upside down. 'Could someone be so kind as to put me up the right way, please?'

Cat flicked her paw and righted boB.

'Thank you.'

Cat now shook her head. She was sure she had heard someone speak, but then again, the journey had been rough. She couldn't hear anything now.

'You okay?' asked Tom, showing concern.

'Sorry-yes, fine,' Cat gave her head another shake. Perhaps she was just hearing things. She decided it must have been caused by the journey; she had most definitely shaken, rocked and rolled. She would shrug it off as one of those things. But if she heard voices again that no one else heard…

'Good,' said Tom. 'I don't suppose, now that we're here, I could…'

'Just be quick,' said Cat, begrudgingly.

'As lightening,' said Tom, already disappearing through the door.

The green hue Darren's face had adopted during the Loo's flight had returned to more of a pinkish one by the time Tom returned.

Tom arrived back jubilant. A large brown bag of doughnuts in one hand and a cardboard tray with two cups on it in the other. He offered Darren a cup from the tray. 'It's mint and ginger tea,' he said, proving he had a heart of sorts where Darren was concerned, 'supposed to be good for the old tummy.'

Darren gratefully took it and had a sip. He grimaced. He thought it tasted awful, but if it helped. 'Thanks.'

'Happy now?' said Cat, aiming her question at Tom.

'With nobs on,' said a smiling Tom. He blew into the hole in the top of the cup and then took a sip. 'Nectar.'

'Good, now get ready to take us to the cottage and no careless thoughts this time.' Cat was taking a firm line with the old duffer for all their sakes.

AMEN TO THAT. (This time, a thought rather than spoken out loud.) The voice thought Cat had enough on her plate.

'Righty-ho,' said Tom, who was only half listening because he had been peering into the doughnut bag. His head appeared from its depths. 'Did you say cottage?'

'Yours.' Cat had decided paying Tom's cottage a visit before going to the Travellers HQ might not be a bad thing. Just to have a quick look round. She wanted to know if boB was telling the truth about Invisible Bob. And perhaps, if he was, she might be able to catch herself another Bob in the process. See if their stories matched. They would have to be on their toes, though, just in case Smokowski and Willy were there with him.

'Okay,' said Tom, concentrating while trying not to think about the money he had just wasted on a cuppa when he could have made one at home for free.

CHAPTER 37

In the shed, Smokowski and Willy watched and waited.

On the lawn, Invisible Bob slowly regained his senses and sat up.

In Tom's cottage, something stirred. Quietly.

CHAPTER 38

Much to everyone's relief, especially Darren's, the journey was a lot smoother this time.

'Out you go then,' said Cat, pushing boB out of the Loo and into Tom's hallway with her paw. 'And try to be quiet.'

'Quiet as a church one,' said boB, making as if zipping his mouth closed to emphasize the point. A pointless point, as no one could see him doing it.

'And be quick about it.'

'Yeah-yeah,' said boB under his breath.

'I can hear you,' growled Cat.

boB decided he best be going. He scooted to the other side of the hall and pressed himself flat against the wall. He was invisible, yes, but BIMBO training – you could never be too careful – had kicked in. He now inched his way along it, carefully, steadily, until he remembered what Cat had said. He now quickly scurried along the hall to the kitchen door. He paused, then skipped inside, literally. His twist on BIMBO training. Don't ask.

'You sure?' said Cat, on boB's return. She wasn't yet sure if she could trust him.

'Empty as my hat,' assured boB.

'You wearing a hat?' said Tom, out of curiosity.

'No, but if I were, under it would be as empty as your cottage.'

'Wouldn't surprise me,' said Cat, affording herself a smile.

'What?' said boB, then realising what Cat meant, 'Oi, not funny.'

'Not if it's true,' smirked Cat.

'Ha,' said Tom, grinning, 'if the hat fits.' He frowned. 'Is that right?'

'Can we go now, please?' said Darren, who, even though the tea had helped, and the journey had been smoother, was still a little green about the gills. He desperately needed some fresh air but would gladly settle for some of Tom's cottage air, even if it always seemed to have the hint of tea and coffee to it.

They left the Loo Indian file with Cat, sniffing the air, leading the way. Behind her came boB so she could keep a magic eye on him. Tom and Darren, taking deep breaths, followed.

The kitchen was reached without drama, and Tom went straight to the cupboard where he kept his cups.

'You can't make a cuppa now,' said Cat.

'I'm not,' said Tom, 'I'm just going to put this in one. Tastes like cardboard.' Referring to the paper cup, he was holding. He then noticed a cup on the kitchen table. Must be the one I was using before all this nonsense started, he thought. He went to retrieve it. It was the one with his name printed on the side. His favourite cup.

He took the top off the paper cup and went to pour the contents into the Tom cup. 'What the—' Tom suddenly exclaimed when he picked up the cup.

'What is it?' said Cat, adopting alert mode.

'It's still got some coffee in it,' said Tom, glaring at it.

'That all?' said Cat, powering down.

'That all?' said Tom, hardly believing his ears. 'You don't waste a cuppa. It's not right.' Then to everyone's horror, he started pouring the coffee from the paper cup into his Tom cup.

'Tom!' said Cat, feeling she should say something.

'Waste not, want not, I say,' said Tom, taking a sip. 'Lovely.' He always thought takeaway hot drinks a little too hot. It was just right now.

'Gross,' said boB, making a face, 'not good man.' Which was rich coming from him considering where he kept his lunch.

Tom ignored all and licked his lips.

Darren, who had watched Tom mix it up, had said nothing as he had been too busy trying not to gag.

Shaking her head, Cat went back to the task in hand; her sniffing had borne fruit. She had picked up three different lingering scents, Smokowski's, that of a stranger she guessed belonged to Willy, and one belonging to a certain magical. So boB was telling the truth, which meant the Chief Traveller was keeping an eye on things. But why? Only one way to find out.

Less than a minute later, they headed for the Travellers HQ.

Less than a minute later, they arrived back at Tom's cottage.

Less than a minute later, after Tom had popped back to the kitchen to pick up the bag of doughnuts he had forgotten, they headed for the Travellers HQ.

CHAPTER 39

'Did you see that?' said Smokowski.

'See what?' said Willy.

'Movement.'

'Where?' said Willy, scrambling to the window.

'In the kitchen.'

Willy squeezed past Smokowski. 'Can't see anything,' he said, scanning the kitchen window, 'you sure you saw something?'

Smokowski was sure. He was adamant. He was dead certain. 'I think so,' he said.

They both peered through the window together.

'Perhaps we should go look?' said Willy.

'Is that wise?' said Smokowski. 'Could be the kidnappers.'

'True,' said Willy, deciding looking in the kitchen window might be a little foolhardy, but they couldn't stay in the shed forever. They decided, for now, to mull on what to do next.

On the lawn, a groggy Invisible Bob struggled to his feet.

Smokowski and Willy continued to mull while he did it.

Getting his bearings, Invisible Bob noticed two familiar faces peering out through one of the shed's dirty windows. That is where he would head next, he decided. See what they were up to.

It was decided. What to do next. Smokowski and Willy would choose between two options regarding what it was they would do. Stay in the shed and become part of the furniture or take a chance and go see what was going on in Tom's kitchen. If anything was. The mulling continued.

Invisible Bob ran towards the shed as fast as his little legs would carry him.

It was decided. What to do next. Smokowski's creaking knees and Willy's complaining back had clubbed together to cast a deciding vote for making a move and for taking a peek through the kitchen window before either of them seized up.

The shed door reached; Invisible Bob started looking for a way in.

The shed door swung open further than Smokowski had intended.

'Careful,' whispered Willy, worrying about drawing attention.

'Sorry,' Smokowski whispered back.

Invisible Bob ducked as Smokowski pulled the door back. 'Aha!' he exclaimed triumphantly at the dodging of the door, not once but twice.

'Sorry?' said Smokowski, 'did you say something?'

'No,' said Willy, 'I thought you had.'

They both did some furtive peering around.

'Must have been the hinges,' suggested a whispering Smokowski when nothing untoward could be seen.

'Must have been,' a whispering Willy agreed.

Silently does it, thought Smokowski, as he went to shut the door behind him. But the door slipped from his overcautious fingers and... Nothing. The door had miraculously stopped short of smashing into its frame.

'Phew,' whispered Willy, still wearing his grimace of expected doom.

'Lucky,' whispered Smokowski, not quite believing the door hadn't slammed but thankful all the same.

But not so lucky for Invisible Bob, trapped as he was between the bottom of the door and the bottom of the frame. He groaned quietly.

Smokowski and Willy, unaware of Invisible Bob's presence, let alone his current predicament, scurried across the lawn and up against the cottage wall. They flattened against it and inched towards the kitchen window. There, with fingers on the window sill, they raised cautious heads and cautiously peered inside.

'Nothing,' whispered Willy, eyes flitting here and there.

'Nothing,' Smokowski agreed.

'Perhaps we should go in?' said Willy, seeking support.

'Perhaps we should,' said Smokowski, not entirely forthcoming with it.

'Okay then,' said Willy, taking a deep breath. He turned the door handle. The door opened a crack. Perhaps the kidnappers were hiding, waiting in ambush for them. He pulled the door to him.

'What is it?' whispered Smokowski.

'Just thinking we should listen for a moment,' said Willy, 'you know, just to check.'

'Very wise,' said Smokowski, who was all for listening.

'Nothing,' said Willy.

'Nothing,' whispered Smokowski, agreeing.

Willy pushed the door open again, this time fully. Eyes wide open, ears straining for the slightest of noises, he and Smokowski stepped into the kitchen.

'I think they've gone,' said Willy, after a moment.

'Who has?' whispered Smokowski.

Willy gave Smokowski a sideways look. 'Whoever it was, you say you saw,' said Willy.

'Oh yes,' said Smokowski.

But just to be on the safe side, Willy went into stealth mode and did a quick recce of Tom's cottage. He returned a few minutes later.

'Anything?' said Smokowski.

'Would we be here if there was?' said Willy.

'Good point,' said Smokowski. He then remembered the attic room. 'Did you go into the attic?'

'No,' said Willy, 'but I listened outside the door. No point stirring a hornets' nest if no need.'

'Good point,' said Smokowski. 'did you hear anything?'

'Where?' said Willy.

'In the attic?' said Smokowski, who was harbouring the possibility of popping up there later if there was no one around. His conscience clear as it was all in a good cause.

'No,' said Willy, 'but I'd advise not going in there just in case,' said Willy. 'You can never tell. Should imagine kidnappers are notoriously quiet.'

'No? Yes,' agreed Smokowski, 'valid advice.'

'Right then,' said Willy, who wasn't overly sure that Smokowski had seen anything, 'let's grab the rest of the clues and get out of Dodge.'

A reluctant Smokowski decided it might be for the best and went to get Tom's cup, the one with Tom's cup written on the side of it. But it wasn't there. 'It's gone!' he exclaimed, throwing whispering to the wind.

'What has?' said Willy.

'Tom's cup.'

'Good grief,' said Willy.

'And look a paper cup. That wasn't there earlier.'

Willy stared at the paper cup suspiciously. So there had been someone here, he thought. But who? Who had taken Tom's cup? Why? 'This isn't good,' said Willy.

'It isn't?' said Smokowski, who was of the mind that if Tom's cup was no longer there, there was a chance Tom and Cat were okay. He smiled to himself at the thought of Tom giving the kidnappers merry hell because he didn't have his favourite cup.

'Too many clues,' said Willy, 'things could get complicated.' Willy listed them. 'Number one, Tom's cup. Number two,' he was counting on his fingers, 'the leftover beverage in said cup, number three the note, number four the…' He paused, thinking. 'Oh yeah, the paper cup and finally the missing cup.'

'But that's only five,' said Smokowski, wondering how five could possibly be complicated and wasn't Tom's cup, here and now gone, just one clue? He then realised how things could become complicated.

'Yes,' said Willy, looking serious, 'but how many are red herons?'

'Herrings,' Smokowski corrected.

'Precisely,' said Willy, now wagging a finger, 'highly fishy.' He wrinkled his forehead. 'We should find somewhere to discuss them.'

'The red herrings?' asked Smokowski, trying to keep track.

'The clues,' said Willy. He looked thoughtful. 'And we need a board. Something to stick the clues to like they do in cop shows.'

Smokowski wasn't sure. He wasn't one for cop shows. Besides, how did they stick a missing cup to a board? Let alone leftover tea, or coffee, or whatever? Both of which weren't here anyway. He voiced his concerns.

'Easy,' said Willy, 'we take photos of them.'

Smokowski pointed out that they were no longer there.

'Then we draw pictures of them,' said Willy, undeterred. 'Can you draw?'

'Stickmen,' said Smokowski, who couldn't draw for toffee.

'The jobs yours then,' said Willy, who couldn't draw for toffee or nuts. 'Now, let's grab what we can and skedaddle.'

Smokowski picked up the paper cup and made for the door as Willy had the note, and the other clues were just memories.

As Smokowski and Willy prepared to skedaddle, a small invisible figure, feeling sorry for himself, had, at last, eased his body from between the shed door and its frame. He ached all over. He wanted to go home. He wanted to make himself disappear. Ah, he thought, just go home then. But he couldn't. He had nothing to report yet unless it was to inform the Chief that door swinging lunatics were on the loose. Though he doubted the Chief would be interested. Invisible Bob sighed a long resigned sigh and headed for the back door to the kitchen. Onwards and upwards, he told himself.

CHAPTER 40

'Oh, sorry, madam,' said Tom, as he left the toilet the Loo had landed in.

The madam in question, alarmed by Tom's intrusion, reached for her handbag and pulled out a rather large gun. 'Who are you?' she demanded.

'He's Tom,' said Cat, slipping from the Loo. 'No idea it was the ladies.'

The madam visibly relaxed when she saw Cat. '*The* Tom?' she asked.

'The one and only,' said Cat.

'Then you must be Cat?' said the madam.

'Pleased to meet you,' said Cat. 'You must be Deirdre.'

'I am,' said a delighted Deidre, pleased that Cat knew who she was.

As Cat and Deirdre exchanged pleasantries, the only thing a rather nervous Tom would find pleasant would be the lowering and the putting away of the gun. Was that a magnum she was pointing at him? And was she really pleased to see him?

Cat smiled at Tom. 'Relax,' she said, 'Deirdre's the new Chief's bodyguard. She's also new.'

'Pleased to meet you,' said Tom, doffing his cap whilst keeping his eyes on the very big gun. Who says men can't multitask? His heart rate slowed considerably as the gun was lowered.

'Is he in?' asked Cat, ignoring the gun situation.

'He is,' said Deirdre, popping the gun back into her handbag. It was quite a large handbag. 'He's expecting you. I'll show you in.'

'Thank you.'

'Hi,' said Darren, peeping over Tom's shoulder now that the area was gun free, 'I'm Darren.'

'Not *the* Darren,' said Deirdre.

'The very one,' said Cat.

'My,' said Deirdre, not believing her luck. So many celebs in one go. 'I don't think he was expecting you.'

'And me,' said boB, pointlessly waving.

'Who said that?' said Deirdre, instinctively going for her gun again.

'Bob,' said Cat, 'he's the backward invisible.'

'Oi!' said boB.

'Oh,' said Deirdre, this time not in the least impressed, 'one of them.'

'Oi!' said boB.

Cat could sympathise.

Deirdre scowled, then turned her attention to the others, the scowl turning into a pleasant smile. 'Follow me, please.'

CHAPTER 41

Lucy smiled at the nice lady who was pouring the tea. She thought she knew her from somewhere but couldn't quite place her. She seemed nice enough, though.

Mary finished pouring the tea, smiled back at Lucy, then gazed at the seascape beyond the window. She could hear Marc upstairs in a bedroom, happily humming a tune. She picked up her tea and glanced over at Kate. Kate smiled back at her. Mary sighed. If only it could always be like this.

'Have you been living around here long?' asked Lucy, snapping Mary from her thoughts.

'Oh, on and off. Quite a while, I suppose,' said Mary, being truthful. The cottage they were in was a safe house, and she had often visited it. It brought thoughts of a time that might have been.

'I can see why,' said Lucy, 'it's lovely here.' She sipped at her tea.

Mary sighed again. She wasn't keen on fogging people, especially family, but it was necessary for their peace of mind and safety. She studied Lucy sipping at her tea, happy but blissfully ignorant of her situation.

Lucy believed she was renting a cottage by the sea for her and the kids. She wasn't sure why she was, but the nice lady sat opposite her, who looked after the cottage and had been nice enough to meet and greet them and provide tea, somehow made any apprehensions just fade and disappear as if they never existed.

Chapter 42

The Chief Traveller was sat brooding when Deirdre popped her head round the door to his office.

'Sir?' said Deirdre, who had had to knock twice without getting a reply even though she had announced Tom and Cat's arrival over the intercom. 'Your visitors.'

'Sorry?' said the Chief, returning from wherever his mind had been. 'Your visitors, sir.'

'Oh yes, send them in. Sorry, away with those darn fairies for a moment there.'

The Chief stepped from behind his desk as Deirdre opened the door to allow Tom and his entourage entry. 'Please come in,' he said as he held out a hand. 'You must be Tom. Heard a lot about you.'

'I'm Darren,' said Darren, shaking the Chief's hand, anyway.

'Ah,' said the Chief, quickly taking his hand back, 'thought you were a tad young.'

Flipping cheek, thought Tom, who had been holding his hand out only for the Chief to walk past him. They had, Tom had to admit, only met once before, at the Chief's inauguration. And then, all the time travellers had been wearing masks to hide their identities from each other; what you didn't know couldn't fatally harm them. Hardly surprising then that the Chief hadn't recognised him. But what was with the ageist remark? How old did he think a pensioner was? Tom humphed and blew out his cheeks. Too young indeed! Darren was at least… Well, he was a lot older than he was, historically speaking.

The Chief now held out his hand to Tom. 'Then you must be Tom?' he said, playing the percentages. 'I've heard a lot about you.'

'All good, I hope,' said Tom, letting recent bygones be bygones.

'Well, some good, some bad,' said the Chief being brutally honest, 'but we can't all be perfect, can we?' He shook Tom's hand.

What the flipping heck did he mean by that? thought Tom, smarting from the remark. Bygones were now, here and now's. Tom frowned darkly at the Chief.

Noticing the frost forming between Tom and the Chief, Cat quickly introduced herself.

'Ah, the famous Cat,' said the Chief, advancing the same hand Tom was glad to be rid of.

'Sorry,' said Cat, 'we don't shake paws.'

'Of course, you don't,' said the Chief, pulling his hand back, 'Silly of me.' He smiled down at her. 'Nice to meet you.'

'And you,' said Cat, not sure she meant it. Unlike Tom, she had never met the man before, and now she had, she felt there was something about him that wasn't right. What though, she wasn't sure.

The Chief suddenly turned to Deirdre. 'I thought you said there were four visitors?' Making a great deal out of looking about the room.

'Yes, sir, I did sir, one of the Bobs arrived with them.'

'A Bob? Which one?'

'The one who spells his name the other way.'

'Ah,' said the Chief.

'Here, boss,' said boB, from one of the seats set in front of the Chief's desk.

What the heck was he doing here with Cat and Tom? thought the Chief. He would have to get him alone. He then remembered the doughnuts. 'Did you get the doughnuts?'

'And the reports so far,' said boB, enjoying seeing the Chief squirm.

'Yes, the reports.' The Chief glanced at Tom and Cat. Did they know what boB meant? No reaction. 'Very important.' But where were the doughnuts? The Chief had been eagerly awaiting the doughnuts. Surely there were doughnuts? 'And the doughnuts?'

'Here,' said Tom, holding up the bag he had got from the café.

'Good man,' extolled the Chief. Tom had suddenly gone up in his estimations. 'Any sprinkles?'

'I don't think so,' said Tom, peering into the bag. 'Nope.'

And down went Tom again. A disappointed Chief took the bag from Tom and asked Deirdre for coffees.

The Chief counted in his head. 'Five,' he said.

'Not for me, thank you,' said Cat, 'not something us cats drink.' She wondered whether to keep to herself she knew all about boB and his "reporting".

'Of course, you don't,' said the Chief, 'can I get you something else?'

'A milk would be nice.'

'A milk?' said the Chief, as if mystified by the thought of such a thing. 'Do we have a milk, Deirdre?'

'Yes, sir.'

'Right, four coffees and a milk it is then.'

'So, your place or mine?' said Willy, as Smokowski carefully closed the back door to Tom's cottage.

'For what?' said Smokowski, eyeing Willy suspiciously.

'As our base,' said Willy. 'We have to have somewhere to set the board up and work from.'

So they really were going to stick missing clues onto a board. Smokowski couldn't see the point of it, but perhaps Willy knew better as he had watched cop programmes. As for going to his place, well, he never had guests, so that was out unless they set up a base in the stockroom. But he didn't like strangers in his shop unless they were customers, and then they wouldn't be allowed in the stockroom. Answer easy, then.

'Yours,' said Smokowski.

'Mine it is then,' said Willy, 'but we'll have to stop off at your place first, though. You'll need to pack some woollies.'

'Woollies?' said Smokowski, wondering why he would need them.

'Yeah, jumpers and the like.'

'I know what a woolly is,' said Smokowski, 'but why would I need one?'

'Because of the cold,' said Willy. 'And I would take a couple of spares too just in case one gets wet.'

Cold! Wet! thought Smokowski. Does the man live in a freezer? He was afraid to ask but did anyway.

'Canada,' said Willy.

Having just dodged another door, as he was thinking about the best way to get into Tom's, Invisible Bob was feeling rather pleased with himself. But as he heard what Willy said, his upturned face took on a look of horror. Grief! he thought, I don't like the sound of that. Invisible Bob didn't have a woolly. He didn't have any clothes at all!

CHAPTER 44

The Chief led everyone to the adjoining conference room, where a large table and several chairs were waiting for them. The four coffees and a milk duly arrived.

Deirdre placed the coffees, milk and sugar and a saucer of milk onto coasters and then laid side plates and napkins beside them.

'Not for me, thanks,' said Cat, declining Deirdre's offer of a doughnut.

'Can I get you anything else?' asked Deirdre, doughnut hovering.

'Milk will be just fine,' said Cat.

Deirdre smiled and nodded and placed doughnuts on the other four plates. She then put the bag with the remaining doughnuts in the centre of the table.

'Ahem!' coughed the Chief.

Without a word, Deirdre removed the bag with the remaining doughnuts from the centre of the table and placed them within the Chief's reach.

'Thank you, Deirdre, that will be all,' said the Chief, eyes fixed on the bag.

'Sir,' said Deirdre, who then left.

'Right,' said Cat, eager to get down to business, 'Mary said you would fill us in on what we had to do next.'

'And so I shall,' said the Chief lifting a doughnut, 'but first coffee and doughnuts.' He took a bite.

'Fair do,' said Tom, who was all for food first, talking later.

Okay, thought Cat, a little weird, but the man appeared focused on the doughnuts. Better he got it out of his system than have his mind wandering while discussing their predicament. 'Whoa!' exclaimed the Chief suddenly, as one of the side plates and the doughnut on it moved as if by magic. 'That's mine!'

'But you've already got one,' boB protested.

'They are both mine,' said the Chief, dragging the plate towards him. 'As are the coffees.'

'But that's not fair,' whined boB.

'Fair?' said the Chief rather haughtily, 'Fair? There is no fair or not fair. I am your boss, and you are my subordinate. It is what it is. You do as I say, and I say you leave and wait with Deirdre until I call you. I don't even know why you're here.'

'The report,' said boB, grinning.

'Ah, yes,' said the Chief caught off balance for a moment, but it was only for a moment, 'bring it with you when I call. Off you go then.'

A miffed boB started to climb down from his chair.

'Wait,' said Cat, appalled by boB's treatment. He was an Invisible Bob, and they could be a pain in the butt occasionally, but there was no call to be so mean. 'He can have my doughnut.'

The Chief gave Cat a sharp look. 'You said you didn't want one.'

'I changed my mind.' Cat looked at Tom. 'Would you mind?'

A speechless Tom, mainly because of the amount of doughnut he had in his mouth, nodded and took one from the bag. He waved it just above the table where boB had been sitting. Tiny invisible hands gratefully grabbed it.

'Thank you,' said boB.

'My pleasure,' said Cat.

The Chief was looking daggers at the floating doughnut. 'I'll speak to you later,' he said.

boB and doughnut reached the floor without mishap and left the room. He left behind him an ominous silence.

'I'm not hungry anymore,' said Darren, breaking it. He was big on injustice.

Tom, his doughnut wedged in his mouth, slowly removed it, or what was left of it, and placed it on his plate. 'Nor me,' he said, wishing he had been a little quicker with his chewing. He stared at his plate.

The Chief stared at everyone. What was wrong with them? But never mind more doughnuts for him. He dunked the doughnut he was holding into his coffee.

Three dunked doughnuts and two coffees later, the Chief decided it was time to talk. 'So,' he said, dabbing at his mouth with a napkin, 'Mary sent you, did she?'

His words were greeted with sullen silence. No one wanted to talk to him. He was an oaf. A bullying oaf. No one had time for bullies. Yet they had to; enough time had already been wasted. Cat answered.

'Yes,' said Cat, thinking the Chief's question a little strange. Wasn't he supposed to be expecting them? 'She left a note saying to contact you, and you would explain what was to be done next.'

The Chief appeared to think on this for a moment. He put a hand to his chin and stroked it. 'Did she say anything else in this note she left you?' he asked, his eyes not leaving Cat.

Cat played what Mary had written through her mind and decided just knowing that Mary had sent them was enough for him. "Who

87

can you trust?" Mary had written. She doubted Mary had meant the Chief, but it was good advice. 'No,' she said, glancing at the others. Darren had fallen asleep, Cat felt he had had a lot in his mind lately, and Tom was in his own little world, not listening, just staring at the half-eaten doughnut on his plate. They weren't going to say anything to contradict her.

'Ah, that's good,' said the Chief, his brow furrowing, 'excellent, but there have been developments since last I spoke to Mary.'

'What sort of developments?' asked Cat.

'Timeline changing developments.'

'I didn't feel anything,' said Cat, who was finely tuned to any ripples; changes in time.

'No, I doubt you would have,' said the Chief, serious looking, 'the ripples were subtle, very subtle, almost non-existent.' He let what he had said sink in. 'But thankfully not so subtle as to go unnoticed by the wall in the operations room.' He now smiled. 'The staff were on it in a flash.' He stood up. 'Follow me.'

Cat nudged Tom from his reverie and told him to wake Darren. The Chief, meanwhile, had gone back to his desk. There, he reached for a wall sconce on the wall behind the desk and pulled on it. A part of the wall immediately began to move, slowly revealing a hidden room beyond.

CHAPTER 45

'Canada?' said an aghast Smokowski.

'Yes,' said Willy.

'You know what?' said Smokowski, now thinking fast. 'On second thoughts, perhaps my place would be better. Closer and all that.' Grief, Canada, he thought.

'Are you sure?' said Willy.

'Quite sure,' said Smokowski, attempting a smile that went slightly awry.

'Your place it is then,' said Willy.

Thank goodness for that, thought Invisible Bob, who was at that moment hanging on for dear life from Smokowski's trouser turn-up. He climbed over the edge and slumped within. There he sighed the sigh of someone who was not about to be frozen solid.

CHAPTER 46

Mary bade Lucy bye for now and strode down the garden path and away. The situation wasn't ideal, but it meant Lucy and the kids were out of harm's way for the moment, and that was the main thing on her mind.

She wanted to see her family as mum and nan one more time before she disappeared from their minds to become a memory you couldn't quite recall. It wasn't something she was comfortable with, but it was a requirement if she was to become the head of the BIMBOs. But before she could do that, she had to get the missing Jam business sorted. So she had things to do.

Mary headed back to Lucy's. She couldn't just disappear. Nor could Lucy and the kids. And that's where her friend would help again.

CHAPTER 47

'Blimey,' said Tom, as he stepped from the Chief's office into the room beyond.

Darren, yawning for the umpteenth time, followed Tom through. Eyes still half-closed, he hadn't yet noticed what had caused Tom's exclamation. Then he did. He blinked. His eyes grew wide. 'Wow!' he said, now fully alert, 'a grotto!'

'The operations room,' said Cat, who had been there before. Though this time it was different, quiet, the usual throng of busy creatures was missing, the room almost devoid of life. It appeared to be running using a skeleton crew.

'Ah yes,' said the Chief, looking down at Cat, 'you've been here before.'

'A while ago,' said Cat, 'but the place was buzzing with activity then.'

'It's like Christmas,' enthused Darren, who could get a tad excitable. That and prone to exaggeration.

The Chief frowned at Darren but ignored him and explained to Cat why the room was so empty. 'It's because of the developments. Top-level security staff only at the moment while you and Tom are here.' He stopped and leaned closer to Cat. 'Don't want anyone blabbing that you haven't been kidnapped, do we?' Just then, the place did begin to buzz as a bumblebee the size of a football flew past.

'Evening Bobby,' said the Chief as the bee passed.

'Evening, sir,' said Bobby.

'Bobby's a shapechanger,' the Chief explained, smiling, 'says he finds it easier to get around the main wall as a bee.'

Cat nodded. Made sense, she thought, the wall is huge. What didn't make sense was the sudden change in the Chief's mood and attitude. Perhaps he felt more relaxed away from the office?

'Bobby the bee,' whispered Tom to Darren as he chuckled to himself, 'couldn't make it up, could you?'

But Darren wasn't listening; he was too excited; he had just seen an elf. 'An elf!' exclaimed Darren with all the joy a young child would show on Christmas morning.

'That's Cedric,' said the Chief, raising an eyebrow, 'Chief of security.' He lowered his eyebrow and greeted the elf. 'Evening Cedric.'

'Sir,' said Cedric.

Darren whispered in Tom's ear. 'Do you think we'll see Santa?'

Tom tutted at the very idea. Was Darren mad? Everyone knew

that Santa and his missus holidayed in Tenby this time of the year.

They crossed the operations room floor with the Chief leading the way and stopped at a wall covered in small light bulbs. Most were off, but a few were flashing.

Tom gave a low whistle as he took in the wall's length, the part he could see that is. 'It's long, isn't it?' he said.

'Some say it's infinite,' said the Chief proudly, 'but then history does go back a long way.'

'What's it for?' asked Darren, watching a flashing light. He wondered what the wall would be like if all the bulbs were on and flashing. Christmas, he suspected.

'It's top-secret.' said the Chief, suddenly turning to stare at Tom and Darren. His eyes adopting a deranged look to them. 'Can you keep a secret?'

Both Tom and Darren shrank away.

'Yeah,' said Tom, not convinced he could.

'I can,' said Darren, who could.

'Good,' said the Chief, his eyes returning to normal. 'Ah, Deirdre.'

'Sir,' said Deirdre, who had been secretly summoned by the Chief, using the blue tooth device secreted in his pocket. The tooth had belonged to an abominable snowman who had had it removed by a dentist in the tech department.

'Impeccable timing,' said the Chief, now smiling at Tom and Darren, 'I was just this second thinking how wonderful it would be if Tom and Darren could partake in a tour of the base, and here you are as if by magic to offer such a service.'

'It would be a pleasure, sir.' Deirdre smiled at Tom and Darren. 'But first, sir, this was just delivered.' She handed him a note. 'The messenger said it was important.' Deirdre now linked arms with Tom and Darren. 'This way, gentlemen, and I suspect a cuppa before we start on the tour wouldn't go amiss?'

'Talking my sort of language now,' said Tom, wondering if he could reclaim his doughnut while they were at it.

Darren, who thought they were already talking a language they could understand, took one long last look at the grotto they were leaving. Perhaps he might get the chance to ask the elf if he could meet Santa.

Deirdre led them away, one happy as Larry, the other as deranged as a turkey looking forward to the festive season.

The Chief watched them leave and then turned his attention to Cat, who was frowning at him. Convenient Deirdre turning up like that, she thought. She was also of the mind that Tom should be in on anything there was to see and hear. He was a Traveller when all was said and done.

'No need for them to see any more than they need to in here,' the Chief said. He was wringing his hands. He could see Cat wasn't happy. 'And I'm afraid they will have to be fogged before you all leave. New protocols, you understand.'

Cat didn't, nor liked it, but was prepared to let it be for the moment; new broom and all that. Besides, she would lift the fog and fill Tom in on all that was said anyway. 'I do,' she lied.

'Good.' The Chief now looked at the note Deirdre had handed him, his face gradually clouding over as he read it.

'A problem?' asked Cat, noticing.

'Sorry? Oh-no.' The Chief screwed up the note and put it in his pocket. 'Just the usual.'

Cat nodded. She knew just how taxing the usual could be. She was thinking of Tom.

With the note read, crumpled and pocketed, the Chief turned and called to a fellow working at a console.

The fellow as wide as he was short, though not particularly rotund, came over and nodded to Cat. 'Sir?'

'I want to introduce you to Cat.'

'How do you do?' said the short wide person.

'Cat, this is mister Widewall. He is in charge of the wall.' All said without the hint of a smile.

'Pleased to meet you,' said Cat, thinking it was perhaps a good thing Tom wasn't about. He could be pretty juvenile at times. She then nearly jumped into the Chief's arms.

'Tom?' said the Chief, alerted by the noise Tom had just made. A snort. 'I thought you were with Deirdre?'

'I was,' said Tom, but the fuse in the kettle blew, and she's gone to look for another one. He had a doughnut in his hand, hidden behind his back. He looked down at Cat and grinned. 'Funny name that,' he whispered, 'made I laugh it did.'

'So I heard,' said Cat, wondering how he had managed to creep up on them without making a noise. Other than the snort of laughter.

'Well,' said the Chief, not impressed by Tom's appearance, 'as you are here.' He had decided, begrudgingly, to carry on with Tom in attendance, at least until another fuse was found. The Chief narrowed his eyes. Was that a doughnut behind Tom's back? He huffed, turned up his nose and turned his back on Tom.

'Now,' said the Chief, 'where were we, Mister Widewall?'

'We were being introduced,' said Mister Widewall. He nodded at Tom. 'Pleased to make your acquaintance.'

Tom, who had sneaked a quick bite when the Chief turned his back, could only nod sheepishly.

The Chief glared at Tom. 'After that.'

'That's as far as we got,' said Cat.

'In that case,' snapped the Chief, 'would you Mister Widewall care to show Cat,' there followed a slight pause, 'and Tom here, what was found.'

'Yes, sir.' Mister Widewall walked over to the console he had been working on and removed a length of crystal from it. He then inserted the crystal into another console. The wall immediately went dark. Except that is for the bulbs that had been flashing. These were now faintly glowing.

Cat knew that the flashing bulbs signified a ripple in time. A warning that someone somewhere was tampering with the past, trying to change history. She could feel ripples. All Magicals could, but they learned from an early age to tune them out. But they were always there, just beneath the senses. Tom couldn't. Travellers couldn't. Instead, they existed in a time bubble, leaving them unaffected by any changes to the present. Changes your ordinary person would take for granted as being the norm. Unless they were very subtle. The travellers would notice a famous landmark suddenly missing but might not notice that chickens now have four legs instead of two. Unless they owned one, that is. Hence the wall. What Cat didn't know was what it was they were showing her at the moment. Bulbs off, some still glowing, nothing out of the ordinary.

'I don't understand,' Cat admitted, 'what is it you're showing me?'

'Look closer.'

Cat did. As did Tom, who had less of a clue than Cat to what it was they should be seeing.

'Ow,' yelled Tom, shaking a finger, 'those bulbs are still flipping hot.'

'That's why we don't touch them,' said the Chief.

Is that a smile? thought Cat, noticing the Chief's lips were twitching.

'Should be a do not touch sign,' Tom moaned.

'We tend to use common sense here,' said the Chief, lips still atremble, 'but if you visit again, I'll have one put up just for you.' As Tom glared at him, his lips also now atremble, the Chief turned to Mister Widewall. 'Mister Widewall, the first aid kit if you please.'

'It's not that bad,' said Tom, being brave while still glaring. He wondered if the sugar on his finger from the doughnut had contributed to his burn. He sucked on the digit in question. What sugar remained tasted burnt.

'Ah,' said Cat, mind back on the job as Tom's finger was treated. She had finally noticed something on the wall. Invisible to the human eye, but not to Cat's, several bulbs that had not been flashing were also faintly glowing. She had had to look hard, but they were there.

'Noticed something?' asked the Chief.

'There are more glowing bulbs than there should be.'

'Exactly.'

'Why?'

'Why indeed?' said the Chief, attention drifting as Mister Widewall returned with the first aid kit. 'Use the salve on him.' Mister Widewall took the salve from the first aid kit.

'Seriously though,' said Cat, losing patience, 'why?'

'Ah, yes. We feel, that is Mary and myself,' said the Chief, 'that they are live time events but disguised in such a way as to make them pretty much unnoticeable to the human and magical eye. Too dull to notice against the regular flashing time tamper warnings you see.'

Sly, thought Cat. 'So, how did you discover what was going on?'

'Serendipity really,' said the Chief. 'The wall alerted us to a bulb having burnt out so, being safety-minded, that part of the wall was isolated so the bulb could be safely replaced.'

'And that's how you noticed the other bulbs were still glowing?'

'Actually, it was Bobby—'

'Sorry,' said Tom, 'the salve tickles.'

The Chief frowned at Tom and then went on with his story. 'As I was saying, Bobby noticed something was awry when he went to replace the bulb. He noticed that several bulbs were still glowing, but that part of the wall, can't remember off-hand which year it covered, anyway, had been clear of flashers, as we call them, so the bulbs should have all been dark.'

Lucky, thought Cat, but what did the flashers have to do with Mary and the missing Jam?

But before she could put her thought into words, Tom interrupted her by thrusting a bandaged hand in front of her face.

'Really?' she said, bemused by the amount of bandage for just a scorched fingertip.

'In case of infection,' Tom explained, 'Mister Widewall,' he stifled a giggle, 'said you could never be too careful.'

'Glad to hear it,' said Cat, mentally shaking her head.

'Do you want to sign it?' said Tom.

'That's plaster casts,' said Cat, who had had enough of the

Tom-foolery so asked the Chief the question that had been on her mind.

'Good question,' said the Chief, 'and the answer to your question is everything. The bulbs have everything to do with the missing Jam.'

He explained that they felt the missing Jam was just a subplot of something bigger. A mere diversion to keep the actual plot from being discovered. Something bigger was afoot. Something to do with the past.

Cat was horrified. If the Chief was correct, then... Then what? She let the situation take form in her mind. Someone takes the Jam. Panic stations. It's recovery a priority because, without it, the Ladies Institute could not replace Mary, and if Mary couldn't take over the reins from the BIMBOs outgoing president, then there would be leaderless chaos. The Ladies Institute, the LISPS, and the BIMBOs would be desperately trying to find the Jam while whoever was trying to change the past would be free to pursue whatever dastardly deed it was they wanted to achieve, happy in the knowledge that those best equipped to stop them would be in no position to do so. Then what? A world changed, that's what, and not for the better. A thought then struck her.

'It has to be an inside job,' said Cat. 'Someone that knows of the changes and the importance of the Jam.'

'Something we looked into,' assured the Chief, 'but after a while, we realised it wasn't that much of a secret. Just about everybody who is anybody knew.'

'I didn't know,' said Tom, who was still in the room nursing his bandaged hand.

The Chief had forgotten he was there and tutted. 'As I said,' he said, 'everybody who is anybody knew.'

Tom glared at the Chief, his face like thunder, but Cat intervened before anything went any further.

'Dead end then,' said Cat, giving Tom a warning look.

'Yes,' said the Chief, 'so we decided to concentrate on the faint ripples instead.' He pointed to the wall. 'And from there, find out what the real plan was and put a stop to it.'

'Then it's up to the Travellers?' said Cat.

'Yes,' said the Chief, 'and no.'

'I don't understand.'

'We don't want anyone to know the ripples are being investigated. We can't place a Traveller somewhere without someone knowing; procedure.'

'So, you're saying you can't trust the Travellers?'

'Apart from a handful of humans and Magicals, we don't know who we can trust.'

Tom, who had only been half-listening to what was being said because he had been watching Bobby buzzing about, now took an interest as his ears pricked up at the mention of Travellers not being trusted. He had already decided he didn't like the new Chief, and he wasn't about to let him get away with bad-mouthing his fellow Travellers.

"'Ere,' said Tom, 'don't go dissing us Travellers, we're completely trustworthy.'

'Dissing?' said the Chief, looking confused.

'Criticising,' said Cat, translating. She would have to have a word with Tom about using words his grandson used; it would get him into trouble someday.

'May I remind you of your great uncle,' said the Chief, hitting back below the belt.

'He was different,' argued Tom, trying to rally but realising he was on a sticky wicket where Rufus was concerned.

'Precisely,' said the Chief.

Cat gave Tom another look. Tom pouted.

'But as I was about to say, if word were to get out, it would more likely be from someone in the ops-room, hence why you are here; people and Magicals we can trust.'

'Oh,' said Tom.

'No one knows you are here. You've been kidnapped, remember. So no one will expect you. You can get in and out with no one being any the wiser.'

Cat was a little surprised. She had expected that she and Tom were here for a reason, but she had thought they would be looking for the Jam, not travelling in time looking for clues as to what was behind the Jam going missing. She then remembered the number of glowing bulbs there had been.

But there must be at least twenty ripples to investigate,' said Cat.

'Twenty-two to be precise,' said the Chief, not helping.

'It'll take ages, and we only have days.'

'In you we trust,' said the Chief, smiling at her. 'Oh, and you Tom.' There was no smile for Tom.

Tom grunted something under his breath.

'Then I suppose we should get started,' said Cat.

'Bravo,' said the Chief, clapping his hands together. 'Off we go then.'

This time Tom growled something under his breath.

'Tom!' hissed Cat, 'language!'

'Well,' said Tom.

CHAPTER 48

Smokowski didn't like the idea of using his stockroom. He liked the idea of Canada even less. The thought of snow, ice, and cold icy wind. He also hated the idea of having to chop wood for a fire. He had a heater in his stockroom. Smokowski had never been to Canada; he didn't want to. Even less so after the description, Willy had painted of the life he lived there.

Willy had lied. He actually lived in a tiny bedsit in London. Too small to entertain guests. He hated it. He was glad he had been quick on his thinking feet coming up with Canada. His jumper had swayed it. Willy had never been to Canada; he didn't want to. Even less so now he had thought about it.

Invisible Bob thought he might like to visit Canada one day, as long as he was warm and there was an abundance of chocolate.

They had stopped at the wholesalers on the way to Smokowski's to pick up the items Willy said they needed. There was a whiteboard on a tripod for sticking things to. A set of markers; various colours. A ball of string: red. Smokowski had wondered at this and was assured by Willy that that was the colour all good detectives used. Posh drawing pins that Smokowski had advised wouldn't stick into the board but couldn't dissuade Willy from buying. Some blue sticky stuff. Rubber gloves. And finally, Willy had insisted they needed a forensic kit to look for fingerprints and check for deoxyribonucleic acid. Smokowski had stared hard at Willy and had said, "doxy what?". Willy had said he had heard it somewhere but wasn't sure what it was but that they should look for it, anyway. The kit would help. Smokowski thought this kit sounded awfully expensive. He was, therefore, pleased to discover the wholesalers didn't stock one. The manager had asked if antiseptic wipes would do instead? Willy hadn't thought so, so they bought a small plastic container, a small paintbrush, sticky-backed plastic and some sherbet instead.

Willy said the container was to collect any dribble from the cup, and the sherbet was to be used for dusting for fingerprints. Smokowski had felt a tad nauseous when Willy had mentioned this and a lot doubtful.

At the till, Smokowski and Willy also discovered they had other items in their trolley; a family pack of chocolate peanuts and a large bar of fudge. As they both thought each other must have added the items, they were paid for without query.

Invisible Bob kept quiet.

The journey to Smokowski's shop from the wholesaler, though it was vital, they got there as quickly as possible for the sake of Tom and Cat, took longer than expected because of rumbling tummies. Smokowski ordered fish and chips and mushy peas to takeaway. Willy decided on pie, chips and gravy. Invisible Bob would have whatever they were having.

'Ah-ha,' said Smokowski, as Willy explained what they would do with the supplies they bought. He popped a chip into his mouth. He chewed, thought, and swallowed. 'But we don't have any photos of suspects, or suspects come to think of it.'

'But if we did,' said Willy, who was trying to explain as simply as he could how the evidence board worked, 'this is where they would go.'

Willy moved his plate to show Smokowski.

Smokowski wished he could remember where he had put the small table. He also wished Willy wouldn't keep bumping knees with him. He also hoped Tom and Cat were okay. He went to fork another chip. That's funny, thought Smokowski as the fork came up empty, where did that go?

Behind him, going as fast as Invisible Bob could carry it, a chip, hovering just above the floor, headed for a convenient hidey-hole.

CHAPTER 49

Deirdre had replaced the fuse in the kettle and popped back to get Tom, but as the Chief had looked happy; sort of; he wasn't yelling, to have Tom with him, she let him be and made coffee for Darren and boB. Even she felt sorry for boB when Darren had told her what had happened in the conference room, so she had taken them back there to see if there were any doughnuts left.

There had been, and now there wasn't. Apart from one, which neither boB nor Darren would touch. boB because after sucking out all the am and licking all the sugar from it, had fainted. A doughnut too far. Thankfully Deirdre had been on hand to resuscitate him with the aid of a stick and a small balloon. Darren, because he had seen what boB had done to it. They now waited in the Chief's office for his return.

'Darren,' greeted the Chief as he entered, 'I hope Deirdre looked after you?'

'She did,' said Darren.

'Good, good.' The Chief scanned the room. 'Is Bob with you?'

'I think so,' said Darren, looking at the empty chairs where he thought boB was.

'Bob?' said the Chief, following Darren's gaze.

A silent second or two later, after remembering no one could see his raised hand, boB answered. 'Here, sir.'

The Chief glanced at one of the chairs and saw nothing on it. 'Good,' he said. He pulled on the wall sconce, closing the wall. He took a seat, leaned on his desk and steepled his fingers. 'I've decided Darren should stay here.' The remark brought different responses.

'Why?' said Darren, miffed. He was looking forward to an adventure.

'If he must,' said Tom, trying to stay neutral but thinking of several reasons why it wasn't a bad idea.

'Your reason?' asked Cat, wondering why the sudden decision.

'Safer for all,' said the Chief, 'we have a guest room he can use.'

'Safer how?' queried Cat.

'Could be a leak,' said the Chief.

'A leak?' said Cat.

'Who's got a leak?' said Tom, holding out a hand and looking up.

'Not that kind of leak,' said the Chief, tutting. 'Informational ones. He knows you haven't been kidnapped. We cannot take the risk.'

'But he would be with us,' said Cat.

'Yes,' said Darren.

'Grief,' said Tom under his breath.

'Twenty-four-seven?' asked the Chief.

It wasn't a guarantee Cat could give. 'No, but…'

'No buts,' said the Chief. 'To put it bluntly, and no disrespect to you, Darren, he will be a liability.'

Couldn't have put it better myself, thought Tom.

'Thirty-one.' said Darren, not helping his cause.

There was no point arguing. The Chief was right, and Cat knew it. She glanced at Darren. 'Sorry, Darren, but I think the Chief is right. Not that you're a liability, but you need to be clued in on the world of the Traveller, and we just haven't got the time to do that.' She felt sorry for him. 'But I promise you, you can come with us some other time.'

'Can he?' said Tom, not meaning to say it out loud.

'Yes, he can,' said Cat, giving Tom an icy stare.

Darren cheered up a tad.

'That's settled then,' said the Chief, pressing a button on the intercom.

'Sir?' said Deirdre on the other end.

'Could you bring in the list, please?'

'Yes, sir.'

'I've had a list drawn up of all the twenty-two ripples. They are numbered. Please, and this is important, follow the list in numerical order. You'll find it less complicated that way.'

The door to the office opened, and Deirdre walked in. She passed the list to the Chief and went to leave, but he stopped her.

'Darren has decided to stay with us for a little while, Deirdre. Could you show him to guest room two please?'

'Yes, sir,' she said, smiling at Darren. 'This way, please.'

A gloomy Darren said his goodbyes and followed Deirdre to the door, where he paused. 'Was I right?' he asked.

'About what?' said Cat.

'Thirty-one being the answer to twenty-four-seven.'

For a second, Cat didn't know what he was talking about. She then sighed. 'Yes,' she said, 'the answer to twenty-four-seven is thirty-one.'

Slightly gladdened by this, Darren left.

'What was that all about?' asked Tom.

'Private joke,' said Cat.

'Right,' said the Chief, handing Tom the list, 'time to go. Good luck.'

'That's it?' said Cat, who had been expecting a deeper briefing.

The Chief, who had started to shuffle a pile of papers together on his desk, put them down and stood up. He looked a little sheepish. 'You're right,' he said. 'There is more.'

I should think so, thought Cat.

'Bob, there, is coming with you.' The Chief pointed to the chair next to the one Darren had been sitting on.

'Here,' said boB, who had moved; Darren's seat was warmer.

'There,' said the Chief.

'He is?' said Cat and Tom almost as one.

'I am?' said boB, just realising what the Chief had just said.

'Yes, you are to work with Tom and Cat and report back to me after each mission.' The Chief faced Tom and Cat. 'It will save you having to waste time coming to me yourself.'

The man keeps making sense, thought Cat, but she wished he would discuss things with Tom and her first. A Bob travelling with them wouldn't have been her first choice of a BIMBO companion. They could be a real pain. It also went a long way to explaining the Darren decision. More spying? What was the Chief up to? She decided to keep quiet for the moment.

Tom was having nearly the same thought. They had just got rid of one liability, and now they were being lumbered with another. Bobs, invisible ones, however they spelt their name, weren't everyone's cup of tea.

The Chief pressed on the intercom.

No one replied.

Drat, thought the Chief, Deirdre must still be attending to Darren. Never mind. 'Right,' he said, 'I have things to do. Important things.' He picked up the papers he was shuffling earlier. 'You know your way out.'

'Think so,' said Tom.

'Yes,' said Cat.

'There's the door then. Oh, and Bob, keep up the good work.'

He waited until they had gone before hurrying across his office to the conference room and the remaining doughnuts. He had no idea boB and Darren had finished them. Nearly finished them. There was one doughnut sitting on its lonesome on a plate. A sucked and licked jam-less and sugarless one. The one boB couldn't finish.

'What the…' exclaimed the Chief, as he peered into the empty doughnut bag. He was not pleased. He suspected their disappearance had something to do with that invisible creature. Drat, he would have to get Deirdre to order more. He then noticed a doughnut sitting all by itself on a plate. He cheered up a little.

'Come to papa,' said the Chief, picking it up. He would take a quick bite and then eat the rest of it with a coffee. He hoped Deirdre wouldn't be too long. He bit into it. Funny, he thought as he chewed, it doesn't appear to have any jam in it. A quick inspection showed it also lacked sugar. Perhaps that's why no one took it? Still, he thought, their loss. He took another bite and headed for the intercom to order coffee.

CHAPTER 50

At Lucy's, Mary's friend had been busy. 'Ta-ra!' she said, 'you can open your eyes now.'

Mary opened her eyes. The resemblance was uncanny. She was not often lost for words, but on this occasion, they deserted her.

'This is Ruth,' said Mary's friend.

'She looks just like her,' said Mary, shaking the shapechangers hand. 'Hello, Ruth.'

'Hello mum,' said Ruth, mimicking Lucy's voice to perfection.

'Incredible,' said an amazed Mary.

'And this is Charmaine and Abdul.'

'Hi grandma,' they said as one.

Mary was doubly impressed. They were the spitting image of Marc and Kate. Triply impressed was on its way.

The kitchen door opened, and another shapechanger walked into the lounge.

'Goodness,' said Mary, looking into her own eyes.

'Hello Mary,' said Mary's double, 'I'm Rhian.' She held out her hand.

'Hi.' Mary shook it and wondered at the weirdness of it, talking and shaking hands with herself.

'They all know what to do?' said Mary, leaving wonder and getting back down to business.

'They do,' assured her friend.

'Then I shall go.'

CHAPTER 51

Dinner over, the whiteboard was now standing, fit for purpose.

Willy was at his car collecting his "forensic kit" string, etcetera.

Smokowski had remembered where he had left the small table and had gone to retrieve it.

Invisible Bob was sprawled in a corner of the stockroom on a pile of unopened toilet rolls. His stomach hurt. Invisible Bobs weren't ones for moderation.

Willy placed his "forensic kit", etcetera, on the table Smokowski had provided. The clues followed: the note that said "Haven't got a clue", the paper cup, the note referring to Tom's cup having had drink still in it, and a note stating Tom's cup had disappeared.

I think we should draw Tom's cup,' mused Willy, 'otherwise things might get complicated.' He handed the markers to Smokowski.

Might? thought Smokowski, taking them. 'We haven't got any paper,' he said, scouring the table.

Willy suddenly looked drained. This case would be harder to crack than he thought.

From the corner of the room, Invisible Bob groaned quietly. A clue to how he was feeling.

CHAPTER 52

'Rude, I call it,' huffed Tom.

'Definitely short on man-management skills,' said Cat.

'Glad he's not my boss,' said boB.

'I thought he was your boss,' said Tom.

'Nah,' said boB, 'I'm just on secondment from the BIMBOs.'

'Well,' said Cat, 'while you're with us, I'm your boss.'

'I thought Tom would be my boss,' said boB, fingers crossed. He knew how tough Cat could be.

'Yeah,' said Tom, 'I'm the Traveller, so I'm in charge.'

'You are,' said Cat, 'but I run things.'

'Right,' said Tom, not entirely sure he understood what Cat had said. He decided it wasn't worth thinking too hard about as long as they knew who was boss. 'As long as you know.'

Knowing exactly what Cat said, boB uncrossed his fingers.

They arrived back at the toilets. Cat went first. 'All clear,' she said.

Tom held the door open, so boB could get in. 'You in?' he asked.

'I'm already in,' said boB, who had followed Cat in.

'Not cool,' said Tom, 'suppose someone had been in there?'

'They can't see me,' said boB, missing the point.

'Not the point,' said Cat, guiding boB to it. 'It's the ladies.'

Tom opened the door to where the Loo waited and stepped inside.

'Okay,' said Cat, when they were all in, 'why are you really with us?'

'Who me?' said boB.

'Yes, you,' said Cat.

'The usual,' said boB, deciding it easier to tell the truth.

'Spying on us.'

'I wouldn't call it spying as such,' said boB, still trying to cover what it obviously was.

'I would and already have,' said Cat. 'Anything else we should know?'

'Don't think so,' said boB, still being honest. 'Like what?'

'Slowing us down?' One of a few reasons Cat could think of.

'Why would he want me to do that?' said boB, sounding genuinely puzzled. 'Reporting is all I was told.'

Cat believed him. 'Good, keep it that way.'

A puzzled boB didn't understand the questioning. Why did— Ah, thought boB, she doesn't trust the Chief for some reason. Well, he decided, it's not for me to get involved.

'So,' said Cat, having finished with boB, 'what's first on the list, Tom?'

Tom took the list the Chief had given him from his pocket and held it up and away from him and then closer. And away again. For a second, it looked as if he was playing an air trombone. He finally found focus.

'You should have your eyes checked,' said Cat.

'I can read it,' said Tom.

'What's it say, big man?' asked boB, accidentally getting in Tom's good books; for the moment.

'Well,' said Tom, preening, 'at number one we have...' He trailed to a stop. He didn't like the look of that. Not one bit. It looked way too dangerous.

'Well, big man,' said Cat smiling to herself, 'what does it say?'

'It says,' said Tom, 'that we have to go back to ten sixty-six during the Norman invasion and find the Duke of Normandy. Who's that?'

'William the Conqueror.'

Tom had heard of him. 'That sounds dangerous.'

It does, thought Cat. 'Does it say why?'

'It seems he invented the first multi-bladed razor just before the Battle.'

Weird, thought Cat, must be something to do with the economy; someone wanting to get rich before they are even born. But what did it have to do with the missing Jam?

'We had better do our homework then,' said Cat, 'check when the battle took place and work back to the day he landed.'

'No need,' said Tom, 'the exact time and date are on here.'

Cat frowned. 'It is?' She had never heard of a ripple case having an exact date and timing before. Still, small mercies, perhaps the list wouldn't take that long to complete. 'When?'

'First of October at four o'clock in the afternoon.'

'Okay, off we go then,' said Cat.

Tom put the list back in his pocket and prepared for a trip to the seaside. He grabbed hold of the flusher and immediately looked in pain.

Cat had to smile. He still grabbed the flusher even though she had admitted to pulling his leg about it the first time they had travelled. He only needed to concentrate.

'Wait,' said Cat, all of a sudden.

'What?' said Tom, hating to be disturbed while straining; thinking.

'We don't know where he was when he discovered the razor.'

'Ten sixty-six,' said Tom, a slight exasperation to his voice.

'Not when, where?'

'Hastings?' said Tom, who thought they knew that.

'Yes,' said Cat, 'but where in Hastings?'

'No idea,' said Tom.

'Don't ask me,' said boB.

'I wasn't going to,' said Cat. 'Tom.'

'Yeah?'

'We need to look at your computer.'

Tom raised his eyebrows. 'Won't Smokowski be there?'

'Let's hope not,' said Cat.

'Home it is then.' Tom grabbed the flusher, concentrated but this time with a slight smile on his face. Cuppa time!

Tom opened his bathroom door a crack and let boB out.

boB, his job to check out the lay of the land, immediately did a shoulder roll across the hall floor. But being short, he only travelled a few inches. So, several rolls later, he landed against the far wall. He pressed his body tight against it. Slowly, boB, keeping tight to the wall, made his way along the hall. A doorway. boB fell to his belly and crawled past. Nothing so far. The place appeared empty. And then, after more wall-hugging, he was at the kitchen door. It was ajar. It was there, as he skirted the door frame, he remembered he was invisible. He quickly glanced towards the bathroom door. It was still open; he could see Tom peering out. Good job he can't see me, thought an embarrassed boB. He dusted himself down and casually walked into the kitchen.

The place was empty.

'Cuppa,' asked Tom as he filled the kettle.

'Nothing for me,' said Cat, who was sitting on a cushion at the kitchen table, starting Tom's laptop up.

'Small one for me, please,' said boB.

'It will have to be in a saucer,' said Tom, eyeing an eggcup and deciding it wouldn't do. 'Milk, sugar?'

'That's fine,' said boB, 'milk, plenty of sugar.'

The laptop came to life as the kettle clicked off. Tom took his cup from his pocket – the one Smokowski had noticed missing – made the tea and placed the cup and saucer on the table. 'Found anything yet?' he asked Cat.

'Not yet,' said Cat.

'Ooh,' said boB poking a finger in his tea, 'could I have more milk, please.'

Tom obliged. 'Biscuit?' he asked, boB still in his good books.

'Chocolate?' said boB, checking his tea again. It was perfect.

'No prob.'

'Then yes, please.'

As Tom turned to get boB his biscuit, he heard a faint splash. Turning back, he saw ripples on the surface of boB's tea and spots of tea on the table.

'boB?' said Tom.

'Sorry,' said boB, 'I slipped.'

'Are you in the saucer?' said Tom, screwing his face in disgust.

'It's good for the skin.' There came the sound of slurping. Tea was disappearing into an invisible hole.

Flipping 'eck, thought Tom, my poor saucer. boB was no longer on Toms Christmas list.

'Ah,' said Cat.

'Got something?'

'Sort of.'

'Sort of?'

'It seems no one knows exactly where the Normans camped.'

'Oh,' said Tom, 'what now?'

'Hastings, I suppose,' said Cat, knowing when she was beaten.

Tom grinned and took a sip of his tea.

boB stayed quiet.

Cat turned the computer off and closed the lid. 'Time to go,' she said.

'I haven't finished my tea yet,' said Tom. The thought of leaving yet another cuppa half-finished sending a shiver down his spine.

'Be quick then.' Cat felt they had wasted enough time already. 'Or bring it with you.' She slipped from the table.

Good idea, thought Tom but… 'Hey,' he said, 'where's the paper cup I had from the café gone?' He had decided Cats idea a good one but didn't want to take his cup with him again.

'Perhaps you tidied,' suggested Cat as she stepped into the hall.

Tom tried to recall if he had but couldn't. Nothing else for it then. It took just two gulps for Tom to empty his cup. He wiped dribble from his chin with a paper towel, stuck a handful of biscuits in his pocket, and went to follow Cat.

'Oi! What about me?' said boB, 'I ain't finished either.'

But Cat had gone.

'Here,' said Tom, handing boB a paper towel, 'I reckon you got ten seconds.'

'Not fair,' moaned boB, scrambling from the saucer and wrapping himself in the paper towel. 'Wait for me!'

CHAPTER 53

The Chief returned to his desk, but instead of using the intercom, he pulled the crumpled note Deirdre had given him and smoothed it flat.

He read it. He reread it. Had things really come to this? he thought. He supposed so. No turning back now.

The Chief opened a drawer and pressed a hidden button. Another drawer opened. A secret drawer for secrets. He popped the note in with the other secrets inside and closed both the drawers.

Note now out of sight; the Chief had a sudden craving for sugar. He pressed a button on the intercom.

CHAPTER 54

They arrived in Hastings. Or at least they hoped it was Hastings; Tom's track record on arriving at the right place was a little sketchy.

Tom quietly opened the door to the cubicle they were in and peeped outside. He was relieved to find they were in the gents this time. He opened the door a little further and listened. They appeared to be alone.

'All clear,' said Tom.

Cat pushed past him. 'Let's check outside,' she said, being well versed with Tom's shortcomings.

They cautiously moved towards the exit. Once again, Tom carefully opened the door. Beyond was a corridor and beyond that was a bar.

'I think we're in a pub,' said Tom.

'I wonder if they sell sarsaparillas?' said boB.

Both Tom and Cat looked down to where the voice had emanated. 'Saspa-what?' said Tom.

'It's a drink.'

'Doubt it,' said Cat, 'and we don't have the time if they did.'

'And you'd need money to pay for it anyway,' said Tom, 'and don't look at me for it.'

'Come on,' said Cat.

They moved on.

'I have money,' said boB.

'Do you?' said Tom, doubting it.

'Yes, and if I give you a couple of pounds, could you buy me a bottle? That's the currency here, isn't it? I have euro's if not.' There came a jingling noise from boB's whereabouts. Two one pound coins appeared in the air a few inches from the ground.

Tom was mortified. Where had he got those from? he thought, not wanting to think about it. 'No,' he said, grimacing.

'Put them away,' said Cat, pulling a face, 'we haven't got time to dilly-dally buying drinks.'

'Tom did,' said boB.

'Grrr,' said Tom.

'And I wasn't happy about that if you remember. Now put the coins away.' As the coins disappeared to the accompaniment of boB huffing, Cat decided it was time to hurry things along. 'Go out for a quick recce Tom and see where we are.'

Tom went, and ten minutes later came back.

Cat wasn't best pleased it had taken him so long; she had started to worry. 'Where have you been?' she demanded.

'There was an offer on crisps, buy one get one half price,' said Tom, producing two packets from a pocket.

Cat prayed for strength, but there was no point moaning. 'And are we in the right place?' she asked.

'Defo,' said Tom.

'You sure?'

'I asked a bloke at the bar.'

'Did you get me a packet?' asked boB.

'No,' said Tom, looking alarmed, 'I would never buy anything for a minor in a pub.'

'I'm not a minor.'

'You're short.'

'Sizest,' said boB, 'and for your information, I'm one hundred and two years old.'

'Go on,' said Tom. 'Never.'

'And it's my birthday today,' boB added.

'Oh, for goodness' sake,' said a despairing Cat, losing patience with the old fool or, in this case, if boB was telling the truth, old fools. 'Give him a packet.'

Tom groaned but did as Cat asked.

'Eat them in the toilet,' said Cat, before boB could open them. Grief, she thought, she never thought to hear herself saying that. 'And as for you, Tom, are you certain we're in Hastings?' She knew she should have gone herself.

'Course I am,' said Tom on the defence. 'After the bloke at the bar gave me a funny look, I thought I'd better check.' He produced a newspaper from his jacket. 'I bought this from across the road.' Tom pointed to the name of the paper. The Hastings and St. Leonards Observer. 'The woman said it was the local Hastings paper. Look, it's even got a picture of a Norman on it.'

It would appear they were in the right place, thought Cat, though why he couldn't have shown her the paper in the first place was beyond her.

'To the Loo,' said Cat.

Next stop October the first, ten sixty-six.

Chapter 55

Smokowski remembered having some paper somewhere. Ah! he thought, the defunct printer. He was in luck. Three dust-covered yellowing sheets. He dusted them down and hoped three would be enough. Now all he had to do was draw Tom's cup.

'Aha!' exclaimed Willy, stepping back from the finished evidence board.

Smokowski had been nodding. A touch away from being fully gone. Almost sleeping on the job while Tom and Cat were in peril. He would feel guilty later on. He opened an eye and looked up. He was on one of the chairs waiting for Willy to finish what he was doing.

'What do you think?' said Willy, stepping to the side like a magician's assistant.

Smokowski looked; he didn't quite know what to think. At the top of the board, Willy had written "THE KIDNAPPING OF TOM AND CAT" in large red letters. A taped length of red string led from the title to the rest of the board. The drawing pins had not pinned, and the blue sticky stuff was nowhere to be seen. It had stuck but hadn't looked quite right against the red string, so Willy had discarded it.

The red string then met eight more pieces of red string that branched off in various directions on the board. They led to the note with "I haven't got a clue" on it, a badly drawn picture of a cup with "Tom" written on it, another to a piece of paper with "unfinished tea" written on it, another to the paper cup, which was now covered in sherbet, which Willy had taped to the board. The other four red strings led to a drawing of Tom's cottage; Willy had added that. He had also added a sketch of the Jam. He had drawn those two while Smokowski had been "nodding". The final two pieces of red string led to blank pieces of paper.

'Well,' said Smokowski, wondering where the drawings of the Jam and Tom's cottage had come from. He also wondered about the two blank pieces of paper. 'As you are the expert here, you could explain it to me?'

'Righto,' said Willy, who had produced a stick from somewhere to use as a pointer, 'we have four clues.' First, he pointed to the note mentioning the unfinished tea. 'I think this is perhaps the most important clue we have. I think it proves beyond doubt that the kidnappers of Tom and Cat took them by surprise.'

On the toilet rolls, Invisible Bob wondered at this; what sort of surprise helps someone kidnap someone?

As if reading Bob's thoughts. 'Which means the kidnap was without warning,' Willy clarified.

Ah, that sort of surprise makes sense, thought Bob, who had recovered from the chip overindulgence and was now tucking into the chocolate peanuts.

Makes sense, thought Smokowski, sitting straighter in his chair.

'The second most important clue has to be the paper cup.' Willy tapped it with his stick. It fell off. Willy picked it up and stuck it back. 'Because I believe the kidnappers realised their mistake of leaving the half-empty cup and returned to take it to cover their tracks, but,' Willy paused, 'they then made the mistake of leaving the paper cup behind in their haste.' He tapped the paper cup again, which this time stayed fast. 'Sadly, as you know, any dribble that might have been on the paper cup had dried and disappeared before we found it. Also sadly, dry or wet, the sherbet was no help, and no fingerprints could be lifted from it.'

Darn waste of good sherbet, thought Invisible Bob, as he stuffed another choccy peanut in his mouth.

Willy now pointed to the poorly drawn picture of Tom's cup. 'I am of the opinion,' said Willy, getting into the swing of things, 'that Tom's cup may well have had nothing to do with the kidnapping. It being just an innocent bystander. It just happened to have the incriminating beverage within.'

Until then, Smokowski had been listening with rising interest, thinking he had perhaps underestimated Willy's detective credentials. He now reviewed this and lowered his opinion.

The stick now waved in front of the drawing of Tom's cottage, which Smokowski thought rather good. Which brought with it the wondering of why Willy hadn't bothered to draw Tom's cup? 'I think this, whilst being a solid clue to where the kidnapping took place, should now be treated as a fact, as we know they are no longer there. Tom and Cat, I mean.'

Go Sherlock, thought Invisible Bob, who was making mental notes of the proceedings, so he had something to report back to the Chief. He stuffed another choccy peanut in his gob.

'And lastly, the note with "haven't got a clue on it".' Willy tapped each word on the note with his stick as he read it.

That's five clues, not four, thought Smokowski.

That's five clues, not four, thought Invisible Bob, who just shrugged and carried on eating.

The stick now pointed at the note. Willy tapped it. 'This I don't think is a clue.'

Ah, thought Smokowski.

Ah, thought Bob.

'This, I believe, is the red heron in the pond.'

Herring, thought Bob.

'Herring,' said Smokowski.

'Quite so,' said Willy, swishing at the note with his stick to flick it from the board. 'Fishy indeed but not a clue.' There was a cracking noise, and the end of the stick snapped off. The note stayed where it was. Willy picked the end of his stick up and placed it on the table. He looked at Smokowski. 'Which leaves me with one conclusion.'

'Yes?' said Smokowski, on the edge of his seat – it was more comfortable there, no cramping.

Yes? thought Invisible Bob, all ears.

'That Tom and Cat have been kidnapped.'

Smokowski sagged back into his seat, cramp or no cramp.

Invisible Bob sighed and continued chewing.

But Willy hadn't finished. 'And those kidnappers left a clue so vital that I have moved it from clue number two to clue numero uno!' Willy went to swap the clues about, but the note mentioning the unfinished tea ripped. So instead, he pointed to the new important clue.

'Tom's cottage,' said Smokowski, 'I thought the paper cup was clue two?'

'It is,' said Willy, looking at the board. He stepped closer to it and tapped the cup. He forgot his stick had snapped.

'Why?' asked Smokowski, sitting up straight again. Not the cramp this time.

'Because, my friend Smokowski, we find out where the cup came from, and I say there we will find Tom and Cats, kidnappers.'

'Well, I'll be,' cried Smokowski, 'I think you've got something there.'

Too right, thought Invisible Bob, choccy peanut poised. Now, that was something he could report. He needed to see the Chief toot-sweet.

'To the café,' said Willy.

'To the Chief,' Invisible Bob whispered.

'But what about the drawing of the jam and the blank paper?' said Smokowski as they went to leave.

'Ah,' said Willy, 'the jam is a picture of the missing Jam, a clue.'

'To the kidnappers?'

'To why it all started.'

A frowning Smokowski thought they knew that; it's why they were there. 'And the blanks?'

'Left blank so we can add pictures of the suspects and victims later on once we have a better idea of who they are.'

Okay, thought Smokowski, blank for the suspects if they manage to suspect someone, but… 'We know who the victims are; Tom and Cat.'

Willy stopped dead in his tracks. 'So they are,' he said. 'Well done. Got any pictures of them?'

'Not on me,' said Smokowski.

'And that is why there are blanks on the board.' Willy headed for the door.

A bemused and slightly worried Smokowski gave Willy's back an incredulous stare, shook his head, and followed.

CHAPTER 56

Tom concentrated for all he was worth. So much so that boB thought he was going to blow a gasket. Hastings, October the first, ten sixty-six was the mantra playing through Tom's head, Hastings, October the first, ten sixty-six.

The landing was smooth. Tom took that as a good sign. It didn't mean that they were in the right place, though. What waited for them outside the Loo door was a mystery. What was certain was, if they were in the days of the Norman invasion, they wouldn't be encased in a cubicle. Not many loos about once you passed a certain time in history. Unless you counted latrines and the like but there, the portable Loo drew the line. No way was the Loo going to land in one of them. They might be deep, for one thing. So the portable always avoided them somehow, and usually out of nostril range and downwind of them. Not that the Loo had them, nostrils. Well, not that anyone knew for sure.

The other slight drawback to there being no cubicles was that the Loo would then be invisible, cloaked. The shell of the portable Loo, as always, still in Tom's back garden. Though occasionally…

Only Tom and Cat knew where it was. Tom, with the help of his Saver and Cat, using her extraordinary senses. The Normans would therefore have no idea it was there; if it was there, with the Normans.

'Ready?' said Cat.

'No,' said Tom, who invariably wasn't. Especially so when the outside might have certain implements that were sharp and dangerous to one's person. But not being ready hadn't stopped him before, so he opened the door a crack. But neither was Tom stupid. He closed the door again before even looking through the gap.

'boB?' said Cat.

'Yes,' said boB, thinking he might not like what came next.

'Do the honours, please.'

'Go outside?'

'Yes.'

'Why me?'

'You're invisible.'

'Always with the invisible,' moaned boB. 'What if we've landed on a cliff edge?'

'What if I throw you out there?' Cat threatened, knowing the Loo wouldn't be so stupid.

'He'll get to the bottom quicker,' said Tom.

'Not helping, Tom.'

'I'll give you a biscuit.' Tom would have trouble sleeping that night.

'Now you're helping,' said Cat.

'Two biscuits,' said boB.

'One and I don't throw you out.'

boB screwed his face up. He had heard that Cat drove a hard bargain. 'Okay, but if there's a chocolate one, I'll have that.'

'Deal,' said Cat.

'Oi!' said Tom. He had just realised he had no idea what biscuits were in his pocket; he had just grabbed a handful. What if there was only one chocolate one? He took them out and sighed a sigh of relief; they were all chocolate. He felt a little better. He handed the one with the least chocolate on it to boB.

'Ta,' said boB.

'Off you go then,' said Cat, as Tom opened the door a crack again.

boB popped his head out of the door. He could see a light. He carefully slipped outside. Tom swiftly shut the door behind him.

boB had been gone nearly fifteen minutes, and Cat was getting worried. Perhaps she shouldn't have sent him out alone.

Tom, on the other hand, had worries of his own; the chocolate was melting on his biscuits. It was on his bandage.

As they fretted, a sudden bump on the side of the Loo brought them both back to the here and now.

'Wath wuz thath?' mumbled Tom, who was at that moment sucking the chocolate off said bandage.

'I don't know,' said Cat, her hackles up.

There followed another bump, followed by muffled speech, which would not have been used in polite company, followed by insistent knocking on the Loo door.

'Phut,' said Tom, removing a piece of linen by blowing it from his lip.

Cat, dodging the errant wet bit of cloth as it landed beside her, whispered through the door. 'boB?'

The knocking continued.

Cat raised her voice.

This time the noise stopped for a moment before resuming.

'Open the door,' said Cat, sure, as the knocking was on low, that it was boB.

Tom, his bandage unravelling, wasn't so keen. 'What if it isn't him?'

'Just do it before he draws attention.'

Tom gingerly did as he was told. The door opened a smidgeon.

'boB?' said Cat as something brushed past her.

'Who were you expecting, the postman?' boB didn't sound happy. And that was because he wasn't. He gingerly fingered the bruise on his forehead. 'You didn't warn me the flipping thing would be invisible! Walked straight into it; twice!'

Oops, thought Cat, so that was what the bumps were. 'You okay?'

'Took me ages to find it again.'

'But you did,' said Tom, helpfully looking on the bright side.

'Yeah,' groaned boB, 'with my head.' He chanced another touch of the bruise. 'Ow!' A bump was coming up. He slumped into a corner of the Loo. He was feeling sorry for himself. Not only had he banged his head, he no longer had his biscuit. 'And I lost my biccy.'

'I'm sure Tom will give you another one.' Cat was feeling sorry for him, but time was running. 'So, boB, what did you see?'

'What?' said Tom.

'Can't remember,' said boB, sulking in his corner. 'I think I've got amoeba; not sure I can remember anything.'

'But you remember losing your biscuit,' smiled Cat.

'And sugar loss,' boB quickly added for good measure, 'I'm feeling pretty weak.'

'Give him a biscuit Tom.' Cat felt boB deserved one, if only for his Oscar performance.

Tom tutted and delved into his pocket. 'I work hard to pay for these, you know,' he said, opening himself to ridicule. It didn't come, Cat had more important things on her mind. Tom handed boB a biscuit.

'Over here,' said boB as he watched the biscuit drift here and there. Then it was in his grasping little fingers. He smiled. He had lied. The other biscuit was safely in his tummy. But he was sure he deserved it; he had been wounded in the line of duty. 'Cheers.'

'You're welcome,' said Tom, which wasn't what he was thinking.

''Ere,' said boB inspecting it, 'where's the chocolate gone?'

'In my pocket,' said Tom, showing boB a chocolate-smeared finger.

boB glared at Tom. Had he done that on purpose? Rubbed the chocolate off?

'Well?' said Cat, 'what's out there?'

'A circus,' said boB. He took a bite of his biscuit.

'Did he say Circus?' said Tom.

'Circus?' said Cat. Grief, she thought, what has Tom got us into now?

119

'Loads of tents,' said boB, whose knowledge of a circus was limited. 'We're in one.' The light boB had seen a chink of daylight showing through the tent flap.

'Tents?' said Tom.

'Sounds like we might be in a camp,' said Cat, dismissing the circus idea.

'Camp?' said Tom. He appeared to have lost the ability to construct a sentence.

'Did you see any Normans?' asked Cat, now with more than an inkling of where they might be.

'Normans?' said Tom. He needed a cuppa.

'There were some blokes wandering about,' said boB, 'but I don't know if any of them were called Norman.'

And Cat had thought Tom was king of trying her patience. She counted to ten. 'Soldiers, Norman soldiers.'

boB had a little think as he gnawed on his biscuit. 'Come to think about it. Some were carrying spears.'

'Spears?' said Tom, who didn't want to say or hear any more on that subject.

'Right, Tom,' said Cat, 'looks like you and I are popping out for a while.'

Tom just knew she was going to say that. 'You sure? You know what I'm like.'

'Yeah,' said Cat, 'but you are also a darned fine Traveller.'

Tom was sure there was a compliment there. 'Okay, but you gotta glamour me. You know, make me invisible.'

Cat had a glamour for every eventuality. 'I'll use a cloaking glamour,' she said, 'but don't go sticking your finger where it shouldn't be.'

Tom reddened. 'It was only once,' he said, in defence.

'Just once could be the difference between keeping your finger or not.'

The thought of the spears came to Tom's mind. He supposed they would also have swords.

'The door Tom.'

It was challenging, but Tom managed it. Not easy to open a door with arms and hands pressed firmly to your sides.

CHAPTER 57

Darren sat on the edge of the bed in guest room number two, feeling sorry for himself.

The Chief didn't trust him. Tom thought him an idiot. Mary had used his mind because it was mostly empty. And to cap it all, he didn't know where Lucy and the kids were. They could still be frozen for all he knew. He sighed. Sometimes he longed for the good old days. If he had stayed there, he would not be here now, getting in the way. But then no, Lucy. No kids. A heavier sigh. Maybe Tom and the Chief were right, but it wasn't easy living in a time you weren't born in. But at least he was in a comfy room.

It had a comfortable enough bed. There was satellite television with a film channel. A small fridge filled with goodies, which he hoped he didn't have to pay for. He had already had a cola and a bar of chocolate. No one had said anything.

Darren stood and went to the window. It had blackout curtains pulled across it. He drew them apart. The window had a picture of a field full of flowers behind it. He tapped the window. No glass, which meant he had tapped the picture. Whatever was behind that felt solid.

Returning to the bed, Darren sat down and wondered where Lucy and the kids could be. They had Mary with them, so that was a bonus, he supposed, but that didn't stop him from feeling useless. He picked up the remote for the television and decided things could be worse.

There was a knock on the door. Perhaps the Chief had changed his mind, thought Darren, opening it.

He hadn't. It was someone intent on proving Darren was right; things could be worse. It was Darren's turn to be kidnapped.

Before Darren could utter a word, someone held something over his nose and mouth. He drifted into unconsciousness. But just before he did, he was sure he had heard a pin drop, a flea scratch, and a bell tinkle.

CHAPTER 58

The paper cup Smokowski and Willy were investigating had a logo on it. A coffee bean with Coffee Coffee Café written around it. A great clue if "Coffee Coffee Café" weren't a massive global coffee shop chain with over one thousand shops dotted about the UK alone. Neither Smokowski nor Willy, not being coffee shop connoisseurs, knew this.

'Onwards and upwards,' said Smokowski, hoping Willy, for Tom and Cats sake, knew what he was doing. Willy's idea about the paper cup was encouraging, though.

'Sideways and backwards,' said Willy, putting his own slant on the saying. He slid the key into the ignition. The Cortina spluttered into life.

'To the Coffee Coffee Café,' said Smokowski.

'Ditto,' said Willy, the bit between his teeth.

'Off we go!' said Smokowski.

'Away we go,' said Willy, releasing the handbrake.

The car lurched forward and then stopped abruptly.

'Problem?' asked Smokowski.

'Just thought,' said Willy, 'You haven't told me where we're going.'

'The Coffee Coffee Café,' said Smokowski.

'I know that,' said Willy, 'but where is it?'

'I don't know,' said Smokowski, 'I thought you knew.'

'You're the local,' said Willy.

'It might not be local,' said Smokowski, revealing a problem.

'Drat,' said Wally, 'I never thought of that.

'Or in this time.' Smokowski felt a sudden weight on his shoulders. They hadn't thought this through, had they?

'Double drat,' said Willy.

'What now?'

'You got a computer?'

'Yes,' said Smokowski.

'Then we better have a look on it to see where this café is,' said Willy, turning the ignition off.

'And if it's in the past?'

'We'll cross that timeline when we get to it,' said Willy, sounding confident.

'They unclipped their seatbelts, got out of the car and set off back to Smokowski's shop.

Invisible Bob, had wandered into the shop and was at that moment staring longingly at the chocolate peanuts in the pick-and-mix, started as the door to the shop opened. Blimey, he thought, who's that? He then heard Smokowski's voice. What are they doing back? Time to go. He took his Hitchhiker from its hiding place. The Hitchhiker was a mini transporter that, like Tom's time machine, could move you sideways in the present time, but unlike Tom's time machine, you had to programme it. It was already linked to the Travellers headquarters. The other thing about the Hitchhiker, which was handy, was that it could also "hitchhike", hence its name, on the back of a time-machines temporal wake, an invisible disturbance that the time machine left as it travelled. Handy for tracking Willy's Cortina when he got back.

Invisible Bob pressed a button and was gone.

CHAPTER 59

Quietly slipping from the Loo, Tom and Cat went to check out their surroundings. boB's observations were right; they were in a tent. No one appeared to be home, which was a bit of luck.

'Seems no one's home,' whispered Tom.

But as they headed to the tent's flap.

'Who's there?' asked a voice of very high pitch from the shadows.

Grief, thought Tom, as his universal translator kicked in, spoke too soon.

'Quick,' whispered Cat, 'the flap.'

Double-time quick march saw Tom and Cat leave the tent and into the midst of the invading Norman army.

'Flipping 'eck!' said Tom, as he looked about him.

'Keep your voice down,' whispered Cat, 'and keep your bits inside the glamour.' She looked left and right, forward and back. 'Right, his way. Keep close.'

Tom started right, then quickly followed Cat left.

Cat leading, Tom following, they twisted, turned, backtracked, and dodged their way through the camp until they arrived at what seemed to be a small wooden castle. From the sound of it, it was full of horses. They crept into the shadows of the wooden palisade that surrounded it.

As Tom got his breath back, Cat weighed up the situation. There were Normans everywhere. There were tents everywhere. There were sharp swords and spears everywhere. Problems, everywhere. Tom had never seen so many swords and spears before. Every one of them, he suspected, had his name on it. Cat looked up into the sky. It was clear, and the sun was high. She worked out that it was not long after one o'clock in the afternoon: plenty of time to stop William from inventing the Williams multi-bladed razor. Not that he really would. Someone would plant it for him to find, complete with instructions. Cat and Tom's job: stop it from happening and apprehend the culprit behind it. What inventing a razor had to do with the missing Jam Cat had no idea. She was in the dark, and Cat didn't like being in the dark; it was dangerous.

'I don't like being in the dark,' said Cat, thinking aloud.

Tom looked skyward.

'I mean with this whole Jam mission.'

'Ah,' said Tom, who could empathise; he spent most of the time in the dark, whatever he was doing.

'But we do what we were sent here to do.'

'Fair do's,' said Tom, his breathing back to normal, but his heart rate was still at a canter with the thought of all that sharp stuff surrounding him. 'What's the plan?'

'High ground,' said Cat.

Tom didn't like the sound of that, clambering up hills. He had only just got his breath back.

But he needn't have fretted; Cat had her mind on something much closer to home. 'I'll climb to the top of that wooden castle,' she said, looking up.

'What about me?' exclaimed Tom, worried by the impending lack of a cloaking glamour.

'You can come with me if you like,' said Cat, smiling at his reaction. A horrified Tom had looked up with a look of sheer not on your Nelly on his face! 'Or, you can stay here in the shadows and wait until I get back.'

It was a unanimous vote, hiding it was.

'Over there,' said Cat, gesturing towards a dip at the foot of the palisade, 'should be safe enough there.'

Tom looked. 'It looks muddy.'

'Up or in.'

Grumbling under his breath and with a face like a wet weekend, Tom started for his hidey-hole. As he did, Cat climbed the fence.

'Remember,' Cat whispered down to him when she had reached the top of the fence, 'keep quiet.'

The dip wasn't deep, but it was shadowy. It wasn't too muddy either, a few bits here and there, but nothing Tom couldn't dodge. Settled, he looked up just in time to see Cats tail disappear from sight. Biscuit time, he thought. Tom took one from his pocket and appraised it. Not bad, some chocolate still on it. He took a bite. He took a second bite. Crunchy. He went to take a third bite, but a sharp pain in his ribs stopped him. At first, he thought he had a touch of indigestion. He then noticed what appeared to be a broom handle pressed against him.

'Who goes there?' demanded a voice from somewhere above Tom.

Tom never had the chance to answer, have a second thought, or time to hide his biscuit as he was hauled out of the dip by two burly soldiers.

'Who are you?' demanded the first soldier who hadn't been the first soldier to speak.

Good question, thought Tom, as he dangled inches from the ground. His international translator had kicked in.

'He dresses strangely,' said the second soldier who had been the first soldier to speak when he had demanded, "who goes there?".

'He is perhaps a fool,' suggested the first soldier.

'Ere, thought Tom, that's a bit harsh, having just met and all.

'He looks like one,' agreed the second soldier.

Now hang about, thought Tom, you can't judge a book by its cover, you know.

'A rather silent fool,' observed the first soldier.

Tom knew when to keep his mouth shut.

'Perhaps we should loosen his tongue,' said the second soldier, reaching for the sword by his side.

That was it. No one was going to meddle with Tom T Tyme's tongue. Tom drew himself up, which was impressive since he was hanging by the shoulders. He would give them a piece of his mind. And he foolishly might have done so if the second soldier hadn't just rested the tip of his sword against Tom's Adam's apple. Complain! Tom couldn't even gulp.

'No,' said the first soldier who appeared to be in charge, 'we take him to the Duke.'

The second soldier smiled as he removed his sword from Tom's throat. 'Good idea, sarge, the Duke will make him talk.'

Tom didn't like the sound of that.

Up above, atop the wooden castle, Cat had seen enough. Or rather, not enough. She had hoped to spot something grand amongst the tents that might help to pinpoint William's whereabouts. A few tents were grander than the majority, but none of them shouted, William the Conqueror lives here. Still, she thought, they had to start somewhere. Memorising where the grander tents were, Cat started down.

At about halfway, Cat heard voices below her. She stopped and looked down to see Tom being manhandled away from his hiding place. Great, she thought, as if she didn't have enough problems. She then had another thought, where is it soldiers might take their captives? To their leader. Suddenly, for Cat, not Tom, things were looking up. She scampered down as fast as she could. It was a break, but she also needed to be close at hand, just in case she was wrong and the soldiers had something else in mind for Tom.

CHAPTER 60

Mary left Lucy's house with a less heavy heart. Lucy and the kids were safe. Their duplicates were better than she ever could have hoped. Things were going well. She almost felt that she could afford to relax a little. But that thought soon changed when she arrived at her destination. No one was there to meet her as planned. Problems?

She summoned her friend, who assured her she would do her best to discover what had happened but wouldn't promise anything as she didn't want to dig too deep and arouse suspicions.

So Mary couldn't relax. All she could do was wait. Wait and worry? No, she decided, waiting was enough for now.

CHAPTER 61

When Invisible Bob arrived in the Travellers Headquarters, the place was in a general but discreet furore.

Someone had kidnapped Darren. Why or how nobody knew. A search was underway of the building in case he was somewhere on the premises. But as the kidnapping of Darren was on a need to know only basis, as with Tom and Cats situation, the search was being carried out in a discreet, casual, looking for something, but not too bothered if they didn't find it, way, by the few in the know.

Deirdre, who had taken tea and crumpets to Darren to cheer him up, discovered Darren was no longer on the premises. She now stood in the Chief's office in front of an animated Chief.

'But someone must have seen something,' cried the Chief, waving his arms.

'Who, Sir? Only a few of us knew he was there,' Deirdre reasoned, 'and of those few, only you, Cedric, and myself have security clearance to be on the guest room's floor.'

'You're saying that one of us is the culprit?' said the Chief, his eyes bulging.

'No,' Deirdre sighed, 'what I'm saying is that there was no one there who could have seen what happened.'

'Problems?' asked Invisible Bob, who had arrived unannounced in the Chief's office. The door had been open, and as he had heard the Chief's voice, he went in.

'Who said that?' said a startled Chief.

'Invisible Bob,' said Invisible Bob.

'What are you doing here?' demanded the Chief, his blood pressure getting higher by the minute.

That's nice, thought Invisible Bob, who was only doing his job. 'You told me to report in if there were any developments.'

'Ah, yes,' said the Chief, calming down a little, 'but now is not a good time.'

'Darren's missing,' Deirdre announced, earning a glare from the Chief. 'Kidnapped, we think.'

'That's quite enough, Deirdre, need to know,' warned the Chief, 'need to know.'

'Sorry, sir,' said Deirdre, who had assumed Invisible Bob would be on that list.

'Now, please return to your office and take Invisible Bob with you.' The Chief turned his back on them and sat at his desk. 'Now.'

Deirdre scurried from the Chief's office and into her own. She closed the door after her, then hesitated. 'Bob, you in here?'

'Here,' said Invisible Bob. 'Blimey, what was all that about?'

'It's the kidnapping,' said Deirdre, 'he blames himself, I think.'

Invisible Bob climbed up onto a chair. 'Not like Cat to let something like that happen,' he mused.

'He wasn't with Cat; he was here in one of the guest rooms.'

Invisible Bob gave a low whistle of astonishment, 'you've got guest rooms here?'

'Yes,' said Deirdre, frowning at nothing on the chair, 'but that's neither here nor there.'

'Anyone see anything?'

'No,' said Deirdre.

'A ransom note?'

'Cedric said he didn't find one.'

Strange, thought Invisible Bob. 'Why wasn't he with Tom and Cat?'

'The Chief's decision. He thought Darren might get in the way. Thought it better for all concerned if he stayed.'

Invisible Bob had met Darren; he didn't think he was that bad. 'Not for Darren.'

'No,' Deirdre agreed. 'Now, I believe you have something to report?'

Invisible Bob told her about Smokowski, Willy, and the paper cup.

CHAPTER 62

With the computer taking a little time to warm up, Smokowski went to put the kettle on.

He made two cups of coffee, put some biscuits from the shop on a plate and took them to the stockroom. The computer still starting up, he decided a change out of his work clothes would be in order. A quick shower first, he thought. When all done, he returned to the stockroom where he sat and read a couple of pages of Grocers Monthly while sipping at his now tepid cuppa. Brew finished; he went and made another couple of cuppas and returned just in time to see the computer spring to life. He nudged Willy awake, who had nodded off waiting for the computer to start, and offered him the fresh brew.

'Wah!' yelled Willy, rocking on his chair, 'we there yet?'

'Drink your coffee,' said Smokowski, handing it to him.

'Ah, ta,' said Willy. He blew on the coffee and took a sip, and looked at a now fully illuminated computer screen. 'What do we know so far?' he asked.

'I need a new computer,' said Smokowski, positioning himself in front of it.

'Eh?'

'Nothing yet.'

The internet connection was pretty quick, not your slower than the snail speed you got in the countryside. Smokowski had had it installed when he got a new landline provider offering a discount.

Within seconds Smokowski had more information regarding "Coffee Coffee Café" than he could cope with.

'Blimey,' said Smokowski, looking at it all, 'where do we start?'

Willy, who felt he knew a thing or two about computers, suggested they ask it where they might find the café they were looking for. He leaned in closer to the computer and spoke to it, asking his question. There was no reply.

'What are you doing?' asked a bemused Smokowski.

'Talking to the computer,' Willy retorted indignantly, 'what does it look like?'

That is exactly what Smokowski thought Willy was doing. 'Why?' he asked.

'That's what you're supposed to do,' Willy explained. 'You ask someone in there called stirrer, or something like that, I think there are a few different ones, a question, and they tell you the answer. They can even turn the lights out for you.'

Smokowski glanced at the screen. 'I don't think my computers got a stirrer,' he said. He knew he had to turn his lights off himself.

'Oh,' said Willy.

'I'll type the question in,' said Smokowski, typing in a request asking for the location of the Coffee Coffee Café. 'Good grief,' he exclaimed when the computer supplied him with an answer.

'What is it?' asked Willy.

'There's over a thousand of them.'

'All local?'

'Countrywide.'

'We only need local.'

'I thought we'd decided the kidnappers might not be local.'

'Drat,' said Willy, 'so we did.' He suddenly adopted a pensive look. 'Then we visit all of them.'

'All of them?' said Smokowski, dismayed by the thought.

'All of them,' said Willy, resolute in his decision.

CHAPTER 63

In the Loo, boB lay stretched out on Cats shelf, finishing the biscuit Tom had given him. He had taken his time. Chocolate digestives were his favourite, along with a long list of other chocolate biscuits, but at the moment, chocolate digestive was top of that list.

Shame about the lack of chocolate, he thought, but thankfully there had enough left on the biscuit to heap into a small pile with his teeth. The last piece would be as a chocolate digestive should be. He savoured the thought. He was ready for it. He closed his eyes, opened his mouth and…

There was a sudden bang on the wall of the Loo followed by a yell of pain. 'Ow!' yelled a voice in distress. There followed quite a few naughty words that boB couldn't understand as they were spoken in what he took to be French. He couldn't speak French. Except for the French word for chocolate: Chocolat. He also knew the Russian word for it: Shokolad. And Welsh: siocled. And more. All Bobs were fluent in the language of chocolate.

The last piece poised again, boB waited. He didn't want further bumps or shouts to spoil the moment. He waited. He waited some more. Nothing. He waited just a little longer. Still nothing. All seemed quiet. The moment had come. boB opened his mouth, closed his eyes and placed the last piece of biscuit in his mouth. Blessed was the chocolate. It was a moment to savour. The next moment wasn't. A shout followed by a crunching blow on the Loo knocked him headfirst from the shelf.

The floor reached, boB bounced and then rolled up against the toilet. boB, being fairly hardy as all Bobs were, quickly got to his feet and brushed himself down. He now heard more voices. As a precaution, he banged on the side of his head. Nope, he could still hear them. And from the sound of it, there were four of them. Four people, all ranting, all raving, all banging on the side of the Loo. This, he thought, couldn't be good.

CHAPTER 64

Flip, thought Tom, wincing as he was lifted off his feet for the umpteenth time, my arms will be black and blue at this rate. The Norman soldiers were none too gentle as they bustled Tom through the camp.

'Ow,' squealed Tom as his arm was pinched.

'Ah,' said the second soldier, 'he makes a sound. Does that hurt fool?'

'What do you think?' said Tom. Drat, he thought, did I say that out loud? 'Oops.' He tried to put a hand over his mouth before he could say anything else, but as his arms were firmly grasped, he couldn't.

The soldiers came to an abrupt halt, causing Tom to jerk backwards from the step he attempted to make.

'You speak our language,' said the first soldier, a sergeant. He gave Tom a menacing stare. He did not look pleased by what he had just heard.

'He *is* a spy,' said the second soldier, excitedly. He was thinking reward.

Tom was speechless. No, he wasn't. 'I'm not,' he said before he could stop himself.

Sarge let go of Tom's arm and grabbed him by the lapels. 'A Saxon fool that speaks our tongue.' He eyeballed Tom, 'Caught creeping about our camp.' He pulled Tom closer until they were almost nose to nose. 'That's a spy in my book.'

'But I…' But it was no good; he didn't have a leg to stand on, literally, since the soldiers had discovered him. They wouldn't believe him. The translator had seen to that. There was now only one way out of the mess he was in; Cat. She would save the day. She usually did. But what if she didn't know his predicament? What if she was still atop the castle? What if… But Tom couldn't take any more "what ifs". His knees suddenly bent as he sagged at the thoughts he was having. The only thing stopping him from sinking to the ground was the sergeant's grip on his lapels.

'Guilty as charged,' said the second soldier, looking on. 'See, he grows faint from it.'

Unbeknown to Tom, Cat, wasn't that far away. She was watching and listening, still and silent, in the shadows of a tent somewhere to Tom's left. She was not happy. She was quite angry. She didn't like what she was hearing or seeing. Tom might be an old fool at times, but he was her old fool.

The soldiers, with Tom sagging between them, started to move. Cat stayed close.

'What do you think a spy is worth?' wondered the second soldier aloud.

'The Duke will decide,' said sarge. 'If anything at all. It's our job.'

The second soldier wasn't listening. 'Silver?' he mused, his eyes almost glazing over at the idea. 'Or gold. It could be gold.'

'You dream,' said sarge.

Sagging but listening, Tom wondered if there was a way out of his predicament. He could try and bribe them to let him go. But what did he have of value that these ruffians might take? Not much. Unless they liked biscuits? Not a lot of chocolate on them but fine biscuits all the same. He doubted they would have tasted anything so good. A plan. What did he have to lose?

As it turned out, it was the biscuit he had offered and any chance of escaping his fate. Sarge had knocked it out of his hand. Tom ruefully stared at it on the floor. It was the one with the most chocolate on it. Woe was he.

'Can you believe that?' said the second soldier, 'trying to bribe us with a biscuit.'

Tom was now being dragged along.

Sarge glared at Tom. 'Spying and now attempted bribery. Serious crimes fool.'

'Biscuits,' laughed the second soldier. 'Unbelievable.'

'It was the best money can buy,' groaned Tom.

Sarge increased the speed of his step. He couldn't wait to see what the Duke made of the devious Saxon creature they had caught.

If Cat had had hands, she would have slapped her forehead. What was he thinking? Didn't he know how much do-do he was in? Still, she thought, on the bright side, one soldier had mentioned a duke. Had to be William. They were taking Tom to their leader. Well done, Tom.

Chapter 65

Report reported, Invisible Bob headed back to Smokowski's shop.

When he got there, the place was empty. Drat, he thought, slipstream it is. He removed the Hitchhiker from its place of safekeeping and was just about to press the button when a thought struck him; chocolate peanuts – the pack from Smokowski's trolley, was empty.

Invisible Bob was now in a dilemma. Did he refill the empty pack or do as he promised and leave the chocolate peanuts alone? He was a tad hungry. And he had meal vouchers provided by the BIMBOs but had never been able to use them. One, because he needed someone to use them for him, and two, because if there were someone available to help him, they wouldn't touch them with a bargepole because of the place he kept them. What was he to do?

'Ah-ha,' said Invisible Bob, slapping a fist into the palm of his hand, 'I'll leave one of the vouchers in the chocolate peanut container.' A eureka moment.

But no, he couldn't; he had made a promise. He looked at the Hitchhiker in his hand. Be brave, he thought, and then pressed the button.

He landed just below the pic-and-mix. Oops, he thought, must have had it on sideways. He began to climb.

CHAPTER 66

As Darren came too, he wondered why his head was aching? He went to move, but that made it worse. The wonder continued. Why was he lying down? He couldn't remember going to bed. And why was the mattress so hard? With some effort, he raised his head and attempted to peer through unhelpful eyelids. Now there was spinning. He decided he must have moved his head too quickly. Best to wait for a few moments before trying again. When he did, the spinning had thankfully stopped. He tried again.

This time he was able to pry his eyelids apart. It took a second or two to focus, and when he did, he realised why his bed was so hard.

'Not again,' groaned Darren as he took in his surroundings. He was in another dungeon. His "bed" was a flagstone floor, the walls made of stone, a light came in through a high window with bars on it, and the door was Oak with a small window and grill at about eye level, depending on how tall you were. Thankfully, this time Darren wasn't on tippy-toes, shackled in chains, a small silver lining.

Head slowly clearing, Darren slowly recalled the events of... When? He realised he didn't know how long he had been here. He recalled the rag over his face and the funny noises he had heard before the blackness had taken him. Had he been kidnapped? Surely not. He struggled to his knees. He waited another couple of seconds before getting to his feet. Now standing, Darren decided he was steady enough to get to the door and hopefully to the bottom of his quandary. Perhaps he might see someone on the other side of it, someone who might tell him what had happened and why he was there.

A couple of paces from the door, Darren stopped. A small door behind the grill in the door's window had opened. Something now poked through the grill.

'Well?' said someone. 'You going to take it or not? I ain't got all day.'

Now, even more, puzzled than he already was, Darren carefully sidled up to the door. He could now see what was poking through the grill. It was a remote control, the sort that turned on a television. He took it.

'Well done,' said the someone. 'Now take this. It's the manual.'

Darren took that, too.

'Enjoy your stay,' said the someone before chuckling into the distance.

'Wait!' yelled Darren, suddenly regaining his senses, 'I want to talk to you.' He pressed his face against the grill and tried again, but it was to no avail. Whoever had been out there had gone. He looked at the remote and its instructions in his hand. Not like the other dungeon then, he thought.

Darren took the instruction manual to the light from the window and read it. It only had two pages. Page one had a list of items and the number you had to press on the remote to receive them. Press A for television. B for chair. C for table and so on. The other page, facing the list of items, also had an instruction:

IF YOU HAVE ANY PROBLEM
UNDERSTANDING THE INSTRUCTIONS
PLEASE PLACE THE REMOTE CONTROL
ON THE FLOOR AND RETIRE A SAFE DISTANCE
Thank you

That's worrying, thought Darren as he read it, but as he didn't have any problems reading the instructions, he pressed button A. It wasn't as if he was going anywhere.

A second later, a section on the wall opened up, and a sixty-inch television appeared. Definitely not like the other dungeon.

He pressed B. This time part of the floor opened up, and a comfy chair and footstool rose into view. Darren couldn't help but forget his predicament for the moment as his eyes feasted on things of which he could only dream. F opened another panel in the wall, and a tray of nibbles appeared.

Predicament now in danger of becoming a distant memory, Darren headed for the chair and picked up another remote control holstered on the arm. There was satellite TV! He had become a child in a toy shop. If only Lucy and the kids could see this. Suddenly the shop closed. He felt guilty. He should try to escape. Find Lucy and the kids. But how? When trapped in a dungeon without any idea of why or where.

He decided the first chance he got; he would make his escape. He couldn't believe the way he was acting. Darren put the TV remote back in its holster and was about to walk back to the door and shout at it when he noticed a sheet of paper lying on the seat of the chair. He picked it up and read it. His eyes opened wide. He looked at his watch. The Sound of Music was showing in half an hour. He had never seen it. He had always wanted to; it was on his wooden pail list. Now he *was* in a dilemma.

He could always watch it when he escaped, he told himself. But he

137

didn't have satellite television. He could always buy the DVD. Settled then. He would try to escape now, this very minute. But what if that is what his kidnappers expected him to do? They could be waiting outside this very moment. Ready to spring a trap. What he should do is to play the game his way. Lull them into a false sense of security. Let them think he has accepted his lot. And then, wham! He would break out when they least expected it. It was decided. He would lull them by watching The Sound of Music, and when it was over, he would make his bid for freedom.

But no. What was he thinking? How shallow was he? He should attempt it now, trap or not. Darren looked at the door and weighed it up. It looked strong, but then he was stronger than people realised. They may have underestimated him. The door did look daunting, though. But no, he had to try. Darren retreated a few steps, psyched himself up, took a run at the door, and shoulder charged it.

Two feet from impact, the little door in the window opened again. The timing had to be perfect. A foot later, a small spray of vapour floated through the grill straight into Darren's face. He went down like a sack of spuds.

On the other side of the door money changed hands.

'Told you,' said someone.

'Good call,' said someone else.

'I'll get the chains then.'

'Better had.'

A skyward glance told Cat that time was getting on. She was worried the window to catch the culprit planting the razor would close if the soldiers didn't get a move on.

The soldiers, mostly soldier two, just soldier two, couldn't help but stop each time a fellow soldier stopped to ask what was going on? Silver was mentioned. Gold was mentioned. Heroism was mentioned. Even medals and promotion, which meant the going had become very slow; there were a lot of soldiers. The sarge tried to move things along, but the mention of silver and gold always held sway.

And so it continued; stop – chat – argue; move on.

A skyward glance told Tom nothing. He didn't even know why he was looking up. Divine intervention, perhaps? A hang-gliding Cat, coming to his rescue? Rain? Now, thought Tom, that might not be a bad idea. No one likes to stop and chat in the rain. But Tom wasn't thinking straight; any sane man would have been glad for the hold-ups. More time for a rescue attempt. A slight reprieve from what was waiting for him. Still, Tom had had enough of his arms being pinched – he doubted there would be any pink skin left showing on them soon – and being prodded and poked by all and sundry while paraded like a prize cow in a show. He decided to say something. He'd had enough.

'Was that a drop of rain I just felt,' said Tom, squinting skyward.

Sarge looked up. 'It's a near clear blue sky fool,' he said.

'Summer rain?'

'It's Autumn.'

'Wouldn't want to be out here in the rain,' said Tom, undaunted, 'could get squishy.'

The second soldier looked up. There was a single white cloud in the sky. A small fluffy one. He glared at Tom. 'You're a bigger fool than I thought,' he said, giving Tom's arm another squeeze. Thankfully for Tom, the spot the soldier pinched no longer had any feeling.

'Just saying,' said Tom.

'Well, don't,' snarled sarge, 'save it for the Duke.' Tom was only dragged a few feet before being stopped again by another group of curious soldiers.

Another idea suddenly popped into Tom's head. He was on a roll, sort of. He had been wondering why Cat hadn't tried to rescue him? She must have noticed he was missing by now. And with her magical powers, she would have had no trouble locating him. Unless, and here is where Tom would have surprised anyone doubting his ability to think beyond the next cuppa, Cat wanted him taken to wherever he was being taken. Wherever that was. Clever Cat. Might be fewer soldiers there. They might even find out where the du— Blimey, thought Tom, the soldiers are taking him to a duke? Could it be the Duke? The Duke of Normandy; William the conqueror? The one they were trying to find? Clever Cat. That was why she hadn't tried to rescue him; she was waiting to see where the Duke was. Tom would have clapped his hands with joy if his arms weren't numb and still being squeezed.

But the soldiers were taking their time, and he didn't know how much of that they had left. He needed them to get a move on, especially if he wanted to keep some pink skin on his arms. Another thought! He would have to have a rest when this was all over.

'I expect this duke you're on about will be wondering where I am,' said Tom, all casual-like.

The soldiers and Tom came to a sudden stop. Tom nearly lost his cap.

'What do you mean?' said sarge warily.

'Just been thinking, that's all,' said Tom. 'If I was this duke bloke you keep talking about, I might have expected the prisoner by now.'

'How so?' said the second soldier. 'He doesn't know about you yet.'

'Ignore him,' said sarge, 'he's talking nonsense.'

Sarge went to walk on, but Tom didn't move; the second soldier was holding fast.

'But he must have meant something by it,' said the second soldier. He took a dagger from his belt. 'I'll make him talk.'

'Whoa,' said Tom, 'I'll talk-I'll talk.'

'See,' said the second soldier, lowering his weapon. 'Told you he was hiding something from us.'

'Are you?' said sarge, squaring up to Tom. 'Speak.'

'Well,' said Tom, 'it's just that, I was thinking, with all those other soldiers you've stopped and spoken to, it's taken a while.'

'Go on.'

'Won't someone have got a message to this duke bloke by now about a prisoner being brought in? Could be looking at his watch this very moment.'

'Watch?'

'Sundial,' said Tom quickly.

'You're right, sarge,' said the second soldier, 'he is a fool.'

But sarge glared at the second soldier. There was something in what the old fool was saying. Why he wanted to meet his fate quicker, he didn't know but… 'He's right,' said Sarge. 'We've dallied too long. The Duke won't be happy if he knows about the prisoner and was expecting him earlier.' He continued glaring at the second soldier. 'And if he is angry, it won't be me taking the blame.' He pulled Tom free from the second soldier and marched double time.

Taken by surprise, Cat also quickened her step. Whatever Tom had just said to the soldiers appeared to have shaken them. The one she thought in charge was now pulling Tom along at a fair old lick while the second one tagged on behind.

It was the turn of Tom's feet and knees to feel the brunt of his captivity as he almost trotted beside the sarge now; his knees were already complaining. He hadn't moved this fast since he saw that five squid note blowing along the street. At least he was getting some feeling back in his left arm, not that it was all that pleasant. He hoped it wouldn't take long now. And just like that, they were there.

'Ere, thought Tom, I'm sure I've been here before.

Well, thought Cat as Tom came to a stop, I'll be, it's the tent we landed in.

Sarge pushed Tom through the tent flaps. Inside, red-faced angry men wielding sticks turned to stare at them.

'What is it,' said a round-faced chap with a moustache and beady eyes, 'can't you see I'm busy?'

'It's the spy, sir,' said sarge. 'Feisty one, lord. Struggled all the way here.' He added, covering himself just in case it was needed.

'He did, lord,' said the second soldier, earning a glare from sarge.

'A spy, you say,' said William the Duke of Normandy, for that was who the round-faced, beady-eyed, moustachioed man was. 'Looks like a fool to me.' He had noted Tom's attire.

Not you too, thought Tom.

'He speaks our language, Lord.'

'Does he.' The Duke stepped towards Tom.

As he approached, Tom noticed a large bruise on the Duke's forehead. A new one by the colour of it.

'Who are you?' asked William, beady eyes noticing smudges of chocolate on Tom's pocket. Not knowing what it was, he turned up his nose in disgust.

'Tom,' said Tom.

'Are you a spy?'

Well, there was a loaded question if ever he'd heard one, thought Tom. He went with the truth. 'No, sir. I mean Lord, I am a fool.'

Not going to go there, thought a smiling Cat, as she crawled through the tent flap.

She disappeared into the shadows and hid behind a large chest. She had to think. A commotion to take their attention from Tom would be no problem. Getting Tom back into the Loo might be. She also had the planting of the razor to deal with. It wasn't four o'clock yet, so there was time. Perhaps she could use whoever plants it to her advantage?

'Yet you speak our language?' said William. 'Explain that to me.'

Yeah, thought Tom, explain that; a hat that can translate.

Good luck with that, thought Cat, as she moved closer to the Loo. If she could position herself close enough to it, she might be able to get boB's attention. What he might do to help, though, she knew not. Pity Darren wasn't here. There, she thought, she'd thought it. Cat made her way past another large chest without as much as one curious thought regarding what might be in them. As a cat, one couldn't be too careful when it came to curious. Coming to the end of it, she stopped. Blast, she thought, as she noticed the other three occupants of the tent. For a fleeting moment, she thought they were there to plant the razor, but then noticed the sticks. The same as the Duke was carrying. Pretend sword fighting? she wondered. Boys and their toys, she thought.

'Well?' demanded William, 'I'm waiting, fool.'

'He was like that when we caught him, Lord,' said soldier two, subtly reminding the Duke who it was that had caught the spy. He could almost taste the gold; or silver. Gold was better, but he would receive whatever was on offer with grace.

But the Duke had other ideas. 'You can go now,' said William. The two soldiers looked at each other. 'Well? Off-off.' The Duke shooed them away with his hand.

'But…' said soldier two, who didn't get to finish his protest as sarge pulled him swiftly away before he could say something he would regret. The Duke glared at him until he left.

Once outside the tent, the second soldier, who felt aggrieved by his lack of reward, immediately walked off to see if he could find the biscuit the fool had dropped. Small compensation, but it had looked rather delicious. He'd have it with a cuppa.

The sarge, scratching at the stubble on his chin, watched the second soldier go. As he did, a thought troubled him. If he didn't know better, he would swear his companion and the fool were related. He shook his head. Nah, he thought. Still, the same nose, the same ears. Even the same gait. But he had known Thonmas la Temps all his life. Nah, a crazy thought. He walked off, never to think of it again.

Luckily for Tom, the interruption by the soldier had given him time to think of something in answer to the Duke's question.

The Duke turned a questioning face to Tom.

'Holidays, Lord,' said Tom.

'Holy days?' asked William, who had all but ruled Tom out of being a spy. A fool, yes, but a spy? He did not think Tom clever enough.

'Yes, Lord, 'said Tom, 'every October.'

The Duke stared at Tom; he said amusing things. Maybe this is just what he needed after a hard day at work. 'Do something funny,' said William. 'Fools make people laugh. Make me laugh.'

I just hope he doesn't try to tell a joke, thought Cat, still crouching behind the chest. But at least if Tom kept the Duke occupied, it would make her job a little easier. But he did better than that. The Duke, calling the other three men to come over to him, inadvertently cleared a path for her to the Loo. Now she could get to it hopefully unseen. But what about the razor? No, she would have to stay put. They might be there at any moment. She couldn't jeopardize the mission. Tom was on his own for now.

'Well?' said William. He wanted a good giggle, but it was also a test. If the fool made him laugh, then the accusation of being a spy would be cast from him. But if he didn't, well, he had ways of finding out the truth. No one would be laughing then.

What jokes do I know? thought Tom, no, maybe not. What did fools do? He thought of ye old court jester. He could fall over; that would make everyone laugh. But they'd soon stop if he couldn't get back up again. What he needed was some of Cat's magic to make him disappear. Where was she? Wait, he thought, disappear, that's it; magic. But he had better not call it that, just in case he ended up tied to a stake. He felt warm enough as it was under the Duke's stare.

'I can do a trick,' said Tom.

'Magic?' frowned William. The other three men followed suit.

'What? Oh-noo,' said Tom, wondering where that had come from and suddenly thinking stakes again. 'No, not magic, no-no. Awful stuff. Shouldn't be allowed. More like what a jester might do.' But what he had in mind would look awfully like magic. Perhaps it was.

143

Either way, he would have to be quick about it.

'Then show me this trick then,' said William, 'and it had better bring a smile to my face.'

It'll bring something, thought Tom. 'Right, I need some space.' He spread his arms apart.

'Give him space,' said William.

'There, behind you will do,' said Tom.

Clever boy, thought Cat, who had been wondering where all this was leading. She now had an idea.

The Duke moved aside and ushered the men beside him to do likewise. They looked at the Duke with a flicker of mischief in their eyes. The Duke smiled. Something funny was about to happen. The four of them waited for Tom to bang his head against the invisible nothingness they had spent the best part of half an hour banging sticks against.

To their dismay, Tom stopped just short of the nothingness. This produced a few disappointed "Oh's" from the watching men. He was now ready. It was now or never. 'I wonder if you might all close your eyes?' He had adopted an on-stage presence.

The Duke narrowed suspicious eyes.

'Just for a moment or two,' said Tom.

'Why?'

'If you see how I do it, it won't be a trick,' said Tom.

The Duke looked Tom up and down. He didn't trust him, but what was the fool going to do? The man had no weapon. Looked about as strong as a kitten. And looked older than anyone he knew. 'Very well,' said William.

The other three men huddled around the Duke. Should there be an unseen plot to harm the Duke, the fool would have to go through them.

'Close your eyes,' said Tom.

The Duke and his men closed their eyes.

'No peeping now.'

'Get on with it.'

'Now count backwards from five and then open your eyes.'

'Five,' said the Duke, who would do the counting. 'Four.'

By the time the Duke had got to three, Tom had opened the Loo door.

Two, saw Tom give a slight bow.

Get inside, you idiot, thought Cat.

'One,' said William. He opened his eyes.

144

The first Coffee Coffee Café Smokowski visited was the closest on the list, and as it wasn't far away, they drove to it.

Paper cup in hand, Smokowski entered the shop, went up to the counter and asked them if they knew who had bought a cuppa in this cup?

This was met with puzzled looks, followed by sympathetic noises and a no. Smokowski was sure he could hear muted sniggering from behind him as he left.

'No?' said Willy, genuinely surprised by the lack of a result.

'It was embarrassing,' said Smokowski, 'they asked me if there was someone they could call.'

'Was there?'

'Of course not,' fumed Smokowski, 'they were of the opinion that I was a few pence short of a shilling.'

'Oh,' said Willy.

'What now?'

'The next shop?' said Willy, brightly.

Smokowski turned on Willy. 'And you suppose we'll get a different reaction?' He was beginning to see the futility of their task. Perhaps he always had.

'I'll go in next time,' said Willy.

Closing his eyes, Smokowski knew Willy would not give up on this hare-brained idea. He sighed. 'Why not?' He felt deflated and feared he would never see Tom or Cat again.

'Righty-ho then,' said Willy, all enthusiastic like. 'Which one's next on the list?'

It had been hard. Really, really, hard. But Invisible Bob had resisted the temptation. The chocolate peanuts were safe. He now sat on the top of the pic-and-mix pondering his decision.

He supposed it made him a better person. He had kept a promise. Why did he feel so glum then? Surely he should feel elated? He shook his head, troubled by his feelings, and climbed down.

By the time Invisible Bob reached the floor, he had come to a conclusion. Eating made him happy, especially chocolate. Not eating, whilst making him hungry, also made him unhappy, especially if he wasn't eating chocolate. How he felt was nothing to do with keeping a promise then; the glum feeling was to do with him being hungry.

Happier now he had cleared that up, he headed for Smokowski's crisps. Okay, not chocolate, but he was hungry, right?

There were eight cardboard boxes of crisps; two rows of four. The front of each box open. Invisible Bob smiled to himself. He had not promised not to snaffle crisps. Suddenly he felt like his old self again and wondered if Smokowski had OXO flavour in stock?

Two packets of crisps later, one beef flavour – the closest he could find to OXO – and one cheese and onion, Invisible Bob felt he could face the world again. He removed his Hitchhiker and pressed a button. A few seconds later, he was sitting in the back of Willy's car.

CHAPTER 70

Three other pairs of eyes opened a moment after the Dukes. Eyes suddenly filled with bewilderment and wonder. A few moments later, the bewilderment and wonder turned to suspicion. The Duke called Tom's name. He called for the fool to show himself. Now four angry voices were all shouting at once. Sticks were raised. Magic and witchcraft were suspected. And they had all experienced the unexplained already. They headed for the nothingness that the Duke had banged his head on. They had put two and two together and had managed to make four. Four raised sticks swung in unison. Four sticks hit nothing with a resounding bang.

That's what the sticks are for, thought Cat. It also explained the bump on the Duke's head. He must have walked into the Loo as boB had. boB, she had never thought until he banged his head on the Loo that the Loo was solid. How had that happened? She couldn't recall it being solid before in its invisible state. Or had it? Thinking about it, she had always taken it for granted that if it was invisible, it was also without substance. It might be worth looking into, in case something was awry. But that was for later; for now, she had the razor to think of. It had to be nearly four o'clock by now.

Inside the Loo, Tom was getting his breath back; it had been a close one.

'Can we go yet?' asked boB, who was eager to be on his merry way, somewhere less dangerous.

Tom looked down. The flusher appeared to be talking to him. 'You holding on to the flusher?'

'Yeah,' said boB, who had clung to it amidst the battering the Loo had been getting earlier.

'Why?'

'Der,' said boB, 'the banging and bumping.'

'What is that?' Tom had noticed it had started a short while after he had got into the loo.

'I don't know,' said boB, clinging tightly. 'It started while you and Cat were out. I think after someone walked into it.' He could empathise. 'And now it's started up again.'

Ah-ha, thought Tom, recalling the Duke's forehead bruise and the sticks. It suddenly fell into place. 'I think they're pretending to sword-fight,' They must have stopped when he arrived and started again after he had disappeared. 'Could be where the Duke got his bruise. Beauty it is, there's a lump too, right in the middle of his forehead.'

boB stared up at Tom. He'd heard rumours about the old boy. 'And that's why they're knocking ten types of chocolate out of your time machine?'

That was strange, thought Tom, how they won the battle of Hastings with such errant swordplay he would never know. 'No discipline, I suspect,' he said.

A frowning boB thought about asking Tom what he was going on about, but decided he didn't want to know. He asked what Cat was doing instead.

'She's…' To his sudden dismay, Tom realised he didn't know. Grief, he thought, what if she doesn't know he's back in the Loo? She could be in danger. Might need help. What did he do? He couldn't go back outside; he would be battered senseless by pretend swords. Thankfully, an idea popped into his head. boB would not like it.

'She's?' said boB.

'I don't know,' Tom admitted.

'You don't know?'

'I haven't seen her since they took me captive.'

'They? Captive?'

'She could be in trouble.'

'Trouble?' To boB's horror, he realised he was beginning to sound like Tom. He fell off the flusher.

'But I have an idea,' said Tom. 'You could look for her, see where she is. See if she needs help.'

'Why me?' said boB, self-preservation kicking in.

'You're invisible.'

'I could get whacked or stepped on.' The whacking of the Loo was still going on.

'Look at it this way,' said Tom, 'the sooner we find out about the razor, the sooner we can go.'

'You go then.'

'I would if I could, but they'll see me,' said Tom, now wondering if Darren would have been the better option. At least Darren wasn't selfish. He would have also been in his element outside. 'And I've got the feeling the Duke would do horrible things to me if he caught me.'

'You shouldn't have upset him.'

Enough was enough, and Tom had had enough. It was time to play the trump card he had only just thought of. 'You're a BIMBO, aren't you?'

A screwed up invisible face with daggers coming from it looked at Tom. No fair, thought boB. But Tom was right. It was boB's duty as a BIMBO to help.

'Okay,' said boB reluctantly, 'but if I get trampled on, it's your fault.'

I could live with that, thought Tom. And because he had thought that and because he felt guilty about thinking it, Tom thought of a way boB wouldn't get trampled on. boB would not like it.

'What!' exclaimed boB, as Tom revealed his idea, 'I'll break something.'

But Tom knew how hardy and resilient Bobs were. 'Only what you land on.'

It was true, Invisible Bobs, however they spelt their name, were tough little so-and-so's. 'Okay,' said boB, 'let's do it.' And he meant it. Suddenly it was an adventure, and Bob's loved adventure. They might complain about it, but it was in their blood. He climbed onto Tom's outstretched hand, ignored the grimacing on Tom's face, and readied himself.

'I have chocolate biscuits with your name on them at home,' said Tom, attempting to sweeten the deal.

It did to a certain extent, but boB wondered if he would ever see them.

'Ready?'

'Not really,' said boB, 'but let's do this.' He was as ready as he would ever be.

'And a bowl of tea so you can get right in there.'

'All right already,' snapped boB, 'I said yes, just do it.' Nerves were fraying.

Opening the door slightly, Tom let fly, launching boB into space. The space above the ranting men with sticks. Tom then quickly closed the door.

Outside the Loo, the whacking of nothing abruptly stopped as high above the men, something invisible screamed.

'Geronimooooo!!' yelled boB for all he was worth.

Is that boB? thought Cat, looking up. A second later, something invisible landed with a thump against the tent's canvas wall.

'What was that?' cried William in a high, squeaky voice.

Bizarre, thought Cat, sounds like he's breathed helium.

'A voice from above,' wailed one man, dropping his stick. He fell to his knees.

'A demon,' wailed another, covering his eyes. 'We have disturbed his nest.'

'What was what?' enquired the third man, who was a little deaf but could hear quite clearly the Dukes highly high voice.

As the Duke and his men did what they were doing, Cat crept to where she thought boB had landed. 'boB?' she whispered.

'Here,' answered a voice that smacked of discomfort.

'You okay?'

'Will be,' said boB. 'Hang about. Ooh, there, that's better.' His Hitchhiker had twisted sideways as he landed. Not an easy thing to put right, considering the space it occupied.

'What happened?' said Cat, one eye still on the lookout for the planting of the razor.

'I've come to help,' said boB, 'Tom's idea,' he admitted, giving Tom the credit, whilst also absolving him of any blame should things go wrong.

'Right then,' said Cat, 'follow me.'

boB followed Cat back to the chest she had been hiding behind.

'Right,' said Cat, 'I want you up there.'

'Where?'

'On the ceiling.'

'Really?' said boB.

'You've come to help me, yes?'

'Yes,' sighed boB.

'Then up you go.'

'What am I supposed to do when I get there?' said boB, thinking it might be important to know.

'Keep your eye open from above. You'll have more chance to see the razor drop than me down here.'

Using magic, Cat raised boB to the ceiling.

In the Loo, Tom was wondering what was going on outside. The whacking had stopped, which was good, he hoped, but he was a tad concerned about the wailing. Should he do something? No, if they needed him, someone would call. He would wait. Tom sat on the toilet and took out a biscuit. To his surprise, it had much more chocolate on it than the ones he had given to boB. He smiled and took a bite. Pity there wasn't a cuppa to go with it.

In the tent, two sets of eyes looked up with trepidation. One pair remained covered. The other looked from one person to the other, wondering what the heck was going on? All was quiet, excluding the occasional sob that came from the man covering his eyes. The Duke's voice broke it. Like Tom, he had had enough. Enough of whacking nothing, seeing nothing and now hearing nothing. He decided everyone was tired. All that they thought they heard or saw or didn't see was likely caused by a nervy imagination. Tightly strung emotions were holding sway. And if those things had happened, for he knew the bump on his forehead was real, he decided why worry? They were way beyond his understanding, anyway. He shouldn't waste time on something he couldn't understand. He had a battle to plan. He wanted to lie down. He would send soldiers to find the fool later. He doubted he would get far in daylight. He also suspected the fool had slipped out of the tent through the flap. A fool had fooled them.

'Right,' said William, 'everyone out.'

'Pardon?' said the slightly deaf man.

'Out!' squealed William.

'Ah,' said the slightly deaf man. He headed for the flap.

The other two men were already there. One, the one who had heard a voice from above, was smilingly serenely as he led the other man, the one with his hands over his eyes, out. He wasn't smiling, just gibbering a little.

With all the men now gone, the Duke stretched and yawned. He headed for his cot. He would forget today. He was determined too. Cat would guarantee that he and the others did.

The tent was quiet again. In fact, so quiet you could hear a pin drop. A bell tinkle. A flea scratch.

'Ow,' said William, as he laid his head on his pillow. He had put his head on something. How did that get there? he thought, as he picked it up. What is it? He wondered. There was also a scrap of paper with it. He picked that up. It was titled "Instructions". Perhaps one of his men had left it. But he would find out later. He needed rest now. He put the razor and instructions aside, checked his pillow just in case there was anything else, and, as all was clear, laid his weary head back down. He was soon fast asleep.

Coast clear, Cat went about her business, taking the razor and instructions and making sure the Duke would remember none of the recent events. She then headed for the Loo.

'Oi!' yelled boB.

Oops, thought Cat. She lowered boB from the ceiling. boB safely down, she knocked on the Loo. 'Tom, it's me.'

Tom carefully opened the door, half a biscuit hidden behind his back. 'What happened?

After dropping the razor and its instructions on the Loo's floor, she went back into the tent and headed for the flap.

'Where're you going?' said Tom, picking the razor up.

151

'Loose ends,' she said over her shoulder.

Ten minutes later, three men were wondering why they had sticks in their hands, and two Norman soldiers were growing increasingly perplexed by a continuous flow of questions asking them what had happened to some spy.

Back at the Loo, Tom had finished his biscuit and was now inspecting the razor. Impressive, he thought, turning it in his hand. 'Wait a minute,' he exclaimed, 'where's me flipping bandage?'

In the tent, boB was scouting for incriminating evidence that might throw some light on who had left the razor.

When Cat arrived back, boB was calling for Tom to open the loo door. They went in together.

'And you saw nothing?' said Cat.

'Nothing,' boB confirmed. He found no incriminating evidence either.

'Then how did they put it there?'

boB shrugged his shoulders to no effect.

'Perhaps it was on the pillow all the time,' Tom suggested.

'It wasn't there while I was on the ceiling,' said boB.

'Then how?' said a mystified Cat. 'I saw nothing.'

'Nor me,' said boB.

'Nor me either,' said Tom.

'You were in the Loo,' said Cat.

'Not all the time,' said Tom.

'Funny thing though,' said boB, 'I thought I heard something.'

'What?' said Tom.

'Nah, doesn't matter,' said boB. It sounded silly now he thought about it.

'It might do,' said Cat, eager to hear.

'All right, but don't laugh.' said boB. 'I thought I heard a pin drop.' He waited for the inevitable laugh, but it didn't receive a single titter.

'I thought I heard a flea scratching,' said Cat. 'Just before William went to his bed.'

'Yes,' said boB, 'just before he went to bed.'

Tom wondered if he should say anything. After all, he was in the Loo when the razor appeared. Drat, he thought, I better had. 'I heard something strange too,' he confided.

'Go on,' said Cat, sensing some hesitation.

'You'll laugh.'

'We didn't at boB,' said Cat. 'Or me.'

Fair do, thought Tom. 'It was when everything went quiet. I got a bit worried, so I put my ear to the wall to see if I could find a clue as to what was going on, and that's when I heard it.'

'Heard what?' said boB.

'A bell tinkling.'

'You sure it wasn't just ringing in your ear?' said Cat.

'How hard did you have your ear pressed against then wall?' said boB.

'Could have been the wall still reverberating after all that whacking and banging,' said Cat.

'That's what I was thinking,' said boB.

Great, thought Tom, they hear something strange, and it's okay, but when I hear something it's "poor old Tom, never mind". He decided to go on the offensive. 'And how do you know it wasn't one of your own fleas?' he said, knowing Cat was scrupulous when it came to personal hygiene. 'And you, wherever you are, you bumped your head if I remember right. Perhaps what you heard was something in your head falling back into place.'

The Loo fell quiet, two of its occupants feeling put in their place.

'Sorry,' said Cat.

'Yeah,' said boB, 'me too.'

'Well,' said Tom.

A contrite Cat decided it was perhaps time to leave the Normans and move on. 'Perhaps we should move on,' she said, 'we've got another twenty-odd more ripples to investigate.'

boB stayed quiet. He had said enough already, especially if he wanted to see another chocolate biscuit.

Tom cocked his head and grasped the flusher. 'Travellers HQ?' he said.

'Please,' said Cat.

CHAPTER 71

Mary's friend had returned. Perhaps she could throw some light on why no one had been there to meet her? She was to be disappointed.

'But someone must know something,' groaned Mary.

'In the inner circle perhaps, but I couldn't get through, not without raising suspicion,' her friend explained. 'The security was too tight.'

'Even for you?'

'Even for me.'

'Something must have happened,' said Mary.

'Perhaps.'

'What do I do now?' said Mary. 'I can't just sit here.'

'You will have to for the moment,' said her friend, placing a comforting hand on Mary's shoulder. 'Two Mary's doing the rounds could cause a problem.'

Her friend was right. She couldn't just up and go. Plans were in place. And if she did, what would happen if those she was waiting for did finally turn up, with a valid excuse, to find her gone. It would turn into a proper farce. So she would have to stay. She had no choice at the moment. Waiting was at last joined by worry.

CHAPTER 72

Again with the aching head, thought Darren, as he returned to the world of the conscious. Funny, he thought, in his dazed state, why doesn't my shoulder hurt? It surely should do; that door had looked solid.

The door! It suddenly occurred to Darren that he didn't know where he was. Had he escaped? His eyes flickered open. What he saw wasn't encouraging; he was still in the dungeon. But some things had changed. The television and chair had gone. And, to his further disappointment, so had the tray of nibbles. What had happened? Grief, he thought, my head hurts. He looked to the door.

More out of desperation than expectation, Darren yelled at the door, demanding some aspirin. He tried again a moment later, but this time not so loud.

To Darren's surprise, the little hatch opened in the door, and a voice shouted through the hatch. 'You'll get some when we bring your gruel. This ain't the Ritz, you know.'

Well, thought Darren, things were finally looking up; gruel, his favourite. All he needed now was for his head to stop throbbing. He went to rub at his forehead to try to ease it, but to his surprise, he found his arm wasn't long enough.

'Oh no,' wailed Darren, looking at the shackle surrounding his wrist. 'How did that happen?'

Head sinking to his chest, eyes closing to his predicament, Darren decided maybe he should be thankful he wasn't hanging by them. He idly splashed his feet in the water. It felt nice. It felt warm. It was— Water?! Darren's eyes snapped open again to find most of the cell floor underwater. Water that was rising. Quite quickly.

CHAPTER 73

The second Coffee Coffee Café was a little further afield, so this time Willy *travelled*. Like Tom's Loo, which could travel to any loo in the world, Willy's car could travel to any vehicle in the world. The nearest empty, stationary vehicle. This time it happened to be a police car.

'Oops,' said Willy.

'What if they come back?' said Smokowski, not fancying being arrested for joyriding in a cop car.

'There's a failsafe,' said Willy. 'If something happens, it automatically switches to the next nearest empty vehicle.'

'What if you're in it?'

'You go with it.'

'What happens if the nearest one is miles away when you get back?' said Smokowski.

'I use this.' Willy showed Smokowski the car key. 'I press this button, and hey presto, all back together again. It works like a Hitchhiker.'

'Ingenious,' said Smokowski.

'Right,' said Willy, 'there it is.'

The second Coffee Coffee Café was across the road from them.

'That's handy,' said Smokowski. Meaning, it was so close he wouldn't have to wait long for Willy to return with the paper cup between his legs, or something like that. 'Here.' He handed Willy the paper cup.

'You not coming?'

'Thought I'd sit this one out,' said Willy, 'seen one, you've seen them all.' He didn't know if that was true, but there was no way he would court embarrassment again.

'As you are then,' said Willy, clambering from the car. 'See you in a mo.' He shut the door then knocked on the window. Smokowski lowered it. 'Keep an eye open for those coppers.' He gave Smokowski a big grin, winked and scuttled off towards the café, waving the paper cup in his hand.

Smokowski watched the poor deluded fool go. He would take no joy from Willy's impending failure. However, he *was* looking forward to discussing the failure and their next move over a cuppa and a nice piece of cake. He had been saving a nice Dundee for a special occasion.

In the back seat, Invisible Bob yawned before scaling the door to look out of the window. He watched Willy enter the café. I wonder if he'll bring back snacks? he thought, a piece of chocolate cake would be nice.

CHAPTER 74

Avoiding the ladies this time, Tom landed the Loo in the Chief Travellers personal washroom.

'Coo,' said Tom, marvelling at the marble hand basin and gold-plated taps, 'there's posh.'

'If you like that sort of thing,' said Cat. 'Personally, I prefer a more refined style.'

'Says the only one in here that washes themselves with their tongue,' said Tom. He paused in thought. 'You don't, do you?'

'No, I don't,' said boB. He used a flannel he kept where he kept everything else. 'Flipping cheek.'

'Only asking,' said Tom.

'If you've finished,' said Cat, who was eager to get on with things. 'Door please, Tom.' As for Tom's remark, she would remember it for future reference but for now, duty called.

'Yah!' yelled the Chief, who hadn't been expecting anyone, especially through that door.

'Only us,' said Tom, quietly smirking at the look on the Chief's face.

'Can't you use the front door like everyone else?' said the Chief, visibly shaken and asking a stupid question. 'At least knock.'

'Have you a toilet by the front door?' asked Tom.

'Do you have a front door?' asked Cat, out of interest.

'Er, I...' said the Chief regretting his stupid question. He pulled himself together. 'Never mind that, what do you want?'

'We have the razor,' said Cat.

'You do? I mean, you have?' said the Chief quickly. 'Well done.'

Tom took the razor from his pocket and handed it to the Chief.

'Well-well,' said the Chief, wondering why there were traces of chocolate on it. 'Any clues to why or who?'

'Sadly no,' said Cat glumly.

'Good,' said the Chief. He looked up from the razor to see Tom and Cat staring at him. He felt boB doing the same. 'I mean, good you stopped the past from being changed.' He gave a nervous laugh. 'But, not good, no, not good, we don't know who put it there or why. Good.'

'What now?' said Tom, who lost track of what the Chief was trying to say on the fourth good.

'What-what?' said the Chief, as he looked at the razor in his hand.

157

'Chief?' said Cat.

'What? Oh, good, carry on,' said the Chief coming back from wherever he had just gone, 'lot's more ripples to sort out, what?'

There was no need to exchange glances to verify that both Tom and Cat were thinking the same thing as they stared at the Chief.

What's going on with the Chief? thought Cat, he's acting a bit odd.

I wonder if we have time for a cuppa, thought Tom, and a biccy. Perhaps they weren't then.

'Any chance of a cuppa?' asked Tom.

Cat kept her thoughts to herself.

'What?' said the Chief.

'Cuppa,' said Tom.

'There isn't time for tea,' said the Chief, suddenly back to his old self and seemingly taken aback at the suggestion. 'The next ripple awaits. Time is running.'

'How long have we got left?' said Cat, sensing something might be amiss.

'Less than we had,' snapped the Chief.

'The lady at Lucy's said we had about two weeks,' Tom chipped in.

'What lady?' said the Chief.

'Mary,' said Cat.

'Mary?' said Tom.

'Not now, Tom,' said Cat.

'Did she?' said the Chief.

'Isn't that what she told you?'

'Do you know what, now you mention it. I believe she did.' The Chief smiled at Cat. 'And now we have even less.'

'You're right,' said Cat, giving the Chief a frown. 'We had better be going.'

As the Chief walked over to the washroom door to usher everyone out, he suddenly remembered Darren. He should tell them. He wouldn't want them to think he was keeping anything from them. But he was extraordinarily busy. There would be questions. Some he wouldn't be able to answer; for various reasons. He placed his hand on the doorknob. Ah, he thought, Deirdre. Deirdre could tell them. But they should be going; time was running. He opened the door. He then remembered boB. Drat, he thought, should hear if he has anything to report. Drat, drat, drat.

'Change of plan,' said the Chief, shutting the washroom door again and narrowly missing Tom in the process. Tom wasn't one to dally if a cuppa wasn't on offer.

'Whoa!' yelled Tom, dodging out of the way.

'Sorry about that,' said the Chief, 'did I clip you?' But before Tom could answer, he carried on talking. 'Just remembered Deirdre has some news for you.'

'What news?' asked Cat.

Ignoring Cat, the Chief went on to say, as the news might take some time explaining, they may as well have a cuppa while they listened to Deirdre.

'Fair do,' said Tom, suddenly forgetting the narrow escape he had just had.

'What news?' said Cat for a second time.

'And while she's telling you,' said the Chief, ignoring Cat for a second time, 'I'll dcbricf boB here. There.'

'Here,' said boB.

'There,' said the Chief.

A glaring Cat, deciding she wouldn't ask a third time, followed Tom, who was already at the door to Deirdre's office.

Having ignored Cats glare, which had caused a little heat beneath his collar, the Chief waited for the door to shut. Door shut; he turned his attention to boB.

'Right,' said the Chief, 'what have you got for me? And make it quick.'

'Aha!' said Smokowski, as Willy emerged from the Coffee Coffee Café. Soon they would be back at the shop making better use of their time trying to find Tom and Cat instead of pointlessly traipsing across the country proffering an empty paper cup to unsuspecting staff and expecting the impossible.

In the backseat, the sudden exclamation from Smokowski caused Invisible Bob to lose his grip on the window and fall headfirst down the gap between the door and the backseat.

'Well?' asked Smokowski smugly as Willy opened the driver's door.

'Bingo,' said Willy, clambering into the driver's seat.

'Bingo?' said Smokowski.

'They remembered who bought it,' said Willy.

'They what?' said Smokowski, not sure he heard right.

'Old boy, wearing a flat cap with flaps at the side tied at the top, they said,' said Willy, feeling extremely pleased with himself. Perhaps I should be a private investigator after all? P I Willy. It had a ring. 'What do you think to me being a private dick?' Willy asked.

Smokowski, his jaw dropping, couldn't believe it. He was stunned. How? he thought. 'How?' he finally asked.

'Get an office first, I suppose, then advertise.'

'What?' said Smokowski.

'If I want to be a PI,' said Willy.

What was he going on about? thought Smokowski. 'How did they know who bought it?' he said.

'Oh,' said Willy, placing the paper cup in the cars only cup holder, a piece of wood with a hole bored in it and bolted to the driver's door. He turned back to Smokowski. 'You okay?' asked Willy, 'You look a little pale.'

'What? Yes, course I am, why shouldn't I be?' said Smokowski, who wasn't. He was gobsmacked. Willy had somehow managed what he couldn't. 'How?' he asked again.

'Well,' said Willy, gearing up to tell of his triumph, 'it appears the cups have a square with squiggles on the side of it.'

'Squiggles?' said Smokowski, not remembering any squiggles or a square.

'Yeah,' said Willy, 'look.' He took the paper cup from the holder. 'Apparently, it can tell them where and when it was bought.' Willy showed the square on the side to Smokowski. 'Marketing, they said. Helps them to map out peoples drinking habits.'

'Map out?' said Smokowski, not following.

'Spying, I call it,' said Willy. 'Anyhow, once it registered on their computer, they could tell the time, the day, and the place where the cup was sold and, as it happens, the place was here.'

'Unbelievable,' said Smokowski.

'I know,' said Willy. 'And if that don't beat all, one of the staff working there right now said they remembered who had bought it.'

'Wonders will never cease,' said Smokowski.

'I know,' said Willy. 'It was because of the doughnuts.'

'Doughnuts?' said Smokowski.

'Yeah, the bloke that bought the coffee also bought doughnuts. The girl behind the counter said she remembered because he bought so many of them.'

A bewildered Smokowski couldn't understand why no one showed the square to the computer in the shop he had visited.

'Ah,' said Willy, 'lucky thing there. It seems the idea's a new one, and it's only being tried in a few shops at the moment. One of them being this one.'

That should have made Smokowski feel a little better, but it didn't. 'Lucky that,' he said.

'Happy they were too, the café people. Proved the system was working.' Willy rummaged in a pocket. 'Look,' he said, 'they even gave me a packet of biscuits as a thank you.'

Of course, they did, thought Smokowski. Not only does he get a clue to the kidnappers identity, but he also gets a flaming reward for doing it!

'We can have them later with a cuppa to celebrate,' said Willy, throwing the packet into the seat behind him. 'Seatbelts on.'

The biscuits landed just as Invisible Bob's head appeared from the gap between the seat and the door. He stared at the biscuits, looked up, and then back again at the biscuits. There is a Deity, he thought.

CHAPTER 76

'Kidnapped?' Cat exclaimed.

'Blimey,' said Tom.

'The Chief didn't tell you?' said Deirdre, surprised.

'Said he was too busy,' said Tom.

Passing the buck, thought Deirdre, but he was the Boss; delegating was in the remit. And so busy, all those notes. He never seemed to have a moment. 'True,' she said, 'he's got a lot on his plate.'

Understandable, thought Cat, he was in an important position. But she felt something was slightly off. What, she couldn't put her claw on.

'Do you know how the kidnappers got in?' said Cat.

'No,' Deirdre admitted, 'but I'll find Cedric. He might know.'

'That would be great,' said Cat.

As Deidre went to go, Tom stopped her. 'The Chief said something about a cuppa.'

'Tom,' hissed Cat.

'What?'

'I'll see what I can do after I've found Cedric.'

'Fair do's,' said Tom.

Deirdre left the room.

'Something's not right,' said Cat, as soon as Deirdre had left the room.

'Yeah,' said Tom, 'should have had the cuppa first.'

'No,' said Cat, 'I mean something's off.'

'Is it?' said Tom, sniffing the air.

'The kidnapping for one,' said Cat, ignoring Tom's nostril activity.

'He's prone to it,' said Tom.

'From the Travellers HQ while it's in lockdown?' frowned Cat.

'We got in,' Tom pointed out.

'I suspect we're allowed to.'

'True.'

'So, how did it happen?'

'What happen?'

'How was Darren kidnapped while in lockdown?'

'Oh,' said Tom, 'I see what you mean.'

Thank goodness for that, thought Cat. 'Well?'

'No idea,' Tom admitted.

Thought not, thought Cat. 'And I'm not sure about those ripples either.'

'We found the razor.'

'I know, but what is the point of planting that? What's it got to do with anything? And it's so convenient.'

Ordinarily, Tom would have tittered at that, what with the Loo, but as Cat was looking so serious. 'How d'you mean?'

'When have we ever had such precise instructions before? It's usually in and out until we strike lucky. Not this time.'

'But that's handy, isn't it?' said Tom, wondering why it should be a problem. 'It means we get the job done all the quicker. I'm all for that.'

'Yes.' Cat couldn't fault Tom's argument. 'But why so many ripples? Anyone would think we were being kept busy for a reason.'

'I thought the Chief gave one, didn't he?' said Tom, a little confused. Especially the ins and outs. It was shaking him all about. 'A plan.'

'Yes,' said Cat, 'but what plan?'

'That's what we're here to find out,' said Tom, proving something wasn't right; Tom being sensible for a change.

'I know, but Mary seemed so concerned about the Jam.'

'Mary?'

Thankfully for Cat, Deirdre took that moment to return with Cedric.

But any hope of light being thrown on the kidnapping was dashed as Cedric admitted he knew no more than Deirdre did. There was one thing that caught Cat's attention, though, and as soon as Cedric left to resume his duties and Deirdre to make a cuppa, she told Tom.

'I didn't realise it wasn't a complete lockdown,' said Cat, surprised to hear it was only the operations room that was in total lockdown while the rest of headquarters was only on tightened security, but as with the ops room reduced staffing.

'Nor me,' said Tom.

'Changes everything.'

'It does?'

'It could mean an inside job.'

'But Cedric said everyone was trusted.'

'Uncle Rufus was trusted,' said Cat. 'Sorry to bring him up again.'

'No,' said Tom, 'fair do's. He's got a lot to answer for.'

'But you get my point?'

'Loud and clear,' said Tom, 'an uncle did it.'

'Did what?'

'Kidnapped Darren.'

'For goodness' sake,' groaned Cat.

'Only joking,' said Tom, on seeing Cat's face. Or am I? he thought, it could have been someone's uncle.

Chapter 77

The water was still rising and had now reached the back of Darren's knees. Soon it would cover the whole floor. Luckily for Darren, he sat on a slight rise in the dungeon floor. Unluckily for Darren, he couldn't stand because his ankles were shackled to the floor.

So this is it, thought Darren as the water lapped about him, the cell would fill, and he would be no more. He had noticed the water appeared to be coming from the top of the far wall. He had also noted the water didn't seem to be seeping out through the door. Sealed. The same with the small hatch, he suspected. Soon the room would be a vast aquarium and him the only fish!

What had he done to deserve this fate? Who would do such a thing? Woe was he in his ignorance. But he would be brave. He was of noble birth. He would not let this terror subdue him. He would meet his fate head-on and laugh in the face of fear. Keep his dignity, if nothing else.

The water crept higher. It was close to his bottom now. His trousers were wet, his pants about to be. It was too much. Darren broke.

'Aargh!' yelled Darren as the water reached his buttocks. His pants were getting wet. He hated his pants being wet. 'Help!' he cried. Being brave was one thing when the enemy was far away, but quite another thing when it crept up your pants. 'Help!' he yelled again. 'I'm too young!'

The door to the dungeon suddenly burst open.

What new terror is this? thought Darren, is it not enough that I will soon be but a cold fish bobbing at the top of its tank. He then remembered he was shackled. Bobbing at the bottom of its tank. What he had failed to notice, as he mind-wailed, was that the water level had subsided a little as some of it gushed out of the open door.

'Flipping 'eck!' said someone, automatically raising the tray carrying gruel and headache tablets as his feet got wet. The owner of the now wet feet called urgently over his shoulder. 'Alwyn, get the plumber. It's happened again!'

CHAPTER 78

Over a cuppa and a mysterious lack of the biscuits, Willy had received, he and Smokowski discussed the description of the suspected kidnapper. Willy had found an empty wrapper on the back seat when he had gone to retrieve the biscuits. Willy couldn't think how but he suspected mice.

'Flat cap, you say?' said Smokowski, who was gradually getting over Willy's triumph. He had decided it was nothing more than a fluke.

'Yeah,' said Willy. 'With flaps on.'

'Flaps,' mused Smokowski. Why did that ring a bell somewhere? he thought.

'And grey hair,' said Willy.

'You never mentioned grey hair before,' said Smokowski.

'I did, didn't I?' said Willy. 'No, you're right, I said old guy. Yeah, old guy with grey hair.'

'Anything else?' urged Smokowski. So far, Willy's description could be anyone down at the OAP club. 'Any unusual markings? Skin colour? Accent?'

'Grey,' said Willy.

'Grey?' said Smokowski, 'grey what?'

'Skin,' said Willy.

'The kidnapper has got grey skin?' said Smokowski, thinking that would narrow it down if any grey-skinned people existed. Perhaps it wasn't kidnapping at all. Maybe it was an alien abduction. Did aliens drink coffee?

'That's what they said,' said Willy, referring to the shop staff, not UFO conspiracists.

'They never thought that strange?' said Smokowski. 'Surely they would have noted that before the cap and grey hair.'

'Well, they never actually said grey skin,' admitted Willy.

'But you just said skin.'

'That's what they said,' said Willy. 'They said the kidnapper's skin had a grey pallor.'

'Grey pallor? Not grey skin?'

'Does it matter?' said Willy.

Flipping 'eck, thought Smokowski. 'Did they say anything else?'

Willy had a think. 'Oh, yeah,' he said at last. 'He was wearing a suit. A grey one.'

More grey, thought Smokowski. He suspected the cap the suspect was wearing was also grey. He also suspected that all the staff in the coffee shop were colour blind.

'But no tie,' added Willy.

'So, our suspected kidnapper, and stop me if I'm wrong, has grey hair, a grey suit, skin of a grey pallor but no tie?'

'Yep,' said Willy. 'Oh, and I've just remembered, his cap was grey too.'

Smokowski closed his eyes. Yes, it was. It was as he had suspected. Which meant either the shop staff *were* all colour blind, or they were pulling Willy's leg, or the kidnapper was one of those street performers that stood still all day down at the town centre.

'And it didn't match,' said Willy.

One of Smokowski's eyes opened. 'What didn't?'

'The suit,' said Willy. 'I remember now. I thought it odd someone going round wearing an odd suit.'

'Odd in what way?' said Smokowski, half expecting Willy to say something stupid like it was weird material or the like.

'I know what you're thinking,' said Willy. Smokowski doubted it. 'The suit was strange. You know, odd strange. That was what I thought they meant at first, you know, odd, strange.'

'Spot on,' said Smokowski, lying.

'Ah-ha, thought you were,' said Willy, who was now wondering if he should have PI Willy painted in gold on the door of his new office.

'Odd in what way?' Smokowski repeated, getting slightly exasperated. He looked into his empty cup. Perhaps something stronger would be in order. He had some dandelion tea somewhere.

'What? Oh yeah, it was different greys.'

Different greys. Smokowski hadn't expected that. 'Different greys?' he said. 'In what way different?'

'The jacket didn't match the trousers.'

'So,' said Smokowski, 'the would-be kidnapper has grey hair, a grey suit that doesn't match, a grey cap, skin of a grey pallor and no tie?'

'That's about it,' said Willy.

As Smokowski put the suspect's description together in his head, he had the feeling, somewhere in the back of his mind, that he should know who this person was.

'Oh,' said Willy, causing the picture in Smokowski's mind to dissolve just as he felt he was on the verge of something. 'There was something else.'

'Yes?'

'He said something.'

166

Could this be the missing piece? thought Smokowski. 'Go on.'

'He said it when the person serving him didn't have what he wanted.'

'Yes?' said Smokowski. 'Go on.' The suspense was unbearable. In the same way, laying on a bed of nails might be to a first-timer.

'They said he said "fair do's",' said Willy. 'But they couldn't recall an accent.'

'What did you just say?' said Smokowski, nearly dropping his cup.

'He didn't have an accent,' said Willy.

'Not that,' said Smokowski. 'Say again what he said?' The picture in his head was reforming.

'Eh, fair do's, I think.'

'You think?' Smokowski almost jumped down Willy's throat saying it.

Backing away slightly, Willy did a quick, I think, rethink. 'No, that's what they said, exactly; you know, verbottom. Why? Is it important?'

The picture in Smokowski's head was complete even though he itched to say verbatim. He animated it. He got it to say "fair do's". He wondered why it had taken him so long to realise? It was Tom. He was all right. Thank goodness for that. The cup belonged to Tom. Which meant Tom was the kidnapper. Hurrah!

'It's Tom,' said Smokowski, grinning from ear to ear. He stood up and did a little jig. 'Tom's the kidnapper.'

Willy moved a little further away and looked in his cup. Perhaps he shouldn't drink anymore? He looked at Smokowski and frowned.

'You talking about your Tom, the one who was kidnapped? The one we're looking for?'

'Yes-yes and yes,' said Smokowski, beaming.

'He kidnapped himself?' said Willy, trying to make sense of what he was being told.

'No,' said Smokowski, still jigging and beaming with the knowledge his mate was safe. 'Don't you see? It was him at the café.'

As one of the worlds up-and-coming detectives, in Willy's mind, he could see that, but if he wasn't the kidnapper? 'So, he's escaped?' he said.

'No,' said Smokowski, 'he was never kidnapped.'

As this sank in, with Smokowski still jigging and beaming, Willy had a thought. 'Then why have we been looking for him,' he said, 'if he wasn't kidnapped?'

The jigging slowed to a stop. The beam on Smokowski's face gradually became a frown. Why were they looking for Tom if he wasn't kidnapped? 'I don't know,' he said.

'He must have escaped,' said Willy, throwing the only logical explanation of Tom's appearance into the ring.

'But surely he would have told someone that he had escaped?' said Smokowski, pouring a little doubt onto the logic.

The nearly great detective thought on this. 'Then we are left with three conclusions,' said Willy, thinking conclusion a great word; he would use it more often. 'He was kidnapped and escaped. He was not kidnapped, in which case, there has been some kinda miscommunication. Or he was out getting coffee and doughnuts for the kidnappers. There, I think that covers the situation.'

'Something's amiss, isn't it?' Smokowski could feel it in his water.

'Or,' said Willy, thinking of another conclusion, 'it's another red heron.'

'Herring,' said Smokowski, automatically.

'Yeah,' agreed Willy, 'it's fishy all right.'

'What do we do now, then?'

'As I see it,' said Willy, 'we have two choices.' He took a sip from his cup. 'Ugh!' he said as the last dregs of cold tea filled his mouth.

'Go on,' said Smokowski, grimacing as Willy dribbled the dregs back into the cup.

Willy wiped his mouth with a hanky and continued with his conclusions. 'Right, yes, well, it's like this. We either continue looking for Tom and Cat, or we report back that we've found Tom and see what that throws up.'

'Talk to Mary?'

'Yes.'

Blimey, thought Invisible Bob, as he sat with his back to a comfy toilet roll whilst finishing the last of Willy's biscuits, I had better tell the Chief.

CHAPTER 79

Having reported all he knew, including the bit about hearing a pin drop just before the razor arrived, boB rejoined Tom and Cat in the Loo on a bit of a high. There hadn't been a lot to report in truth, but the Chief had actually thanked him before wandering away to his desk with a thoughtful look on his face.

'Kidnapped?' said boB, wondering why the Chief hadn't told him.
'Yes,' said Cat.
'Shouldn't we look for him?'
'It would have been my choice given the chance, but we have a job to do. I'm sure everything is being done to find him,' said Cat, not overly confident it was or if the list was all it was supposed to be. But upwards and onwards. 'Where next, Tom?'
'Oh,' said Tom, as he read the next mission on the list. He had thoughts on Darren too but kept them to himself; he couldn't have everyone thinking he might miss the lad. Besides, he was sure Darren could look after himself.
'Is that a good "oh" or a bad "oh"?' said Cat.
'Depends,' said Tom, 'whether you like plays or not.'
'What's a play?' said boB.
'Something performed on stage.'
'What's a stage?' asked boB.
Cat, who liked the odd foray into the world of theatre, was intrigued. 'Go on,' she said.
'Seems Shakespeare will invent moving pictures,' said Tom.
'What?' said Cat, thinking the idea ridiculous. 'Does it say when?'
'Just a mo,' said Tom, tracing a finger along a line. 'Ah, here we are, Monday the twenty-third of April, fifteen ninety-one.'
'Wow,' said boB, 'three ninety-one in the afternoon, now that is precise.'
'That's the year,' said Cat, wondering whether boB knew there were only sixty minutes in an hour.
'At least it doesn't sound dangerous,' said Tom.
'No,' said Cat, 'Is there a time on this one?'
'No,' said Tom.
In a way that eased Cat's mind a little. One, it didn't appear to be dangerous, and two, no precise time to it; both reassuring. Her suspicion

levels would have been higher if they had. This one smacked of one of your run-of-the-mill jobs. But they would see. But again, why? Profiteering perhaps? But again, she thought, what did it have to do with the missing Jam? Yeah, as the Chief said, the Jam could be just a ruse to keep eyes away from what was truly going on, but surely there had to be some link? Then again, she could just be overthinking things. Mary had sent them to the Chief, so she would have to trust they knew what they were doing.

'Okay,' said Cat, 'back to the cottage then and let's see what that date has in store for us.'

Wahoo! thought Tom, as the prospect of another cuppa loomed large. It would also give him the opportunity to clean the chocolate from his pocket. Such a waste.

boB, who couldn't read minds, nonetheless read Toms on this occasion. It wasn't hard; Tom-home-cuppa. Okay, not the intended pocket cleaning, but no one's perfect.

It didn't take Cat long to find what she was looking for, and although it didn't appear to be a dangerous assignment, it would take a little while for them to locate the exact whereabouts and time of the plant.

'Tom,' said Cat, 'did the list mention where Shakespeare was when he invented it?'

'I don'th fink tho,' said Tom, mouth full of biscuit.

'Ith wude ta tork wiff yer mooth thull,' said boB, ditto.

'Do you think you could have a look?'

Note removed from his pocket, Tom did just that after swallowing the last of his biscuit. 'No,' he said before turning to boB. 'You can talk.'

Drat, thought Cat, they have the year; they have the date; but not the exact time, which was fair enough but time-consuming, but more importantly, where would Shakespeare be on the date they had. Was he going to be in Stratford-upon-Avon or London? As they didn't know, it looked like they would have to be in two places at once. One thing she thought might be important was the date, the twenty-third of April, generally regarded as the Bards birthday. Going on that, Cat thought it more likely he would be home in Stratford celebrating his birthday rather than London, but she couldn't be one hundred percent certain.

CHAPTER 80

'He's what?' exclaimed Mary, as her friend, who had just arrived, told her about Darren.

'Kidnapped,' said her friend.

'But how? I thought he was with Tom and Cat.'

'I can't find out,' said her friend, 'I got word about his abduction, but that's all. The security is even tighter now than it was.' Her friend also admitted she had no idea if Darren had been with Tom and Cat when it happened.

'What next?' said Mary. 'It's all getting out of hand.'

'I don't know. It's all getting complicated.'

It was, thought Mary, but what could she do? Not sit on her hands anymore, that's for sure. But what she could do with them was another thing entirely. Mary made a decision.

'I'm coming with you.'

'But I thought we decided two Mary's wondering about wasn't a good idea,' her friend cautioned. 'And what if the ones you're waiting for turn up?'

'I know, but I can't just sit around waiting. Will you pop back now and again to check?'

Mary's friend wasn't going to argue; she knew when Mary had her mind made up, it stayed made. 'Okay. Where do you want to go?'

That was something Mary hadn't thought about. Where did she go? She could see the Chief, but that might cause problems. No one knew they were working together to find the Jam. And anyway, from what her friend had just said, it might not be an easy thing to do. Only one thing for it then, she would go back to Lucy's. See what she could do from there. If anything.

CHAPTER 81

It was decided it would be easier to drive to Lucy's, where Mary had said she was going, than a sideways hop, and just as well they did as there wasn't a car in sight when they arrived. So they parked out of sight, round a corner; Smokowski's idea, the thought of something fishy going on, erring him on the side of caution. In the back seat, Invisible Bob was getting ready to dodge closing doors. He had stayed rather than report back to the Chief at the moment, feeling, even though he had more than enough to report, there was more to come and soon. He didn't want to be away if something important happened. Truth be told, he was just plain nosy. Smokowski opened his door, and Invisible Bob made a dash for it.

'Do you think she's here?' said Willy, crouching behind his car.

'We'll soon find out,' said Smokowski.

'Okay, what's the plan?' asked Willy.

Plan, thought Smokowski. He hadn't thought about a plan. 'Knock on the door?' he said.

'Perhaps we should do a quick recce first?' suggested Willy.

'Good idea,' said Smokowski, still erring. The thing was, he didn't know why it was a good idea. After all, all they had to do was knock on the door and tell Mary what they knew. Simple. Or was it? Something was going on. Perhaps it wasn't such a bad idea. He would more than likely laugh about it when he was old. Or at least, older.

'After three,' said Willy.

'One,' said Smokowski, as Willy said three

'Oi,' said Smokowski, 'wait for me.'

CHAPTER 82

The plumber arrived and fixed the water pipe. The water had gone down quickly and had only managed, despite Darren's cries to the contrary, to dampen his pants ever so slightly. His trouser legs were soaked through, as was his sleeves, which was his fault as had left his arms slumped in front of him while bemoaning his watery fate. He now stood, wearing only his semi-soggy underpants.

'It's all we have in your size,' explained Alwyn, one of Darren's guards.

Darren took what they offered and put it on. 'But I look stupid,' he wailed.

'Better stupid than wet,' said Arwen, Darren's other guard.

'What is it?' asked Darren, pulling at the bottom edge. There was a whisper of a cold draft in the cell, and whatever Darren now wore invited it to visit his nether regions.

'It's called a tall bird,' said Alwyn.

'Tabard,' Arwen corrected.

'Is it?'

'Yes.'

'Fancy that.'

'It was in the fancy dress chest.'

'Oh,' said Darren, giving his new clothes a dubious look. It reminded him of the clothing of his day. But then again, it also looked uncannily like a sack the potatoes that Smokowski ordered came in. 'I thought at first it was a sack with holes cut in it.'

'Yeah, well,' said Alwyn, mouth twitching.

'Beggars can't be choosers,' said Arwen. 'Which reminds me.' He disappeared from the cell for a moment before returning with the tray he had earlier held aloft, containing the bowl of gruel, a spoon, a glass of water, and two aspirins. He handed it to Darren. 'It's a bit cold now, I'm afraid.'

Arwen looked at Alwyn. Alwyn looked at Arwen. 'What yer think?' said Alwyn. He had something in his hand.

'Suppose,' said Arwen, 'wouldn't hurt.'

Arwen and Alwyn were feeling a little sorry for the lad. It *was* a potato sack. And it *was* their fault he got wet. They should have got the plumber out the last time instead of trying to fix it themselves.

'Here,' said Alwyn, placing the remote control and the manual on the tray. 'Don't make us regret it and have to chain you again.'

'Thank you,' said Darren, wondering if he should push his luck a little while his jailers were in a giving mood? Chains or no chains, that was the question? Or possibly the answer to his question? What did he have to lose?

'Who are we?' said Arwen. He glanced at Alwyn, who just shrugged. Arwen decided there wouldn't be any harm in telling the lad. 'Just jailers,' he said.

'But we didn't kidnap you,' said Alwyn, receiving a sharp look from Arwen.

But deciding no harm done, Arwen told Darren a little more. 'No,' he said, 'we didn't. We're just freelance jailers. Hired on a see nothing, hear nothing, know nothing basis.'

'Sometimes we do see things,' said Alwyn.

'Okay,' said Arwen, 'we do sometimes see things but only what we need to see.'

'And hear things,' said Alwyn, 'sometimes.'

Arwen frowned at his fellow jailer. 'Sometimes,' he agreed, 'but only what we need to hear.'

'And we do know some things too,' said Alwyn.

Arwen now glared at Alwyn.

Darren decided, if he wanted to ask anything else, he had better do it now before the tide turned completely.

'So, if you didn't kidnap me, who did?' said Darren.

The jailers exchanged a furtive glance. Some things they saw, some things they didn't. Some things they heard, some things they didn't. Some things they knew, some things they didn't. Some things were dangerous, some things weren't. This thing fell into the dangerous category. They didn't know for sure, but they had an idea. They had heard the sounds. And the sounds were something not to be messed with.

'Can't help you there,' said Arwen.

'No,' said Alwyn.

Saying no more, they left Darren alone in the cell, Arwen carrying Darren's underpants at arm's length.

CHAPTER 83

Deirdre popped her head around the door that connected her office with the Chiefs. She had never seen him so agitated. She hoped all was well with him; he had a job to do. He looked her way, but whether he saw her, Deirdre didn't know. She quickly closed the door.

The Chief was pacing back and forth, mumbling to himself. Although boB's report was pleasing, a few doubts had now set in. A few worries. Where was Invisible Bob for one? He should have reported in again by now.

'What was happening?' muttered the Chief to himself, mid-forth.

The Chief paced back. He was in the dark. The last note hadn't been part of the plan. What did it mean? 'Maybe I should tell someone,' he said, a little louder than he had meant. He glanced at the door to Deirdre's office. He thought he had heard something, but the door was closed.

There had been a plan. A good plan. But he didn't feel part of it anymore. 'What should I do?' he wailed. He glanced at the door again.

What was that? thought the Chief, mid-pace. He stood still. He listened. Nothing, he decided. His mind playing tricks. No, there. The Chief strained his ears. Was that the sound of a pin dropping? No. A flea scratching? Then nothing; silence. He was letting his imagination run away with him. He then heard, quite plainly, a bell tinkle.

The Chief's face grew pale. Why were they coming here now? he thought. Something's wrong. It wasn't part of the plan. Perhaps, if he were quiet, they wouldn't know he was there? He looked for a place to hide. The ops room! He ran. But to no avail. They were there, with him. And then they weren't, and neither was he.

CHAPTER 84

It was just after midnight in Shakespeare's home in Stratford-upon-Avon, and Cat had been right; the bard was home. That very moment he was upstairs in bed, fast asleep.

But Cat still had reservations.

'Why?' said Tom.

'It's all too easy,' said Cat.

Tom, who liked easy, couldn't see why she was so worried.

'Usually, I wouldn't be,' Cat admitted, 'but these ripples are different.' Cat wanted to check the London address as well, just to be on the safe side.

'But if he's here, why do we need to?' said Tom, another sensible question. 'The list says he will discover it today. He's here, and we're here.'

'I know,' said Cat, 'but doesn't it seem strange that we are finding out about it before it happens?' Cat had a point. The usual ripple announced that something in the past had changed. These gave notice that a change would happen before it did. 'I just want to check, humour me.' Cat had a theory. It was probably wrong, but she wanted to know anyway. She wondered, as the list didn't say where Shakespeare would be, if that meant the invention would be in the same place he was? In most ripples, the place was known. This one, it wasn't. It sounded stupid in her own head if she was being truthful, but what if the date of the invention was right, but the day Shakespeare received it was different? Coincidence? He might find it later when he went to London. There might be a note with a date with it. His birthday. Would he then claim he invented it on his birthday? It would nicely cover any counterclaims by the sender. Shakespeare was not to know someone from the future planted it. So the date would then be in line with the list. If that was to happen, they might have to go back again. More time-wasting.

'Suppose,' said Tom, not entirely sure he was following.

Overthinking it if you ask me, thought boB, knowing no one would. So he went off to find something to eat.

'We need to find out his London address,' said Cat.

Yuk, thought boB, finding some stale cheese and a half cup of small beer.

After a stealthy look through Shakespeare's belonging's, they found what they were looking for, the address of his London lodgings.

'So, who's going?' asked Tom.

A certain small invisible person thought he knew the answer to this.

'Have you got your Hitchhiker boB?'

'Yes,' said boB, giving himself a gold star.

'Good,' said Cat. 'Tom will take you to London and come back. I'll wait here just in case someone turns up.'

'What if no one appears my end?' said boB.

'If someone turns up here, we'll come collect you,' said Cat. 'If someone turns up your end, you travel to us so we can come pick it up.' No one knew for sure what shape or form the moving pictures invention would take.

'And if something turns up at both places?' said boB.

It was something Cat hadn't thought of. A double bluff. Grief, she thought, I'm sure I'm overthinking this. But to be on the safe side. 'Then we stay at both places until the day ends, or we have two of them.'

Me and my big mouth, thought boB.

You and your big mouth, thought Tom, wishing he'd brought a flask of coffee with him.

CHAPTER 85

Followed by Invisible Bob, who was keeping a discreet distance as he didn't want to be stepped on, Smokowski and Willy made their way to Lucy's house.

Sideways, backwards, suddenly duck behind something, the progress was slow. Behind Smokowski and Willy and their erratic behaviour, a bemused Invisible Bob wondered the reasoning behind it. What were they expecting to happen? What were they expecting to find? Why couldn't they just walk up to the door and knock? But it wasn't his place to say. Oh, no. None of his business. Not that they would listen to him. Besides, it would mean him blowing his cover. Also, it was funny to watch.

'That hedge,' said Smokowski, who had had training on how to duck behind hedges when on duty.

'Which hedge?' said Willy, keeping his head down.

'The privet,' said Smokowski, heading for it.

'What's a privet?' said Willy, changing direction.

'The one by the lamppost,' said Smokowski.

'Why didn't you say so?' said Willy.

'I did,' said Smokowski, 'three times.' His voice was getting lower the closer they got to Lucy's.

They reached the hedge which sat across the road from Lucy's and ducked down behind it. Invisible Bob sidled up a few seconds later and sat beside the hedge in full view of the house. No one could see him, so why not?

'There,' whispered Smokowski, with a modicum of triumph, 'we can see the front of Lucy's from here.'

Nothing looked untoward.

'Now what?' said Willy.

Yes, thought Invisible Bob, now what?

'We wait,' said Smokowski.

'For what?' said Willy.

Yes, thought Invisible Bob, for what? He couldn't wait.

'To see who comes and goes,' said Smokowski.

'Oh,' said Willy, 'good idea.'

Oh, for pity's sake, thought Invisible Bob, we could be here all day. He decided to take matters into his own hands.

Casually strolling across the road, after looking both ways and making sure the way was clear of traffic, Invisible Bob headed for the front door. His idea was to knock on it. Wait for it to open. Then shout at the top of his voice that Smokowski and Willy were across the road hiding behind the hedge. Then, as chaos reigned, he would pop indoors, grab a bite to eat and then return to watch the fun. That is what he planned. Not what he planned happened.

He squeezed through the bars on the front gate, ran up the garden path, pulled himself up onto the front doorstep and knocked all sorts of nonsense out of the front door. Then, happy with his work, he hid to one side, ready to yell at the top of his voice when the door opened. He didn't have long to wait.

The door opened. Someone stepped out. And just as Invisible Bob opened his mouth to give Smokowski and Willy away, the someone that had stepped out suddenly stooped down and grabbed Invisible Bob by the scruff of his neck. Thankfully for Invisible Bob, the skin on the back of his neck was akin to that of a kitten – Bobs' mums would frequently grip their offspring by the neck between their teeth and carry them from one place to another. The shout Invisible Bob had intended became a shriek. Someone then stepped back inside and closed the door behind them.

'Did you see that?' whispered an agog Smokowski.

'Saw it and heard it,' whispered Willy, equally agog.

'Who knocked on the door?'

'No idea,' whispered Willy. 'Who screamed?'

'No idea,' whispered Smokowski.

'Who was that who opened the door?' asked Willy.

'Lucy, I think,' said Smokowski.

'Ah,' said Willy, vaguely remembering a photo on Mary's desk. 'What do you think she picked up?'

'No idea,' said Smokowski. 'But whatever it was, it didn't like it judging by the noise it made.'

'Looked like she was picking up a kitten,' said Willy, 'you know, the way she was holding it.'

Um, thought Smokowski, it did. 'Couldn't see a kitten though,' he said.

'Unless it was an invisible kitten,' said Willy.

Invisible! Both Willy and Smokowski suddenly had the same thought.

'A Magical,' said Willy.

'An invisible one,' said Smokowski. He had the sudden feeling that perhaps he had met this particular Magical before.

'Holy Molly,' said Willy when Smokowski told him his thoughts.

'Moly,' said Smokowski.

'That his name?' said Willy.

'No,' said Smokowski, 'it's Holy Moly.'

'A religious Moly, eh?' said Willy.

Thankfully, the inane conversation stopped when the front door to Lucy's opened, and a voice called out. 'We know you're out there,' it said.

Smokowski and Willy ducked lower.

'Tell tit,' whispered Willy, aiming his remark at the Magical he gathered had told on them.

'Perhaps we should go in,' Smokowski whispered, 'now they know we're here?'

'It could be a trap,' said Willy.

'Don't be silly,' said Smokowski, 'that was Lucy at the door.'

'True,' said Willy. 'Perhaps we should then.' He started to rise, but as he did, Smokowski grabbed his arm and stopped him. 'What?'

'I just had a thought,' said Smokowski, 'that was Lucy.'

'Thought we had covered that,' said Willy.

'Yes,' said Smokowski, 'but the Lucy I know doesn't know Tom is a traveller, let alone know what a Magical is.'

'So?' said Willy, being a little obtuse.

Smokowski sighed and explained.

'Oh,' said Willy, slowly sinking back down. 'What now?'

'I have no idea,' said Smokowski.

The plot had just thickened considerably.

CHAPTER 86

Her ear pressed against the door to the Chief's office, Deirdre listened intently. The Chief had missed his latest coffee break and wasn't answering the intercom. She had heard him talking to himself a few minutes earlier, his voice gradually getting louder and louder until, suddenly, all had gone quiet.

She wondered if she should go in, but he could be grumpy if she just walked in unannounced while he was busy. Still, she had to know what was going on behind the door, even if it meant feeling the Chief's ire. She went in.

It was empty. The boardroom was empty. Deirdre went to the Chief's private washroom and knocked on the door. There was no answer. She tried again, and this time when no one answered, she pushed the door. It opened, and again, the room was empty. One more place to try, she thought, the operations room. But no one had seen him for a while.

Deirdre returned to the Chief's office and sat in his chair. What now? she thought.

CHAPTER 87

With boB firmly ensconced in Shakespeare's London lodgings, Tom returned to Cat.

'Anything there?' asked Cat, as Tom emerged from the Loo.

'All clear so far,' said Tom, wondering if tea or coffee had been invented yet. His tummy rumbled.

'Why don't you see if you can find something to eat?' suggested Cat, all too aware of what a rumbling Tom tum meant; discovery if they weren't careful in this case. 'I believe boB was scavenging for something over there.'

Tom went to investigate and was delighted to find some pies. He stuck a finger in one of them and pulled out a plum. Nice, he thought. He returned with both pies, a piece of cheese and a jug of ale.

'You happy now?'

'S'poth,' said Tom, his mouth full of pie.

Tom's rumbling taken care of, he and Cat settled down to wait.

Meanwhile, in London, boB had had the same idea as Tom. To his dismay, he was less fortunate than Tom. He had found nothing but a dry crust of bread. Thank goodness he had thought to pack a flask and sandwiches. He settled back to sip tea and munch on thin slices of bread filled with inch thick chocolate spread. Happily, the spread hadn't melted.

The day stretched on. Tom had finished a pie and half the ale. The household awoke. Cat put a glamour over her and Tom's hiding place, just in case. Birthday greetings were given. Presents were presented. Cheers were raised. A "Ta-ra" was said. A cloth was raised. There was silence. Words were raised. Questions were asked. Where were the birthday pies? Where was the jug of ale? Cat glared at Tom. Tom went to whistle but thought better of it. Fingers were pointed. William was blamed. He pleaded his innocence. Yeah, right, thought Tom, before remembering who had taken them. A huff set in. Wife would not talk to husband. The front door slammed. William went to the inn. Night had drawn in. A wife had gone to bed. Later a husband, worse-for-wear, arrived home. Stairs were climbed. An argument ensued. A gift was pledged. Silence. A giggle. More silence. Strange noises. boB had not arrived from London. It was now just past eleven. Cat was tense. Surely something would happen soon.

'Quiet,' whispered Cat.

Halfway through his second pie, Tom stopped mid-chew. He hadn't thought he was making that much noise. He was about to complain when he was aware of a noise. Was that the sound of a flea scratching?

Cat had thought she had heard a pin drop.

Together, they now thought they heard a bell tinkle.

Tom went to say something, but Cat hushed him.

Silence followed.

Cat waited.

Tom tried not to chew, so swallowed instead.

'The same sounds as in the tent,' whispered Cat.

'What do you think it means?' asked Tom, grimacing as the lump of pie forced its way down his gullet. He would suffer from indigestion; he just knew it. He wasn't wrong.

Cat had put two and two together and arrived at an answer. 'I think it's here,' she said.

'What is?' said Tom, wincing as indigestion announced its arrival.

'The thing we've been waiting for.'

Oh yeah, thought Tom. 'Where do you think it is?'

'Come on.'

There followed a further search of Shakespeare's house. A painstakingly slow one; they had no idea what they were looking for. It could be in any shape or form. It could be anything.

Time was nearly up. There were only a few more minutes left until midnight when a noise from upstairs stopped Tom and Cat in their tracks.

'Quick,' whispered Cat, 'Hide.' Someone was coming down the stairs.

The someone was William Shakespeare. He had awoken with a thirst and needed a drink. Having reached the table Tom and Cat were hiding under, he noticed something not there earlier. 'What's this,' he said, picking it up. 'Another birthday present I'll be bound.'

Cat and Tom heard him put his candle down.

'I say,' said Shakespeare, 'how amusing.'

Under the table, Tom and Cat could hear the flicking of paper. Tom looked at Cat. Cat looked at Tom. The one place they hadn't looked. It had been so obvious. But it couldn't be, could it? thought Cat, it couldn't be that simple? She thought she knew what the sound of flicking paper might mean. Tom, on the other hand, didn't; he was more concerned with the cramp in his calf. He needed to stretch his leg. He couldn't take it much longer.

'Tom,' said Cat suddenly, 'run to the Loo, make as much noise as you can about it.' Tom just stared at her. 'Now?'

No idea why, but pleased nonetheless because of his cramped calf, Tom rolled from under the table and ran, limped, to the Loo. All the while moaning at the pain in his leg.

Frightened half out of his wits, Shakespeare staggered backwards into a chair. Cat moved quickly. She leapt onto the table, grabbed something from it with a paw, saw that Tom was labouring, shouted for him to hurry, glamoured the bard, and ran for the Loo, arriving a second or two before Tom did. Tom slammed the door shut behind them.

'London, James,' said Cat, 'and be quick about it.'

'Eh?' said Tom.

'London.'

As Tom and Cat travelled sideways to London, Shakespeare's wife appeared at the top of the stairs, enquiring if he was all right. It appeared he was. He had fallen asleep on the kitchen chair.

What a dream he had had. But the more he thought of it, the more Shakespeare remembered. The dream had been so real. Cat, in her haste, had not hidden everything from Shakespeare's mind with her glamour. Yet amazingly, his play, "The Tale of the Amazing Talking Cat", was not a hit.

CHAPTER 88

'Are they still behind the hedge?' asked Mary, the real one.

'Yes,' said Lucy's double. She still had Invisible Bob between finger and thumb. He hung there, limp and dejected.

'He said anything yet?' said Mary, referring to Invisible Bob, as she stared at Lucy's hand.

'Not yet.'

'Best put him in something for now then,' said Mary. She wanted to know what he was doing here but, for the moment, she had more pressing problems; Smokowski and Willy.

Invisible Bob offered no resistance as Lucy carried him away.

'Oh,' said Mary, 'and make sure there are air holes.'

'Will do,' said Lucy's double.

You're an air hole, thought the disgruntled Bob.

'Okay, what now?' said Mary's friend.

'We go get them,' said Mary.

CHAPTER 89

The foray into the world of Shakespeare had been a success, with the moving pictures retrieved. They turned out to be nothing more than a wad of paper stuck together with a stick man drawn on it, who ran when you flicked the pages. Crude, but a man of Shakespeare's intelligence may have made something from it. Thin though, Cat had thought. It hardly seemed to be worth the bother. She wondered about that. She was becoming increasingly suspicious. And there was the thing with the noises; the same ones both times. Something else was going on, but what?

boB had been asleep when Tom and Cat had arrived but had missed nothing. They waited until midnight; nothing. Cat, it seemed, had been over-cautious, but better safe than sorry. From there, they returned to the Travellers HQ to disturbing news.

'When? How?' said Cat when Deirdre broke the news about the Chief's disappearance.

'Gone AWOL, eh?' said Tom, nodding sagely.

'Blimey!' said boB.

'What do we do now?' said Tom.

'What he said,' said boB.

'Can I speak to Cedric?' asked Cat.

'You could,' said Deirdre, frowning, 'but I've no idea where he is either. It appears he's disappeared as well.'

'When?' asked Cat.

'Blimey,' said Tom, 'perhaps we should skedaddle toot sweet before we disappear too.'

'Flipping 'eck!' said boB, 'to the Loo.'

'Whoa,' said Cat, putting her paw down, 'no one's going anywhere until we find out just what is going on here.'

'But we could be next,' Tom protested.

boB, who had got halfway to the Loo, carried on. He wasn't going to disappear! Well, no more than was usual.

'Deirdre?' said Cat.

'No one is sure,' said Deirdre, 'but at a guess, I'd say he disappeared at about the same time as the Chief.'

Just coincidence, or is he in on it? thought Cat. She decided not to air her speculations, not yet.

'What do I do with this?' said Tom, holding out the wad of moving images they had taken from Shakespeare.

'I'll take it and put it in the cupboard with the razor,' said Deirdre, taking the wad of paper from Tom.

'You have a cupboard for them?' said Tom.

'Sort of,' said Deirdre, 'we keep them there until they are destroyed.' She returned and suggested a move to the boardroom to discuss what they did next if that was okay with everyone. It was. 'Now,' she said, 'I expect everyone could do with a brew before we start.'

'What's that?' yelled boB from the washroom.

'A cuppa,' Tom shouted. 'What the—'

'Sorry,' said boB, who had taken but a second to return. He had used Tom as a ladder to reach the table. 'Any biscuits?' he asked.

'I'll look,' said Deirdre, 'Cat?'

Up all day and night, why not? 'Milk, please.' Cat looked at Tom as he smiled at the thought of a biscuit. It's all right for some, she thought. He had slept through most of it.

'Well, this is a right to do, isn't it?' said Tom when Deirdre left.

'Something's not right,' said boB.

'You think?' said Tom, doing a bit of head shaking.

'He's right though, Tom,' said Cat, 'something most definitely not right. I've felt it for some time now.'

'How d'ya mean?' said Tom.

'Nothing I can point to,' said Cat, 'more niggles, the ripples for one. The way they're so neatly set out. And the way the Chief has been acting.'

'He was a bit in and out,' agreed boB.

'And Darren not coming with us and then disappearing like that,' said Tom.

'I hadn't thought about that, to be honest,' said Cat, thinking it added fuel to the flames; coincidence again? But the more she thought about it.

'And the spying,' said boB. Tom and Cat looked at him. 'I mean reporting. Like what the Chief asked me to do.'

'Yes,' said Cat, giving boB a wry smile, 'and that.' But for Cat, the jury was out on that one. If she were in charge of an operation, she would want to know what was going on in the field. It just depended if the knowledge retrieved was for the good of the operation or personal benefit. Until they found the Chief, they wouldn't know for sure.

A few minutes later, Deirdre returned with coffee's, milk, and a tin of biscuits which she handed out. As she did, she saw something on Cat and Tom's faces which troubled her; she hadn't bothered with boB's. Deirdre didn't want to pry but felt she ought to ask if there was something wrong.

'Why do you ask that?' said Cat.

'Any chocolate biscuits?' asked boB, trying to peer in the tin.

'Have what you're given,' said Tom before turning to Deirdre. 'Any chocolate ones?'

Ever the host, Deirdre produced a small packet of chocolate biscuits. She had brought them just in case.

'Ah,' said Tom, 'my favourites.' He dished them out, one for boB, two for him. He was bigger.

With the children quiet, the adults could now talk.

'I just wondered,' said Deirdre, replying to Cat's question. 'You looked worried when I came in. Thought maybe you were talking about the way the Chief's been acting lately.'

Not sure whether to involve Deirdre, Cat nonetheless decided to ask her how much she knew.

'I know about the ripples,' said Deirdre.

'What else?' said Cat.

'I know everything the Chief knows.' Deirdre's turn to be wary. 'I wouldn't be much of a bodyguard or secretary come to that if I didn't make my charges business my own.'

Cat didn't know quite what to make of that, but, she supposed, she knew all of Tom's business; some she didn't want to, so it made sense on some level.

'Yet you said you thought there was something wrong with the Chief but didn't know why.' See what you say to that, thought Cat.

'Business plans I know, but the Chief wasn't very forthcoming about his personal life,' said Deirdre, giving a reasonable answer.

'You think he might have problems in his personal life?'

'Could have, I suppose.'

Cat wondered if Deirdre was more outside looking in than she thought where the Chief was concerned; not a bad thing. Otherwise, you could be in each other's pockets all the time. She glanced at Tom; he was dunking a biscuit. And no one in their right mind would want to be in one of Tom's pockets. She shuddered just thinking about it.

'So, you know he is working with Mary?' said Cat, thinking it was time to put their cards on the table.

'Yes,' said Deidre. 'I know Mary sent you to help find out about the ripples. The Chief said I was to help in any way I could.'

'Oi,' said Tom, 'that's mine.'

'You had more than me,' wailed boB.

'I'm bigger than you,' said Tom.

'No fair,' cried boB.

Ignoring the squabbling, Cat gave Deirdre one of her rare moggie smiles. Whatever was going on, she didn't think Deirdre was a part of it. Cat drank her milk.

'What now?' Deirdre asked when Cat had finished.

'I see it this way,' said Cat, 'we have two choices; Ripples or Mary.'

'Why Mary?' said Deirdre, 'I would have thought the list more important.'

'I've been having doubts about the Ripples. They don't appear, to me, to be getting us anywhere.' Cat had a thought. 'Tom, out of curiosity, what's next on the list?'

Tom, half an eye on nothing, just in case it stole a biscuit, reached into his pocket and took out the list. He read it. 'It say-oi!' A biscuit had moved on his plate. He decided, against better judgement, it might be safer if the biscuits were in his pocket out of the way.

'No fair,' whined boB, as he watched them go in.

'Tom,' urged Cat.

'Right,' said Tom, 'where was I?' He flicked the list straight and ran a finger down it to number three. 'Ah, here we are. Flipping goosegogs!'

'What is it?' said Cat, noticing the blood had drained from Tom's face.

'I didn't think they really existed,' said Tom.

'What existed?' said Cat.

'Those great big hairy things that live up mountains and the like.'

'What things?' asked an exasperated Cat.

'I think he means a Yeti,' said boB. 'Horrible grumpy things they are.'

'Do I?' said Tom.

'Grief,' groaned Cat, 'give the list to Deirdre. Could you read it please so we can get some sense?'

Tom huffed but handed the list over.

Whether she had ever done it before is not known, but once you were acquainted with Tom, it was habit-forming; Deirdre rolled her eyes and looked at Cat with what could have been a look of sympathy. 'Sherpa,' she said.

'That's it,' said Tom, 'we've got to find a Sherpa.'

'A Sherpa's not a great big hairy thing,' said boB, who, as he had not met a Sherpa, didn't have a clue if they were or not. But everyone knew what he meant. But Cat and Deirdre knew what he meant.

'What's a Sherpa then?' said Tom.

'Not a Yeti,' said boB, chuckling.

'A mountain guide,' Deirdre explained.

'Ah,' said Tom, 'doesn't sound too dangerous then, to be fair.'

'On top of Everest,' said Deirdre, reading more.

'On top of Everest?' said Tom. 'That's high, isn't it?'

'As high as an elephant I should imagine,' said boB, who at only a few inches tall couldn't imagine anything taller than an elephant. He knew there were trees and buildings that were taller, but he didn't have to imagine them.

'Just over five miles high, if I remember right,' said Deirdre, blowing boB's mind. boB looked up, trying to imagine a five-mile high elephant, lost his balance and fell off the edge of the table.

'Why have we got to find a Sherpa on the top of Everest?' asked Cat, trying to bring the conversation back from the surreal.

'Says here, he invents a special lightweight material near the top of Everest that will replace tent canvas.' Deirdre read on. 'He does it just before the first-ever attempt to reach the summit.'

Profit again, thought Cat. 'Does it say the name of the Sherpa perchance?' she asked.

'No.'

Cat really could not see any reason for the ripples except to put them in danger and waste their time. She made her mind up; they were going to see Mary. But whether she was still at Lucy's was another thing.

'Right,' said Cat, 'let's go find Mary. See if we can get some answers. We'll try Lucy's first to see if she's there.' She didn't know if Mary could help, but with the Chief gone, there was no one else.

'Who's Mary?' said Tom.

boB chuckled.

'She is,' said Deirdre.

'You know that for a fact?' said Cat, hopes rising.

'According to the Chief,' said Deirdre.

'Great, Lucy's it is then.'

'Can I come with you?' said Deirdre. 'I seem to be a tad redundant here until the Chief's found.'

'You're not going to look for him?' said Cat.

'The best Magicals we have at HQ are looking for him. I doubt I would make a difference.'

Again with the sense, thought Cat. 'Why not then?' she said. Cat found she liked Deirdre, but whether she trusted her was another thing. She would have to earn that, but at the moment, apart from the backroom staff, she was the last of the inner circle left. Suspicious? But then perhaps she might be the next to disappear? Cat couldn't blame her for wanting to go from here with that hanging over her. But whatever, Cat felt it best to keep her close. Good or bad.

'Excellent,' said Deirdre smiling, 'I'll get my gun.'

Cat frowned but said nothing. She was a bodyguard, and it was part of her equipment.

'Cat?' said Tom. 'Who's Mary?'

'Good news,' said Cat, deflecting rather than ignoring Tom, 'we're going to Lucy's.'

'Fair do's,' said Tom, Mary already slipping from his mind.

CHAPTER 90

Darren was halfway through watching the Sound of Music when the door to his cell flew open.

'Company for you,' said Alwyn, who stepped aside to let Arwen past. He was leading a tall man dressed in black with a hood over his head.

'Who is he?' asked Darren, pausing the television.

'We don't know, but then again, it's not for us to know,' said Arwen.

'No,' said Alwyn.

'On a need-to-know basis,' said Arwen.

'And we know nothing,' said Alwyn.

'We know some things,' said Arwen, giving Alwyn a sharp look.

'I suppose we do,' conceded Alwyn.

'But we don't know him,' said Arwen.

'No,' said Alwyn, 'nor you.' Meaning Darren.

'We know him a bit,' said Arwen, meaning Darren.

'I suppose,' admitted Alwyn.

'Come on,' said Arwen, 'job done.' He led Alwyn out and closed the door behind them.

'Hello?' said Darren to the man in black, who was in danger of walking into the wall.

There was a muffled reply. Perhaps I should take his hood off? thought Darren, perhaps not. He didn't want to upset anyone. Maybe the man liked wearing it. Maybe it was a hat of some sort. The man spoke again, muffled as before but louder. It could be something to do with him walking into the wall. Perhaps he should have taken the man's hood off. Time for decisive action, thought Darren. He took the man's hood off.

'Chief?' cried Darren when he did.

CHAPTER 91

Smokowski and Willy were still discussing the where's, wherefores, why's and why nots of what to do next when a shadow fell across them. They instantly fell quiet. Turning slowly, they looked up from their crouching, from behind the hedge they crouched behind, straight into the face of a stern-looking Mary who had arms crossed and legs akimbo. A rolling pin in one of her hands wouldn't have looked amiss.

'Hello, boss,' said Willy quietly.

'I want to know what you are doing, why you are doing it, and why have you got one of the Bob's working with you?' demanded Mary, ignoring Willy's meek greeting.

'We-what?' said Smokowski.

'Willy!' snapped Mary.

'A Bob?' said a clueless Willy.

'Invisible Bob, to be precise,' said Mary. 'But forget him for a moment and tell me what the heck you are doing crouching behind this bush when you should be looking for Tom and Cat?'

'It's a hedge,' said Smokowski, who received a glare for his effort.

'We found him,' said Willy, hoping he didn't receive one.

'Who?'

'Tom,' said Smokowski.

'You had better come inside,' said Mary.

CHAPTER 92

The door to Lucy's bathroom opened just enough to allow a small invisible head to peep through the gap.

'See anything?' whispered Tom.

'Nope,' said boB.

'Go out a little further,' encouraged Tom. He was also encouraging boB with the toe of his shoe; gently like.

'Oi!' said boB, 'watch what yer poking with those size nines of yours.'

'Keep it down,' whispered Cat.

'Sorry,' whispered boB.

'Anything yet?' asked Cat, as boB, helped by Tom's shoe, ventured further into the hall. The plan was for boB to check out the lie of the land before Tom went in to keep Lucy and the kids busy – she hoped he wouldn't ask too many questions about Mary – while she had a word with Mary.

boB took another step. Then another.

'Anything?'

'Noooooo!' screamed boB, as he unexpectedly left the hall floor on an upward trajectory.

'What the heck was that?' whispered Tom, goosebumps rising.

'boB, I think,' said Cat. 'Quick, close the door.' She didn't know what was out there, but she needed time to think before acting.

Tom went to do as asked but was a second too late. He couldn't hold it. The door pushed open. A figure stood in the doorway. Tom took on a defensive stance; behind Cat.

'Mary?' said Cat cautiously. She sensed all was not as it seemed.

CHAPTER 93

The Chief looked dazed, was dazed, walls could be unforgiving.

'Chief?' said Darren, looking worried, 'you okay?'

With eyes glazed over, the Chief turned towards the voice he had just heard. 'Chief?' he said, a deep furrowing of his brow, which must have hurt because that was where the bump was coming up.

'Yes,' said Darren.

'Chief of what?' asked the Chief.

Oh-oh, thought Darren, something's up. Perhaps it's the bump?

'Travelling,' said Darren, 'you're the Chief Traveller.' Somewhere not so distant, a gasp was heard. Darren frowned, looked at the door, no one there, and turned back to the Chief. 'Don't you remember?'

The Chief's eyes suddenly filled with tears. 'If only I could forget,' he wailed forlornly.

Okay, thought Darren, this is confusing. Does he know who he is or not? Could it be a concussion? That's it, a concussion. Funny things concussions.

'It wasn't my fault,' wailed the Chief, tears running down his cheeks.

'Walls can be quite hard,' said Darren, running with his diagnosis.

'It wasn't my fault.'

'So you said,' said Darren, wondering if it was the Chief's way of blaming him for not removing the hood in time? That or his head's broken.

'You don't understand,' said the Chief, his teary eyes boring into Darren's. 'I've been a bad person.'

Ah, thought Darren, the doughnuts. He must be talking about the doughnuts. At least he hoped he was talking about the doughnuts.

'Perhaps you should sit down,' said Darren, pointing to the chair.

'It wasn't my fault,' the Chief repeated.

'It's comfy,' said Darren, not sure what else to say or do. What about CPR? No, perhaps not. 'How about I turn the telly off?'

'It wasn't my fault,' said the Chief, beginning to sound as if he was on a loop.

'Lovely day,' said Darren, pointing to the ceiling. 'Ah-well. Here.' He took the Chief by the arm and attempted to coax him to the chair.

But the Chief was having none of it and pulled his arm away. 'I've been a bad person, and bad people don't sit in chairs. They stand in corners.'

195

'Oh, right,' said Darren, 'well, we have four of them. Take your pick.'
Looking thoroughly dejected, the Chief shuffled towards a corner. 'Except that one,' said Darren quickly. 'Sorry, it's still a bit wet there.' Stopping in mid-shuffle, the Chief turned slightly and shuffled in another direction, telling Darren that it wasn't his fault as he went.

Watching the Chief settle in his chosen corner, his head bent and resting on the stones of the wall, Darren couldn't help but think this was a right puckle – packle – predicament.

CHAPTER 94

With boB dangling from her hand, Mary led Tom, Cat and Deirdre through to the lounge.

'Hey Tom, how's it hanging?' said Marc/Abdul as Tom entered.

'Eh,' said Tom. 'Marc?' He looked like Marc, sounded like Marc, but Marc never called him Tom.

'Not Marc,' said Mary, seeing the baffled look on Tom's face. 'that's Abdul.' The look deepened.

'Cat,' exclaimed Kate/Charmaine, when she walked in, 'heard a lot about you.'

'Katie knows about you?' said a gobsmacked Tom. Until then, he had thought Cat's identity was unknown to Lucy and the kids. True, they had seen a cat wandering here and there at home, but only as a cat, a stray.

'Don't worry,' said Cat, 'I'll get you all caught up in a moment.' She had worked out all was not as it seemed. She wondered where the real Lucy and kids were?

'You will?' said Tom, his face a mixture of emotions, mostly bewilderment. 'In what?'

'Sit down, Tom, and I'll explain in a minute.'

A perplexed Tom was finding it hard to understand the last few minutes. First, a woman Cat say's is Mary, his ex-wife, opened the loo door. Then Marc, his grandson, acts strangely. And then, to cap it all, Kate knows about Cat. What in the world of madness was going on? What next; Lucy rides in on a tiger dressed as a cod? The tiger dressed as a cod, not Lucy. Was he going mad?

'Hi Dad,' said Lucy, walking in from the kitchen.

Thank goodness for that, thought a relieved Tom, some sense at last. He smiled at her. Perhaps some answers? It was a good thing Tom was sitting down because just as he was about to ask Lucy what was going on, she, thinking all knew what was afoot, morphed into her true self, Ruth. He fainted.

'Ruth,' scolded Mary/Rhian, 'time and a place.' This was the Mary that had greeted everyone and grabbed boB, his "Oi!" giving him away.

'Sorry,' said Ruth, 'too soon?' She became Lucy again. 'Is he okay?'

'He's fine,' said Cat, after finding a pulse with her nose. Might be for the best, she thought, thinking about it. She had to find out what was going on, and with Tom sure to be asking a multitude of questions, it would be easier with him having forty winks while she did.

Just then, the front door opened, and Smokowski and Willy walked in, herded by Mary, the real one.

Poor old Smokowski's eyes widened when he saw Cat. Wider still when he saw Tom slumped in a chair.

'He's resting,' said Cat.

'Oh,' said Smokowski, who decided he would leave his questions for later; he had a more pressing matter at the moment. Namely, Mary's hand shoving him in the back.

With Smokowski and Willy safely ensconced on a sofa, Mary scanned the room. She smiled grimly. 'I see all the gang's here,' she said. 'The question is, why are you all here?'

CHAPTER 95

The small hatch in the door stood open. Arwen, who had been spying on the prisoners through it but a second ago, had just gasped and quickly turned away.

'What's up?' said Alwyn.

'Darren took the other blokes mask off.'

'Good grief,' exclaimed Alwyn, getting up from his chair. 'Shut it quickly.'

Arwen did, but it was too late. He knew something.

'It's too late, isn't it?' said Alwyn.

'I know something,' wailed a stricken Arwen.

'Quickly,' said Alwyn, 'sit down; I'll get you a cup of tea.' Alwyn scampered off to get one with plenty of sweeteners in it. He had heard sweet tea was supposed to be good for shock.

When he got back with it, Arwen was looking a little grey about the edges. 'Here,' said Alwyn, 'drink this.'

'It won't do any good,' groaned Arwen. 'I saw something. I saw who was under the hood.' He took a sip and spat it straight out again. 'Yuk,' he spluttered. 'You know I don't take sugar!'

'There wasn't any in there,' said Alwyn, 'I used sweeteners.'

Arwen scowled at him and put the cup down.

'But it can't be that bad.'

'It was,' said Arwen, 'tasted flipping 'orrible.'

'Not the tea, I mean what you saw,' said Alwyn. 'As long as you don't know who it is, you're all right. We know Darren, but we don't know who he is.'

'But I do,' wailed Arwen, 'it's the Chief Traveller.'

'LA-LA-LA-LA!!' resounded around the guardroom as soon as Arwen got to "it's the". Alwyn, with his fingers in his ears, did not want to know. No need both of them knowing. Who would hire them on a need-to-know basis if they both knew things they shouldn't need to know? With fingers still firmly in earholes, he scampered off. He had heard that sweet tea was good for thinking. He liked sugar. It also got him out of earshot.

CHAPTER 96

As Mary waited for an answer from the many faces looking at each other to see who would go first, she noticed Tom, who she had thought was asleep, had a strange look on his face. 'Is he all right?' she asked.

Lucy/Ruth admitted her mistake.

'Oh,' said Mary. Might be for the best, she thought, echoing Cat, less to deal with. She now addressed the faces. 'As no one seems eager to offer an answer, I'll get the ball rolling. Smokowski?'

A rabbit caught in headlights would not do justice to describe the look on Smokowski's face at that moment.

'Er,' said Smokowski, 'I, that is we,' sharing the blame should there be any, 'found Tom, so came to tell you.' He cast a quick glance in Tom's direction. He was still out for the count.

'You said,' said Mary, 'and that is all?'

'You said we had to find him, and we did,' said Willy, coming to aid his comrade-in-searching.

'That I did,' said Mary, casting a quick stern eye over Smokowski and a slower one over Willy, 'and as you succeeded in your mission, I want to congratulate you both on a job well done.'

Smokowski and Willy felt relief roll over them. They didn't know why; they had done nothing wrong. A moment later, the relief rolled off again.

'Just one more thing though,' said Mary, her gaze intensifying, 'why was Invisible Bob working with you?'

Willy and Smokowski immediately tried to talk at once, each trying to get themselves heard over the other.

'Willy,' snapped Mary, bringing order, 'you tell me.'

'We didn't know,' said Willy.

'It's true,' said Smokowski.

Mary had figured as much.

'Okay,' said Mary, 'Rhian, can you please take Smokowski and Willy to the kitchen and make them a cuppa? Rhian/Mary nodded. 'Good, and when you're done, could you bring those invisible rascals back in with you? Thank you.' Rhian led them into the kitchen.

'Did someone mention a cuppa?' Tom had come round.

'And Rhian, could you bring one in for Tom, please?'

'Will do.'

'And a biscuit?' said Tom.

'I'll have a look,' said Rhian.

Although Tom's hearing was still sharp, especially at the mention of a cuppa, he was still dazed. Who were these people? he thought, who was this woman giving the orders?

Now Tom was back with them. Mary decided her next questions would be for him and Cat. She would ignore the Deirdre woman for the moment. She would also save the question she would like to ask for later. No one was going anywhere for the moment. So, intrigued as she was by all the goings-on that had been going on, she would focus on Tom and Cat.

'So,' said Mary, 'how did they find you?'

'To be honest,' said Cat, 'I've no idea.'

'Nor me,' said Tom, studying Mary in a not so discreet way. Cat decided it might be for the best to give his memory a little jog. Tom blinked. 'Wait a minute,' he exclaimed, 'is that you, Mary?' He hadn't seen her in years.

'Yes,' said Mary, 'but before you ask me any questions you might have, I would like answers to my questions first.'

Fair do, thought Tom. Who, when he thought about it, didn't actually have any others.

'They discovered Tom had been in a café,' said Rhian/Mary, relaying from the kitchen what Smokowski and Willy had told her after hearing the question.

'Why were you in a Café?' said Mary, who was aghast. They were supposed to have been kidnapped, keeping out of sight. They should have been somewhere else.

'I'm sorry,' said Cat, who then told Mary about how they had discovered boB, that he was working for the Chief, and the need for doughnuts, which was why Tom had been in a café.

'The Bob was spying for the Chief?' said a stunned Mary when Cat had finished. 'Why?'

'They both were,' said Rhian/Mary, coming from the kitchen with a cuppa and biscuits for Tom.

'Both of them?' said Mary.

'And according to Smokowski, it was Willy who'd discovered Tom had been there,' said Rhian/Mary. 'Something to do with a paper cup and a note amongst other things.' She went to hand Tom the cuppa she had brought for him, but he was too busy trying to free his hand from between the arm and seat of the chair he was sitting on. 'Tom, your cuppa.' Tom looked up.

Thankfully Cat, alive to the situation, caught the cup and saucer in an antigravity field before any harm could be done. The sight of another Mary looming large had been too much for Tom's mind to take in, and he had shut down again.

'What happened?' said a concerned Mary.

'One too many Marys,' said Cat.

'I'm so sorry,' said Rhian/Mary, 'I didn't think.'

'Not your fault,' said Mary, 'none of us did.' She walked over to Tom, leaned down, and lifted one of his eyelids. He seemed to be there still, somewhere. Some people's minds, confronted by something as unusual as Tom had just experienced, would shut down, sometimes for good. Thankfully, it hadn't happened often and only, so far, to people of above-average intelligence. Tom was way safe of that.

'I'll glamour him when he comes round,' said Cat, hoping he could cope with so many glamours in the space of such a short time. First Lucy morphing, now this. Some people— No, thought Cat, he'll be okay. And thinking of Lucy, where was she? And, on that matter, the kids? She asked.

'They're safe,' said Mary, 'but that's all I'm saying for the moment.' She put a hand to her ear and wiggled it for Cat's eyes only. Her way of saying you never know who might be listening. Cat nodded. 'Now, what cup and what note?'

Rhian/Mary relayed what Smokowski and Willy had told her about the cup.

'I remember Tom swopping the paper cup for his cup at the cottage,' said Cat.

'And this note?' said Mary.

'They thought it a clue to finding Tom and Cat,' said Rhian/Mary.

'What did it say?'

'Haven't got a clue,' said Rhian/Mary.

'They wouldn't tell you?' said Mary, preparing to have a word with them herself.

'No,' smiled Rhian/Mary, 'that's what it said on the note.'

'Oh,' said Mary, calming down, 'how odd.'

'A-hem,' coughed Cat, 'I can throw some light on that, I wrote it.'

'You?' said Mary, 'Sorry for my ignorance, but I didn't know cats could write.'

'I used magic,' Cat confessed. 'I thought I'd give it a go. Never know if it might come in handy one day.'

'But why write haven't got a clue?'

'Tom asked me what I was going to write, and I said...' Cat raised her eyebrows.

'So, Willy's not an aspiring detective then?' said Mary.

'Sound like they happened on us by accident,' said Cat.

'To be fair, Willy did use the paper cup to find them,' said Rhian/Mary.

'I suppose,' said Mary, musing. Secretly she was pleased Willy had. Maybe give credit where credit's due? But later, when she was sure he wasn't on the wrong side. Now though, it was time to talk to those Invisible's.

'I'll get them,' said Rhian/Mary.

'And Rhian.'

'Yes?'

'Perhaps you could be you again?'

'Ah.' Rhian/Mary was just Rhian again.

'And one other thing,' said Mary as Rhian went to go, 'make sure we can see them.'

'Will do.'

'But not every bit of them,' added Mary, pulling a face.

Rhian smiled and went to get them.

CHAPTER 97

'Hi,' said Cedric cheerily as he knocked on Deirdre's office door. 'I have cakes.' The cakes were a surprise for Deirdre to cheer her up. The kidnapping of Darren on her watch, their watch, had upset her.

After a few more knocks and no answer, Cedric tentatively opened the door. No Deirdre. He checked the ladies, again tentatively. He then tried the Chief's office and got no answer there either. Where was everyone? he wondered, staff meeting? Cedric checked the conference room and, finding no one there, checked the Chief's washroom. All empty. Strange, thought Cedric, neither Deirdre nor the Chief wandered far from home. Only one place left.

After checking the ops room and being told that Deirdre had been looking for the Chief earlier, Cedric started to worry. It was procedure for anyone who left the Travellers Headquarters to report to him or his second in command to book them out. But he hadn't been here, and it was the second in command's day off. Cedric chewed on his lip. Should not have slipped out to buy cakes, he thought. Worse, he had told no one he was going. He needed to get to his security detail fast and find out if anyone knew anything.

CHAPTER 98

'Hello?' called Darren through the small grill in the door. 'Anyone there?' No one answered. All was quiet on the other side of the door; it had been for some time.

What do I do? wondered Darren. Surely they wouldn't leave me here for all eternity? A prisoner, shut in with a man who appeared to be edging towards insanity. He took a quick peep behind him at the Chief, still in the corner but now sitting on the floor swaying back and forth. He could only just make out what the Chief was saying; he was telling the world, repeatedly in a whisper, interspersed here and there with the odd whimper and sob, that he was a naughty person.

Darren tried again, but this time a little louder. Still no answer. A prisoner, shut in with a budding lunatic. Worse still; a prisoner wearing a potato sack. Where was the dignity in that? Oh, woe was he. And why hadn't they given him his clothes back yet? They had to be dry by now? Darren scratched at his neck. He was sure the sack was host to a multitude of fleas. Louder still this time, Darren hollered at the grill.

'What?' asked someone so close to the grill it made Darren jump. It took Darren a moment or two to recover. 'I-er,' he stammered.

'Ain't got all day yer know.' It was Arwen.

'I need to get out,' said Darren, with all the authority of someone with none. He scratched at an armpit.

'Don't we all,' said Arwen, sounding a little down.

'You need to get out as well?' said an unsure Darren.

'Yeah,' said Arwen, 'but mine is a situation, not a dungeon.'

With no idea of what Arwen was talking about, Darren asked where his clothes were while he had an audience.

'Life-threatening,' said Arwen, not listening to Darren. His mind weighed down as it was.

'What is?' asked Darren, suddenly alert. His clothes could wait.

'The situation,' said Arwen.

'Oh,' said Darren, cautiously relieved. He didn't sound unwell, thought Darren. Unless he was covered in spots. Spots could be dangerous. And as Darren couldn't see Arwen. 'You got spots?'

'What?' said Arwen.

'You got spots?'

'Bit personal,' said Arwen.

'I only ask as spots can sometimes be a life-threatening situation,' said Darren.

'Oi!' shouted someone on Arwen's side of the door. 'No fraternising with the prisoners.' It was Alwyn, who was just returning with a third sugary cuppa. The last two had done nothing to calm his nerves. He now doubted the third one would either.

'He wants his clothes back,' said Arwen.

'And to be let out,' said Darren quickly.

'Can't do that,' said Alwyn, placing his cup on the jailer's table. 'But I think your clothes might be dry by now.' He put a hand on Arwen's shoulder. 'Arwen here will go look, won't you?'

'Me? Dogsbody is what I am,' said Arwen. He walked away huffing.

'I don't mind if they're slightly damp,' shouted Darren after Arwen.

'Now,' said Alwyn, sidling up to the door grill when Arwen was safely out of sight, 'I have a proposition for you.'

'A proposition?' said Darren.

'Aye,' said Alwyn. 'There's a little situation that has cropped up.'

'Is it life-threatening?'

Eyebrows rose on the other side of the door. 'Dangerous,' said Alwyn, 'but hopefully not life-threatening.'

Two situations, thought Darren, what's the chances?

'It's like this,' said Alwyn, 'someone knows something they shouldn't, and it needs to be put right.'

'I see,' said Darren, who didn't. Behind him, the Chief was now facing the other way and had thankfully gone quiet. This was perhaps due to a bruise on the back of his head caused by a rather thrusting backward sway.

'So desperate times need desperate measures,' said Alwyn, 'and that's where you come in.'

'Ah,' said Darren. Come in where? thought Darren, he wasn't out yet to come in. Maybe he meant the room behind the door. Aha, thought Darren, now we're getting somewhere. There was one slight problem that Darren could see, though; he had nothing to measure with. Perhaps they did.

With his hopes rising, Darren asked Alwyn if he meant the dungeon door when he'd said that's where he came in?

'Maybe, maybe not,' said Alwyn.

'Oh,' said Darren.

'We need your help,' said Alwyn. 'That's what I meant by where you come in.'

'My help?' said Darren.

'Yes,' said Alwyn, 'to get us out of it.'

Get them out of it? puzzled Darren, didn't he mean, get them out of there? He didn't understand what was going on. But if Alwyn did mean *it*, what did that mean? He should ask.

But before he could, Arwen arrived back with Darren's clothes. Nearly all of Darren's clothes. His underpants were missing. Alwyn had purposely hidden them to give him more time to discuss his plan with Darren. A hidden delicate to help a delicate situation.

'Where're my underpants?' demanded Darren.

'They were there when I hung your clothes up,' said Arwen.

'Better go look for them,' said Alwyn, 'we don't want our prisoner to get a cold, do we? Questions might be asked.'

Backing from the cell and shutting the door after him, a grumbling Arwen ambled over to the stairs that led to the rooms above.

When Arwen was safely out of sight, Alwyn, cuppa in hand, resumed the conversation with Darren.

'You have to bribe Arwen to let you go,' said Alwyn. He sipped at his tea. It was the only way Alwyn could think of getting around the situation he and Arwen were in. The situation of knowing something they shouldn't like Arwen did. And although he was innocent, the powers that be would find him guilty by association.

'Bribe Arwen?'

'Do you repeat everything someone says to you?'

'Repeat?' said Darren. Tom would have been proud of him.

'Never mind,' said Alwyn. 'It's like this, and tell no one I told you what I'm about to tell you, okay?' Darren nodded. 'There would be heck to pay if what I told you got out. The Guild of Jailers would never forgive us, and they put on quite a do on the day of Winter Solstice.' Alwyn had a faraway look in his eye as he spoke. There followed a pause and a sigh as he remembered. 'Anyway,' said Alwyn, pulling himself together, 'as I was saying, bribe Arwen with more than our present employers are paying us. It's how it works.' He tapped a finger to his nose and winked. 'No one is supposed to know. A trade secret, you see. You are then our employers, and you can then tell us to open the door, close our eyes, and count to a hundred.'

'What then?'

'We open them and discover you've escaped somehow while we weren't looking.'

'But shouldn't I bribe both of you?' said Darren, beginning to see the light and playing into Alwyn's hands.

'Hmmm,' said Alwyn, relieved that Darren was brighter than he looked, 'you have a point. Tell you what then, this is how it'll go.'

How it would go was Alwyn would make an excuse to leave them alone, then Darren would approach Arwen with the bribe. That way Alwyn would know nothing about it. Which meant, and Alwyn never mentioned this to Darren, that if something went wrong and the finger of blame was pointed – even though it was legal and proper, except where he, Alwyn, had illegally told Darren about the escape clause, but no one would need to know that – it would be pointed at Arwen, leaving him in the clear.

'How much?' said Darren, thinking this sort of shenanigans wouldn't have happened in his time. Jailers were not for buying then. The very idea was more than their life was worth. A life-threatening situation. Oh! Is that what Arwen had meant? he wondered.

'You must guess,' said Alwyn.

'Can't you give me a clue?'

'Shh, he's coming.' Arwen was coming down the steps carrying Darren's missing item of clothing. 'But if it helps, we are reasonably cheap.'

But Darren had one more question. 'What does that someone know that he shouldn't?'

'He knows who that is in the corner,' said Alwyn. He had a gulp of tea and started for the table.

'Oh,' said Darren, 'you mean the Chief Traveller.'

The mouthful of tea Alwyn had just taken suddenly sprayed from his mouth. Luckily, it missed Darren's underpants. 'Drat,' said Alwyn, or words to that effect, as he wiped tea from his chin and Arwen's surprised face.

CHAPTER 99

'Not fair,' wailed Invisible Bob as he and boB were carried into the lounge.

'What isn't?' enquired Mary, who had her back to them as a minor disturbance had drawn her attention.

The disturbance was Tom. 'What-where-who?' he spluttered as he suddenly rejoined the world about him. He sat up, eyes wide. He looked at Mary. Glanced at the Bobs. Studied Rhian. 'What the...'

'I'll fill you in in a minute,' said Cat, patting Tom on the knee.

'But?'

'In a minute,' soothed Cat. She had decided against glamouring him again, so instead hit him with a relaxation spell. 'There-there.'

With a mind now filled with fluffy clouds and the sound of whales singing, Tom sank back into his chair, thinking what a wonderful world.

Disturbance over, Invisible Bob continued with his whining. 'Look,' he said, holding his arms out so Mary could see his disgruntlement.

Mary turned and just managed to stifle a chuckle. 'Oh,' is all she could say.

'Well?' squealed Bob.

'Rhian?' said Mary, raising an eyebrow.

'Sorry,' said Rhian. 'I had to improvise. The only male clothes I could find to fit them were on some toy soldiers, but they all looked the same. So it's the only way we would be able to tell them apart.'

'I'm taller,' said an indignant Invisible Bob.

'You are not,' argued boB.

'Sindy or Barbie?' asked an amused Cat.

'Barbie,' said Rhian, grinning.

'Fetching,' said Cat, smiling.

'It is not,' growled a scowling Invisible Bob, who was modelling a two-piece ensemble comprising a red Bolero jacket edged in gold with matching culottes. The jacket was more like a coat on him, but the culottes, which were short, fitted him perfectly.

'Why is Invisible Bob wearing a skirt?' asked Tom, who had drifted from his clouds for a moment.

'I'm not,' wailed Invisible Bob.

'He is,' sniggered boB.

'Enough!' snapped Mary, deciding enough was enough. It was time to get down to business. The questioning of the Bobs. 'Dress or no dress, you're in it, get over it.' She went over to the Bobs who were in large glass jars on the sideboard. As well as dressed in toy clothes, they were also doused in flour. 'Now, what was it exactly you were doing for the Chief?'

The Bobs adopted furtive looks under the flour and exchanged a glance.

'Well!' bellowed Mary, making them and some in the room jump.

'I didn't want to do it!' wailed boB, 'he made me do it.' He pointed at the other jar.

'I did not,' wailed Invisible Bob, 'it was—'

'I don't want to hear who or why. I want to know what?!' Mary had raised her voice even higher, and now there was anger in it. 'Tell me.'

The two Bobs wilted under Mary's glare. Who would break first? But there was a matter of honour at stake. Bobs' never blabbed. Bobs' weren't grasses. At least not until there was a very good reason to do so. The two Bobs exchanged glances. Was Mary's rising anger a good enough reason? No. They folded their arms and took on stubborn looks.

'I have a phone,' said Mary, her voice now a threatening whisper as she changed tack. The Bobs gave her a wary look. 'It has a camera on it.'

Invisible Bob's invisible face turned white under the flour. He would be a laughing stock dressed as he was. A very good reason to blab had reared its ugly head. He gave boB a helpless look. boB returned a sympathetic one and nodded. Bobs' knew when they were beaten. They would blab, but it would be an honourable one, which was more than could be said for Mary's below the belt tactics. Invisible Bob blabbed.

When they had blabbed their all – boB had joined in out of solidarity – Mary had them returned to the kitchen.

'Well,' said Mary, flopping onto a chair. 'What was he thinking?'

'Perhaps it was his way of keeping an eye on things,' said Cat, thinking she would have done the same in his position.

'Maybe,' said Mary, who was thinking the same. She glanced at Tom. He looked bemused but chilled out. She wondered if it was time to give him a clear head and bring him back into the here and now? Would be fair, she thought. 'Cat, I think it's time to bring Tom up to speed.'

Up to speed and back to his state of normal, Tom shook his head. 'Well,' he said, 'wonders will never cease.'

'Indeed,' said Mary.

Tom licked his lips. He was thirsty. Relaxing could do that to you.

'A cuppa Tom?' said Mary.

Cuppa on its way, Mary pondered aloud on where they had got to before Tom was enlightened.

'The Chief,' said Deirdre. Apart from the briefest hello on arrival, she had kept herself to herself until now. Mary stared hard at her. Deirdre stood her ground where others might have wilted. 'I'm sure he had only good intentions.'

'And you are?' Cat had introduced Deirdre as just that, no more when they had arrived.

'Deirdre,' said Deirdre, 'I'm the Chief's secretary and bodyguard.'

'Multitasking, eh?'

'It's what I'm paid to do.'

After a moment of appraisal, Mary decided she liked her. An honest face, a responsible attitude, and, it would appear, not shy of hard work. But still, she stayed wary of her. 'Why do you say the Chief's intentions were good?'

'Tea up,' said Rhian, bringing Tom his cuppa and biscuits.

'Coo, ta,' said Tom on seeing the chocolate digestives. He immediately dunked one, which immediately broke in half. The half in the cup, now floating on top of the tea. 'Drat.'

Intrigued, Deirdre watched Tom try to retrieve the floating half from his cuppa. There was always something to boggle a new acquaintance's mind when getting to know Tom. 'Sorry,' said Deirdre, realising what she was doing. 'Because he's a good person.'

'A lot of good people do bad things,' said Mary.

'I know, but he changed just before Tom and Cat arrived.'

'How so?'

'He became distant. Worried about something. It was as if he had something on his mind.'

This prompted Cat to air the doubts she had been having about the Chief.

'But I'm sure he wouldn't do anything wrong,' said Deirdre.

'Then,' said Mary, 'why didn't he do as we had arranged?'

Ears pricking, Cat asked Mary what she meant.

Even Tom's attention drifted from his tea and the sinking biscuit he had failed to retrieve. Licking soggy crumbs from his fingers, he waited for Mary's response.

'I had given him strict instructions that when you Cat, Tom and Darren arrived at the Travellers, he was to send you directly to me at the scene of the crime at the Ladies Institute HQ. Posthaste I had told him.'

'Crime?' queried Tom.

'The missing Jam,' whispered Cat.

'Oh yeah,' said Tom, slightly embarrassed. He had forgotten all about the Jam in the general melee of the past couple of days.

'I take it the Chief never mentioned this to you?' Mary asked Cat.

'No,' said Cat.

'Maybe he forgot,' said Deirdre. 'He's had a lot on his plate lately.'

'Maybe he did, maybe he didn't,' said Mary, 'but until his whereabouts come to light, and we can ask him, I think we should err on the side of he didn't, whatever the reason.'

'So,' said Cat, 'what now?'

'We do what we should have done in the first place,' said Mary. 'Tom, take us to HQ. The sooner we find who took the Jam, the better.'

Downing the last of his tea – one never knew when the next one would happen along – Tom forgot about the soggy biscuit remains at the bottom and began choking and sputtering on them.

'You okay?' said Mary, preparing to slap him on the back.

'Fine,' coughed Tom.

'Good, let's catch that thief red-handed.'

'How're we going to do that?' whispered Tom.

'I suspect we'll find out,' Cat whispered back.

Mary turned to Deirdre. 'Would you like to come? Might be handy having someone along who can handle themselves.' What she meant was: I want you to come along so I can keep an eye on you. Mary thought it prudent to bring along the person who had been closest to the Chief the last couple of days.

'I'd love too,' said Deirdre.

'That's settled then,' said Mary, 'but before we go, I want to introduce the friend who has been helping me. She's been waiting in the kitchen. Mary went to fetch her. She also wanted to give her the heads up as to what was in the offing.

At last, thought Cat, wondering who Mary's mysterious helper was, but Cat was to be disappointed. Mary's friend had already left.

A little disappointed that her friend had left without a goodbye, Mary left a note to let her friend know where they were going and returned to the lounge.

'Sorry people,' said Mary, 'but I'm afraid my friend has been called away. But never mind. Rhian, you're in charge until we get back. Mind you watch those scallywags in the kitchen. We don't want them going anywhere.'

'They won't,' said Rhian.

'Okay, let's go,' said Mary, 'and Tom, please wipe those soggy crumbs from your top lip.'

CHAPTER 100

A happy family scene. A parent and her children huddled around a board game. Laughing and smiling as one went up a ladder, and another slithered down a snake. Except there was something wrong with this scene. It was not a natural family scene, not natural at all.

The boy, the youngest of the family, would usually have snorted derision at the mention of a game not played on a computer or console.

The girl, head usually stuck between the pages of music and fashion magazines, would have been appalled at the suggestion of a children's board game. Didn't her mother know how old she was?

As for mother, ordinarily, she would have found the game, rubbed the dust off it, and wondered why they didn't play board games anymore before putting it back.

The scene was not natural at all. Fogging did that to you sometimes.

Kate laughed as her mother's counter slithered down a snake.

'Oh-no,' wailed Lucy, feigning horror.

'Bad luck, mum,' said Marc, grinning as now he was in the lead.

'What was that?' said Kate.

'What was what?' asked Lucy.

'I thought I heard a pin drop.'

'That's funny,' said Marc, 'I thought I heard a flea scratching.'

'Now you mention it,' said Lucy, 'I thought I heard a bell tinkling.'

There then came a sudden knock-knock-knocking on the door.

'I wonder who that can be?' said Lucy, standing.

'Perhaps it's dad,' said Marc, who found he couldn't remember him all that well.

'Yes, dad,' said Kate, 'perhaps he's got a film.' She didn't know why she thought that.

'And a curry,' said Lucy, heading for the door. She suddenly stopped in her tracks. Curry? Where did that come from? And why was the thought of it tugging at her mind? More strange thoughts now surfaced. Darren? Her husband. Why was it so difficult for her to visualise him? And then it wasn't. It could be Darren. But if it was, why didn't he have a key? Because they were on holiday. Not at home. The realisation now brought a flood of memories back to her. Something wasn't right.

And as she had those thoughts, those realisations, the front door to the cottage was kicked in.

'Removals!' said the first through the door.

CHAPTER 101

Darren managed to scrape together a bribe that outdid the wages Arwen and Alwyn were promised by their present employers. And, after a few minutes of arguing between themselves, as to who should have searched Darren in the first place before putting him in the cell and why they hadn't, between them, noticed he had stuff in his pockets when they dried his clothes, Alwyn and Arwen accepted the bribe.

And what a bribe it was. A magic looking glass that made things bigger than they were when you looked at them through it. A many bladed weapon that Darren called a combi-tool. A combi-cool is what Arwen had called it. And lastly, a packet containing small flannels that were already wet and smelled of lemons. You could wash at any time with them without the need for water. They decided they would trade them at the earliest opportunity. Whoever heard of a clean jailer?

But all in all, a fair payment. Far better than the two copper pennies and spa day for two on offer. As neither Arwen nor Alwyn had known what a spa day was, the copper pennies had swung the deal. Darren had said he thought it was a day in a shop as Mister Smokowski, a shopkeeper, and his boss, had mentioned it sometimes as he wailed aloud at some of the bargains some other shops managed to offer. "How do they do it?" He would say. So it was left at that, with no one the wiser.

'Ready yet?' called Darren from the cell.

'Not yet,' came the reply from the other side of the cell door.

Two cups stood empty on the guardroom table. Beside them were two rucksacks in the process of being hurriedly packed.

'Only take what we need,' said Alwyn, folding and packing his favourite pair of leather lederhosen, black, tight, yet surprisingly comfortable.

'I haven't enough room,' wailed Arwen, 'I need everything.'

'Well, you don't need that,' said Alwyn, gently removing the handle of a toilet potty from Arwen's grip. Where the rest of the potty was, only Arwen knew. He threw the handle over his shoulder.

'Oh,' said Arwen, who hadn't realised what he was doing. He slumped into a chair. It was all getting to him, knowing something. 'Sorry,' he sighed, 'I'm all of a dither.'

'No sugar Sherlock,' said Alwyn, who *had* noticed. And talking of sugar, Alwyn had an idea that might save time. 'Tell you what,' he said, 'why don't you make yourself a cuppa and then sit there while I finish the packing?' Time was of the essence. The sooner they were away, the better. Even though what they were doing was legal; legal-ish, he didn't wholly trust their now ex-employers to agree; they were the sort of *not people* you didn't want to get on the wrong side of.

CHAPTER 102

'Flusher,' said Tom, 'check.' He wiggled the flusher handle. 'Toilet seat down, check.'

Sat on her shelf, Cat stared at Tom. This is new, she thought.

'Door shut,' he continued, 'check.'

'What are you doing?' whispered Cat.

'Pre-flight checks,' said Tom, looking at Cat as if she was crazy.

'Why?' said Cat, 'you've never done it before.'

'Ha-ha,' laughed Tom, looking at Mary and Deirdre. 'She will have her little joke.'

There's only one little joke here, thought Cat. And then she understood. He was trying to show off to the ladies.

'Can't be too careful,' said Tom, looking for all the world the idiot he was trying not to be as he gave the ladies a cheesy grin. 'All ready? Good. Then check.'

'Tom,' hissed Cat, 'get on with it.'

Tom narrowed his eyes at Cat but continued. 'Hold tight, please!' He said, reminiscent of the days of bus ticket collectors. He closed his eyes, followed this with a wiggle of the flusher, and then took on the look of the constipated.

'Is he okay?' asked Deirdre.

'Open to opinion,' said Cat.

'We're here,' announced Tom. 'All ashore who's going ashore.'

Shaking her head, Cat jumped from the shelf and asked Mary to see if Tom was right.

'Of course, we are,' said an indignant Tom.

'Looks like we've landed in the executive toilet,' said Mary.

'All present and correct,' said Tom, saluting smartly. 'All ashore—'

'Tom!' snapped Cat.

'Only saying,' said Tom, pouting.

Confident they were where they were supposed to be, Cat led the way out of the Loo, followed by Mary, Deirdre and, bringing up the rear, Tom. He felt the ship's captain should always be the last to leave, especially when one was travelling into the unknown. Once out of the executive toilet, Mary led them to her office.

CHAPTER 103

'What about now?' said Darren.

'Flipping 'eck,' said Alwyn to himself. As the only one packing, he was doing the best he could. 'Nearly there.'

'You said that just now,' said Darren.

'And I will again if you keep on with the same question.' said Alwyn, desperately shoving stuff in the rucksacks.

'How about now?' said Darren, hoping the slight change to the wording would somehow move things along.

'Grrr,' growled Alwyn.

Darren decided it might be better to wait before he asked again.

An exasperated Alwyn, with no help, or help that only hindered, from Arwen, who was still in a dither, even worse maybe, the sugary cuppa hadn't worked at all, was close to finishing. Alwyn hadn't a clue where Arwen had got the full-size stuffed giraffe from or where he had been keeping it and didn't waste time asking him. It lay on the floor with the potty handle and other similar detritus.

'There,' said Alwyn, 'finished.'

Hurrah! thought Darren, an ear pressed against the grill.

'Right,' said Alwyn, 'get ready to open the door.'

Hand on the door handle, Arwen waited.

'Now-Wait!' Alwyn's nose had wrinkled. What was that smell? He sniffed. It was coming from Arwen's rucksack. He carefully opened it.

At the door, Arwen had adopted a worried look.

'What the—' cried Alwyn, as he pulled from the rucksack a kipper that had seen much, much better days. 'No-no-no,' he cried.

'But you never know when we might need it,' wailed Arwen.

Now holding his nose, Alwyn threw the offending fish into the corner with Arwen's other "you never know" offerings. It landed with a splat.

'Now,' said Alwyn, 'time to open the door.'

On the other side of the door, Darren wasn't sure what Alwyn said. 'Did you say now?' he whispered.

'Yes,' said Alwyn, whose hearing was above average.

'Great,' said Darren, holding back a little jig.

The door handle turned. The door opened. The jailers stepped back. Darren took a step towards the open door.

'Wait!' said Alwyn, 'we haven't started counting yet.'

'Oh yes,' said Darren, remembering. 'Sorry.'

'One. Two.' The counting was slow and solemn.

'Now?' said Darren.

'Three, yes. Four.'

With the Chief on his arm, Darren stepped through the doorway.

'Five. Six.'

Darren second step was tentative. Was he really about to escape?

'Seven. Eight.'

The third step taken was when Darren realised the Chief was no longer holding his arm.

'Nine. Ten.'

'Oh drat,' said Darren, returning to the cell.

'Eleven. Problem? twelve.'

'I've lost the Chief,' said Darren, from inside. A quick scan of the cell found the Chief had returned to his corner.

'Thirteen. What? Fourteen.'

In the corner, the Chief was refusing to move. He would take his punishment. He didn't deserve to be free.

'Fifteen. Sixteen.'

'He won't come out of the corner,' yelled Darren.

'Seventeen. Drat, eighteen. Hang about, nineteen.'

'Twenty. This will do it, twenty-one.' Alwyn took something from his pocket and walked into the cell and across to the Chief. 'Twenty-two.'

'What's that?' said Darren, as he spied something in Alwyn's hand.

'Twenty-three. Elsie, twenty-four,' said Alwyn.

'Elsie?'

'Yeah, twenty-five. My cosh, twenty-six.'

'Cosh?' But before Darren's mind could fully comprehend the consequences of what this meant, it was too late to do anything about it.

'Twenty-seven.' The thud of a cosh hitting home. 'Twenty-eight. You had better, twenty-nine, pick him up, thirty, and go, thirty-one.'

'But-why-I,' stuttered a stunned Darren.

'Easier, thirty-two. Quicker, thirty-three,' said Alwyn, as he left.

Darren rushed over to the Chief. He had yet another bump, but at least the wailing and rocking had stopped. Darren supposed he should be grateful. He heaved the Chief, who was lighter than he looked, to his relief, onto his shoulder and carried him from the cell.

'Thirty-four. Thirty-five. Thirty-six.'

Once outside, Alwyn gave Darren directions for his escape.

'Thirty-seven. Up the stairs, thirty-eight. Door to the right, thirty-nine.'

Not needing to be told twice, Darren bounded, as best he could with the Chief over his shoulder, up the stairs and at the top, headed for the door on the right. Below him, he could still hear them counting.

'All the fours, forty-four.'

'What?' said Alwyn.

'Bingo,' yelled Arwen.

'Forty-five,' said Alwyn, frowning at Arwen and wondering if he might not be better off on his own.

With some weight shifting, Darren opened the door. Bright sunlight flooded the landing. Well, I'll be, thought Darren as his eyes grew accustomed to the light, I think I know where I am.

Shifting weight to his other shoulder, Darren glanced behind him to see if there was anyone about, there wasn't, and took his first steps to freedom down yet another set of stairs. This one in a spiral. At the bottom, he should have made with the swift removal from the area, but curiosity had got the better of him. He wanted to gaze upon the castle that had held him captive. He took a few steps away from the bottom step. He gazed. He frowned. There was no castle, just a large warehouse with the door he had made his escape from standing open above him.

As he stood there, dumbfounded, the sound of counting drifted down to his ears. Oops, he thought, time to make tracks. Stopping at the edge of the pavement he, looked both ways, then checked again. All clear, he headed for the opening to an alley. An alley that he hoped would lead him to where he hoped it would take him.

'The keys to the door, twenty-one.' Arwen had lost the plot.

'Seventy-eight,' said Alwyn, scowling at him.

And then a sudden moment of clarity. 'Do you think we should go now?' said Arwen, catching Alwyn by surprise.

'What? Seventy-nine. No, we have to count to one hundred,' said Alwyn, 'it's the rule, eighty.'

'But what if they arrive before we finish?'

'Eighty-one.' Blimey, thought Alwyn, what if they did? Alwyn decided it might be best if they didn't find out. There would be no eighty-two this day. The next time they had to count, he would count to one hundred and nineteen to make up for it. 'Let's go,' said Alwyn.

'Top of the shop, ninety,' said Arwen, clarity's moment now over.

Grabbing Arwen's arm, Alwyn dragged him up the stairs. At the top, as he reached for the handle of the left door, staff, he thought he heard a noise from behind it. A pin dropping? There was no time to spare. Alwyn pulled Arwen through the door Darren had left open, and they ran for their lives. Or, in Arwen's case, dragged.

CHAPTER 104

They never knew what hit them! Perhaps because nothing had. All it had taken was a snap of the fingers, and Lucy, Kate, and Marc froze where they stood. Three statues to be removed and relocated with the minimum of fuss.

'Quickly now,' said one remover, lifting Lucy, 'the boss wants it done as fast and quietly as possible.'

'And kicking the door down was doing it quietly, was it?' said a second remover.

'Yeah,' said the first remover.'

The second remover laughed.

'Strewth, this one is heavier than it looks,' said the third remover, picking up Marc.

'How is that?' said the second, shouldering Kate.

The third was joking. Magicals didn't need brute strength. 'Just getting in the role,' he said. 'I thought all removals people said that?'

'Who knows,' said the first.

'Who cares,' said the second.

The third shrugged.

'Come on,' said the first, 'we got to get them back to the house pronto.'

Once outside the cottage, the three removers, along with their victims, disappeared into thin air.

Chapter 105

As they walked, Mary told them about the meeting she had had with the Chief. The plan had been for Tom and Cat to travel to the Ladies Institute Headquarters where Mary was waiting, and on arriving, they would go back in time to find out when exactly the Jam had gone missing and from there find out who had taken it. It sounded a bit of a hit and miss idea, but Mary explained how it would work.

Tom and Cat would go back in time to the first day the Jam was placed in the Ladies Institute HQ. From there, they would then travel on ten years. If the Jam were still there, they would then repeat the process until they discovered when the Jam went missing.

'But that would take ages,' said Deirdre.

'Not really,' said Mary. 'Once we've discovered when the Jam went missing, it's then just a case of backtracking until it shows up again. We would then finally end up in the year it was taken.'

'The year?' said Deirdre, still thinking it a considerable amount of time to sift through.

'And then,' said Mary, as if reading Deirdre's mind, 'we could work out the month in the same way as the years until we had the day, the second.'

'Clever,' Deirdre had to admit. 'But you would still need to find the culprit.'

'True,' said Mary, 'but once we knew when it went missing, it would take no time at all to track down who had taken it.'

'How?'

'Sorry,' said Mary, 'but on a need-to-know basis.' She smiled and tapped the side of her nose with her finger.

'So,' said Cat, who had been listening intently, 'I take it we're not here to chat about what should have happened.'

'No,' said Mary, smiling at Cat, 'we still have time before the ceremony to still pursue the plan.'

'We had better get started then,' said Cat, returning Mary's smile. She turned to Tom, who was standing by her side, who had been standing by her side. 'Tom?'

Bored by the talk of there and back again, Tom had wandered off to inspect something that had caught the corner of his eye when they had entered Mary's office. The front of his trousers was now soaking wet.

'You're supposed to put a paper cup under the nozzle before

221

pressing the button,' said Mary, shaking her head as she watched him prance about waving the front of his soggy trousers. The water had been hot.

'Ah,' said Tom, thinking perhaps he should have asked how the coffee machine worked before touching it.

'I suppose you missed what we were talking about?' said Cat, giving Tom no sympathy.

'Jam,' said Tom, no let up on the prancing.

'What about it?' said Cat, not about to let Tom off the hook.

'We got to find it.'

'Well done,' said Mary, handing Tom a tea towel.

'But why don't we just replace it with one from the past?' said Tom. 'No one would know, and we could find the missing one later.'

For a moment, there was a stunned silence. Tom hadn't even looked remotely constipated.

'He makes a good point,' said Cat, wondering where that had sprung from. It was a brilliant idea. Why hadn't anyone thought of it already?

'Yes,' said Mary, 'but it's an idea we had already mulled over. Even though they are technically the same Jam, they develop a distinctive quality of their own as time passes. No two Jams are the same. Day to day, they undergo a subtle change. Think growth rings on a tree, but so much more intricate. So sadly, no other one will do. We need the one that should have been there when I went to get it.'

'Who else can remove it?' asked Cat, taking a different tack.

'No one,' said Mary. 'It's protected.'

'Then how was someone able to take it then?' said Deirdre.

'And how would we be able to open the place it's kept in without you?' said Cat, now wondering why Mary hadn't already gone back in time to see when it was taken. A question that needed an answer. 'Why didn't you go back? You were going to get the missing one.'

'Ah,' said Mary, 'we tried, but it appears they can only be opened by the head of the L I at that particular time. As you can imagine, a near-impossible task as some, sadly, are not with us anymore.'

'Oh,' said Cat, 'but then, as Deirdre pointed out, how did they do it?'

'With magic,' said Mary, 'strong magic. It is the only conclusion, and that is why you need to go, Cat. Only the strongest of magic could open the Jams hiding place, so we need someone equal to that task.'

Across the room, Tom, who was only half-listening to the conversation the ladies were having, finished with the trouser wiping the best he could and put the tea towel beside the coffee machine. But although he had not been paying as much attention as he should have been, something he had heard had got him thinking.

Jam with rings in it, Tom pondered, why does that ring a bell somewhere? And then he had it. 'Don't suppose you have any Swiss rolls lying around, do you, Mary?'

'No Tom,' said Mary, 'afraid not.'

Back to normal then, thought Cat, sighing. But there was no time to dwell on the vagaries of Tom Tyme, as someone was knocking at the door. 'We expecting anyone else?' she asked.

'No,' said Mary, giving the door a quizzical look.

'What do we do?' said Deirdre.

'We answer the door,' said Mary. 'It might be nothing but... Cat.'

'On it,' said Cat, getting into a defensive position.

'Can I help?' said Deirdre, taking her gun from its holster.

'Can't hurt,' said Mary.

'What about me?' said Tom.

'The cups are in the cupboard in the corner.'

'Cheers,' said Tom.

'Mary went to the door and opened it.

Chapter 106

Perturbed by the news that the Chief had disappeared and his security detail had no idea where Deirdre was, Cedric headed to speak to whoever was in charge of the Travellers HQ now.

A few minutes later, it suddenly dawned on Cedric that the person he was looking for might actually be him. What did he do now? he thought.

A few minutes later, Cedric had an idea. He needed to contact a time traveller. But not any old time traveller, he needed The time traveller; Tom. Cat would know what to do.

The problem was, they were supposedly kidnapped. Plus, they could be anywhere on their mission. In that case, he should contact... But there was no one. But someone should know what was going on. But who? Someone who might be able to get a message to those that matter. But he had to be careful; he didn't want to let any secrets slip. Then it came to him.

Cedric took to his heels. He'd had an idea. He needed to get to the file room where all the details of every Traveller were, ASAP. Perhaps there would be something in Tom's file that could help him. A contact number? His next of kin? Someone or something that might help; know how to contact Tom or Cat in an emergency. Another problem, unbeknown to Cedric, was he hadn't been privy to the whole story.

CHAPTER 107

An alley that he hoped would lead him to where he hoped it would take him proved to be just that. Darren had been right. It had led to another street, that had led to another alley, that had led to another street. He was now on a street he knew. A street that led to a street with a certain shop in it; Smokowski's.

But there was a problem, that street was long, and Smokowski's was at the other end to where Darren would emerge. Add to that the burden that was the Chief, even though he had recovered enough from the whack Alwyn had given him to stagger on his own two feet. At least he didn't have to duck into doorways now the Chief was no longer on his shoulder. However, that didn't stop people from giving them a sideways glance or stepping to the other side of the road to avoid them. But who could blame them when the Chief kept wailing to the world how much of a bad person he was? So, even though the Chief was moving on his own two feet and they didn't have to keep popping into the odd doorway to hide, the journey would still take some time.

Darren's mind also whirred with worries. Would Smokowski be there? Why would he? If he wasn't, who was running it? Should it have been him? Say it wasn't open because he wasn't there. And on a weekday. Oh woe was he, Smokowski wouldn't be pleased. Oh yeah, and there was them that had kidnapped them and put them in the dungeon. Would they be looking for them? Would he remember where he had got to in the Sound of Music?

Slinging an arm of the stumbling moaning Chief around his neck, Darren gathered the Chief to him and stepped up his pace. He just hoped his family hadn't gone to the cinema to see the film with the monkeys in it without him. Woe was he.

CHAPTER 108

The door to the files room was locked as the room was a secure unit. The Travellers identities within were kept secret from the worlds and each other; a safeguard put in place should they find themselves in an awkward situation. Only the top brass – of which he was at the moment – could obtain them. But of course, Tom was different; he was a sort of open secret to some people in the job and some Magicals due to his exploits and other things.

Cedric stared at the keypad consul and the retina scan above it. Only the Chief traveller had the authorisation to enter the files room. But this was an emergency, and he wasn't here. Neither was anyone else of consequence, which meant that he, Cedric, was in charge. He tentatively tapped his personnel number into the keyboard.

'Hello, Cedric, head of security. How can I help you?' said a voice.

'Er,' said Cedric, who hadn't expected the keyboard to speak to him. 'I think I'm in charge now. I mean, I am in charge now and need to enter the files room.'

'I will check,' said the keyboard.

Everything went quiet for a moment before the keyboard spoke again. This time it appeared to be talking to itself.

'Not here,' said the keyboard.

'Not here. Not here.'

'No longer here.'

Cedric wondered what that meant.

'Ah, found you.' Silence.

Cedric thought he could hear a whirring.

'Please look into the retina scan, Cedric.'

Cedric stepped forward and looked into the scanner.

'Closer, please.'

Cedric moved closer. His eyelashes were touching the small screen.

'Closer, please.'

This is crazy, thought Cedric, pressing his eyeball against the scanner.

'Perfect,' said the keyboard. 'You are now Head of the Travellers Headquarters until further notice. *Tee-hee.* You may enter the files room.'

Did the keyboard just laugh? thought Cedric. But he had no time to worry about that; he had a file to find. And so he entered the files room, oblivious to the inky black ring circling his right eye.

CHAPTER 109

With Cat at the ready to do what she did if there was trouble, Deirdre poised, ready with her gun, and Tom out of the way, looking for a paper cup, Mary opened the door wide.

The sight that met their eyes drew different reactions. Mary breathed a sigh of relief; Rhian must have passed on the message. Deirdre raised an eyebrow but kept her gun levelled. Tom's mouth fell open. Cat powered down and smiled.

'Brandy?' said Cat. 'What are you doing here?'

'Good grief,' said Tom, dropping the paper cup he had just found.

Mary beckoned for her to come in and closed the door behind her. 'This is the friend who's been helping me.' She smiled at Tom. 'I believe you and Cat already know Brandy.'

Coughing, an embarrassed cough, Tom noticed Brandy still had something in her belly button. He sniffed at the air. He knew he shouldn't. He knew what would happen. The smell of Brandy's perfume could be eye-watering. Then he had a second sniff. That's funny, he thought, why aren't my eyes stinging? She must have changed her perfume. That wasn't like her.

At the same time as Tom was questioning Brandy's change in perfume, Mary noticed that Deirdre hadn't lowered her gun, and Cat had a sudden gut feeling that something was wrong.

'You can lower the gun now,' said Mary.

'Sorry,' said Deirdre, 'but I'll be the judge of that.' She slowly moved sideways until she was standing beside Tom.

'But she's a friend,' said Mary, dismayed by Deirdre's reaction. 'Cat, explain to Deirdre who Brandy is.'

'Ah,' said Brandy, speaking for the first time, 'but I'm not Brandy.'

Tom immediately had a moment of déjà vu. Not again, he thought, as he realised the reason for the lack of watering eyes.

With her cat senses spot on, as usual, Cat prepared to pounce.

'Whoa there, kitty,' said Deirdre, seeing Cat tense, 'move, and Tom here gets it.' She had sidled up to Tom and now held her gun to his cap.

The cup Tom had retrieved now fell to the floor again. His usual greyness had become ashen. He wondered if he would ever have a cuppa again. It was this thought, not the gun, that made Tom's knees suddenly wobble. Deirdre grabbed him by the collar to stop him from falling.

If there was a moment to act, it was then as Tom wobbled, but at,

227

sensing Deirdre meant business, stayed her hand. She doubted even magic could stop a bullet that close to Tom's cap.

'What is the meaning of this?' Mary demanded of Deirdre. 'And if you are not Brandy, who are you?'

'Sherry,' said not Brandy, 'I'm Brandy's evil twin.'

'Evil twin?' said Cat. It was the first she had heard of it. 'She hasn't got a twin.'

'Well,' said Sherry, wiggling her head and shoulders, 'not technically her twin.' She smiled and looked thoughtful for a moment. 'Or her sister. Or particularly evil either, to be honest. Just a job.' She held up a hand and rubbed her finger and thumb together. 'A particularly lucrative one I couldn't say no to, to be honest.'

'You're a shapechanger,' said Tom.

'What? Oh no, I just look remarkably like her. Handy for what Deirdre had in mind.' Sherry glanced at Deirdre. 'She found me, you see and told me all about her plan. One with which I totally agree.

'So, you're a BIMBO?' said Cat.

'No,' said Sherry pretending to look hurt, 'just a little empty-headed sometimes.' She laughed. 'No, not a BIMBO, but I am magical, so don't try anything.'

'But just in case you decide it might be worth taking a chance,' said Deirdre, poking her gun into Tom's cap, 'let me let you into a little secret that might help dissuade you further.'

'What secret?' said Cat.

'As of this moment.' Deirdre quickly glanced at her watch. 'Yes, as of now, we have everyone Tom here cares about tucked up nicely at his daughter's house.' She glared at Cat. 'So behave yourself if you know what's good for everyone.'

Having no choice but to do as Deirdre said, Cat let herself relax. She wondered how she could have been so wrong about someone?

'She's lying,' said Mary, confident Lucy and the kids were safe.

'Am I?' said Deirdre.

'Nice cottage,' said Sherry, 'shame about the door.'

'No,' said Mary, visibly shaken.

'Yes,' said Sherry.

'What are you talking about?' said Cat.

'She,' said Sherry, nodding at Mary, 'had Lucy and the brats hidden away, but they're home now.'

'So, you're behind all this,' snapped Mary, as Sherry approached her with a pair of handcuffs.

'No,' said Sherry, 'weren't you listening? Deirdre is the one to thank for all this.'

As Sherry put the handcuffs on Mary, Deirdre, gun trained closely on Tom, opened a cupboard and pulled from it a special cat carrier, one from where magic couldn't escape.

'Inside Cat,' snarled Deidre.

Oh-oh, thought Tom, she isn't going to like that.

A low growl confirmed Tom's thought. But what could she do? Nothing now, she decided. She would have to bide her time. She was sure she would have her moment. Until then— Cat reluctantly walked into the carrier.

'Good,' said Deidre, locking the carrier door. She then pushed Tom from her and lowered her gun.

'You'd better not have hurt Lucy or the kids?' warned Tom.

'You'll see for yourself soon enough,' said Deirdre, 'it's time to go home. Lucy's, that is.'

'Why are you doing this?' said Cat.

'Ask Mary,' was the cryptic reply. 'Now move.'

Sherry picked up the cat carrier and followed as Tom and Mary were ushered back to the Loo.

CHAPTER 110

They were fast – which was stretching it a tad – coming to the end of the street that led to the next one where Smokowski's shop was, mainly due to the Chief picking up the pace as Darren pulled him along by the hand. The Chief was still rambling but had kicked up a couple of gears from stumbling along to ambling to intermittent promenade strolling. Still not fast, but Darren wasn't about to complain. They were nearly there.

'Nearly there,' said Darren, grabbing the Chief to stop him from going back the way they had come. 'Not long now.'

The Chief's eyes rolled in their sockets at the news. His speed had improved, but his comprehension was worsening. Darren hoped there would be someone at the shop that could help him.

As they reached the corner to Smokowski's street, Darren stopped. The Chief didn't. Darren quickly swung the Chief around in an arc and pushed him up against the wall of the house they were standing beside. He now peeped around the corner.

'Oh no,' he said. Someone was standing at the door of Smokowski's.

'Bad person,' said the Chief.

'You know them?' said Darren, suddenly hopeful the Chief had taken a turn for the better.

But no. 'I'm a bad person,' said the Chief. He then turned around and faced the wall.

Sighing, Darren peeped back around the corner. They were still there. What did he do now? There was only one thing for it; he would have to get closer. He needed to know if the person at the door was friend or foe. He spoke to the Chief and told him to stay where he was. He didn't know if he would, but he had to take the chance.

'What do bad people do?' said Darren.

'Stand on the naughty step,' said the Chief.

'Yes,' said Darren, 'what else?'

'They stand in the corner.'

'Yes,' said Darren, 'and as this is a corner, you have to stay here and face the wall.'

'Face the wall.'

'Well done.'

Darren, fingers crossed, now inched round the corner into Smokowski's street.

CHAPTER 111

The file room was humongous. No computer filing here; all were on paper, old school. No, thought Cedric, nothing was going to be easy.

He stepped into a corridor that led to others, each with a designated letter of the alphabet above it. Twenty-six corridors. Two more, covering retired Travellers and future Travellers – the next in line to take over from the retired – branched off. He stared in amazement and wondered how there could be so many Travellers. Why so many? Surely they would step on each other's toes? But as he thought about the area they had to cover, the size of the world, the human one, and then the Magical worlds, he understood. Thankfully, Cedric only had to trawl the T's.

A little while later, Cedric was standing outside corridor T. He stepped in. A further, little while later, Cedric finally found what he was looking for, a sign for TOM T TYME. He pulled on the handle of the file room and walked in.

'Crikey,' exclaimed Cedric at the sight that met him. The room was half full of files, and the room wasn't small. For someone who hadn't been travelling that long, it was a lot. Where did he start?

'Where do I start?' Cedric said to himself.

'Hello, how may I be of assistance?' asked a familiar voice.

'Er?' said Cedric, taken a little by surprise.

'Sorry,' said the voice, 'I scanned the files but found nothing relating to "er".'

'What?'

'Good news. I have found several thousand references to "what". I will start in chronological order. The first instance of "what" was recorded just after Tom T Tyme's first mission. The Chief Traveller at the time wrote, and I quote: "What have we done? Th—'

'Stop,' said Cedric, who had gathered his wits and realised the voice belonged to the keyboard. He was now a little excited. Perhaps it wasn't going to take as long as he had expected.

'Is that a request for a search or a command to stop?'

'Er, no forget that. Stop searching.'

'As you command.'

'Thank you, er, keyboard,' said Cedric.

'Please call me Iris.'

'Oh, okay,' said Cedric, not sure what to make of that. 'Are you a computer?'

'Yes,' said Iris, 'I am files and depositories, dealing with certain aspects of files, namely Travellers and number twos.'

Did he hear that right? 'Number twos?'

'Yes, number one deposits, external deposits, are dealt with by another computer. I control number two deposits, internal deposits.'

'Ah,' said Cedric, none the wiser. 'Can you help me then?'

'Yes, and please call me Iris, it's my favourite flower. Now, what can I help you with, Cedric?

After explaining his predicament, Iris came back to him with a name that might help him with his quest.

'Smokowski?' said Cedric, feeling he had heard that name before somewhere.

'Yes, he is registered as first contact. Here is his address.'

'Thank you,' said Cedric, heading for the door. He just hoped this Smokowski character could help.

Cedric reached the exit, turned the handle but found it locked. 'Iris?'

'Please press your eye to the retina scan, please.'

'But I did that on the way in. Why do I have to do it again?'

'Security Cedric.'

Sighing, Cedric did as was asked.

'No, Cedric, the other eye now.'

Good grief, thought Cedric, but he didn't have time to argue.

'Closer, please.'

Cedric moved closer.

'Thank you, Cedric, you are cleared to leave.'

The door opened, and Cedric bolted. He had only one thing on his mind; find Smokowski.

Behind him, the door was tutted shut. Well, thought the computer, not even a thank you or goodbye. Which the computer supposed made what she had done all the sweeter. Cedric was heading out into the world looking like a Panda. Iris tittered.

CHAPTER 112

An angry Smokowski sat on the sofa in Lucy's lounge with an equally angry Willy beside him, both feeling completely useless. Between their feet, still in their containers now covered by cardboard taped down, were the Bobs. Air holes had been provided.

Ruth/Lucy, Abdul/Marc, Charmaine/Kate, and Rhian/Mary were nowhere to be seen.

Ten minutes earlier.

The doorbell chimed, and as no one was expected by that entrance – the occupants all focused on the bathroom door as they were – they treated the sound with caution.

Abdul ran upstairs to look through the landing window so he could see who was at the door. What he saw was a complete surprise.

Standing on the doorstep was Lucy, Kate, and Marc. There was no sign of Mary. What did it mean? After a swift discussion, where Rhian suggested things must have taken an upturn, and Mary had dropped them off for safekeeping, they decided to open the door. Besides, they couldn't just leave them standing there.

Ruth, shed of the Lucy disguise, opened the door.

'Hi,' said Lucy, 'mum sent us.'

There it was then, the reason that they were no longer in hiding.

Ruth let them in but couldn't help but feel that they appeared somewhat distant. But then, if glamouring had occurred, which she expected it had, it was one of the telltale signs.

'Come in,' said Ruth.

Smokowski and Willy, who had been wolfing down tea and dunking choccy biscuits in the kitchen – Tom would not be pleased – got up and entered the lounge just as Lucy and the kids entered from the hall. In the kitchen, the two Bobs were whisked from sight and into a cupboard by Charmaine. She and the others could be explained away, but there was not enough explanation in the world to cover the existence of the Bobs.

'Lucy,' said Smokowski, 'how are you?'

'Fine,' said Lucy, sounding distant, 'just fine.'

Smokowski cast a concerned glance at the others but guessed, as Ruth had, that they were recovering from a glamouring or were still in one. Still, he thought, he had better make introductions, but as he didn't know what Lucy knew, he would keep to the basics, for now; just their names.

In the kitchen cupboard, the two Bobs exchanged a concerned glance.

'Did you hear that?' said boB.

'The sound of a flea scratching?'

'More a pin dropping.'

'A bell tinkling,' they said as one.

'Oh-no!' said boB.

They then heard a pop!

'What was that?' said Invisible Bob.

'Sounded like a popping sound,' said boB.

What it was, was the sound of Charmaine disappearing from the kitchens field of existence. Where she was now was anyone's guess.

Meanwhile, in the lounge, Smokowski had started his introductions.

'This is Willy,' said Smokowski, 'he's an old friend.'

'Pleased to meet yer,' said Willy, bowing slightly.

'Hello,' said Lucy, appearing distracted.

'And this is—'

'Into the kitchen now,' said Lucy, interrupting Smokowski's attempt at introducing Ruth.

'Okay, mum,' said Kate and Marc together. They headed towards the kitchen, followed by Lucy.

'Hurry now, or dinner will get cold.'

Alarm bells instantly rang in Smokowski's head. What dinner? Glamouring wouldn't do that. Something was wrong. He went to air his concerns to Ruth just as a popping noise filled the air. Ruth disappeared before his eyes.

Now also alert to something amiss – Ruth disappearing, the clue – Willy turned to Smokowski. 'What's happening?'

'Nothing good,' said Smokowski.

The door to the hall suddenly flew open, and Abdul burst in. 'They're here,' he yelled.

'Who is?' said Willy.

'Didn't you hear? We've got to get out.'

'Hear what?' said Smokowski.

'The pin drop,' said Abdul. 'Come on.'

'Come to think of it,' said Willy, 'I thought I heard a flea scratching.'

'We have to go.'

'Now you say, I thought I heard a bell tinkle,' said Smokowski.

'Now!'

The door from the kitchen now took a turn bursting open. The sound of clicking fingers and Abdul went the same way as the others.

Wide-eyed, mouths open, Smokowski and Willy stared at the creature standing in the kitchen doorway. They had heard of them but had never seen one in the flesh.

'My name is Pin,' said the creature. He smiled an awful yet sweet smile. 'Now, are you going to behave, or are we going to have a scuffle?' Pin clicked the knuckles in each hand and walked in. Behind him were two others. One of them was carrying the containers holding the Bobs.

They knew they would have little chance against these creatures, so Smokowski and Willy tamely sat on the sofa.

'Good choice. Now, if you behave yourselves, you won't disappear like the others.'

With Smokowski, Willy, and the Bobs subdued, the creatures, known to Lucy as the removers, each took a position and settled down to wait. Pin sat in the lounge watching over the old boys and the Bobs. Flea was in the kitchen with Lucy and the kids. Belle was waiting in the hall by the bathroom door, ready to greet their boss, who would arrive anytime now.

CHAPTER 113

The door to Smokowski's shop was locked. What now? thought Cedric. Perhaps there was a back door? But that still solved nothing if Smokowski wasn't home. Why hadn't he asked for a backup name? Because he had been too excited to think when he found out the computer could do the work for him. Drat, he thought, I have to go back to HQ.

Dejected, despondent, other words starting with D, Cedric was about to head back when he noticed someone acting suspiciously a little way up the street. Why he stopped, he didn't know, but something was pricking at his elf senses.

A little way up the street, Darren threw himself against a hedge when the person at Smokowski's door suddenly looked his way. Unfortunately, the hedge wasn't very thick, and Darren fell through it into the garden beyond.

'Oi!' shouted a voice from above. 'What yer doing in me garden? Yer vandal!'

Desperately trying to disentangle his feet from the hedge so he could stand, Darren, looked up. Leaning out of an upper window was an elderly woman shaking her fist at him.

'Sorry,' said Darren, 'it was an accident.'

An apology was not enough, as the elderly lady was now threatening to call the police if he didn't get off her gnome.

Darren had wondered what he was lying on. He got to his feet. Just needed to stand the gnome up, say sorry again, and be off, he thought. But to his horror, when he went to stand the gnome upright, its head fell off.

'Murderer,' wailed the elderly lady as she saw the damage.

'I'll get some glue,' said Darren, starting to panic.

'Had him fifty years yer murderer,' yelled the elderly lady who had decided the police wouldn't be needed. She would deal with the idiot herself. She had a baseball bat for just such circumstances. It took but a second to find, but to her dismay, it was heavier than when she had last used it some twenty years ago. Still, that was not about to stop her. She started dragging it along the floor. She was sure she could still do some damage with it.

Seeing the suspicious person fall through a hedge, Cedric went into security mode. This needed investigating. Finding Tom forgotten for the moment, he headed up the street to find out what was happening.

A determined Cedric arrived at the garden with the hedge just as a dishevelled Darren appeared at the garden gate.

'Darren?' said Cedric, so surprised, he nearly fell off the kerb.

'Agh?' said an equally surprised Darren, amazed to see an elf standing there when Christmas was so far away. He then recognised Cedric from the Travellers Headquarters. 'Cedric?'

'What are you doing here?' said Cedric. 'I thought you'd been kidnapped.'

'We escaped,' said Darren, 'the Chief and me.'

'The Chief?' Cedric's mind boggled. 'How?'

But before Darren could answer, there came a bump-bump-bump noise from the house. The elderly lady was coming down the stairs.

'Quick,' said Darren, 'it's the owner of the gnome.' He pointed. Cedric looked.

'Oh dear,' said Cedric without feeling. He and gnomes, real ones, had history. 'We should go. Where's the Chief?'

'Round the corner, this way.'

To Darren's relief, the Chief was still there, facing the wall. He quickly explained the situation. Cedric did the same. They each grabbed hold of the Chief's arms and headed for Smokowski's. Darren had a key.

The trouble was, they had to pass the garden with the damaged hedge and headless gnome. Darren kept his head down, hoping to dodge the owner, but the elderly lady appeared at the gate as they reached it.

''Ere,' said the elderly lady, 'you seen a gnome murderer?'

Cedric politely said he hadn't, while Darren sank his head even further and said nothing. The Chief muttered something about a bad person.

'Too right there, guvnor,' said the elderly lady sadly, shaking her head, 'don't know what's 'appening with the world today.' As she spoke, she began staring hard at Cedric. 'Pah,' she said, then waved her hand at them dismissively and wandered over to her broken gnome. 'Flipping vandals,' she muttered as she looked at it. And as Cedric and Darren propelled the Chief away from the garden, the old lady despaired of the day's fashions. Why on earth would yer try to look like a panda with pointy ears? she thought. 'Pah,' she muttered before wandering indoors to get some glue.

CHAPTER 114

Tom went through the motions, as one does in a Loo, but was stretching it out as he tried to think of a way out of the mess they were in.

'In your own time,' said Deirdre, who suspected Tom was up to something. It was the lack of a constipated expression that was giving him away.

I am, thought Tom, who then flinched as the cold barrel of Deirdre's gun touched the side of his nose. At that point, he decided perhaps she didn't mean what she said.

'Can't be rushed,' said Tom. But as the end of the barrel was now threatening to force its way up his nostril, he thought perhaps he should. Tom took on the look of the constipated, wiggled the flusher, and thought of Lucy's bathroom.

'Good boy,' said Deirdre, relaxing the pressure on Tom's nostril, 'but no more of the funny stuff.

In the cat carrier, perched on the toilet seat, Cat was doing some thinking. She would have to bide her time. Wait for the right moment. She settled down to wait for it.

Squashed in a corner, between Deirdre and Sherry, Mary looked from Cat to Tom to Deirdre and finally to Sherry. She, too, was waiting for her moment, but that was to come.

Sherry was painting her nails.

CHAPTER 115

As Darren went to unlock the door to Smokowski's, Cedric kept an eye out for customers. It was the last thing they needed.

'Quick,' said Cedric, as the Chief, gradually losing the will to stand, started to slip down the window. 'I can't hold him up much longer.'

'I can't remember which key it is,' said Darren, starting to panic.

Peering around Darren's arm, Cedric had a look to see if he could help; being in security, he was good with locks. He frowned. 'But you've only got two keys,' said Cedric.

'I know,' said Darren, 'but which one?'

Oh dear, thought Cedric, as he grabbed at the sliding Chief, no wonder the Chief hadn't wanted him on the mission. 'Try them both,' he said.

'Good idea,' said Darren, looking at the keys in a new light. He tried the first. It didn't fit. He tried the second. Neither did that. Panic set in again.

'You tried the same one twice,' said Cedric, hardly believing what he was seeing. 'There, try that one with the blue top.'

Key tried. Door unlocked. Success. Then the Chief buckled. Cedric lost his grip. Darren was hit in the back. And all three landed with a crash on the welcome mat.

They lay there for a moment, winded, bewildered, and unconscious before Cedric and Darren managed to scramble to their feet. The Chief was still being "welcomed".

"'Ere,' said a voice startling those awake, 'is 'e all right?'

The voice belonged to a little old lady. Smokowski knew her well and always trembled at the sight of her. She was a haggler.

'He's fine,' said Cedric, getting it together.

'Good,' said the old lady. 'Now, can I have a pint of semi-skinned, please?' She stepped over the prostrate Chief with a sprightly step. She squinted at Cedric. 'Why do you look like a Panda?' she asked.

'Panda?' said Cedric.

'Meant to say,' said Darren.

Cedric gave him a quizzical look.

'When yer ready,' said the old lady.

'We're closed,' said Darren.

'Looks open to me,' said the old lady, planting her feet firmly. She wasn't going anywhere without a fight.

'Right,' said Darren, knowing when to back down, 'a pint of skinned milk.' Skinned? He thought it best not to say anything, so went to the chiller with only two things on his mind; get milk, get rid of her.

'How much is that?' said the old woman when Darren returned. She knew full well how much it cost, but mistakes are sometimes made.

Drat, thought Darren, he had forgotten about that. What now? He didn't want to open the till. He had an idea. 'Do you need a receipt?' he asked. If she didn't, he reasoned, he could just take the money and leave it on the counter for later.

'Yes,' said the old lady, scenting blood.

Then he remembered he couldn't open the till anyway. Smokowski had the only key. More quick thinking was needed. His next words were out of his mouth before he could stop them. 'It's free,' he said.

'Free?' said the old lady, looking at Darren as if he had two heads.

'Yes,' said Darren. More thinking on his feet. 'Every twentieth customer gets a free pint, today only.' Oh, woe, what would Smokowski think? Darren imagined him turning in his apron.

'Well, I won't say no,' said the old lady, not believing her luck; two freebies in one day. She snatched the milk from Darren's hand and stuffed it in her bag before triumphantly stalking from the shop, carefully navigating the Chief as she went.

Pulling the Chief clear, Darren quickly closed and locked the door at the first attempt.

'Where to?' said Cedric, wanting to move the Chief away from window prying eyes.

'Out, back.'

They lifted the Chief and carried him to the stockroom.

CHAPTER 116

'Still nothing,' said Belle, replying to Pin from her station outside Lucy's bathroom, even though he could see from where he was standing.

'Something's wrong,' said Pin, in the doorway between the lounge and the hall. 'We should have heard something by now.'

'I heard that Cat is one tough cookie,' said Belle, 'perhaps she put up a bit of a fight.'

'Maybe,' said Pin, 'maybe.' There had already been one problem; the one called Darren wasn't there when they had gone to get him, disappeared along with the Chief. He would have stern words with the jailers when he found them. 'But be ready for trouble,' he warned.

'Always,' said Belle, nodding grimly.

CHAPTER 117

They had placed the Chief on a chair. Darren sat on another, and Cedric brought Darren up to speed on all he knew since Darren's kidnapping.

'Well, she wasn't in the same place as the Chief and me,' said Darren, after learning of Deirdre's disappearance. 'At least I don't think so. The guards never said. Perhaps there's a lady's dungeon somewhere.'

'I suppose,' said Cedric, not sure what to think.

'So, why were you looking for Mister Smokowski?'

'I thought he might know where Tom and Cat might be.'

'I doubt it,' said Darren. He told Cedric how Mary had set Smokowski and Willy on a wild goose chase. 'But you mustn't tell anyone,' he quickly added, realising that he may just have let out a secret.

'I won't,' said Cedric. 'It looks like I've been on a wild goose chase of my own.'

'Yeah,' said Darren. 'It's a pity we couldn't follow his trail.'

'Smokowski's? How would we do that?'

'No, Tom's,' said Darren. 'Mister Smokowski once told me he had done it. A right old adventure, he had said, like travelling in a rainbow.'

'Why, of course,' said Cedric, smacking the fist of one hand into the flat of the other and making Darren jump, 'we need a Hitchhiker.' They wouldn't be able to find Smokowski with it, but they might find Tom. They could cut out the middleman.

CHAPTER 118

'Oops,' said Tom, as they arrived at the wrong Lucy's bathroom for the second time. 'My bad.'

'You do it again, and there will be consequences,' growled Deirdre. One mistake she was prepared to ignore. Dodderers made mistakes. But twice?

In the cat carrier, Cat was smiling. Don't underestimate the Tom.

'Sorry,' said Tom, 'you're making me nervous. Can't you lower the gun?'

'What a good idea,' said Deirdre, lowering the barrel, 'that way I can shoot you in the foot if you do it again.'

Oops, thought Tom, perhaps he should heed the warning; his shoes were almost new. He concentrated again. This time about *his*, Lucy's bathroom.

'Okay, Sherry,' said Deirdre, now confident that Tom would now toe the line, 'get ready, just in case.'

'Will do, boss,' said Sherry, continuing to paint her nails. She had started on her toes.

The Loo came to a halt. Well, that's that, thought Tom. Though what that was, he didn't rightly know. But it had to be something bad. He needed a cuppa. And a biscuit. He then remembered he had some. Did he dare? He slid a hand very slowly into his pocket. Drat, he thought, as his fingers touched his Saver, wrong one. Then Tom's eyes suddenly brightened as if a light had come on behind them. The Saver would get them out of this jam. It had before. All he had to do was concentrate on whatever he wanted the Saver to become, and voila!

The only problem with that was, the Saver rarely did what Tom wanted it to do.

CHAPTER 119

Smokowski nudged Invisible Bob's container, which nudged boB's container, which then nudged Willy. Willy glanced at Smokowski, who gave a quick nod towards Pin.

'Something's up,' whispered Smokowski.

'Yeah, I noticed,' whispered Willy, 'what you want to do?'

'I don't think we can take them,' whispered Smokowski. He knew they wouldn't stand a chance against the removers, but he couldn't just sit there. He had to do something for Lucy and the kids' sake. Who knew what was going to happen? 'But if we can cause a distraction when their boss arrives, one of us might be able to get Lucy and the kids out of here.'

A nodding Willy agreed. 'Who does what?' he whispered.

At their feet, the Bobs were listening intently. They would help if asked, as long as it wasn't too dangerous for them.

'I'll cause the distraction while you get Lucy and the kids out. Your car's not parked too far away.'

'Good plan,' whispered Willy. He looked down. 'What about them?'

'Oi!' whispered boB, taking the word right out of Invisible Bob's mouth.

'We are here, you know,' whispered Invisible Bob, taking the words right out of boB's mouth.

'Sorry,' whispered Smokowski. 'Will you help?'

'Will it be dangerous?' asked boB.

'What do you think?' whispered Smokowski. 'You know what they are, right?'

They knew all right. They exchanged a glance. Both nodded.

'Okay, we'll help,' whispered Invisible Bob.

'We're BIMBOs,' said boB, 'it's our duty.' For all their faults and talent for the easy way out, when they donned their BIMBO hats, they were there for whoever needed them. They wouldn't attack feet, though. Feet were off-limits. Bobs' could get squashed by feet. They could get squashed by anything but feet was not the way to go.

'Good,' whispered Smokowski, 'just wait for the word.'

'Which word?'

Smokowski glared at him.

'Okay-okay,' said Invisible Bob.

'Just one thing,' whispered boB, 'how are we going to get out?'

'When the time comes, Willy and I will release you.' Thankfully, because the removers didn't think two old duffers would be a problem, they hadn't restrained them.

Across the room, Pin had noticed Smokowski and Willy whispering between themselves but had put it down to two old duffers talking about what old duffers talked about. At a guess, bunions, or the like. Nothing for him to worry about there.

Some who knew Smokowski, and those that knew Willy, would say that was a mistake.

CHAPTER 120

It didn't take long for Cedric to find Smokowski's Hitchhiker. The Hitchhiker latched on to the time-machines slipstream, and you then followed its path.

'We can't,' said Darren, dismayed they were taking something without the owner's permission, especially Smokowski's, 'he won't like it.'

'It's an emergency,' said Cedric.

'But what if he finds out?' said Darren.

'He will find out,' said Cedric, 'so don't worry about it until then.' That didn't offer Darren any comfort. 'But don't worry, I'll take the blame; head of security, you know.' He added after seeing Darren's face.

Darren felt better, but not a lot.

'So,' said Cedric, 'can you remember from where the last place Tom travelled from was?' If they could find that out, it would cut the journey time. The drawback with the Hitchhiker was it didn't take you straight from A to B, from where you were to the time machine; it took you to all the stops in-between. It would take time to catch up.

'I think it was the Travellers HQ,' said Darren.

'Drat,' said Cedric, 'we can't go there, too risky.' It wasn't looking good. 'Before that?'

'Lucy's,' said Darren, 'that's where we started from.' Everyone called it Lucy's, even though it was his house as well.

'Lucy's it is then,' said Cedric. He went to start the Hitchhiker.

'Perhaps we should walk,' said Darren, thinking, if Lucy and the kids were there, their sudden appearance in the house might not be a good idea, especially as Cedric was an elf. He explained his reasoning.

'Fair point,' said Cedric. 'How far is it?'

'Not far.'

'Good, let's go.'

'What about the Chief?'

'We'll have to leave him.'

'Better check on him first.'

The Chief was checked on. He was dozing. They placed a bottle of water and a packet of biscuits within reach. A small window with bars – handy should he decide to wander – opened to get air. The stockroom door locked. All checked again.

'Let's go,' said Cedric.

'Do you think there'll be trouble?' said Darren.

'When?'

'Whenever. You know, from whoever's behind all this.'

'I wouldn't bet against it,' said Cedric, all serious.

'In that case,' said Darren before disappearing back into the stockroom. He reappeared moments later, wearing something and carrying something.

'Really?' said Cedric.

'Courage,' said Darren, 'reminds me of the old days, although it's not exactly what I would have worn.' His fingers tightened around the thing in his hand.

'It's not real, you know?' said Cedric gently.

'I know,' said Darren. But he would not be put off, even though nothing he wore fitted.

'Fair enough,' said Cedric, thinking whatever floats your boat. 'Let's go.'

'Wait,' said Darren.

'What now?' Cedric was losing patience.

'What about…' Darren made circular movements around one of his eyes.

'Oh yeah,' said Cedric, who had forgotten all about the black rings. 'No time now, but do me a favour and remind me when we have a moment, will you?' He would have a word with that computer when he got back.

'And,' said Darren, pointing to his ears. Arriving on the doorstep with an elf was nearly as bad as emerging from the bathroom with one.

'I'll say I was at a fancy dress party.'

It was good enough for Darren.

They finally left Smokowski's and headed for Lucy's with steely, determined looks on their faces. The face without the Panda rings looking slightly more convincing but only just.

CHAPTER 121

Resembling a gurning champion in the making, Tom concentrated the hardest he had ever concentrated in his life. Tom had to get this just right; the Saver wasn't always to be relied on to get you what you wanted, especially in his hands. He had to clear his mind of everything but what he needed. The trouble was, he didn't know what he needed.

Many things now raced through Tom's mind, all of which he was desperately trying to ignore. Concentrate boy, thought Tom, concentrate, oh-oh I'm drifting. Doughnuts popped into his head. A doughnut would be nice, but not now. The thought left. But it was a small victory as others tried to take its place. He had to fight them. He needed something concrete. No, don't think that! He quickly pushed it away. He needed to calm down. Slow down. Take a breath. Relax. Push away the thoughts. He needed to float. His mind started to clear at last. Now all he had to do was— Oh no! No!

Too late.

CHAPTER 122

They seem agitated, thought Smokowski. Flea had joined Pin in the lounge. Something was up. Smokowski hoped so. He then realised their plan might have suddenly just got a lot easier. With Flea in the room, that meant no one was now guarding Lucy and the kids. His ears now pricked up. Was something happening? Pin was moving towards the hall door.

'That was something,' said Pin, moving his head to one side as if he had heard something. 'I'm sure of it.' He started towards the hall. 'Belle?'

'Something,' confirmed Belle.

'Get ready,' said Pin.

Any minute now, thought Smokowski.

CHAPTER 123

If Cedric had thought he looked conspicuous because of his Panda appearance and pointy ears, then he was right. But Darren had managed to put him in the shade. Thankfully, as it was still early, there were not that many people about, and those that had come across the duo had either quickly crossed the road or put their appearance down to a late-night fancy dress – badly dressed – party and had hurried past. Thankfully, they were nearly at Lucy's and had just passed the hedge where Smokowski and Willy had earlier hidden.

'It's what people imagine I wore,' said Darren when Cedric mentioned what he was wearing. Idle chat mingled with small talk along the way, but finally, Cedric cracked and had had to ask about Darren's attire for the sake of his sanity.

'I can imagine,' said Cedric, who really couldn't. And he doubted anyone else could imagine what Darren was wearing unless they were fiction writers with a weird mind.

They soon arrived at Lucy's, but as they approached the front gate, there was the sound of an almighty crash from within the house.

'What was that?' exclaimed a startled Darren.

'I don't know,' said Cedric, 'but I think we should investigate.'

Suddenly worried that Lucy and the kids might be in there and in trouble, Darren ran to the door. Close behind was Cedric. Appearances forgotten.

As they did, someone inside Lucy's spotted them. Spotted a chap with pointy ears wearing Panda makeup charging up the garden path beside a knight straight from the legend of King Arthur adorned in plastic armour and a plastic Viking helmet. An eyebrow was raised.

CHAPTER 124

Well, Tom got what he wanted, or not really what he wanted. Still, the Saver had done its job and had come to his rescue.

'Agh! Yelled Tom as the Saver burst into life.
    'What the—' Mary didn't finish her sentence because of the sudden squidging against the Loo wall.
    The cat carrier groaned as sudden pressure pushed at its side. Inside, a shocked Cat lay as flat as she could.
    As Sherry took her turn at being squidged, the nail polish bottle she was holding flew from her hand, while the brush in her other one painted a red line across the hand that no longer held the bottle.
    Snarling with rage, Deirdre tried to raise her gun but felt it ripped from her hand as she slammed against a Loo wall.
    Two walls and a door had bodies squashed against them. On the other wall, the cat carrier was close to coming apart. That left the floor and the ceiling. The floor was clear, except for the Savers interpretation of help, which just left the ceiling, and that was where Tom was, pressed against it. He could feel things breaking due to the pressure. Drat, he thought, there go my biscuits.
    The pressure in the Loo was building. The walls were holding, but the door was bulging.
    Then, suddenly, all heck broke loose. The door could take no more and burst from its hinges.
    For those close to being crushed, it wasn't a bad thing.

CHAPTER 125

As the full force of Lucy's bathroom door hit Belle head-on, Pin noticed an odd sight running towards the house.

'You watch them,' Pin ordered Flea, 'while I deal with the circus we got coming to the door.'

'What about Belle?' said Flea, as he watched her struggle to free herself from under the door.

'She can look after herself.' Pin went to the front door.

'Now,' hissed Smokowski, and together with Willy, they removed the lids from the Bob's containers.

The doorbell rang.

Why did he do that? thought Cedric.

'Oh, hang about,' said Darren, 'I've got a key.'

Cedric said nothing.

As key approached keyhole, the door suddenly flew open and Pin filled the frame.

'Cripes,' stuttered Cedric as he realised what was standing before him.

'Who are you?' demanded Darren, not knowing who or what was filling the doorframe. He raised his sword when there was no answer. 'Then have at you, varlet.' He had heard it said in a movie.

Finally freeing herself from the door, it surprised Belle to find Sherry lying on top of it. She checked she was okay and went to the gap the door had left. As she reached it, the Saver, now in the form of a self-inflating dinghy with Mary and Deirdre clinging onto it for dear life, sprang from the Loo and knocked her down again. Tom was rolled along the ceiling before being dropped onto the cat carrier, finishing its demolition. He rolled, groaning, to the floor. On the toilet seat, the cat carrier lay broken. Inside, Cat could only stare on in utter amazement.

In the lounge, Smokowski, boB, and Invisible Bob attacked Flea as he stared at the scene unfolding in the hall.

'Aha!' shouted Smokowski as his special training kicked in. He landed a vicious karate chop to the back of Flea's neck. The Bob's, who went for his ankles, were careful to dodge his size twelves. Willy headed for the kitchen as fast as he could.

A confused Pin grabbed Darren's plastic sword and crushed it in his hand. The next thing he grabbed was Darren and Cedric and pulled them inside.

Getting to her feet again, Belle helped Sherry and Deirdre to theirs. Cat, now free and finished with being amazed, leapt into action. She had aimed her leap at Belle. Knowing what she was, Cat deemed her the main danger. But she hadn't taken into account how quick they could be and, missing her target, landed on the fully inflated dinghy, bounced, and careered sideways down the hall.

A dazed Mary, her hands still cuffed, struggled to her knees.

Meanwhile, inside the Loo, Tom was lying on the floor, staring at the ceiling, wondering what had happened. Then it hit him. The dinghy, pushed back into the Loo by Belle and Sherry, landed on his head.

Strong hands threw Darren and Cedric along the hall, which now resembled the aftermath of the fancy dress party they never went to.

Cedric instantly sprang to his feet. Darren struggled with the plastic Viking helmet that had wedged itself on his face.

A strong left leg sent boB into orbit. He landed on the floor in a cloud of flour. Invisible Bob grimly held on to Flea's right leg by sinking his teeth in it.

'Why you little-oi!' growled Flea, his growl cut short by Smokowski's karate chop landing on the back of his neck.

Smokowski's aim was true, but before he could be pleased with himself, his hand bounced back from Flea's neck and struck him squarely on the nose.

Willy was in the kitchen. The plan had gone well. Apart from the bit where he now stood, arms in the air, as Rhian aimed a crossbow at him.

'But you disappeared.'

'Did I?' said Rhian, giving Willy a sly smile. 'Now, back in there and don't try anything stupid.'

Behind Rhian, Lucy and the kids sat staring into space, oblivious to all that was going on.

In the hall, Cat landed beside Darren.

'That you Darren?' said Cat when she got upright.

'Yeth,' groaned Darren.

Now with it again, Cat helped him remove his helmet.

'Phew!' said Darren, his face a sweaty bright red. 'Thanks.'

Above them, Pin had Cedric by his ears.

'I think Cedric needs your help,' said Cat, who wanted to ask Darren how he had got there but guessed the question would have to wait for later, as right now people, she had spied Deirdre pulling Mary to her feet, needed her help. Cat bounded back along the hall whence she had bounced. Her target, not Deirdre, but Belle again. She didn't know how she would fare; she had never fought a fairy before, let alone an Uber one.

The door from the kitchen opened, and Willy walked into the lounge.

The first to notice was boB who was trying hard to remove the flour from his head and hands. His clothes lay on the floor.

The second was Flea. 'Well done,' he said as Rhian appeared behind Willy. 'Ow!' Invisible Bob was still biting and had noticed nothing but the disgusting taste of the Uber fairy's skin. Flea leaned down and flicked him away with the back of his hand. A dazed Invisible Bob landed on the sofa. 'Look after them while I help the others.' Flea limped towards the hall. His calf would smart for a while, but no real damage.

Sitting against the sofa, Smokowski was holding his nose. Thankfully it was only swollen and nothing worse, but he was having trouble focusing. He now noticed Willy. At least he thought it was Willy as he looked at him through a kaleidoscope of stars and colourful flashes, and if it was him, why did he have his hands in the air?

In the hall, Cat was getting on top of things. Deirdre was pinned under the dinghy in the bathroom doorway. Just a little magic used. She now closed in on Belle again, who was sporting a spectacular bump on her forehead where the bathroom door had magically hit her.

Sherry had squeezed back into the Loo, where she gathered her nail brush and polish.

Having heroically turned onto his stomach, Tom now crawled past Sherry, making for a gap between the bathroom door post and Deirdre. He ignored her potty mouth as he squeezed past her.

At the other end of the hall Darren, who had kept all his strength from his other life, crashed a plastic gauntleted fist as hard as he could into the side of Pin's head.

Pin dropped Cedric and grabbed Darren by the besague – even though the armour was plastic, it was accurate to the last detail – causing his eyes to water.

Staggering between the warring factions, Mary decided she needed to do something to help. But what could she do, handcuffed as she was? She looked about and noticed of all things an oar. It must have come with the dinghy. She stooped and picked it up, picked a target and was just about to swing it when a loud voice called for everyone to stop.

Pin dropped Darren. Belle grinned. Deirdre moaned. Mary dropped her oar. Darren groaned. Cedric sat against a wall feeling sorry for himself as he nursed sore ears that were no longer pointy but round and puffy. The Bob's huddled together on the sofa. Smokowski was getting up onto all fours. Tom, who had just squeezed into the hall, was staring and wondering what the heck had happened to Lucy's hallway. Flea was holding his left ear, which was ringing from the closeness of the shout. He had only just got up after tripping over one of Darren's feet.

Rhian, who had watched the melee from her vantage point between lounge and hall, had shouted. She now smiled as she pointed the crossbow at Willy. Melee over, the vanquished were rounded up.

Under the threat of more besague pulling and more ear twisting, the subdued Cedric and Darren were dragged by their arms and deposited on the lounge floor.

The limp hardly showing now, Flea helped Belle remove Deirdre from her predicament and, with Deirdre's help, herded Cat and Mary into the lounge with the others. Mary slumped into a chair while Cat settled on the arm.

And last but not least, a drained Tom was hoisted onto Belle's shoulder and carried to the lounge where she put him on the sofa beside Willy.

Now back on the floor, Smokowski sat wedged between their feet. The stars and flashes had all but subsided, but the groans were still there whenever he gingerly touched his nose.

Back in their containers, the Bobs sat on the windowsill where they could be kept a close eye on.

With nearly everyone in the lounge, Sherry was still in the bathroom trying to pick fluff from her nail brush, and all under control, Rhian could return to the kitchen to look after Lucy and the kids. Flea and Belle took up the role of guards and stood grim-faced in each of the lounge doorways. And Pin, well, he just glared, daring anyone to move.

CHAPTER 126

The atmosphere in the lounge had become less tense after Deirdre allowed Tom, Mary, and Darren, to look in on Lucy and the kids to put their minds at rest concerning their safety.

'So you took the Jam,' said Cat, when Tom, Darren and Mary, returned to where they had been sitting, 'But why? What is it all about?'

'All in good time,' said Deirdre.

Watching and listening while he idly played with the biscuit crumbs in his pocket, Tom suddenly realised he hadn't had a cuppa for who knew how long. He wondered if anyone would mind if he had one? They had let him see Lucy and the kids, so why not? It wouldn't hurt to ask, he told himself, as he built up the courage. He asked.

To his and everyone else's surprise, Deirdre said yes. She called for Rhian and asked her to make everyone a drink. She turned to Mary.

'You might think we're the bad guys in all this, but, as you can see, we can be quite civil,' said Deirdre.

Mary doubted she was a bad person, misinformed perhaps, but not bad. 'So why did you do it?'

'Come now, Mary,' said Deirdre, taking a cup of tea from the tray Rhian had passed to Flea. 'Why do you think?'

Still, on the arm of the chair where Mary sat, Cat declined a saucer of milk offered her and waited for Mary's answer.

Mary obliged. 'To stop the ceremony?'

'Spot on,' said Deirdre, tipping her cup to Mary.

'Why?' said Mary.

'To cause a delay,' said Cat. 'With the LISPS and BIMBOs out of commission, they could put their plan into action without any interference.'

'What? No,' said Deirdre. 'I told you we're not bad. We want a delay but want the BIMBOs and LISPS working and keeping the worlds safe.'

'Then what?' said Cat.

'Sorry,' said Tom, who had produced a noisy slurp as he sipped at his cuppa. 'Carry on.'

'Simple,' said Deidre, ignoring Tom, 'to stop someone untrustworthy from becoming the head of the BIMBOs.' She gave Mary a hard stare.

'What!' exclaimed Mary. 'Of course, I'm trustworthy. What nonsense. I've been the head of the Ladies Institute for years.'

'Perhaps,' said Deirdre, 'but the boss says otherwise. That's why you are still wearing your handcuffs.' She watched mystified looks form on faces. 'Oh, and I never took the Jam. The boss did.'

'I thought you were in charge?' said Cat.

'Yeah,' said Tom, ready to join in now he had finished his cuppa.

'I never said that,' said Deirdre.

'It's the Chief, isn't it?' said boB. It explained a lot, he thought.

'No,' said Deirdre, 'the poor man was forced to help. I hated writing those notes he received telling him what to do next.'

'You wrote them,' said Cat, 'why?'

'Just part of the plan. We didn't know who we could trust.'

'The boss is here,' said Sherry, appearing from the hall. She leaned against the door frame.

'Here?' said Deirdre, looking confused. That wasn't part of the plan. Her job was to hold up the ceremony and when, and only when it was too late for it to go ahead, the boss would appear and reveal the truth about Mary to the world.

'So who is the boss?' asked Smokowski.

'I don't know. I've never met him,' said Deirdre.

'Him?' said Mary.

'Or her,' said Deirdre, looking expectantly at the door Sherry was leaning beside. It was her turn to sport a puzzled look. 'I thought you said the boss was here?'

'She is,' said Sherry.

'Where?' said Deirdre.

'There,' said Mary.

All faces looked at Mary, who was pointing in Rhian's direction.

'What is this?' said Deirdre.

'Rhian is the boss,' said Mary. 'I apologise for not letting you all in on her little secret, but I couldn't make a move until all involved were in one place which, without, you Deirdre, wouldn't have been possible.'

'You're lying,' said Deirdre. 'Rhian was working for you until she realised the truth.' She turned to look at Rhian, who was sporting a poker face and was slowly edging towards the kitchen. 'Rhian?'

'I've no idea what she's talking about,' said Rhian.

'And what truth was that?' said Mary, ignoring Rhian.

'That you can't be trusted.'

'And who do you think started that rumour?' said Mary. 'Sorry, Deirdre, but you've been duped. You all have.'

'What is going on?' whispered a confused Smokowski.

'Who knows?' said Tom.

'Now,' said Mary, 'if everyone behaves, no one will get hurt.'

'Now,' whispered Sherry to one of her bangles.

There was a sudden clatter from the direction of the kitchen. Seconds later, Rhian dropped her crossbow and writhed as if doused in itching powder, her arms frantically reaching here and there across her body.

At the same time, the front door opened, and a horde of "grannies", dressed in black, poured through it.

Special teams of BIMBOs and LISPS had been called into action. The BIMBOs, headed by a secret force of invisible Bobettes, had attacked via the rear. It was they that were climbing all over Rhian and forcing her to the floor. The LISPS, meanwhile, who had entered through the front, now faced the Uber fairies and Deirdre.

'Quick,' said Doris, as Pin tried to make a break for it, 'he's trying to get away.' But a double-baked rock cake, thrown by Mabel, stopped him in his tracks. He slumped to the floor. The rock cake, coated with a contact knockout serum, reacted with Pin's blood from the cut the cake had caused. Other, less tough opponents could be knocked out just by contact. A second earlier, Mabel, bravely fighting its effects, had crumpled to the floor; she had forgotten to put her gloves on. The other Uber fairies and Deirdre went quietly. But at the door, Deirdre stopped and turned.

'I don't understand,' she said.

'It will all be explained to you in a cell,' said Mary. 'Take them away.'

A subdued Rhian was carried away amidst wolf whistles aimed at the two containers on the windowsill. The Bobettes would return later to exchange a few phone numbers with the Bobs. LISPS escorted Deirdre and the Uber fairies from the house, Pin on a stretcher, Mabel on another, and into black Maria's van. Maria was the only chimney sweep in the LISPS.

'What just happened?' said Smokowski.

'Yeah,' said Willy, 'and why hasn't she gone with the others?' He pointed at Sherry.

'Yeah,' said Darren, with no idea who she was.

Cedric said nothing, too preoccupied with his ears.

'I'll let her explain,' said Mary, opening the floor to Sherry.

'I need a drink first,' said Tom. This time a plain simple old cuppa wouldn't do. He needed something stronger. He wondered if his daughter had any maple syrup in the house. 'Lucy!' he suddenly shouted, remembering she was in the kitchen. But when he got there, Lucy and the kids were missing.

'We took them to a new safe place,' said Sherry, who had followed him in, 'they won't remember anything.'

Tom turned on his heels. 'Says you,' he said, teeth grinding, fists clenching.

'Says Brandy, Tom,' said Cat, having been enlightened by Mary.

'Brandy?' exclaimed Tom, 'but-what?'

'She'll explain when you've got that drink,' said Cat. 'Something for everyone, I think.'

CHAPTER 127

All had been explained. All had ended well. Perhaps not so well for Rhian or the Chief to some extent, but for everyone else, all's well that ends well.

Shapechanger Rhian was a disgruntled distant relative of the outgoing head of the BIMBOs who felt she should have been considered for the job, not a non-Magical. But that had only been a gripe, not her real motive; there was a darker reason behind her actions. With the BIMBOs and the LISPS in disarray, she intended to plant operatives of her own into the organisations, and then, with their backing, she would take over the BIMBOs and the LISPS as well. The worlds would then have been her playground to do with them as she wanted. Thankfully, when she had taken the Jam, morphed as Mary, it had only been a copy. The real Jam hid away in a vault somewhere deep within the bowels of the Ladies Institute's Headquarters. So the ceremony was never in any danger. But Mary and the Ladies Institute, after discovering the theft, had decided to let things play out, see what happened, find out who was behind it and why. Brandy went undercover to do just that, and her discreet enquiries led her to Rhian. Tom and Cat were supposed to go to the Ladies Institute Headquarters, but only because Mary wanted to tell them what was happening, To see if they could help on the quiet, nothing to do with retrieving the Jam. Something she couldn't say in the end, with Deirdre tagging along. The Chief Traveller, not privy to what the Ladies Institute was doing – the less that knew, the better – had been told to send Tom and Cat to help find the Jam. Deirdre had passed this info on to her boss. The rest is history. With the capture of Rhian, arrests of her Magical and non-Magical supporters soon followed.

The Uber fairies, warrior fairies, taken into custody by the fairy colony they had come from were, although misled by Rhian and not part of her Magical cohorts, convicted of stupidity and excess force when opening a door. The result; seven weeks of community service cleaning cobwebs and stripped of their Uber rank.

Thinking it for the best, despite seeing charges against her dropped, the Travellers relieved Deirdre of her position. The feeling was, she had suffered enough. No law against being taken for a fool. She intended to open a day spa with a shop attached.

Ruth, Charmaine and Abdul were tracked down to a dimension filled with questions no one wanted to answer. They returned unharmed.

The Chief's family, used as leverage to ensure he did as he was told, were discovered safe and well living in a five-star hotel in their minds. They had been at home all the time, hidden in the attic. As for the Chief, his good name tarnished, not because of his involvement in the shenanigans, but because it emerged he was a big horrible bully, mainly where Bobs were concerned, was dismissed and given permanent gardening leave. He hated gardening.

For outstanding detective work and in the way of an apology from Mary for not trusting him, she, with the support of the Travellers, appointed Willy as the new Chief Traveller, provided he got rid of his jumper.

After recovering from the shock of discovering some of his stock had been given away for free, a delighted Smokowski found he was to be the sole supplier of chocolate peanuts to the BIMBOs. A reward for his sterling help. It transpired it was not only Invisible Bob's that liked that particular treat. They were to be part of a BIMBO agents field rations. Smokowski's hands had nearly caught fire with all the rubbing together when he had heard the news.

Also landing on his feet was Cedric. For showing great initiative in the field, Cedric was appointed as a security consultant to the LISPS and personal bodyguard to Willy. He also kept his old job as Head of Security in a delegatory role. Other security officers would get the cakes if needed. He also remembered to remove the black rings around his eyes.

The computer in charge of the Travellers files was reprimanded for the practical jokes and given the job as Cedric's assistant. The practical joker was actually a female elf called Iris, who operated the computer. She would also fill in as secretary to Willy until they found someone to fill the post. Rumour has it that Cedric and Iris intend to get hitched. It had been the first ever computer dating between elves.

The identity of Sherry was dismissed for bad taste by Brandy, who vowed never to wear cheap nail varnish again. Mary asked her to be her chief advisor. Brandy accepted but would continue her job with the LISPS.

The reward for the Bobs was chocolate and medals for bravery, not chocolate ones. boB also receiving a medal of honour in the face of having to wear culottes. They also received numerous offers of dates from the Bobettes.

Lucy and the kids were glamoured and taken back to the cottage. There, their memories of their last moments before being frozen were mixed with new ones of an impending holiday. A happy Darren, begrudgingly awarded a pay rise by Smokowski and awarded free family cinema tickets for life by the Ladies Institute for services rendered, met them there later. Mary joined them after the ceremony, which had gone without a hitch. Now in charge, she set the rules where visiting family was concerned.

The jailers, Arwen and Alwyn, were never heard of again. But a pair of plumbers, specializing in dungeon drainage, smelling of lemons and looking remarkably like them, appeared a few months later.

As for Tom and Cat, after everyone had left, they went home to Tom's cottage, where Cat had to explain who the woman in the handcuffs was. Tom was mortified. Why hadn't she said something earlier? A cuppa and choccy biscuits were called for, but to Tom's shock and horror he found the cupboard bare, or at least the biscuit tin was. Leaving Cat tucking into cold chicken and a saucer of milk, and the memory of Mary once again disappearing to the back of his mind, he headed for the shops. But it was not to Smokowski's that he headed. No, Darren had told him of a shop that held pamper days, whatever they were, and offered deals such as buy one, get one free. He arrived at the shop with trepidation but left a happy, contented man. But had wondered at the sign above the biscuits that read:

BOGOF

He puzzled about it all the way home, where he decided it must be the owner's name. He wondered if they knew Smokowski.

We now travel forward two weeks to Tom's kitchen.

Chapter 128

'What are you doing?' said Cat, as she wandered into Tom's kitchen. He had been quiet for a while now, so she thought she had better check in on him.

'Listening to my breathing.'

'Why?' said Cat, suddenly concerned. 'Are you ill?'

'No. It's called focused medication.'

'Meditation,' corrected Cat, who had heard of it.

'That's what I said,' said Tom. 'It's supposed to help with a wandering mind. Saw it on the thingamabob.' He nodded at the laptop. 'Now, if you don't mind, I need to medicate?'

Of course, you do, thought Cat smiling. She turned and headed back to what she had been doing. Halfway there, she heard Tom filling the kettle. She smiled again.

Back to the present.